THE
HOUSE
ON
SUNFLOWER
LANE

GWENNA McALLIS

ISBN 979-8-9885669-7-7 (paperback)
ISBN 979-8-9885669-6-0 (hardcover)
ISBN 979-8-9885669-8-4 (ebook)

Cover design by MiblArt

Published by Oracle Hawk Press

Author website: www.gwennamcallis.com

For my daughters,
who made me brave.

ONE

Shannon

August 16, 2022

I STEPPED INSIDE THE hotel lobby, moving across dingy, outdated carpet with mud-caked bare feet, my sleeping toddler growing heavy on my shoulder. Her forehead, hot and damp, rested on my collarbone. Her stuffed cat hung limp in her hand.

The automatic doors closed behind me with a hiss as a cluster of too-bright fluorescent lights overhead blinded me. My breath hitched when I read the wall clock mounted behind the front desk.

Was it *really* almost 3 a.m.?

I inhaled sharply, taking in the scent of bleach and mildew and burnt coffee as I approached the counter. My teeth were chattering now, not from cold, but from the adrenaline spike that had finally crashed, leaving my whole body shaking.

The clerk behind the desk looked up from his phone, startled. His eyes flicked to my filthy shoeless feet, then to my daughter, then back to my face.

"I-I need a room," I said, too aware of my voice's shakiness. I cleared my throat and tried to steady it as I added, "Please."

He stared for a second too long, taking in how feral and shaken I must have looked, clearly wondering if he should call someone. The cops. Maybe DHR.

I glanced at his nametag. *Brian.*

Brian started typing on his computer keyboard. "One queen okay?"

I gaped at him, the question taking a moment to process. "Um, sure. That's fine."

"Name?" he asked, eyes still on the computer screen.

"Shannon Holl—" I started, then stopped. My mouth went dry. I shifted my daughter on my hip. "Sorry. I, um, I used to be Shannon Holloway. But it's Reed now." I swallowed. "Shannon Reed."

I hadn't said it out loud in a long time. It sounded so foreign on my lips. Tears pricked my eyes, and I blinked fast.

Brian didn't notice. "ID and credit card?"

I fumbled for my wallet with one hand, trying not to jostle my child awake. My fingers, still trembling, were clumsy. It took me three tries to unzip the right pocket of my purse. The clerk waited, quiet, watching me too closely. I handed everything over without meeting his eyes.

He swiped my credit card and handed my things back to me, along with a receipt and a hotel-branded key card.

"Alright, Shannon. I've got you in room 334. Elevator is to your right."

"Thanks."

His eyes passed over me once more, and I turned away before he could say anything else. Before he could ask questions I couldn't answer.

The elevator dinged as the door slid open. I moved inside and pressed 3. The ride up felt too slow and claustrophobic. I wished I'd taken the stairs.

Room 334 was a musty box. White walls and a wallpaper border straight out of the nineties. The navy carpet crunched against the bottoms of my feet, gritty on my exposed skin.

I dropped my bag, locked the door, and wedged a dining chair beneath the knob. A useless little ritual to make myself feel better.

Somewhere down the hall, a door slammed hard enough to shake the walls.

Hazel flinched against me, a weak, startled sound escaping her lips.

"It's okay," I murmured into her brown curls.

I crossed to the bed and eased her down onto the mattress. She sat up, rubbing her eyes with the backs of her fists. My stomach lurched all over again when I took in her unicorn nightgown, the hem damp and smeared with dirt. Her three-year-old body suddenly seemed so small.

She blinked up at me, confused. "Mommy?"

"I'm right here."

Her gaze drifted around the unfamiliar room. "Where are we?"

"A hotel."

She frowned, thinking. "We left the house?"

"We did."

A pause stretched between us.

Then she whispered, "Good."

Two

Shannon

January 2019

I FELT, ALMOST IMMEDIATELY, that the house on Sunflower Lane was the one.

Marc and I had begun house-hunting after the 2018 holiday season ended. I was nineteen weeks pregnant at the time, and making a zillion trips up the stairs to our cramped little apartment on the third floor was already becoming, quite literally, a pain in the butt. And the calves. And the back.

That one-bedroom, seven-hundred-square-feet hamster cage with plumbing was the best we could afford back in 2017, when we'd moved to Huntsville, Alabama, for Marc's first engineering job. He convinced me that tiny apartment was temporary, and thankfully, he was right.

By 2018, Marc had climbed a little higher at work, and the bills weren't draining us quite as hard. And now, in 2019, with our first baby due in June, we officially needed more space.

I found a realtor, Tom Altamira, who was highly recommended in the Huntsville Happenings Facebook group, and we started looking for our first house.

Tom seemed like a nice guy. Pleasant. Professional. He had warm brown skin and tight black curls that somehow stayed where they were supposed to be, even in the Alabama humidity. His face was clean-shaven, with a strong, square jaw and a smile that came easily.

He dressed like someone who took pride in his work. Neatly pressed button-downs, pleated slacks, leather shoes so shiny you could probably see your reflection in them. Sometimes he wore a jacket and a tie, too.

Tom looked like a real adult who had it all together.

Marc and I . . . not so much.

Marc was tall and lanky, all limbs, always wiping his glasses or losing them. He wore wrinkled plaid shirts, the same jeans he'd had in college, and sneakers that squeaked when he walked. His five o'clock shadow was permanent, and his dark hair never stayed flat no matter what he did. He wasn't so much careless as perpetually distracted, the kind of guy who forgot to eat because he was too busy reverse-engineering the dishwasher or something in his head.

Meanwhile, I wore the same two maternity tops in rotation, both already pilled and stretched in places they shouldn't be. My hair lived in a ponytail, I'd long since given up on makeup, and between the hormonal brain fog and constant puking that still hadn't gone away in the second trimester, I wasn't good for much.

Touring homes with Tom Altamira felt like tagging along beside a J.Crew ad.

But we liked him.

Tom stayed upbeat, but after processing our pre-approval paperwork, he leveled with us: the usual loans were off the table. Our debt-to-income ratio was too high, thanks to our student loans.

What we *did* qualify for was something called a USDA Rural Development loan, one of those "zero-down" programs for people willing to live in a town with nothing but a gas station and twenty churches. It would cover the full mortgage, which was good, because we had nothing set aside for a down payment. But it also meant Huntsville proper was off-limits.

Life in the country wasn't what we'd pictured, but dreams change. We just needed some place safe to build a life together.

Tom took us all over Madison County, exploring the furthest reaches of rural proximity to Huntsville. We drove what felt like every back road in the county, checking out every half-decent listing we could find.

We bounced down neglected, potholed highways and passed through some of the worst poverty I'd ever seen. Dilapidated single-wide trailers that should have been condemned but were still very much inhabited, their yards strewn with heaps of old tires, rusted-out vehicles, and literal garbage. Confederate flags flew next to homemade political signs, cheap particle board with *In Don We Trust* painted in the penmanship of a first-grader.

I cringed. My hands drifted to my pregnant belly, instinctively protective. I couldn't stop thinking about schools. Access to healthcare. Clean water. What kind of childhood could I give our baby way out here?

There were no parks. No libraries. No mommy-and-me music classes or baby swim lessons.

Would she be the only kid in her class without camo coveralls and a hunting license? Would he be able to make friends? Would she be safe? What if he got sick and the nearest urgent care was almost an hour away?

For the first time, I wondered if staying in our tiny, overpriced apartment might've been the better move.

As uncomfortable as I felt driving through the outer stretches of the county, I felt even more awkward dragging Tom Altamira out there with us.

I watched him sometimes, his quiet scanning of the houses, the way he adjusted his posture depending on who was watching. We never talked about it. But the silence of those moments said enough.

After touring one house with a lifted Dodge Ram in the driveway that had *"Speak English or Go Home"* stuck across the back window, Marc and I agreed, without really saying it, that we'd stick as close to the Huntsville city limits as we could.

I'd grown up in Alabama. I'd seen this kind of thing before. But something about it felt different now. Maybe it was the baby. Maybe it was Tom Altamira.

Or maybe I was just finally seeing things for what they were.

We kept looking.

We saw a dozen houses in two weeks. Just when I was ready to call it quits, we pulled into the gravel driveway of 119 Sunflower Lane.

It wasn't much. Just a simple, small, one-level farmhouse tucked behind a curtain of bare-limbed trees. The porch sagged a little. The once-white painted clapboard was chipped and faded.

But the name got me. *Sunflower Lane.*

There weren't any sunflowers. Not in January. But I did see the brittle remains of last summer's stalks, drooping and withered, looming at the edge of the driveway next to a rusted, leaning mailbox.

Tom Altamira climbed out of his car, iPad in hand, and met us in front of the porch.

"Alright, guys," he began, tapping the screen of his tablet, "this place has got three bedrooms, two baths, and it's on just over five acres. It's zoned for Madison County Elementary in Gurley." His chestnut brown eyes met mine. "It's a Blue Ribbon school, actually. My buddy's kids go there, and they love it." He glanced back down. "Low taxes, easy commute to Huntsville. About a thirty-five-minute drive to the Arsenal. And it still qualifies for a USDA loan."

Marc nodded, planting his hands on his hips as he scanned the house's façade. "Checks all the boxes," he said.

Tom grinned. "I was hoping you'd agree with me on that."

I lingered at the edge of the driveway, eyes drinking in the expansive front porch. I imagined it with hanging ferns. Wind chimes. Potted marigolds and petunias. A pair of rocking chairs. I saw myself out here with coffee and a book, listening to falling rain and faint rolls of thunder. It was the kind of thing I'd been craving without even realizing it.

This could be it, I thought.

It felt right. Almost familiar in a way I couldn't explain, like the house had been waiting for us all along.

Tom unlocked the front door. When it didn't budge, he gave it a hard shove with his shoulder. The frame groaned, then gave way with a squeal as it swung open.

Marc was the first inside. A frown creased his forehead as he scoped the place out. "Floor slopes a little."

"Yeah," Tom said, tapping his iPad once more. "It was built in 1960. That's not uncommon in a home this age. Likely foundation settling. I don't see any signs of water damage."

I stepped inside behind them and glanced around. The living room was nothing fancy, a bit narrow with sickly yellow walls and scuffed baseboards. The outdated carpet was an unfortunate shade of baby-food green, but I wanted to believe original hardwoods lurked underneath. Having been built in 1960, there was a good chance they did.

That was one of the things I loved most about old houses—the way they had layers. Immaculate hardwoods concealed beneath ugly carpet. Perfectly usable fireplaces bricked over. Little secrets tucked beneath the surface, waiting to be uncovered.

I thought of my parents' old house on Sand Mountain, my dad peeling back the wallpaper in our hall bathroom in the nineties and finding the prettiest robin's-egg blue paint underneath. Someone else's favorite color perhaps, sealed away for decades. It had felt like discovering buried treasure.

I loved things like that. New builds felt cold and sterile to me. Bland and lifeless. Forgettable.

Not here. This place left an impression.

In the far corner, near the big front window, there was a little alcove just wide enough for a chair.

I stopped, already picturing it.

"Ooh, that's where my reading nook will go," I said, mostly to myself, halfway kidding. "Big cozy chair. String lights. Some floating wall shelves."

Marc didn't respond. He was crouched by a wall, tapping on it for reasons perhaps only an engineer would understand.

Tom, however, peered up from his iPad. "Reading nook, huh?"

I smiled. "Yeah. I've always wanted one."

"I can totally see it. That looks like the perfect spot for one."

I nodded, losing myself in the image: an oversized armchair the color of moss. The golden glow of fairy lights tacked across the ceiling. A steaming mug of coffee atop a thrifted side table. A storm outside, and nowhere to be but here.

A sudden chill skittered across the back of my neck. I touched the spot absently and glanced behind me at the front door. It was closed. Probably a draft from one of the old windows, I told myself. The single-hung panes felt paper-thin, barely a barrier between us and the cold January air. That might be an issue for the utility bill. We might need to replace them, and that sounded expensive.

I shivered and turned toward the hallway, where Marc and Tom had already disappeared. I gave the nook one last glance and followed the sound of voices, stepping deeper into the house that might be ours.

I found the guys in the hall bathroom. The space was aggressively pink. Tub, toilet, sink, walls, floor . . . all pink.

It didn't get much better from there. The entire house felt frozen in time, like nothing had been updated since it was built in the sixties. We wandered room to room, wincing at the realities while imagining the possibilities.

The curling, floral, grandma-core wallpaper in the hallway and dining room needed scraping. That grimy, baby-food carpet had to go. Almost everything would need updating, but honestly, that seemed to be in the house's favor at the time. It would be our project. A chance to start fresh and truly make it our own.

The exterior was the same. The chipped clapboard needed paint, the roof probably needed replacing, and the yard was terribly overgrown. Out back, there was an old barn that looked like it might collapse if you stared at it too hard.

That is, until Marc and Tom tugged open the heavy wooden doors and revealed its dusty, cluttered interior.

"Whoa," Marc breathed, stepping inside. "Look at all this."

Tools. So many tools. Fully stocked shelves lined the walls, someone's collection abandoned beneath dust and cobwebs. Rusted coffee cans filled to the brim with nails and screws. Paint cans so old the labels had faded. A dozen clamps, measuring tapes, and levels. A heavy-duty drill set and a set of socket wrenches lay open like they'd just been used.

It looked like someone had once poured their weekends into this space, started a dozen projects with the best of intentions, then just stopped.

"Is all this stuff included?" Marc asked, poking through a bin of screwdrivers, their handles dulled with age but still very much intact.

Tom scratched the back of his neck. "I'd have to double-check with the seller, but I mean, the house is empty. I doubt they're coming back for any of this."

Marc lit up like he'd hit the jackpot. I could see him taking mental inventory of what could be salvaged, scrubbed clean, and made useful again. He had a knack for that sort of thing, seeing the worth in what others tossed out. My dad did, too. The pair of them would have a field day out here.

I lingered in the doorway, hand resting on the curve of my belly, taking it all in. We didn't own many tools. There just wasn't room in our cramped apartment. This felt like a gift from the house itself. Like it had been waiting for someone to pick up where the last person left off.

Marc called it luck. Tom called it a solid find.

But I called it a sign.

Swept up in the thrill of possibility, we put in an offer that day.

We were naïve, fueled by HGTV marathons and misplaced DIY overconfidence, but we believed we could turn this old place into something beautiful. Something perfect for our growing family.

We were too enchanted to wonder why it had been sitting empty for so long. Too hopeful to ask why someone had abandoned their tools, their paint cans, and left their neatly stacked lumber to rot in the barn.

Looking back, it's easy to see all the things we missed.

But that day, all we saw was potential.

The house somehow convinced us we belonged there.

THREE

Shannon

March 2019

THE DAY WE CLOSED on the house, we ate a celebratory dinner cross-legged on the empty living room floor, balancing takeout containers on an unopened box labeled *KITCHEN—FRAGILE*. The food was lukewarm, and the Gerber-chic carpet beneath us was disgusting, but we couldn't stop smiling. We'd already brought over a couple of boxes after signing the final paperwork that same afternoon. We couldn't help ourselves.

Marc flipped to a fresh sheet on his yellow legal pad, pushed his glasses up the bridge of his nose, and clicked the top of his pen like he meant business.

"Okay," he said, grinning. "Operation Nesting. Let's go."

I shifted, trying to find a position that didn't cut off my breath or send a bolt of pain through my back. I was twenty-nine weeks pregnant now, solidly in the third trimester, and our little girl was growing more active by the day. Even sitting still was a struggle, especially on the floor.

Marc scrawled *OPERATION NESTING* across the top of the page in all caps, underlined it, and started the list we'd been building in our heads for weeks:

- *Crib*

- *Curtains for nursery*

- *Paint (light green or yellow?)*

- *Rip out the Linda Blair pea soup carpet*

- *Plant hydrangeas out front*

"Hydrangeas?" I asked, raising an eyebrow.

"They were your mom's favorite," he said. "And they're perennials. They're cheerful. Hopeful."

He shrugged like he hadn't just activated every hormonal switch in my body. My throat tightened as my eyes burned with tears. "That's so sweet, Marc."

"I have my moments."

I leaned back on one hand, the other resting on my belly, where I could feel little Hazel stretching, pressing against me. The room fell silent except for the faint rustle of wind outside and the distant creak of settling beams. My eyes swept across the empty walls, the faded trim, the boxes stacked near the door.

It was our blank canvas. It needed so much work, but it was *ours*.

Everything had gone surprisingly smoothly. Just a few hours ago, we'd been sitting in a sleek conference room downtown, signing a stack of paperwork with our realtor, Tom, and an attorney named Preston something. The seller hadn't even bothered to come. She'd signed the documents from California.

"She never even came to see it," Tom had told us. "Inherited it from her mom and just wanted it off her hands."

The monthly mortgage payment was less than a third of what we'd paid in rent. For a whole house and five acres.

It felt like fate. Like a door had opened just for us.

We wouldn't officially move in until the following weekend, when my dad could come up with his truck and help us haul furniture.

But the second we got the keys, we had to celebrate.

We were homeowners.

Marc rose to his feet and began pacing the room, tapping the end of his pen on his legal pad and muttering things like "replace outlet covers" and "paint trim."

I stayed seated for a minute longer, soaking it in. The way the golden hour sunlight filtered through the dusty windows. We needed curtains, I realized. And blinds. Anyone could see straight in. Not that there were neighbors close enough to do so, but still.

The house was surrounded by thick trees on either side. As I looked out, I caught sight of the woods at the edge of the property, dark and shadowy in the waning daylight.

I told myself it was beautiful. Peaceful.

But something about the trees and their shadows, so still, so close, made the back of my neck prickle.

I suddenly needed to pee.

I pushed up off the floor with a grunt and stretched, brushing dust from the back of my leggings. Marc had wandered into the hallway, still scribbling things and mumbling to himself.

The hall bathroom was closer, but I found myself drifting past it, toward the master. I hadn't actually looked at it since we first toured the place, and I wanted to see it again.

The master bath was entirely cobalt blue. Blue tile, blue toilet, blue tub. In theory, blue was supposed to be calming. Tranquil. Serene.

But this blue wasn't like that.

Under the flickering overhead light, it felt cold. Hollow. Almost sad.

I did my business and washed my hands beneath a sputtering faucet, making a mental note to bring soap next time. After wiping my hands dry on my leggings, I decided to have a look inside the vanity drawers beneath the sink.

They were swollen with age, squeaky on their tracks, and their insides were coated with a fine, powdery dust. Old makeup, maybe, or something long-decayed.

I grimaced. Before I could move my things in here, I would need to remove all of the drawers and give them a good cleaning.

Gingerly, I tugged open a third drawer. I noticed something tucked into the very back.

A small pink cardboard box, faded and soft at the corners like it had been handled often, long ago. I extracted it carefully and lifted the lid.

A corsage lay inside.

Or what was left of one. The flowers had dried to near paper. Sprigs of baby's breath tucked alongside three roses. I guessed they were once pink, though they had curled inward and gone pale. A length of ribbon cinched the base, its original blue faded to a dusty gray.

Beneath the flowers was a small cream-colored card with scalloped edges, the florist's name embossed in gold along the top. A message had been added beneath it in black pen. Not the careful cursive of a shopgirl, but something more masculine, slightly messy:

> *For Fern. Always.*
> *- R*

For a long moment, I stood there, staring at it. A deep, unexpected sadness struck me—a level of sorrow I didn't understand.

I tucked the note back beneath the dried flowers, then closed the lid and placed the box where I'd found it.

I kept thinking about it for days after.

Those wilted flowers.

That note.

For Fern. Always.

Four

Fern

April 1961

The bathroom was blessedly quiet apart from the electric buzz of the overhead light, a harsh, grating sound that throbbed behind her eyes. Fern stood at the vanity, robe knotted at her waist, ratty slippers not doing much to cushion her aching feet. She leaned against the countertop and breathed.

In.

Out.

Again.

Reluctantly, she raised her eyes to the mirror. She could scarcely bear the sight of her own reflection. When had she let herself get this far gone? Bags beneath her eyes. Wrinkles beginning to form at their corners. She was only twenty-nine, but she looked so much older.

She supposed domestic life would do that to a woman.

Day after day of humdrum repetition, an eternal checklist with no reward. Cleaning. Mending. Cooking. Laundry. Childcare. A thankless job. She kept the entire household running and had nothing to show for it.

She'd trudged through the bedtime routine—supper, bath, tuck-in with a lullaby—with all the patience she could scrape together before slipping away to her own bathroom for a moment of peace.

She'd put Ray's supper plate in the oven. Maybe it would still be warm whenever he decided to come home. Or maybe it wouldn't.

She sort of hoped it wouldn't.

The bitterness of the thought sat heavily in her chest. It hurt. More than she wanted to admit.

Ray said the long nights at Redstone Arsenal were necessary now. The Soviets had sent a man into space, and now it was all hands on deck. Everything was classified. Everything was urgent.

She'd wanted to believe him. She really had.

But lately, that belief was wearing thin.

Her gaze drifted to the vanity cabinet. She pulled open the drawer.

The corsage was still there, nestled in its box. The roses had long since dried, their once-vibrant pink faded to a soft, dusty blush. Their sweet fragrance grew fainter by the day.

She lifted the card with careful fingers.

> *For Fern. Always.*
> *—R*

A lump formed in her throat.

That night bloomed in her memory. The thrill of it. Raymond in his pressed shirt and tie, the warmth of his hand on her lower back as he led her down the steps of her mother's house.

She'd worn her sister's dress, a gauzy, tea-length affair in periwinkle blue. *It matches your eyes,* Ray had said.

He'd given her the corsage then. Tied it to her wrist with trembling fingers while her mother snapped a photograph.

They had danced for hours. Afterward, they'd parked by the lake and kissed until Fern's cheeks burned.

She blinked down at the dried flowers.

It felt like a lifetime ago.

A different Fern.

Perhaps because it was.

She slipped the card back inside the box, closed the lid, and returned it to the drawer.

The silence was suddenly unbearable. The loneliness pressed against her ribs like a fist.

She reached for the little transistor radio on the windowsill and turned the volume low, just enough to quell the quiet. She caught a familiar voice mid-chorus. Patsy Cline, velvety-smooth, crooning about falling apart over a love gone wrong.

The melody warped through a hiss of static, dipping in and out of key until a string of pops and crackles drowned out the tune entirely.

For a moment, she thought she heard something else beneath the noise. A garbled whisper caught between stations.

She turned the dial a notch, and it was gone.

FIVE

Shannon

March 2019

THE RADIO CRACKLED WITH static as I turned off Sunflower Lane and guided my CR-V down the gravel driveway to our new home.

My hand rested on my swollen belly as Hazel shifted inside me, a slow, rolling flutter that made my stomach roil. Up ahead, the trees parted, and the house came into view.

Our house.

I parked beneath the big oak and climbed out into the pre-dawn darkness. The sudden silence made my ears roar. No traffic, no neighbors. Nothing but my breath and the ticking of the cooling engine behind me.

It should've felt peaceful, but instead, it was almost oppressive.

Maybe I just wasn't used to the country anymore. I hadn't been anywhere this remote since visiting Granny Jean as a kid. Nights at her house were so dark the sky felt endless, scattered with a million bright stars.

Gravel crunched behind me as Marc's Corolla rolled up the drive, followed by Dad in his overcompensating Chevy Silverado with the trailer hitched to the back. The thing groaned as it stopped, weighed down by the contents of our apartment.

Dad had driven up from Sand Mountain at some ungodly hour to help us move out. He and Marc did all the heavy lifting while I shuffled between boxes, pausing every twenty minutes or so to throw up. Third trimester or not, the morning sickness hadn't let up. Zofran barely touched it.

I met Marc and Dad in the driveway, my hands suddenly sweaty as I studied Dad's face. He hadn't seen the house in person, only the touched-up photos from the Zillow listing. What would he think about the place?

The house was all shadows. I hadn't expected it to be *this* dark, but out here, away from the city, there were no street lamps. We had five secluded acres to ourselves, and almost half of that was wooded.

Our only light source was the moon hanging in the sky over our heads. It cast a strange, ethereal, silver glow across the house's façade. The effect was a little unsettling.

Dad whistled, and I jumped. "Shoo-wee, y'all got your work cut out for you," he declared, planting his hands on either side of his round belly as he surveyed the front of the house. He hooked his thumbs behind his red elastic suspenders and they stretched with the tension.

He was wearing his get-shit-done outfit. Scuffed, once-white tennis shoes. Acid-washed dad jeans held up by those red suspenders he'd had since the nineties. A faded gray T-shirt with *Crimson Tide - 2012 National Champions* across the front. The shirt stretched taut across his midsection. Our bellies were beginning to match.

"But this old place has good bones," he said. He took a few steps closer to the house, reached out, and tugged on the bottom of a load-bearing porch post as though testing its sturdiness. "Solid. Don't make 'em like that anymore."

Marc nodded behind him.

"These slip-shod new builds they're throwing up overnight all over the place don't even compare," Dad went on. He glanced at me, and I thought I detected a bit of pride in his gaze. "You got something with real potential here, Shanny. As long as y'all are willing to put in the work."

"Yes, sir," I said.

"We're looking forward to that part, actually," Marc said, grinning. "Wait 'til you see the barn."

I smiled faintly while they talked, my eyes drifting toward the tree line. The woods gathered at the edge of the property, denser and darker than I remembered. A breeze rustled through the trees, the branches swaying in unison, whispering. For a second, I thought I saw movement deeper inside, something pale between the trunks, but when I blinked, it was gone.

Hazel kicked inside me, so hard this time I gasped. I pressed my palm to my stomach and tried to laugh. "I think she's ready to see the place," I said.

Dad grinned. "Then let's get y'all moved in."

But as we walked toward the porch, I couldn't shake the feeling that something in the woods was watching us.

Six

<hr>

THE HOUSE FELT DIFFERENT the second the truck pulled away.

Marc and my dad had gone back for the final load—one last trip to clear out the apartment and hand over the keys. I'd volunteered to stay behind and start cleaning. I was no help with the heavy lifting right now, and someone needed to make the place livable before we started unpacking.

The carpets were filthy. Dust coated every surface. The cabinets and countertops all begged to be scrubbed clean.

I rolled up my sleeves, but I didn't start right away. The silence settled thick around me, heavy in the absence of other people. Behind me, the house creaked in unfamiliar ways.

"Well, it's just us now," I murmured to my belly. "We've got a lot of work to do."

I pulled on rubber gloves, masked up, and got busy wiping, scrubbing, and sweeping every surface until it started to feel less like someone else's gross old house and more like a blank slate.

I found the box that contained my essential oil diffuser, plugged it in on the kitchen counter, and filled it with beads of citrus oil. Wispy clouds spiraled upward, the bright, lemony scent slowly overtaking the mustiness clinging to the walls.

Around ten, I began to feel achy and tired, so I took a break from cleaning. I peeled off my gloves and washed my hands at the kitchen sink, taking a moment to appreciate the view beyond it.

A large, arched window hung above the deep, double-basin sink—the only arched window in the house. It was one of my favorite features, one of the things that stood out from our first tour. It let in so much light, and the view was stunning.

I peered through the now pristine glass panes, drinking it in. Morning sunlight filtered through the leaves of mature oaks, the old barn with its faded red paint up on the hill, the flat, cleared patch next to it that would be perfect for a big vegetable garden. Maybe a chicken coop, too. I didn't know the first thing about keeping chickens, but everyone had to start somewhere, right?

The possibilities unfolded in my mind's eye. I mentally installed bird feeders and planted fruit trees, laid winding brick pathways flanked by colorful flower beds. We could pave a patio, add a picnic table and a grill for Marc. He'd always wanted a grill. I pictured a tire swing hanging from the big oak on the left, a little playhouse with a mud kitchen beside it.

I dried my hands on a paper towel (still hadn't found the clean towels yet) and smiled to myself. Folding my palms around my belly, I felt my eyes sting just a little. This was the perfect place to raise a child.

We were going to build a life here. Make memories here.

I grabbed a pack of peanut butter crackers from my purse and downed half of them over the sink, imagining our future as I ate. After a few long gulps from my water bottle, I decided to wander the house to see how it looked with our things.

Never mind that our stuff was all boxed up.

It was here. In our house.

We had a freaking house.

I could barely believe it.

I moved into the hallway, peeking into each room like I was seeing it all for the first time. It was dark in the hall, and I reached instinctively for a light switch, but there wasn't one. Weird. I glanced up and found there wasn't even an overhead light. Maybe we could install one.

I proceeded on through the dim, shadowy space and stopped at the first bedroom on the left, the smallest one, which we'd already decided would make the perfect nursery.

Sunlight spilled through the bare windows, illuminating the changing table I'd scored on Facebook Marketplace, the glider with soft gray cushions I'd thrifted, and the still-boxed crib leaning against the wall (an early gift from my dad, even though the shower was a few weeks away).

I paused in the doorway, hand on my abdomen, admiring the cozy space.

This was going to be our little girl's room.

The baby kicked so hard, it knocked the wind out of me.

"Jeez," I said, wincing as I rubbed my belly. A solid lump pressed back against my palm. Her foot, maybe. "You okay in there?"

I let out a soft laugh and crossed the threshold, my shadow stretching across the dingy green carpet. I tried to picture what the room would look like in a few weeks. Soft curtains on the windows, pastel walls, a mobile with little forest animals spinning lazily above the crib.

My gaze drifted to the closet. Two white bifold doors, shut tight.

"This'll be your room, you know," I said, my voice quieter now. She shifted again, as if answering. "Yeah. We'll fix it up. Make it special for you."

As I moved closer to the closet, I noticed a dull patch on the carpet just in front of the doors. A dark, faintly oily splatter, like something had spilled there decades ago and seeped too deep to clean.

I frowned. This carpet really had to go before the baby came.

My eyes wandered back to the doors themselves, and a chill slipped down my spine like someone had traced it with a fingertip.

I couldn't have said why, but the thought of opening those doors made my stomach twist.

I told myself I'd deal with that room later.

Maybe when Marc was back, and I wouldn't have to be in there alone.

Seven

The final weeks of pregnancy passed in a blur of unpacking boxes, Braxton Hicks contractions, and approximately one thousand trips to Lowe's. I worked my last week at the graphic design firm in May, though I was mostly useless those last few days. Too swollen to sit comfortably, too distracted to focus, too consumed by the nesting instinct to care about designing brochures.

I probably could've toughed it out a few more weeks to keep the maternity leave benefits, but I couldn't make myself care.

Every spare hour was spent getting the house ready for our daughter. Marc ripped out all of the hideous pea-green carpet and uncovered the original oak hardwoods I'd been hoping for. They were scratched and stained and warped from water damage in places, and we didn't have time or money to refinish them yet, but with some well-placed rugs, it was a vast improvement over the carpet.

We swapped out rusted vent covers, patched a few holes in the walls, and learned how to rewire an outlet from YouTube. Marc stayed up late after work painting the nursery a soft mint green that took three coats to look right. I hung watercolor prints of woodland animals on the walls and installed blackout curtains I found on clearance at Target.

Ninety percent of the house still looked like the "before" footage from a home renovation show, but we were making progress.

Then all that progress skidded to a halt—indefinitely—on June 19, 2019.

At 4:12 PM, after twenty-seven hours of labor, Hazel Jean Holloway entered the world. She was rosy and round, and she announced herself with the faintest little whimper of a cry, like she didn't want to be a bother.

She weighed nine pounds, two ounces. One of the nurses said she looked like a Butterball turkey. I didn't laugh.

She was perfect.

We brought her home two days later, bundled in a fuzzy blanket and a knitted hat far too warm for the humid Alabama summer. Her cheeks flushed pink the moment we stepped outside, but she didn't make a sound.

The house felt different with Hazel inside it.

Not in some magical, glowy, *motherhood-is-beautiful* kind of way, but in a *we have no idea what the hell we're doing and we haven't slept in days* kind of way.

Our routines vanished overnight. The days and nights blurred together in one endless loop of crying and rocking and feeding. The coffee pot stayed on day and night, but the caffeine didn't make a dent in the fatigue.

At first, I blamed the weird shift in the house on that. The chaos. The utter, complete exhaustion. The unstable postpartum hormones.

But something else had changed, too.

And it wasn't just us.

It started with footsteps.

Heavy, unmistakable footfalls on the wooden floorboards, sharp enough to make me sit up straight in the dark.

At first, I thought I was hallucinating.

It only happened at night, always in those odd, half-conscious times between wakefulness and sleep. This was a common phenomenon; I know because I Googled it. According to Wikipedia, the transitional period before the onset of sleep is called *hypnagogia*. That's when people experience things like sleep paralysis, lucid dreaming, and hallucinations.

On top of this, I was a new mother, majorly sleep-deprived and riding the postpartum hormonal rollercoaster. My mental state was questionable most days during the first three months of Hazel's life, so I dismissed what I heard for a long time.

After all, Marc never heard the footsteps.

But Marc never heard Hazel screaming for milk half a dozen times a night either, damn him. The way he continually slept through her crying flabbergasted me. And enraged me. Every night, at nine o'clock, eleven, one, three, I dragged my weary, aching, still-bleeding body out of bed, scooped a wailing, red-faced Hazel out of her bedside bassinet, and whipped out a sore, chapped boob to quell her.

I sat in the glider, rocking back and forth as I fed her with my body, glaring contemptuously at Marc as he snored away, oblivious, useless, on the bed.

Yes, the glider was originally in the nursery, but it only took about two nights of constant wakeups before I had Marc move it into our room. Getting in and out of bed over and over to make the long walk down the cold, dark hallway got old fast. I was extremely uncomfortable and in a lot of pain. Hazel's big head had ripped me open, and I had stitches in my crotch; plus, of course, I would be passing blood and chunks of uterine tissue for about six weeks, which meant I was wearing bulky, chafing, horrendous adult diapers for the foreseeable future. The shorter walk from my bed to the glider in the corner of our bedroom helped with the pain and exhaustion.

Though it did mean I had to sit there and look at my sleeping husband.

I began to resent him.

His long, restful, blissfully uninterrupted nights infuriated me. I was running on about four non-consecutive hours of sleep each day, and I was miserable. I snapped at him constantly. I didn't enjoy my time with Hazel.

This, of course, made me feel insanely guilty. I was supposed to be *enjoying every moment*, treasuring these quiet bonding sessions I had alone with my daughter at my breast in the wee hours, but dammit, I just wanted some sleep. I craved it to the point of tears. My body required sleep just like anyone else's does, but I was the mama. No sleep for me.

I felt myself sliding off the rails. I *had* to find a way to cope with the persistent nighttime wakeups. I relied on my phone to keep me from dozing off and dropping Hazel or smothering her with my boob (two of my constant fears). I took to scrolling social media for hours in an effort to stay awake. This was unhealthy and made everything worse, so I turned to online shopping. Also unhealthy. And expensive. Marc and I started arguing about the number of packages suddenly showing up on our doorstep.

Those first few months were an unpleasant blur. No one came over to help us out. All of my co-workers, our extended family members, everyone who had asked nosy questions during my pregnancy, brought gifts to my baby showers, gushed about how wonderful things were going to be—I never heard from them. Not even a text.

I went days without showering because I couldn't figure out how to manage it. I tried leaving Hazel in her bassinet while I hopped in the shower, but I couldn't bear her incessant screaming. Wet wipes and dry shampoo became my best friends.

I was too overwhelmed and exhausted to cook. Hazel cried every time I put her down, and it felt too unsafe to cook while holding her. After work most days, Marc brought home takeout from the city—whatever I wanted—in an attempt to appease me. I often ate lo mein with Hazel attached to my nipple. Marc and I both gained weight.

I didn't go back to work. As hard as things were at home, I almost had a mental breakdown when we discussed sending Hazel to daycare. The budget would be tight, but we could make it on Marc's income.

There was no home renovation, no yard work. Still-packed boxes sat in corners, neglected. We were purely surviving.

But as the months passed and Hazel grew, things got better. I kept her alive. Somehow, she was healthy and thriving because of me.

We celebrated our first holiday season at Sunflower Lane. We got a real tree and everything. We took Hazel out of the house for a Christmas get-together with Marc's family in Birmingham, where everyone fussed over her adorableness. We drove to my dad's house on Sand Mountain and had an obligatory, not-very-festive lunch with him at the nearest Cracker Barrel.

In January, we welcomed a new year. Hazel was taking naps now, actual two-hour-long naps in her crib in the nursery, and with these newfound little pockets of freedom, I began feeling human again. I started cooking meals in my new kitchen. With the baby monitor always close by, I unpacked the rest of our long-ignored boxes, and the house began to feel like home.

One Tuesday, during one of Hazel's afternoon naps, I was trying to decide which cabinets would be best for storing the dishes and kitchen gadgets we used most infrequently, things like a glass serving platter, popsicle molds, and the Instant Pot I'd used maybe twice. This kitchen was far bigger than the one at our apartment, but I was already running out of space to organize things as neatly as I wanted.

I reached over my head and slid the glass serving tray into the last empty upper cabinet, then stopped to listen when the baby monitor crackled with static.

A terrifyingly familiar sound followed.

Footsteps.

My heart quickened as I reached for the parent unit and clicked up the volume.

A distinct *thunk, thunk, thunk* across creaking floorboards.

My ears pricked up and my spine tingled as I realized I could hear the sound behind me now, too, coming from the hallway.

Marc was at work.

Someone was in the house.

Protective mother mode fully activated, I seized the nearest thing I could use as a weapon—a chef's knife—and bolted toward the sound, fully prepared to defend my baby. I dashed through the dining room, the living room, like a madwoman, then whipped around the corner into the hallway, where I would come face-to-face with our intruder.

Only the hallway was empty.

The nursery was empty, too.

I rushed to the crib to check on Hazel and found her sleeping, the rise and fall of her little chest regular and rhythmic. My own breath was ragged and uneven as my eyes tracked across the room, examining every inch of space, but there was nothing out of the ordinary.

I stood still and listened.

The house was so quiet, I could hear my racing heartbeat.

Still gripping the knife, I moved from room to room, flicking on light switches, banishing the shadows, and searching every nook and cranny of the house, just to make sure we *really* were alone.

We were.

What was happening?

I stared at the giant chef's knife in my hand and wondered if maybe I was losing touch with reality. Postpartum psychosis was a thing. The doctor's office had given me a handout on it, among a dozen other things that could potentially go wrong after childbirth. Hallucinations and paranoia were things to watch out for.

Jesus.

This was bad.

As I passed Hazel's nursery again, on my way to return the knife to the kitchen, I felt it.

The tiny hairs on my arms stood on end.

Someone was watching me.

I turned, heart pounding, and saw no one at all.

Eight

Several unseasonably warm days rolled through in February, the kind of Southern false spring that made everything feel hopeful again. The sun was high, the sky a sharp blue, and for the first time in weeks, I didn't need a coat to step outdoors.

It felt good to be outside. I wanted so badly to believe that normal had returned. That the footsteps I'd been hearing were nothing. That I hadn't stood frozen in the hallway clutching a chef's knife like a crazy person.

Today was different. Bright and warm and full of promise.

I set Hazel's new quilted bouncer at the base of the porch steps and buckled her in facing the yard. The bouncer was a game-changer; I had a safe place to put her while I worked, and for the first time in what felt like forever, I could use both of my hands.

I got to work on the flower beds out front, desperate to tame the mess. They'd been wild when we moved in, choked with weeds and half-dead shrubs, the kind of neglect that takes years to accumulate. Spring fever had me believing I could undo it in a single morning.

I knelt beside the porch with gardening gloves on, tugging at stubborn roots and straining my lower back as I threw my weight into it. I cleaned up garbage left behind by the last owner. Plastic plant tags. Broken pot shards. I trimmed the azaleas down to neat, orderly spheres. I didn't know if that's what you were supposed to do this time of year, but I needed them to look better.

Hazel cooed softly from her bouncer, seemingly just as pleased as I was to be outside. For the first time since we'd moved in, I felt capable. Like I could finally take action and really make this place ours.

The renovations had all been put on hold after Hazel was born. We'd meant to pick them back up, but between newborn chaos and recovery, it just hadn't happened. Now, though? I was almost eight months postpartum. I had my body back, more or less. No job to clock into. No deadlines to meet. Just lots of time and, finally, the energy to start doing things again.

I began planning which perennials I would plant along the porch after the last frost date. Hydrangeas, for my mom. Marc had mentioned those once. Wisteria. That would look so charming if I let it climb up the porch columns. Maybe gardenias and irises. Out back by the barn, I pictured a row of sunflowers and a small vegetable garden. I could start seeds indoors soon.

I'd just torn open a fresh bag of brown mulch, the woody scent of it oddly comforting, when a voice behind me made my heart skip.

"Hey, there."

A bubbly, singsong voice. Girlish, with a thick Southern drawl.

I turned to look over my shoulder.

A woman stood a couple of yards behind me. She was thin, maybe in her late forties or fifties, though her age was hard to pin down. She looked crispy. Her leathery skin told a story of too many hours in the tanning bed, and her shoulder-length, bleached-blonde hair looked just as fried. She wore white Nikes and a hot pink tennis dress that clung to her bony frame.

Where had she come from?

I glanced past her, searching for a car, but there wasn't one. She'd walked here.

"Didn't mean to startle you, hon," she said, voice syrupy sweet. "I was out on my walk and I saw you working in the yard. Thought I'd stop by and introduce myself. I'm your neighbor. Kim Gillespie."

My eyes scanned our yard, checking the tree-lined sides of our property, following the gravel driveway out to Sunflower Lane, to the cornfield across the road, as though I expected to find a house I'd somehow missed before.

We weren't right up on them, but I supposed we *did* have neighbors. There were other houses on our road; I just hadn't paid them much attention.

Kim seemed to sense my confusion and gestured toward the left. "I live over at one-twelve. It's the big brick house over thataway."

"Ohhh, okay," I said, pretending to know which one she was referring to. I couldn't picture it for the life of me. I let the bag of mulch fall over and pushed myself off the ground. "It's nice to meet you, Kim. I'm Shannon."

"Shannon. I have a cousin named Shannon. I've seen a man out here a few times. That your husband?"

"Yes, ma'am," I said, dusting the dirt off my pants.

"Oh, good, good. I'm so glad to hear that. I was hoping you weren't living at *this* place all alone."

I blinked, taken aback slightly by the odd comment.

Her thin, overplucked brows shot up. "Y'all sure are brave, I'll tell you that."

I assumed Kim from the "big brick house" was being a little uppity and referring to the less-than-ideal state of our little old house. "We do have our work cut out for us," I admitted with a shrug.

Kim tilted her head. "You do know the stories about this place, right?"

I frowned. "Um, I'm not sure what you mean."

Her brown eyes widened with incredulity. "Are y'all not from around here?"

"No, not really."

"Well, let me just tell you, this house is haunted," she said bluntly, planting her hands on her hips. "I swear to Jesus, it is. Miss Fern? The old lady that owned it before you? She died in the house."

My stomach knotted at this unexpected revelation. I didn't really believe in ghosts. Nevertheless, my mind went to the mysterious footsteps I'd been hearing all this time.

The knowledge that a person had lost their life in my home... it made me feel a little sick. More than just sick, actually. Perhaps thanks to my still-not-back-to-normal postpartum hormones, I felt my eyes growing misty.

"Lord, you really didn't know that," Kim said. "I'm sorry to be the bearer of bad news."

She didn't look sorry. She looked downright delighted to deliver such a juicy scoop.

I sucked in a deep breath through my nose, hoping it would dry up my tear ducts.

Kim shifted her weight from one foot to the other. "Well, all I'll say is y'all just need to be careful. Mmkay?" Her intonation was overly dramatic, but her eyes seemed genuine. "And listen, if you ever need anything, I'm just right down the road. Come by any time."

"Thank you."

She reached into a pocket and removed a slip of paper. "I wrote my name and number down for you, just in case you need it. Call me. Or text me. I know most folks your age like to text. How old are you, anyway?"

I took the paper from her and glanced down at it. Of course she had it ready. She'd *planned* this interaction.

"I'm thirty," I replied.

"Oh. Wow. I didn't think you were *that* old."

Damn. This lady had no filter.

My curt reply was out of my mouth before I could stop it: "I use sunscreen."

Kim fell quiet. Her eyes traveled beyond me, apparently discovering Hazel in her bouncer for the first time. "You have a baby!"

Her high-pitched squeal hurt my ears. "Yep."

"Aw, Lordy, he is just precious! Look at those fat little cheeks!"

"She's a girl," I said flatly.

Didn't her pink floral onesie give that away? It was always *he* first, no matter what she wore. People were always making the same assumption at the grocery store, at restaurants, wherever we went. Why did everyone assume babies were boys unless proven otherwise? It annoyed me to no end.

Kim pushed past me and went to the bouncer. She squatted down to place herself at eye level with Hazel.

I held my breath. *Don't touch her. Please don't touch her.*

"Hi, there, girly! Ain't you just a cutie patootie?" She glanced up at me. "What's her name?"

"Hazel."

"Hazel?" She laughed softly. "Now *that's* an old-timey name. Don't think I've heard that one on anybody under eighty. You know, I had an Aunt Hazel. She lived down in Randolph County. Lived to be ninety-seven."

I smiled politely. "It was my mom's middle name. I wanted to honor her."

"Oh, that's sweet. What happened to your momma?"

"Cancer."

"Aw, I'm sorry to hear that, hon." Kim leaned down even closer to Hazel and slipped right back into her grating baby talk. "Well, you wear that name better than any old lady I know. You are just too sweet, little lady. You are! Yes, you are!"

I'd seen a few headlines about a new virus going around, and I really wished she would back the hell up.

Thankfully, she kept her hands to herself and straightened. "You need to keep a close eye on her. I mean it. A real close eye."

I braced for a follow-up joke. Something gross and cliché, like *better get a shotgun, the boys'll be lining up to date her.* But Kim didn't say it.

Instead, she looked genuinely uneasy.

"Well," she said after a beat. "I'll get out of your hair. I don't like sticking around this old place longer than I have to. Nice meeting you, Shannon."

"You too."

She turned toward the driveway, then paused. Glanced back. But her eyes didn't meet mine. They fixed on the line of trees beyond the yard, a cluster of shadows despite the mid-morning light.

"Y'all be careful around those woods," Kim said, her voice lower now. "Things get lost in there." Her eyes stayed on the trees. "Not all of 'em come back."

NINE

Fern

June 1961

THE SHOVEL MET THE earth with a dull thud, turning over another clump of stubborn red clay. Fern pressed her boot down on the edge and leaned into it with her whole weight, jaw clenched tight. The flower bed along the front porch looked more like a graveyard than anything else. All the lovely perennials she'd planted back in April had shriveled by June, their stems dried up and brittle, like skeletons, their roots blackened with rot.

Nothing wanted to grow here. Not even weeds.

It was disheartening. Fern knew this place needed some color, some natural beauty, but they'd been here a year now, and her efforts always failed. It felt like the house itself was rejecting her, resisting her every attempt to make it feel like home.

She'd grown things successfully her whole life. She'd worked the land from girlhood in rural Georgia, and always thought of herself as having a green thumb. Maybe the soil here was just different. Maybe it needed proper amendments she wasn't familiar with. She'd ask her neighbor Colene about it after service on Sunday.

For now, she aimed to rip everything out of this cursed ground.

Fern leaned the shovel against the house and knelt down, gloved hand wrapping around the base of a desiccated gladiolus. She gave it a tug just as a flicker of motion in her periphery caught her eye. She tossed the bulb aside and looked up.

Joyce was dancing along the edge of the tree line, giggling to herself as she spun, the flared skirt of her robin's egg blue dress fanning out with every twirl.

Fern frowned. That was her *good* dress. "Joycie!" she called.

Joyce stopped and turned to her. "What?"

Ma'am, Fern corrected her silently. She didn't feel like yelling it across the yard. Joyce already knew better.

"Come here! I don't like you so close to the woods."

She could see Joyce roll her eyes even from a distance. Such a strong-willed child. But she started toward Fern anyway, skipping through the grass.

As she drew close, Fern could see the stains on the dress.

"Joyce, what have you done to your dress?" she gasped. "Why are you wearing your good one out here? Is that mud?"

"This one's my favorite," Joyce said simply, as if that explained everything.

Fern sighed, but despite herself, she felt a small swell of pride. She'd sewn the dress herself, and it *was* some of her best work. It suited Joyce so well.

"I know, darling, but it isn't one for romping around in." She plucked a pine needle from Joyce's disheveled sandy brown hair and studied her more closely. "Were you out in the woods?"

Joyce glanced away and shrugged.

"I've told you time and time again, I don't like you going out there by yourself."

"I wasn't by myself. Shirley was with me."

"Shirley?" Fern's eyes darted around the yard. "Where is she now?"

"She went back home."

"Did *her* mother know where you were?"

"No."

"*No, ma'am,*" Fern corrected with a huff. "I'm sure Mrs. Colene would tell you the same thing. Y'all know wild animals live out there. Coyotes and snakes and Lord knows what else. What if one of you had stepped on a snake and gotten bit? What would you have done, out there all alone? Your father and I wouldn't have even known where to look for you. It isn't safe, Joyce. I need you to listen to me."

Joyce clasped her hands behind her back as her eyes dropped to the ground. "I know."

"Then why do you keep disobeying us?"

Her blue eyes snapped up to meet Fern's. "Loretta told us to."

Fern blinked. "Loretta told you to?"

Joyce gave a little shrug, her eyes shifting sideways.

Fern followed her daughter's gaze toward the woods. The midday sun overhead burned down on them, but in the trees, it was black as night.

"I don't want to hear any more about Loretta telling you to do things," Fern said firmly. "It's not funny, and it's not very Christlike. You have to take responsibility for your own actions."

Joyce didn't argue. But her small shoulders lifted as she drew in a breath. When she exhaled, her voice came out quiet: "She said those woods have secrets."

Fern froze for a moment, her eyes scanning the tree line once more. A breeze rustled the pine branches, and for a moment, the air felt far colder than it should've for June.

"Well," she said, trying to keep her voice steady as she ignored the prickle of unease crawling across the back of her neck, "secrets are for Christmas and birthday parties. Not the woods. And certainly not for little girls out there by themselves."

The screen door creaked open and slammed shut. Raymond's polished loafers clacked across the floorboards, louder than they needed to be, leaving behind a trail of red mud from the front yard. He wore black slacks and a pale blue dress shirt that Fern had pressed for him yesterday, its sleeves rolled to the elbow. A striped tie, loosened but still knotted at his throat, swung slightly with each step. He smelled of aftershave and machine oil and something else. Something sweet and floral and unfamiliar.

Was it . . . perfume?

Fern looked up from the sink, still scrubbing a dinner plate. "Hey, honey," she said, forcing a smile. "Your supper's in the oven. Want me to take it out for you?"

Raymond didn't answer right away. He dropped his briefcase on the table and looked around the kitchen, nose wrinkling. "Smells like beans."

"It *is* beans. With cornbread."

He grunted. "No meat?"

"We had chicken last night," she replied. "And I put some fatback in the beans."

Another grunt.

She watched her husband give the room a once-over, his eyes skipping from the pile of dirty dishes she was working on to the cluttered table and the basket of laundry she hadn't put away yet. "What in God's name have you been doing all day, Fern? This place looks like a pigsty."

Fern bit her tongue hard and stared out the big arched window above the sink. "I've been working outside." She nodded toward the view of the yard, where the last rays of sun had long since faded to darkness. "The flower beds were in rough shape."

He glanced down at his muddy shoes, then back to her. "That explains *this* mess then," he huffed. "And that took you all day?"

Heat rose in Fern's cheeks. "Well, Raymond, the meals didn't cook themselves, and the maid didn't wash and hang out the laundry," Fern shot back. "And the nanny didn't—"

"Alright, I get it, Fern. Quit acting like you have something to prove."

"Don't I, though? It sure feels like it when you walk in and say such things, as though I've been sitting on my rear-end watching television all day."

He leaned down and began untying his shoes. "I'll take my plate in the living room. Need to go over some notes before Friday."

Fern sighed as she wiped her hands dry on a dish towel, resisting the urge to snap back *Notes on what? How to be an ass?* She held her tongue, as always, as she slipped on an oven mitt and pulled Raymond's plate from the warm oven.

As she set it on the counter, she added, "Joyce waited up for ages to show you her drawing." She didn't look at him when she said it.

Just peeled off the mitt and turned back to the sink. "She was so excited for you to see it. But she finally gave up and went to bed."

He snorted. "You let her stay up so far past her bedtime?"

Fern blinked at him, incredulous. "She's seven, Raymond. You're always working late, all she wants is to see you, to—"

"She needs routine, Fern. What's it gonna be like when school starts back in the fall? You're too soft."

Fern stared down at the soapy water. Joyce had drawn him a rocket ship, bright red and blue, with smoke trailing out behind it and a tiny American flag in the corner. She'd even written *NASA* across the side, though the *S* was backward.

She was so proud that her daddy was helping send the first men to the moon.

Fern swallowed the lump growing in her throat, blinking fast as tears threatened to fall. She'd told Joyce he'd love it. That he'd take it to work, hang it up in his office. She felt like a liar now, and her heart ached for her little girl.

Behind her, Raymond retrieved his plate without so much as a thanks. As he carried it off down the hall, Fern realized how often Raymond disappeared into separate rooms lately. He came home from work later and later, and every night, he sat alone. Saying less. Needing less. *Giving* less.

For the first time, it struck Fern that she couldn't remember the last thing he'd said that made her laugh. Or the last time he'd touched her.

She stared down at the soapy dishwater as it went cold, feeling lonelier than ever before.

TEN

Shannon

March 2020

AS THE WEEKS PASSED, I gave less and less thought to my strange interaction with Kim Gillespie, the pushy neighbor who'd shown up in my yard with nosy questions and more info than I'd ever asked for. There was too much other shit going on to think about it.

Hazel went through a developmental leap, then a horrible sleep regression, all while the news headlines grew more and more alarming. COVID-19 was raging out of control. People were dying from it all over the world while the people in charge insisted everything was fine.

Groceries became consistently out of stock, and toilet paper—God, the toilet paper—vanished from the shelves. People began wearing masks. Schools went virtual. All businesses deemed non-essential closed.

My dad thought the whole thing was overblown. "You don't shut down the world for a dern cold," he'd said over the phone, furious that Cracker Barrel had closed its dining room. He said he'd rather die than eat a microwaved biscuit from a to-go box.

I asked him not to come over and begged him to be careful. "You're high risk, Dad," I told him. "You've got heart problems."

He brushed me off. Said I was overreacting. That I couldn't keep Hazel in a bubble forever. That he missed his only grandchild.

The guilt gnawed at me, but I held my ground. I couldn't risk her getting sick. Not when everything was so unknown, so chaotic, so out of control.

All around us, people were still arguing about whether COVID was even real, even as tens of thousands of Americans died in a single month.

Then Mr. Charles died.

Mr. Charles was one of Dad's oldest friends. They met for biscuits at Hardee's every Tuesday and Friday, rain or shine, and sat in the same booth by the window, swapping stories about the good ol' days, trash-talking college football, pretending the world wasn't changing around them. When Mr. Charles caught the virus, Dad said it was just "a bad cough." When he was hospitalized, Dad stopped answering my texts. When he died three days later, Dad called me and couldn't say anything for almost a full minute.

"Didn't even get to say goodbye," he said finally. "They wouldn't let me in the hospital."

After that, Dad changed. He started wearing a cloth face mask, one with Big Al on it, the big dumb elephant mascot of the University of Alabama. Dad's greatest love, right behind Cracker Barrel and Home Depot.

He stopped pushing to come inside the house. He never outright apologized for what he'd said early on in the pandemic, but he began dropping off care packages on our porch. Diapers, wipes, random canned foods, batteries, a pack of those soft, pink-frosted cookies I liked as a kid. One such delivery contained a little note he'd scrawled out on a Hardee's napkin:

Love y'all. Be safe.

We waved at each other through the window. Hazel clapped her hands when she saw him. Dad and I both tried not to cry.

Things softened between us. I stopped dreading his calls and started looking forward to them. He asked about Hazel's sleep, my sleep, and whether Marc was pulling his weight.

"We're managing," I told him.

This was mostly true. Marc's job had gone fully remote, so we were both home twenty-four-seven. I took care of Hazel while Marc worked in the spare-bedroom-turned-office.

For the first couple of weeks, it was amazing. We'd never spent so much time together. We made big breakfasts, took turns rocking Hazel to sleep, and ate all our meals together.

But as the weeks became months, and months quietly turned into a new year, the days blurred together. Cabin fever set in hard.

Marc working from home became Marc living at work. All boundaries vanished. He spent more and more time behind his closed office door, like the rest of the house no longer existed. If he wasn't on a Zoom call or working on a report, he wandered aimlessly, restless and irritable, like he didn't know what to do with himself anymore.

He started snapping at me over nothing. We bickered constantly about the dumbest things. Laundry, the right way to load the dishwasher, who drank the last of the coffee. But more than anything, we argued about the state of the house.

The place felt smaller by the day. Every creak of the damaged floorboards we never got around to refinishing, every draft through an outdated window we couldn't afford to replace—it all felt suffocating now. We'd come here with plans and Pinterest boards, dreaming about custom renovations and reading nooks.

Now we just felt stuck.

I think we both hoped that if we just fixed *something*, anything, it might knock us out of this rut and break the tension between us. Help us remember why we bought this house in the first place.

But with COVID driving prices up and our income sliced in half, even the most basic remodeling supplies were out of reach.

Then I remembered the barn.

We had barely touched it since we moved in, and Marc had lit up like a kid on Christmas when he'd first seen all those tools. Maybe if we could dig through what was out there, repurpose what we found, we could get to work.

And maybe, hopefully, that would shake us out of whatever this was.

On a chilly day in April 2021, two whole years after we'd bought the place, Marc tugged open the heavy barn doors without a word. There was none of that old spark. No wide-eyed excitement. Just a resigned sigh as the hinges groaned open.

The smell of dust and rodent urine hit us immediately. The air inside was colder, still and stale.

Everything was just as we'd left it. Paint cans with faded labels. Tins of screws and nails. It all looked the same, but something about the barn felt heavier now. Less like potential and more like a red flag we'd ignored two years ago.

Marc half-heartedly picked through a box of tangled extension cords while I sorted through the wall shelves.

We spent the better part of the afternoon out there, working mostly in silence. Hazel was safely corralled with toys and board books in a toddler play yard just outside the barn doors, nearly two now and too quick for me to trust on open ground. For a while, she babbled to her stuffed unicorn, then switched to pointing at birds overhead.

Every once in a while, I peeked out to check on her, mostly an excuse to get away from Marc. He was so quiet, so sullen, I felt like I was doing something wrong just by breathing in the same space as him.

One time, I found some mystery tool and asked if he knew what it was. He let out this exaggerated sigh like I'd asked him to perform some Herculean feat.

I didn't say anything. I put it back and kept digging.

This wasn't how it was supposed to be.

We were supposed to be the couple that fixed things. That took something old and neglected and made it beautiful again. That was the whole reason we bought this place. To build something together.

What was happening to us?

I moved toward the back of the barn, where the shadows gathered and formed a dusky curtain, the perfect refuge for lurking wildlife. I braved it reluctantly, desperate to find something useful. Something that might reignite Marc's excitement.

I nudged aside a warped sheet of plywood leaning against the wall, holding my breath in anticipation of movement—a flash of fur, the sound of tiny feet scampering away—but nothing stirred.

Instead, I caught sight of something large wedged in the corner: a vintage chest freezer. Buried beneath a precarious stack of chewed-up cardboard boxes, old garden hoses, and broken furniture legs that stretched nearly to the rafters, its once-white exterior was now a grimy yellow. It looked like it hadn't been touched in decades.

"Hey, there's a deep freezer back here," I called over my shoulder. "You think there's electricity?"

I waited, hoping for a positive reaction. Marc had always dreamed about having a workshop to putter around in. If this place was wired, maybe it would revive his excitement.

But all I got was a shrug. "Doubt it," he muttered, not even turning around.

Something in me sank. I turned back to the pile without replying and stepped closer to check it out. I didn't hear it humming. My eyes searched until I spotted the end of its frayed cord flopped uselessly over the edge, unplugged.

Definitely not in use. Probably hadn't been in years.

I stood there for a long moment, just staring at it.

There was something about the freezer that made the back of my neck prickle. It sat still and silent, buried beneath decades of cobwebs and junk, but I couldn't shake the feeling that it was . . . hiding something.

Then my eyes caught on something else.

Propped between a broken dining chair and a tattered cardboard box was a narrow wooden plank, partially hidden under a length of old hose. I reached for it and brushed away a layer of dust with the sleeve of my hoodie.

Chipped at the edges, maybe a foot long, it had streaky black letters faded with age:

Joyce's Clubhouse
LORETTA KEEP OUT

The last line had been underlined three times. Bits of glitter clung stubbornly to the wood, sealed beneath clear glue. A child's project from long ago.

I stared at it, heart thudding. I didn't know why it unsettled me.

"Hey," I called out again, softer this time. "Did you see this?"

"Shannon, if it doesn't have a DeWalt logo on it, I don't care."

I gaped at him for a second, disappointed but not surprised. "Why are you being such a jerk?" I asked. "You were so excited about all this stuff when we bought the place. What happened?"

He didn't answer. Just kept fiddling with a box of screws like I wasn't even there.

Eleven

I went to bed alone that night. Again. The third time that week.

When we finally gave up on finding treasures in the barn, Marc went straight back into his office and shut the door behind him. He never came out. Not even for dinner.

I waited as long as I could, hoping he'd emerge. That he'd sit with me, eat with me, ask about my day with Hazel, ask about anything. But the hours dragged on, and the only sounds from his corner of the house were the occasional clack of his keyboard.

By nine, I'd bathed Hazel, nursed her, and put her down in her crib for the night. I showered, changed into an oversized T-shirt, and crawled into our cold, empty bed. I lay there, wide awake, staring up at the ceiling fan spinning above me in the darkness, my entire body crawling with a jitteriness that meant sleep wasn't happening any time soon.

By midnight, I was still awake. And still alone.

What was he doing in there?

He said his job had become more demanding. More video calls. More reports. But what kind of reports had to be written at midnight? What kind of job made a man work around the clock, day after day, night after night?

And I'll admit it; sometimes I lingered outside in the hallway to listen through the door, and all I ever heard was silence. No Zoom calls, no typing, no click of his mouse. Nothing.

I'd never said it out loud, but the thought had been simmering in the back of my mind for weeks. Maybe he'd lost his job and was too ashamed to tell me. Maybe he was playing video games in there all day, hiding from the world. Hiding from me.

Or maybe it was something worse.

A sick, cold thought wormed its way into my brain, one that only came late at night when I was too tired to think rationally and too wound up to stop myself: What if he was having an affair?

I knew it didn't make sense. We were both home all the time. He never left the house anymore except to pick up groceries. But that was the thing, wasn't it? It didn't have to be someone local. Not these days. It could be entirely online. Private messages. Webcam stuff. Digital cheating.

I shut my eyes, trying to chase the thoughts away. I hated thinking like this. I hated what this house, this year, this silence had turned me into. I didn't want to be this version of myself. Suspicious. Bitter. Lonely. Someone who tiptoed around, spying on their husband, and spiraled alone in bed at midnight.

That wasn't who I was. It wasn't who we were.

But Marc had changed. Something in him had gone quiet. Shut down.

And maybe I had changed, too.

I rolled onto my side and stared at the empty space beside me.

The baby monitor on my nightstand crackled.

I froze, listening.

Soft rustling drifted through the speaker, followed by the sound of Hazel's voice. Gentle babbling at first, then a giggle.

I smiled. Maybe she was dreaming.

Then her giggle escalated into a full-on belly laugh, the kind of laugh that made her whole body shake with joy, like when we played peekaboo or when I made silly faces at her.

I sat up.

That wasn't dream laughter. That was real. Alert and reactive.

A hopeful thought flickered through my mind: *Maybe Marc went in to check on her.* Maybe he was finally trying. Maybe he'd remembered how to be a dad.

No, something about it felt off.

Not bad, exactly. But strange. Wrong.

I swung my legs over the side of the bed and stepped into my house slippers, shrugging on my bathrobe as I moved. The hallway was colder than it should've been. I pulled the robe tighter and padded quietly to the nursery, my ears straining to hear more.

I pushed open Hazel's door.

In the bluish glow of the nightlight, I could see her outline in the crib. Hazel was sitting up, smiling, the whites of her eyes sparkling in the dark.

"Hey, what are you doing wide awake?" I whispered, moving to the crib and resting my hand on the railing.

She gave me a fleeting glance, then turned her gaze beyond me, eyes still twinkling with joy. Her grin widened, and she waved.

My heart lurched.

She wasn't waving at me.

She was looking *past* me. Grinning, waving, laughing at something directly over my right shoulder.

A cold, electric dread climbed my spine.

I didn't turn around. I couldn't.

Every part of me screamed *don't look.*

I scooped Hazel up, clutching her to my chest. She squealed with laughter, twisting to peer over my shoulder.

"Bye-bye!" she said.

I bolted out of the room, refusing to see whatever she was still waving at behind me. We didn't stop moving until we were down the hall and safely in my bedroom.

She slept with me that night.

TWELVE

Fern

March 1962

A SCREAM TORE THROUGH the darkness and ripped Fern out of sleep.

She jerked upright in bed, heart hammering. For a moment, she couldn't place the sound, was only aware of the thud of her pulse in her ears and the tightness in her chest. The house was so quiet she could hear the grandfather clock ticking in the living room.

"Ray?" she mumbled, reaching out for her husband in the darkness.

The other side of the bed was empty, the sheets cold and unwrinkled.

She frowned. He *still* hadn't come home?

Another cry came from down the hall, high-pitched and frantic. Joyce.

Fern threw back the covers and darted across the room. Out in the hallway, the air was sharp and frigid. It bit at her bare ankles as she hurried toward Joyce's door.

She found her daughter sitting up in bed, fists clutching her quilt, her face streaked with tears.

"What is it, darling?" Fern asked, settling onto the bed beside her. She pulled Joyce's trembling frame against her chest. "What's wrong?"

The whites of Joyce's eyes shone wide in the darkness as they darted toward the window.

"She was here," she whispered.

Fern followed her gaze. The curtains billowed faintly, as though something had just brushed against them.

"Who?"

"The lady," Joyce's voice cracked. "She was standing right here, smiling at me."

Fern felt her scalp prickle. "You had a nightmare, sweetheart. No one's here."

Joyce shook her head urgently. "She left. She went outside when she heard you comin'."

Fern's throat went dry. She pushed herself up, crossed the room, and parted the curtains just enough to peer through.

The backyard was drenched in pale moonlight, the grass sparkling silver beneath a layer of frost. The woods at the edge of the property stood black and still.

Nothing moved.

Yet the cold deepened. A crawling, damp chill that settled against her skin. She drew the curtain closed.

"There's nothing out there," she said as firmly as she could manage, hoping Joyce didn't pick up on the tremor in her voice.

When she turned back, Joyce was weeping quietly, eyes fixed on the window.

"Oh, Joycie. Sometimes, nightmares feel so real, but—"

Down the hall, the groan of a floorboard cut her off. The sound was long and slow, like a man tentatively shifting his weight.

"Raymond?" Fern called out.

Silence.

Another pop. Then another.

Footsteps.

Heavy, dragging footsteps. Slow. Deliberate.

Fern moved to the doorway. She gripped the frame as she peered into the hall. "Ray?"

Nothing.

Only the hum of the furnace and the slow, menacing tick of the clock down the hall.

"She said Daddy isn't here," Joyce murmured. "She told me he isn't coming back."

The words hit Fern like a slap.

"Joyce," she said, her voice quavering now. "Don't say that."

"*She* said it. Not me."

Fern sucked in a ragged breath, gathering her resolve. "Stay here, Joyce."

She stepped into the hall. The floor planks announced her presence with too-loud pops.

"Ray?" she called again.

No answer.

She moved to the front of the house, where her bare feet met the soft edge of the living room carpet. At the entryway, her eyes landed on the empty hook where his coat should've hung.

Her stomach tightened.

The key rack beside the door was empty, too.

She crossed to the window and pressed her palm against the cold glass. The ground shimmered faintly with dew, hardening to ice in the moonlight. The whole yard looked frozen.

No car. No tire tracks.

He'd never stayed out this late. She glanced at the grandfather clock. Ten minutes past three.

She stood there until the chill reached her bones.

Behind her, the clock kept ticking.

Thirteen

Shannon

April 2021

MORNING LIGHT POURED THROUGH the dining room windows, too cheerful for how I felt. I slouched over the table in my robe, clutching my coffee, willing myself awake.

Hazel sat in her booster beside me, calm and focused as she skewered banana slices with her tiny fork. Blueberry yogurt smudged her chin, and a little blob clung to her curls where she'd brushed them back. She didn't seem to notice.

I was too distracted to care. I kept replaying last night on loop. Hazel's laughter. Her innocent little wave. The way her eyes locked on something behind me.

Bye-bye!

My skin crawled all over again.

I glanced at the baby monitor unit perched on the edge of the kitchen counter. Audio only, no screen. I needed something better. I needed to see what was happening in Hazel's room when I wasn't there.

I'd drive into Huntsville today and buy a camera.

And I had to talk to Marc, really talk to him, before I lost my mind.

He never came to bed last night. It was nearly nine now, and his office door was still closed. I hadn't knocked. I didn't want to set him off, give him another reason to be angry with me. But now it was getting absurd. He couldn't just lock himself away, pretending his wife and daughter didn't exist.

I had to know what he was doing in there.

I needed to know if he was even okay.

What if something had happened? It wasn't crazy to wonder, not with the way he'd been pulling further away from me day after day. He'd been hiding away in that room for weeks now.

Images of worst-case scenarios bombarded my brain, one after another. Marc slumped over in his desk chair, not breathing. Marc curled up in a ball on the floor, enduring a silent, spiraling breakdown I should've seen coming.

What if he couldn't even ask for help?

What if I'd missed the signs?

A *clunk* followed by a tiny *"uh-oh"* yanked me back to the present.

I glanced over to find Hazel staring at the floor, her fork lying amidst a messy ring of banana slices.

"Hazel, don't do that!" I snapped, too sharply.

Her little face crumpled. "Sowwy, Mama."

My chest tightened with instant regret. "No, no, I'm sorry, baby," I murmured, setting down my mug and leaning over to retrieve her fork. "Mama's just . . . tired, okay? I'm sorry."

She blinked up at me with her solemn blue eyes, then smiled, forgiving me immediately.

I sighed. I wasn't just tired. I was unraveling. And if I didn't open that office door soon, I was going to make myself sick with all the awful possibilities I'd imagined.

I wiped her fork with a napkin and handed it back.

"Stay here, sweetie," I told her, rising to my feet. I kissed her forehead. "I'll be right back."

She was contained. Sticky, but safe. I just needed five minutes. That's all. I turned and made my way toward Marc's door.

The hallway was dim, as always. We still hadn't installed an overhead light. The crack at the bottom of Marc's office door showed nothing but darkness.

I swallowed hard and knocked. "Marc?"

Silence.

I pressed my ear against the wood. I couldn't hear a thing.

My fingers trembled as I turned the knob. I pushed the door open and flicked on the light.

The smell hit me first. Stale food. Old coffee. Something sour and rotting beneath it all. I lifted my hand to cover my nose, gagging as I stepped inside.

Trash littered the floor. Food wrappers, empty soda cans, crusted takeout containers. A line of half-drunk water and Gatorade bottles stood along the windowsill. Marc had always been tidy. A bit of a neat freak, even. This wasn't just clutter.

This was collapse.

Near the back wall, I spotted a sleeping bag and a pillow, flattened from regular use.

When had he brought them in here? How long had he been sleeping on the floor?

His desk chair was pulled out at a crooked angle, like he'd left in a hurry. The desk itself was buried in unopened mail, loose papers, and unwashed coffee mugs I hadn't seen in days.

His laptop was gone.

Dread twisted my gut.

Above the desk, tacked to the wall, hung a piece of lined notebook paper. I thought it was a to-do list until I stepped close enough to read the single line he'd written at the top in small, cramped letters:

I don't belong here.

A chill swept over me.

I backed away from the desk slowly, eyes scanning the room again for something, anything, that might explain this.

Had he left it for me to find?

I ran down the hall to the living room window, shoved aside the blinds, and looked out toward the driveway.

His Corolla was gone.

My breath hitched. I hurried back into the dining room, where my phone waited beside my coffee.

Hazel smiled at me as I rejoined her. "Mama!"

I barely acknowledged her as I grabbed my phone and checked for missed calls or texts. There were none. He'd just left.

I stood frozen, mind scrambling.

Where would he go?

Why didn't he say anything?

What was happening to him?

I called him. It rang three times, then went to voicemail. I hung up before the greeting and tried again, pacing in slow circles as each unanswered ring tightened my chest.

I opened our text message thread, thumb hovering over the keyboard, unsure of what to say. *Where are you? Are you okay? Please come home.*

I couldn't type any of them.

"Down," Hazel whined, tugging on the straps of her booster seat. "I done."

I forced a shaky breath and helped her down. "Come on. Let's go wash those sticky hands."

We headed for the bathroom. Hazel climbed onto her little stepstool, reaching for the faucet. I helped her turn the water on, and she began lathering her hands, quietly absorbed in watching the water stream over her fingers.

The click of the front door lock sent a jolt through me.

Marc was home.

Trembling, I crouched down so Hazel and I were eye-level. "Stay right here, okay?" I whispered. "Play with the bubbles."

She nodded eagerly.

I stepped into the living room just as Marc opened the front door.

"Where the hell were you?" I demanded.

Marc didn't look at me as he dropped his keys into the bowl by the entry. "I needed to get out for a bit."

"You didn't tell me you were leaving. You didn't answer your phone. You've been holed up in that disgusting mess doing God knows—" I stopped myself. I hadn't meant to bring that up yet.

His shoulders stiffened. "I'm not doing this right now."

"Well, *I* am," I shot back. "Because something is going on with you, Marc. You're not yourself. You're pulling away, you're—" I forced myself to slow down, take a breath, and proceed carefully. "I'm worried about you."

He finally turned to look at me. "I just needed some damn space, Shannon. That's all."

"From what? Me? Hazel?"

His silence stung.

"You're scaring me, Marc. I think you need to talk to someone. A doctor. A therapist, maybe. Please."

"I don't need therapy," he huffed. "Why are you getting so worked up over this?"

"You don't come to bed anymore. You never leave that office. You don't ever spend time with us anymore."

"What're you even talking about? I was in that damn barn with you all day yesterday."

"Right, but after that, I never saw you again." My voice cracked as I went on. "You didn't say goodnight. You didn't check on us. Hazel was up at midnight laughing at something in her bedroom. She was waving and giggling and, I don't know, Marc, it was so creepy."

He gave a humorless dry laugh. "Can you hear yourself? *You* sound like the one who needs therapy."

I scoffed. "I'm being serious. Something's gotta change. We can't go on like this."

He stared at me for a second, then shook his head slowly, like I was a problem he didn't have time to deal with. "You want something to change? Fine. Start by backing the hell off."

I blinked, stunned. He'd never talked to me like that before.

"That's not fair," I said, my voice cracking. "I'm trying to hold this house together while you disappear into that room and act like we don't even exist."

He turned away, already retreating down the hall.

"Marc!" I called after him. "Please. Just *listen* to me." My heart pounded as I finally said the thing I'd been swallowing for weeks. "I'm tired of being alone in this marriage and pretending I'm not. I need you to show up. I need you to care."

That's when he snapped. He spun back around, eyes bloodshot, jaw clenched, and spat out, "I need you to get out of my ass."

Then he slammed the office door in my face.

Fourteen

THE REST OF THAT spring passed in a fog of silence and surveillance. I got a security camera and mounted it on the wall in Hazel's nursery, the lens aimed at the closet. I stayed up late night after night, watching hours of footage, combing through every frame like I might catch something that would explain everything. But I only ever saw Hazel sleeping, breathing, stirring. Occasionally babbling into the dark.

I was tempted to put a camera in Marc's office, too, but I couldn't bring myself to do it.

He disappeared into that room completely. He stopped eating with us. Stopped talking to me. Stopped being a person I recognized.

The following summer was a season of secrets.

Marc took more and more "drives to clear his head." I stopped asking where he went. Hazel turned two and learned how to sing most of "Twinkle, Twinkle, Little Star." I learned how to smile in front of her and cry in the shower.

Fall brought the end, quiet and cruel.

One morning, bleary-eyed and on my way to start the coffee maker, I found a manila envelope on the kitchen counter. A neon sticky note sat on top, Marc's handwriting scrawled across it:

I'm done. Sorry.

Inside was a packet of divorce papers. He'd already signed them.

My marriage was over. Like that. No discussion. No attempt at repair. Not even the decency of a goodbye.

The winter that followed barely felt real.

The divorce was finalized in a seven-minute hearing over the phone. The Omicron variant was surging, so legal proceedings were happening remotely. Judge Tanaka's voice crackled through my iPhone speaker, brisk and impersonal as he declared the matter concluded. Then the line went dead.

I put away my phone and made boxed mac and cheese while Hazel stood in her learning tower beside me, carefully stirring the noodles with a wooden spoon as I fought back tears.

Marc didn't ask for joint custody. He wasn't even interested in the occasional weekend or holiday. He gave up our little girl with a cold, unsettling detachment that gutted me. I could never understand how easily he let her go.

After that, nothing else he did surprised me—except when he signed a quitclaim deed that gave me the house while he agreed to keep paying the mortgage. The judge thought it was best for Hazel and me to stay in the family home. Stability mattered more than anything, and truthfully, I couldn't have afforded rent on my own. The mortgage payment was only five hundred seventy-five dollars a month, but Marc agreeing to keep covering it still shocked me. I guess maybe he felt guilty. Or maybe he just wanted out that badly.

Dad told me to sell the house now that it was in my name and move back in with him. He said he'd help with Hazel while I went back to work full-time. I appreciated it, but I couldn't go back to Sand Mountain. There weren't many opportunities there for

Hazel or me, and moving back in with my dad felt like undoing everything I'd worked for. I'd already escaped that place once, and returning felt like slipping backward into a version of myself I didn't want to be again.

So I stayed in the house on Sunflower Lane.

And that winter nearly broke me.

Those long, cold, dark nights were the worst.

I woke often to Hazel's voice on the baby monitor—soft, hushed tones I couldn't understand. When I pulled up the camera feed, she'd be perched at the edge of her floor bed, facing the closet, holding a one-sided conversation with someone I couldn't see, in words I couldn't quite make out.

I stopped making her sleep in there. I pulled her into my bed, where she curled against me like a cat. I told myself it was for her safety, but the truth was I couldn't face the dark alone anymore. Not after everything.

The new year came without fanfare. 2022. No countdown, no kiss at midnight, just me and Hazel in our pajamas, watching *Bluey* while the neighborhood fireworks cracked somewhere beyond the tree line.

But something shifted in me after that. Maybe it was the symbolism of a fresh year. Maybe it was the way Hazel looked at me, like I was still her whole world, even when mine had shattered. But I woke up on January first with something I hadn't felt in months.

Resolve.

If Marc wasn't coming back, I had to come back to myself.

I stopped waiting for the camera footage to show me anything. Stopped letting the past dictate every second of my present. I was still scared of what might be in this house, of what tomorrow held, but I had a child who needed me to keep going.

I needed a plan for the future, something that belonged to Hazel and me alone.

I needed to make some money.

I reached out to the design firm I'd worked for when I was pregnant, but they'd downsized during COVID and couldn't take me back. So I started freelancing. Fiverr, Upwork, anything I could get. I designed logos for Etsy shops. Made e-book covers for indie authors on a budget. I got up early and worked while Hazel slept. It was slow, unstable, and paid like crap. But it was something.

It was mine.

Marc never called. Never texted. He'd completely cut us out of his life. But the child support and mortgage were always paid on time, so I knew he was still out there somewhere, still fulfilling some part of his duty.

By the time summer rolled around again, Hazel was speaking nonstop in complete sentences and planning her third birthday party with the wide-eyed exhilaration only a toddler could muster. She wanted purple balloons, a cat cake, and a sparkly purple dress, and she wanted Grandy to come.

Grandy was her name for my dad; a mispronunciation of *Granddaddy* that had stuck. Dad adored it.

Hazel had never had a real birthday party, thanks to COVID. But it was 2022 now, and the world was mostly back to normal.

And so were we.

I'd landed a few regular design clients and started to believe, for the first time, that I might actually make this work. We had routines now. Grocery runs on Mondays. Library story time on Tuesday. Homemade pizza on Fridays. Pancakes on Saturdays.

Hazel's constant chatter and giggles filled the house, and more and more, I laughed with her.

I rearranged the living room. Bought fresh flowers—bright golden sunflowers for our little house on Sunflower Lane. I started lighting candles for no reason other than I liked how warm and cozy they made the place feel.

The fear and loneliness hadn't vanished completely, but I wasn't ruled by it anymore. I was building something new. Just the two of us.

I really thought the worst had already happened.

I thought I'd already hit rock bottom and clawed my way out.

But the house was only getting started with us.

FIFTEEN

Shannon

June 19, 2022

BY MIDMORNING, THE ALABAMA heat was already cruel.

It was Hazel's third birthday, and I'd done everything I could to make it feel like a celebration. I'd set up the party beneath the big oak trees out beside the barn, hoping the shade would help, but it wasn't much of a reprieve.

Balloons drooped. The frosting on the cake threatened to melt. The colorful paper streamers I'd strung between the trees curled in the humidity.

I'd gone all out with the decorations. Hazel was deep in a cat obsession, so naturally, I leaned into the theme. Kitty-cat plates, napkins, cups, plastic tablecloths, and balloons. But the pièce de résistance—a giant yellow tabby piñata—hung from one of the oaks, swaying slightly in the breeze, its paper eyes wide and un-blinking.

And then there was the cake. A full-on cat in the round, baked from scratch by yours truly and brought to life with a DIY topper kit I found on Amazon. Against all odds, it actually turned out alright, if I do say so myself.

Hazel loved it. She twirled across the patchy grass in her sparkly purple dress, chasing the bubbles my dad blew from a unicorn-shaped wand. Her curls stuck to her damp neck. She was beaming.

She didn't seem to notice that no one had come.

We'd invited several people. Some kids her age we'd met at library story time. Even a sweet cashier from the Piggly Wiggly who knew us by name and always gave Hazel a sticker, Miss Phyllis. I'd handed out invitations. Sent follow-up texts.

The people I used to count on, Marc's family, my former co-workers, friends from before the divorce, they had all drifted away months ago.

So I cast a wider net. Tried to start fresh.

No one came.

And Marc? Not even a call or a text.

My dad tried to make up for it.

He'd shown up with a glittery pink gift bag so aggressively sparkly it nearly blinded me in the sunlight. Pink and purple polka dot tissue paper puffed out of the top like the icing of a giant cupcake. The contrast of the sparkly gift against his well-worn Crimson Tide T-shirt and leather-belted dad jorts made me grin.

He helped me hang streamers, made funny voices for Hazel's stuffed animals, and played DJ with a little Bluetooth speaker that kept overheating in the sun.

"You did a good job, Shanny," he said, patting my shoulder with his sun-spotted hand. "She's gonna remember that cake. How hard her mama worked on it. That's what sticks."

I swallowed and tried to believe him.

I poked three candles into the cat cake, and we sang "Happy Birthday" together, just me and Dad, our two voices painfully off-key and drifting in and out of sync. Hazel didn't mind. She clapped and grinned, cheeks pink with summer heat and joy.

I cut the cake into generous squares and passed them around.

Dad took one bite and grunted in approval. "That is the best dern cake I've ever had," he said, through a mouthful of buttercream and cat-shaped sprinkles.

When Hazel finished licking the icing off her fingers, she looked up at me expectantly. "I open presents now?"

I smiled and nodded. "Of course, baby. Go ahead."

She bounced over to the gift pile, just two bags, one from me and one from Dad. Her fingers hovered over the sparkly pink bag, but I gently nudged the smaller one next to it.

"Why don't you open mine first?"

"Okay!" she chirped, already yanking out the tissue paper.

Inside was a pair of purple glittery cat ears on a soft headband, a new coloring book, and a pack of washable markers I'd ordered online.

She gasped and immediately shoved the ears onto her head, grinning wide. "Tank you, Mommy!" she cried, then barreled onto my lap and threw her arms around me.

I held her tight and kissed the top of her head. "You're so welcome, sweetie."

For a moment, the empty chairs and unanswered texts didn't matter. Hazel's joy was enough. It made everything worth it.

She let go and turned, her eyes locking on the sparkling pink bag. "Now Grandy's!"

She seized it and tore into the polka dot tissue paper with glee, and a delighted gasp burst from her when she pulled out a plush yellow tabby cat.

"I lub it!" she squealed, hugging it tight against her chest and burying her nose in the soft fur.

Dad laughed. "Your mama told me you loved yellow kitty-cats. I used to have a real tomcat that looked just like this 'un when I was a little boy. His name was Ernie." His eyebrows danced as he turned to me and added, "Little booger was mean as hell, too."

I grinned. "And I'm sure you had nothing to do with that."

Hazel looked up from her new toy, smiling. "A yellow cat used to live here, too," she said. "A long time ago."

I blinked. "What do you mean?"

She just shrugged and started petting the stuffed animal like it was alive.

I looked at Dad, who gave a small, bewildered shake of his head.

"Well, Hazelnut, what are you gon' name this here kitty-cat?" he asked her.

She paused for a second too long. Her little brows furrowed as she tilted her head to the side, like she was listening to something. Then she looked up at us, face suddenly serious.

"Loretta."

A strange prickle crept along the back of my neck. "What?"

She didn't look up from the cat. "Her name's Loretta."

Dad gave me a puzzled glance, then looked back at Hazel. "That's a mighty grown-up name for a little kitty," he said gently. "Where'd you hear it?"

Hazel looked up, completely unfazed. "That's what the closet lady calls me sometimes."

My chest tightened, and I had to swallow hard before I spoke. "The closet lady?"

She just shrugged, still cradling the plush cat. "She's nice. She lives in my closet."

All I could think about in that moment was the smaller version of my daughter in her crib, waving at the closet behind me, laughing at something I couldn't see.

Bye-bye!

And now . . . Loretta.

It wasn't a name I'd ever said around her. We didn't know anyone named Loretta, and it wasn't a character from a book or a show.

But I'd seen it once. Deep inside the barn. Faded and scrawled across a warped wooden sign, tucked behind rusted tools and spiderwebs.

Joyce's Clubhouse.

LORETTA KEEP OUT.

The sound of Dad chuckling pulled me back to the present. "Well, if the closet lady's real, I hope she's payin' your mama rent."

I turned to him, shaking my head. "Dad," I chided.

"I'm just joking, Shanny." He pushed himself up from his seat with a grunt. "Now if y'all will excuse me a minute, I gotta go make sure your plumbin' still works. That cat better not eat my cake while I'm gone."

Hazel giggled.

"Be back in a few." He patted me on the back, then leaned in and muttered with a wink, "But if the closet lady's on the shitter, we're gonna have a problem."

I rolled my eyes, then watched him cross the yard. His gait was wobblier than I remembered, his spine more hunched, the gray at his temples more pronounced.

When did he start looking so old?

The last few years had aged us all, but suddenly I saw it in him, etched into the lines of his face, the careful way he moved.

He shielded his eyes from the sun and slipped inside the back door.

I shifted in my camp chair, the cloth seat creaking beneath me, and took a slow sip of sweet tea. Hazel hummed nearby, busily playing with her new toys. But my mind wouldn't settle. It kept circling back to Loretta. And the closet.

The afternoon sun filtered through the oak leaves, dappling the grass in speckled patterns. Cicadas droned in the distance. It should've felt peaceful. But something about the stillness made me uneasy.

I glanced toward the back door.

Dad had been gone a while.

A breeze stirred the streamers. I took another swig of tea, trying to shake the bad feeling slithering up my spine.

Then I saw him.

Dad was crossing the yard, moving more slowly than before.

Something was wrong.

His face had gone pale. Grayish, almost. A thin sheen of sweat glistened on his forehead, shimmering in the sunlight. His lips were pressed into a thin, tight line.

He wasn't looking at me.

His eyes were on the house.

"Dad?" I stood up.

A pause. A flicker of something in his expression. Hesitation? Fear? Then he forced a half-hearted chuckle, waving a hand. "Yeah, yeah. Just got a little lightheaded in there."

I frowned. "Lightheaded?"

"Yeah, yeah, you know." He gestured vaguely. "Probably the heat. And that bathroom's got no airflow. I ought to put a fan in there."

His gaze snapped to the back door again and held there.

I followed his line of sight. The door stood ajar, a narrow slice of darkness gaping open like a mouth.

"You should drink some water," I told him, moving to a cooler I'd stocked with bottled water and canned sodas for the no-shows. I reached in, pulled out an icy bottle, and handed it to him.

His hand trembled as he took it from me.

"Dad, are you—"

"I-I thought I saw something in there."

I froze. "What do you mean?"

Dad didn't answer right away. He stared down at the plastic bottle in his hand, shoulders stiff. The water sloshed slightly in his tremulous grip.

"Dad," I said again, more firmly this time.

He exhaled through his nose. "Probably nothing. Just thought I saw someone. Just for a second."

My heart thudded. "Where?"

"Hazel's room."

The air thickened, congealed around me. I opened my mouth, but no sound came out.

He finally looked at me, and there was something in his eyes I had never seen before.

Fear.

His lips parted to speak, but his inhale caught. One hand went to his chest.

"Dad?"

The water bottle slipped from his other hand and hit the ground with a dull thud.

"Dad!" I lunged forward.

He staggered back a step, blinking rapidly. His hand clutched at his shirt, mouth working soundlessly. He kept trying and managed to rasp, "Hazel . . . get her out."

His knees buckled.

I caught his arm, but his weight collapsed against me. The two of us went down hard.

"Dad!" My voice cracked with panic.

He was gasping, one hand still pressed to his chest. His lips moved like he was trying to say more, but no sound came. Just one last shudder of breath.

Then nothing.

I pressed my fingers to his neck. Searched for a pulse.

There wasn't one.

And just a few feet away, Hazel stood frozen, her eyes wide and shining. Her little arms wrapped tight around the yellow cat.

Watching.

Sixteen

I DON'T REMEMBER MUCH after Dad collapsed. Just flashes. The wail of sirens approaching. Red lights bouncing off the barn.

I must've called 911. The call was in my phone log, but I have no memory of making it.

My first clear moment was of sitting in the grass beside Dad, stunned, holding Hazel as she cried hot tears into my shirt.

The paramedics' voices cut through the fog, low and clipped. Efficient. Detached. Saying words I wasn't ready to hear.

Dad was gone.

The weeks after Dad's death blurred together into a mess of difficult phone calls, funeral homes, legal paperwork, and attorneys. At least he'd finally sat down and made a will after Mr. Charles died during the height of the pandemic. I was thankful for that.

But there wasn't much to sort through. Dad hadn't owned a home in years.

We lost the one I grew up in after Mom got sick. They tried so hard to keep up with the bills, but in America, cancer doesn't just take your loved ones. It takes your savings. Your credit. Your entire family's future.

The debt piled up, and eventually, he had to file for bankruptcy. The house went with it. After that, he moved into a rental on the edge of town and never looked back.

Now, all these years later, there wasn't much left. Just the lease on the house he'd rented and his truck, which wasn't paid off, and I couldn't afford the payments. The little bit of money he had built back up in savings went toward the funerary expenses and his final bills.

I cleaned out the rental by myself. I put on cartoons for Hazel while I bagged up his clothes, boxed his old records, and tried to decide what to keep and what to donate. I cried as I cleaned the food out of his fridge and tossed out his heart medications. It was the hardest thing I'd ever done.

I didn't keep much.

His leather wallet.

His favorite flannel shirt, the one he layered over Crimson Tide T-shirts on chilly mornings, its green-and-blue plaid fabric soft from decades of wear.

His go-to coffee mug—a tacky green one that said *I Don't Snore, I'm Dreaming of a Tractor*, the words half-faded beside a chipped image of a John Deere. A silly Father's Day gift I'd given him a lifetime ago, back when I thought dumb jokes on coffee cups were peak humor. He'd used it daily ever since.

I kept his old classic country records, too. Merle Haggard. Waylon Jennings. Johnny Cash. I wasn't allowed to touch them when I was little. That collection was his baby, always meticulously neat and alphabetized, even as everything else in the house fell into chaos and disarray. I couldn't let them go.

I took the record player, too. I didn't know where I'd put it or when I'd use it, but I couldn't stand the thought of it ending up on a shelf at Goodwill for five bucks.

By the end of July, it was all over. His home was empty, his things were in my house, and I was trying to find a new normal.

But every time I closed my eyes, I relived that moment.

The thud of his water bottle hitting the ground. The terror in his eyes. Those final words rasping from his lips:

Hazel . . . get her out.

His last moments looped in my head, over and over. No matter what I did, I couldn't shake it.

I knew I was dealing with trauma. I tried writing about it in my journal, hoping that naming it might help lessen the grip it had on me. I tried deep breathing. I tried grounding exercises.

But grief had its hands around my throat.

Most nights, it felt like the only thing keeping me from falling apart was the warm weight of Hazel's body curled up against me. I'd lie awake beside her in the dark, night after night, staring up at the ceiling as my brain spiraled, refusing to sleep for hours.

One such night, the second week of August, we lay just like that. Her breathing was slow and steady. Mine wasn't.

I watched her in the dimness, noticing the subtle changes in her body, her face. The roundness of her cheeks was fading, her features shifting into something older. A lump formed in my throat. When had she started looking more like a little girl than a baby?

I noticed Loretta, the stuffed yellow tabby, tucked beneath one arm. Seeing it made my chest ache. Images of Dad collapsing slipped into my thoughts again, uninvited.

"Mommy?"

Hazel's voice—so small, so innocent—was such a stark contrast to my grim thoughts, I felt tears sting my eyes. I blinked hard. Swallowed.

"Yeah, baby?" I managed at last, brushing a stray curl from her forehead. Her skin was so soft and smooth. Warm. Alive.

"Mommy, did Grandy say bye to you?"

Something inside me cracked. "What?"

Hazel's mouth parted in a long yawn. She'd asked her question so casually, like it was nothing. Like it wasn't the worst thing I had heard in weeks.

"Did Grandy tell you bye?" Hazel repeated.

I felt my pulse pounding in my throat. Hazel was three years old. I should have just nodded, smiled, given her some soft, comforting lie. *Yes, of course, baby. He did. And he loved us so much.*

But I didn't. I couldn't.

I watched her tiny fingers curl tighter around Loretta's plush fur. "He didn't tell *me* bye," she said.

Dear God.

What a gut punch.

What the hell could I say to that?

My eyes flooded with tears. There was no stopping them this time. They spilled over, hot and bitter, flowing freely down my cheeks. I reached over and squeezed her hand. "I know, sweetie." My voice trembled as I said it. "I know. He just... he didn't have time."

Hazel peered up at me. She blinked, long and hard, and I could see the wheels in her head turning, working things out. I held my breath and braced myself. Whatever she asked or said next, I knew it would be difficult. It would hurt.

"The closet lady said she's sorry."

My gut clenched hard. "What do you mean?"

She yawned again and settled deeper into her pillow. "She told me she saw him. Grandy. He saw her, too. At my birthday party. And he got scared."

A chill curled through my chest. "What lady, Hazel? Who are you talking about?"

"The lady that lives in my closet."

I stared in disbelief.

"She said she's sorry. She didn't mean for him to get hurt." Hazel rubbed at her eyes with the back of her hand, getting sleepier by the second. "I know she didn't. Because she's nice."

A slow, cold tingle crept down my spine. My body tensed, muscles coiling tight, and before I could stop myself, I glanced over my shoulder, half-expecting to find a ghost woman standing at the foot of my bed.

The bedroom door was pulled shut like always.

Nothing was there.

But beyond the door, down the hall, past the bathroom, was Hazel's room. I could almost *feel* the closet from here. Like it knew we were talking about it.

I held Hazel a little tighter.

She was already, somehow, drifting toward sleep again. I watched her breaths come and go, slow and even, her little arms still curled around Loretta.

Maybe I should have shaken her gently awake and pressed her for more information. I could've asked what the lady in her closet looked like, what else she'd said.

But I didn't.

My exhaustion—physical, emotional, and intense—won out. I wasn't going to wake a toddler who'd refused to nap all day and spent the last hour stalling bedtime in every way possible.

Not when my own pulse was hammering, when the weight of what she'd said to me just now sat like lead in my stomach.

She saw him. Grandy. He saw her, too.

I stayed quiet. I held her close. I lay there in the dark, eyes wide open, listening to the silence, trying not to think about the closet.

Instead, my mind replayed Dad's final moments. He'd gone inside to use the bathroom. He'd returned ashen, breathless, and panicked.

He'd seen something. Inside the house. Something so unexpected, so terrifying, he collapsed minutes later.

I hadn't let myself question it until now. I hadn't considered the possibility that perhaps his last words had meant more than I'd thought.

Hazel . . . get her out.

Now Hazel's own words echoed in my head.

She saw him. Grandy. He saw her, too. At my birthday party.

What if the nursery camera had captured something?

Careful not to wake Hazel, I rolled over and grabbed my phone from the nightstand where it lay plugged in, charging.

I found the security camera app, the one I'd installed in her room ages ago. Not once had it captured anything strange. Not that I'd seen, anyway. But I hadn't looked closely in months.

I pulled up the recording history with trembling fingers and thumbed through the dates until I found the right one.

Sunday, June 19. Hazel's third birthday.

There were several recordings from that day, but only one during the time of the party.

MOTION DETECTED - 1:19 PM

I tapped play.

The black-and-white, bird's-eye view of Hazel's room appeared. Everything looked normal. Bright midday sunlight streamed through her curtains. The covers on her toddler bed were neatly made. Her toys and books had all been put away for the party.

Out in the hallway, visible through the open bedroom door—Dad.

He walked by, headed toward the bathroom. Just a blur of motion, nothing out of the ordinary, then he was gone.

For a long moment, the room remained still.

I thought that was it. I expected the footage to end, but the lighting in the room dimmed, just barely. The curtains fluttered, as though caught in a gentle breeze.

The bifold closet doors shifted.

A metallic screech sounded as one panel folded open partway on its track, slow and hesitant.

My breath caught in my throat.

A shadow—though not quite a shadow, more like a ripple or a heat distortion—moved forward from within the closet.

The audio fuzzed with static.

A whisper.

Garbled. Indistinct. But definitely a voice.

Then a sound from the hallway. Footsteps. Dad, walking back toward the party.

He passed the nursery doorway again, but this time, he stopped.

He didn't move. Just stood there, frozen.

Even through the grainy footage, I could see his sudden terror. The way his shoulders jerked. That quick, stumbling step back, like he'd seen something he couldn't process.

The bifold closet door snapped shut in a blur, slamming along the metal track with a sharp, metallic clang.

The clip ended.

My hands were shaking so hard, I could barely hold my phone. But I watched it again. And again. My stomach twisted into a tight, painful knot as I accepted this impossible reality.

Something had been in Hazel's room.

My dad saw it.

And now he was dead.

I wanted to scream. I wanted to call someone, anyone, and say, *Look at this video. Please tell me I'm not losing it.*

But there was no one. No Marc. No Dad. Just me, awake in the dark, in this creepy old house full of secrets.

I set the phone down and stared into the blackness.

I needed answers.

Seventeen

Fern

September 1962

THE CHEST FREEZER GROANED across the barn floor, its metal base scraping crooked furrows through the dry-packed earth. Fern's back screamed, sweat dripping down her spine as she braced both arms against the edge and shoved with her full weight.

"Come on, damn you," she hissed, her boots skidding against the dirt floor.

The freezer should've been packed by now. Corn. Okra. Pole beans. All the summer harvest put up for winter. That's what she'd bought it for, what she'd *planned* for, back when she still believed anything would grow on this godforsaken land.

But nothing survived here.

Not her flowers.

Not her vegetables.

Not her marriage.

She thought of what Colene Henderson had said a few weeks ago, out behind the fellowship hall after service.

"I hate to be the one to tell you this," her friend had murmured, eyes lowered, "but I saw Raymond downtown last week. He was at the diner with that secretary from the Arsenal. They looked… familiar."

Fern had thanked her, driven home in silence, and tried not to picture it. But the image had taken up residence in her mind. Raymond cozied up in a booth next to some slim young blonde in smart business attire. He was looking at her the way he used to look at Fern.

Maybe it wasn't true. Maybe it was. Either way, he wasn't coming back.

"Waste of money," she muttered now. "Waste of time. Waste of damn near everything."

She rammed her hip against the side of the freezer, barely inching it forward. Breath short and fury rising, she slammed a fist into its lid, rattling the coils inside.

After all of that, here she was. Doing this alone. Just like everything else, since Raymond left.

The house had changed since he'd gone. The nights felt longer now, heavier. Lights flickered for no reason. Doors she knew she'd latched creaked open after dark. Joyce kept having those awful nightmares.

And now, this.

Fern had found the old trapdoor cracked open the night before, muddy footprints leading down into the dark. The thought still turned her stomach. Joyce had been playing down there again, she assumed.

"It's dangerous," she'd told her daughter, but Joyce only grinned and called it her clubhouse.

"Not anymore," Fern whispered now. She clenched her jaw with resolve and gave the freezer one final shove.

It scraped into place with an ear-splitting screech, covering the door completely.

Fern stepped back and planted her hands on her hips, chest heaving. "There. That's better."

She wiped her forehead with the hem of her apron and stood still, catching her breath. Dust floated in slow spirals through the slats of light cutting across the barn.

Behind her, something creaked.

"Mother?"

She jumped.

Joyce stood in the doorway, backlit by the late afternoon sun, her tangled hair glowing like a wild halo.

Fern's hand flew to her racing heart. "Mercy, child! Don't sneak up on me like that."

"I was looking for Buttercup. I saw her run out here behind you."

"You're supposed to be inside."

"But you're out here. I thought it would be okay."

Fern frowned. "Well, it's not. Get back in the house."

Joyce glanced at the freezer. "What're you doin' with that?"

"Moving it where it belongs," Fern snapped. "Now get back to the house. I mean it."

Joyce looked down. "Yes, ma'am."

As she turned to go, a flash of yellow fur streaked past her feet. Buttercup. The tabby cat they'd gotten to take care of the mice. She leapt to the top of the freezer and stared at Fern, tail flicking back and forth.

"There you are," Joyce said with relief. She scooped the cat into her arms. Buttercup let out a soft mewl as Joyce hugged her close.

Fern watched the pair of them disappear into the sunlight, Joyce's bare feet padding back toward the house. Her soles were filthy, she observed. That girl would *never* keep her shoes on. Fern had given up nagging her about it ages ago.

The barn was quiet again. Fern stood still, ears ringing in the silence as she stared at the piles of junk and half-finished projects Raymond had abandoned. Tools gathering dust. Scrap wood stacked like it was waiting to become something. Old paint cans turning to rust.

It would've taken so little, she thought. Just a spark. One match, and the whole place could go up in smoke.

She needed to get back to the house. Evening was coming, and she had to start supper. It would be a simple one tonight. She no longer had to fool with meat and potatoes for every meal. No more fussing to placate a man's temper.

She turned to leave.

But before she reached the barn door, she paused. Looked back.

The freezer sat askew in the shadows. Its pale enamel gleamed in the patchy light, too bright, too clean for this place.

Her eyes dropped to the darkness beneath it.

A cold knot tightened in her chest.

Fern pressed her lips together, stepped into the fading light, and pulled the barn door shut behind her with a hard, echoing thud.

Eighteen

Shannon

August 12, 2022

I hated going into the spare-bedroom-turned-office. It felt just as haunted as Hazel's room, only the ghost in here was my ex-husband. His scent was long gone, but his presence remained. A ring from his coffee mug on the desk. His favorite pen still rested on the mousepad, clicky-top down, pen tip exposed and ready, like he'd be back any minute.

I sank onto his desk chair and yanked open the bottom drawer of the filing cabinet. I thumbed through tax returns, appliance warranties, and old instruction manuals until I found what I was looking for. The thick manila envelope from our closing day, slightly bent at the corners. I hadn't touched it since we moved in.

The original deed was tucked in the back.

Grantees: Marc and Shannon Holloway.

Grantor: Joyce Marshall.

I stared at her name. Joyce Marshall. It didn't spark recognition, but it unsettled me all the same. I whispered it under my breath once, then repeated it, louder, like hearing it aloud might knock something loose in my brain.

Her mailing address was printed just beneath her name:

914 Summerwind Avenue, Apt. B, San Diego, California.

That's right. The seller, the daughter of the woman who'd lived here before us, had handled the sale remotely. She'd hired a company to clear out her mother's home and signed the papers from across the country. I remembered that now.

San Diego. Joyce Marshall had put a whole country between herself and this place.

And now I was starting to wonder why.

I shut the folder and went to my laptop, my palms growing sweaty with anxiety. I opened the browser and typed:

Joyce Marshall San Diego California

I hit enter.

I found her in the third search result.

> *Joyce Ann Marshall, 64, of San Diego, California, passed away on December 14, 2020, due to complications from COVID-19. Born and raised in North Alabama, Joyce relocated to California as a young woman, where she spent the remainder of her life.*
>
> *Known for her independence, dry wit, and love for animals, Joyce volunteered for decades at a local no-kill animal shelter. She fostered numerous cats over the years and helped place countless pets in loving homes.*
>
> *She is preceded in death by her husband of thirty-seven years, Robert Marshall. A private memorial was held*

by close friends. In lieu of flowers, please consider do-nations in Joyce's memory to your local animal shelter.

A square photo sat beside the text. It wasn't a formal portrait, more like something a friend had snapped with their phone. A middle-aged woman with silver-blonde hair stood on a patio, her gray linen shirt fluttering in the breeze. Palm trees arched behind her, and blue ocean waves shimmered in the distance. She cradled a silky black cat in her arms, its eyes half-closed in the sunny embrace.

Joyce wore the faint, uncertain smile of someone more comfortable behind the camera than in front of it. Her eyes, though.

Shannon leaned closer to the screen.

There was something in them. Something tired. Something knowing.

The woman in the photo looked like she'd spent her whole life running from ghosts.

Shannon's skin prickled. She eased back against the chair and rubbed her palms over her face, exhaling hard. She hadn't even known the woman, but an ache settled in her chest after reading her obituary.

She'd been hoping, maybe foolishly, that she might be able to contact her. That she could ask Joyce what she remembered, what she'd seen, what had happened here.

But Joyce was gone. And with her, the truth about this house.

Except that might not be the case.

There was still one person around here who *loved* to talk. Who always seemed to know more than she should.

Shannon picked up her phone, pulled up her contacts, and found Kim Gillespie's name.

The smell of vanilla-cinnamon plug-in air freshener punched me in the face before I even stepped all the way inside Kim's house. My ears flinched at the high-pitched yapping of her tiny dog, and Hazel scrambled up my leg in terror, nails digging into my skin.

"Get over here, Booboo, you hush now!" Kim hollered from the other side of the screen door, approaching from somewhere deeper in the house. "Lord have mercy, you'd think I was gettin' robbed."

The dog—some unholy mix of Yorkie and feral alley rat—launched itself at the screen door with the ferocity of a pit bull. Hazel whimpered and clung tighter to me.

Kim strode up to the door, her platinum blonde ponytail pulled back high and tight like always. She wore black leggings, a bright coral sports bra peeking out from beneath a zippered hoodie, and a full face of makeup that had not smudged in the Alabama summer heat. She scooped up the tiny dog and swatted his rear-end. "Sorry, he don't know how to act around strangers. I'll put him in my room. Y'all come on in."

She smiled as she held the door open for us, and I accepted her invitation.

The screen door hadn't even shut behind us when the wall of heat and fragrance inside Kim's house smothered me. Scented plug-ins, maybe six of them, all working overtime to mask whatever lurked beneath. Probably dog stink. My eyes watered.

Hazel clung to me like a spider monkey, wide-eyed and trembling at the relentless, yappy barking.

"Y'all have a seat in the living room, I'll be back in a second," Kim told us, carrying the little terror down the hallway.

Hazel didn't let go of me. Her eyes were wide as she took in the unfamiliar surroundings.

The living room was spotless and obnoxiously Pinterest-perfect. Pale gray furniture, about a dozen black-and-white buffalo check throw pillows, a towering stone fireplace, its mantel decked out in farmhouse-chic knick-knacks, including a cotton wreath mounted in the center of a distressed mirror made to look like a vintage window frame. Crosses, family photos, and whitewashed signs took up almost every inch of wall space. *Blessed. Family. Live Laugh Love.* Clearly, Kim was keeping Hobby Lobby in business.

I found a spot on the couch that wasn't covered in decorative throw blankets and pulled Hazel onto my lap.

Kim rushed back into the room. "Now then. Sorry about that." Booboo barked one last time from behind a closed bedroom door, scratching like he had a personal vendetta against us. "Knock it off!" she shouted, then turned back to us and smiled. "Do y'all want somethin' to drink? I've got some Crystal Light."

The heat in the house was starting to make my skin crawl, so I nodded. "Yes, please."

"And maybe a snack for the little one?" she said sweetly, waving at Hazel. "Don't worry, I keep healthy stuff on hand."

She disappeared into what I assumed was the kitchen.

Hazel shifted on my lap and leaned in close, pinching her nostrils shut. "I don't like it here. It smells bad."

I shushed her instinctively, then quietly added, "I know. We won't stay long."

Kim returned with a tray that held two Rae Dunn glasses filled with pink Crystal Light, one child's sippy cup, and one of those 100-calorie packs of diet cookies that tasted like cardboard and sadness. She set it down on the coffee table next to a mason jar of artificial eucalyptus and a stack of coasters shaped like paw prints.

I gave her a polite thank you and sipped the Crystal Light, grateful for the hydration. Hazel scooted over onto the couch, settling down right next to me, and brought the sippy cup to her lips.

Kim perched on an oversized ottoman and crossed one leg over the other, her dark brown eyes on my daughter. "Good gracious, she's gotten so big. She is a doll, Shannon. I mean it. Just a doll."

I smiled with pride and stole a glance at Hazel myself. She *did* look extra adorable today with her curly pigtails and little olive-green corduroy overalls, which she'd proudly paired with her favorite cat T-shirt, silver glittery ballet flats, and purple crew socks. Quite the fashion choice, but I wasn't about to say a word. That kind of confidence didn't need taming; it needed protecting.

Kim's gaze slid back to me. Her eyes gleamed like she couldn't wait to spill the tea. "So," she said, voice dropping just a bit. "Let's get down to business. Stuff's been happening in your house, huh?"

I hesitated and glanced at Hazel. I didn't want to talk about any of this in front of her, but I didn't have a choice. Without childcare, she had to go wherever I went.

"You've been hearing things?" Kim went on. "Feeling weird energy or something?"

I swallowed hard. "Um, well, she's been talking to someone," I said carefully, bobbing my head toward Hazel. "In her closet."

Kim's overplucked eyebrows shot up. "Oh, honey."

"And my dad, he, um . . ." I trailed off. "He saw something. Right before . . ." I gulped. "It scared him."

Kim nodded solemnly. "It's that house. I told you, Shannon. Something ain't right over there. Never has been."

I drew in a deep breath. "I need to know about the people who lived there before us."

Kim leaned back a bit, folding her arms over her chest. "Well, I told you a little about Miss Fern already. Fern Carlisle. Sweet little woman. Quiet. Always used to see her sittin' out on her front porch when I was walkin'. She—" Her eyes darted to Hazel, then back to me. "She D-I-E-D in the house."

Hazel looked up at the sudden hush in Kim's tone. I gave her an uneasy smile and reached for the 100-calorie snack pack on the coffee table. "Want a snack, baby?"

She nodded, eyes bright. I opened it for her and passed it her way. "Tank you, Mommy."

"What nice manners," Kim exclaimed warmly.

Hazel smiled. I waited until she turned her attention back to her snack, then faced Kim again. "What happened to her?" I asked. "Miss Fern?"

"It was her heart," Kim whispered. "She had one of them *conditions*. And she was diabetic. They say it was peaceful, but . . . I don't know. She lived there sixty years, Shannon. Her husband built the place for her. Never wanted to leave."

I nodded slowly. "Because she loved it so much?"

Kim gave me a look. "Because she was *waiting*."

The hairs on my arms rose.

"Waiting for what?"

"For her little girl to come back."

I swallowed, thinking of the obituary. That photo of sixty-year-old Joyce Marshall with the ocean behind her, a cat in her arms and sorrow in her eyes. A woman who had run as far as she could and still hadn't managed to outrun the past.

"I guess she never did," I said softly. "I found her obituary this morning. I don't think she had any intention of ever coming back from California."

"Oh, you're thinking of Joyce."

I looked at her. "Yes?"

"Fern had *two* daughters," she said. "You're talking about Joyce, the one who sold you the place. Joyce was the oldest girl." Her eyes widened as she went on. "But the younger one . . . well . . . she went out into those woods one day. Never came back."

I felt the color drain from my face. "What? When did this happen?"

"Back in the sixties, way back before my time. She was just a little kid. Like, three or four years old." Kim shook her head sadly. She eyed Hazel and lowered her voice further. "They never found her. No trace. No clues. Miss Fern never got any answers."

My stomach churned.

Kim's lips pressed into a line. "She never would let them declare her, you know, D-E-A-D. Always said she was still out there somewhere. She wouldn't move. Wouldn't ever leave the house. She turned into a real hermit, especially towards the end."

I looked out the window. From here, I could see the thick woods that lined our property across the road. The shadowy grove loomed like a wall, dark and quiet and watching.

Kim saw where I was looking. "You okay, Shannon?"

I wasn't sure. I had one more question, and I was pretty sure I already knew the answer.

"Do you know what the younger daughter's name was?"

Kim nodded. "Of course. Her name was Loretta."

NINETEEN

Fern

October 1962

SWEAT TRICKLED DOWN FERN'S forehead and seeped through her eyebrows as she pinned Joyce's blue dress on the clothesline. October wasn't supposed to be this darn hot. Where was the crisp breeze that called for cardigans and pumpkin bread? The humid air clung to her like a damp sheet.

She hated the heat. Always had. But the older she got, the more she loathed it. It turned chores like this into punishment. A high-pitched buzz whined in her right ear, and she smacked at it with her wrist.

A mosquito.

In October.

October was not supposed to be like this.

Fern huffed as she bent down, pulled one of Loretta's little blouses from her laundry basket, and tossed it over the line. Her nose wrinkled in disgust. The fabric smelled like Tide and . . . something else. Something sour. Something rotten. She sniffed it again and recoiled.

She crouched next to the basket and began apprehensively rummaging through the damp clothes, half-expecting to find a dead mouse curled up among the fabric. But blessedly, she found nothing out of the ordinary except for that lingering, putrid smell.

"Am I having a stroke?" she muttered, rubbing her nose with the back of her hand. Wasn't that one of the signs? Smelling phantom odors?

She reached for another dress, and as her fingers brushed the wet, thin cotton, a flicker of movement caught her eye.

Loretta stood at the far edge of the yard, just past the old oak tree, her bare feet almost touching the tall weeds that separated their land from the dense, wild woods. She was absolutely still, arms at her sides, Miss Flossie clutched in her right hand.

She never went anywhere without that stuffed rabbit, and it showed. Miss Flossie's once-pink fur was now dingy and matted, the silk lining its long ears frayed and worn thin. One seam along its side sagged open just enough to show the white stuffing inside. Fern had been meaning to mend it, but she never seemed to remember until it was too late in the day.

She shaded her eyes with her hand and called out, "Loretta? What are you doing over there?"

Loretta didn't respond.

A shiver crawled down Fern's spine despite the heat. She dropped the clothespin and wiped her palms on her apron as she started across the lawn.

What had transfixed Loretta so?

A snake?

Fern's mother used to tell the story of how, at age four, Fern had been "charmed" by a black snake in the garden. Said she stood there in a daze, eyes wide and blank, until her mother broke the spell. Fern didn't remember it. But her mother loved to tell that tale.

She prayed this wasn't the same thing.

As she drew closer, her breath snagged in her throat. Loretta's big brown eyes were wide and glassy. Her lips moved without sound as she whispered something frantically.

Fern hunched beside her and gently touched her arm. "Loretta? What are you looking at?"

Loretta didn't blink. Didn't flinch. Her skin was cool beneath Fern's hand. Still, she whispered, eyes locked on the trees.

Fern caught the scent again. Rot. Stronger this time, clinging to Loretta's hair like she'd pressed her head against something wet and decaying in the yard.

Loretta's lips kept moving, and Fern leaned in close to listen.

"She's waiting," she murmured. "She's waiting for me."

A spike of cold ran through Fern's chest. "Who is, sweetheart?"

This question seemed to snap Loretta out of her fugue. Her eyes unclouded as she turned to Fern. "Huh?"

"Who's waiting?" Fern turned, squinting into the woods, scanning for any movement. A neighbor. A deer. Anything.

But there was nothing. Only shadows.

She looked back to see tears pooling in Loretta's eyes as she squeezed Miss Flossie the rabbit tighter. "I'm scared, Mama."

"Oh, sweetheart, come here." Fern gathered Loretta into her arms and pulled her against her chest, whispering all the vague reassurances she could muster until the girl's breathing evened out. "It's all right. Mama's here."

Loretta's little body trembled against her, an involuntary motion so intense, it unnerved Fern.

"It's all right, darling," she said, running a hand over her daughter's back. "There's nothing to be afraid of." She wasn't sure she believed that last part herself, but she said it anyway, almost like a talisman.

After a few moments, Loretta sucked in a shaky breath and wriggled free from the embrace. She wiped the wetness from her cheeks with the back of her hand and sank onto the grass, still sniffling quietly.

"Good girl. You stay right there while I finish up this laundry," Fern told her. "Won't take but a few minutes, alright? Stay close."

"Okay, Mama." Her wide eyes stayed on the tree line as she smoothed the rabbit's tattered ear flat.

Fern turned back to her work. She dug a damp slip from her basket, flung it over the line, and pinned up one side. A sudden breeze knocked it askew before she could grab another clothespin, billowing the white nylon fabric about like a ghost.

She shivered in the cooler air. Maybe fall was on its way after all.

A shriek cut through the air, echoing across the yard.

"Mama!" Joyce cried. "The cat scratched me!"

Fern sighed as she glanced up and saw Joyce barreling off the back porch toward her, clutching her hand. Behind her, Buttercup bolted under the porch steps, tail puffed out and back arched.

"Lord have mercy," Fern muttered. She bent for another clothespin and dropped it, her fingers too slick with sweat. The mosquito buzzed at her ear again, its whining sharp and grating. She smacked at it and missed, cursing under her breath.

Joyce reached her side and held out her hand. A thin line of red bloomed across her palm.

"Were you aggravating that poor cat again?"

"No!"

"Run back in the house and wash it. I'll put some iodine on it in a minute. Just let me get the rest of this on the line before it's too wrinkled."

"But Mama, it hurts!"

Fern bent to retrieve the dropped clothespin. When she straightened, her eyes flicked back to Joyce's pouty face. "I know. It'll feel better in a bit."

She started to reach for a blouse in the laundry basket, then froze. The cicadas had gone silent, their song cut off mid-buzz. Joyce quieted too, shifting uneasily at her side. The back of Fern's neck went cold.

Slowly, she turned.

Loretta was no longer sitting on the patch of grass.

"Loretta?" Fern's voice cracked. She turned back to Joyce. "Where'd your sister go?"

Joyce only shrugged.

"Loretta!" Fern's gaze tore over the yard. No stuffed rabbit. No child. Her breath seized in her chest. She bolted for the woods, Joyce trailing behind. "Loretta!"

The woods swallowed her voice.

Somewhere up ahead in the trees, Fern thought she heard a laugh—or a cry. The sound echoed unnaturally in the thick air, bouncing from one trunk to another. Sweat stung her eyes as she shoved branches aside. "Loretta, come here this instant!"

A limb whipped her across the cheek. She barely noticed the sting.

"Loretta!"

Fern screamed until her voice gave out, but only silence answered back.

Hours later, lantern light bobbed through the shadowy woods like fireflies. Men's voices carried through the trees—neighboring farmers, volunteer firemen, and the sheriff's deputies all calling Loretta's name. Tracking hounds whined as they led the way, noses down against the forest floor, pulling their leashes taut as they searched for her scent.

Fern walked among the crowd in a daze, each step heavy. Her dress clung to her bark-scraped legs, her throat raw from screaming. The world blurred around her, distant and unreal. The lanterns, the shouting, the crunch of boots on dry leaves and twigs. It all felt like a dream.

The only things anchoring her were Joyce's small hand clinging to her skirt, and the steady grip of Colene Henderson leading her forward step by step.

"That's it, Fern," Colene murmured, though her voice quavered. "We'll find her."

Fern stared into the forest where the lantern beams wrestled with the shadows.

She's waiting for me.

The words echoed through Fern's head as clearly as though Loretta had whispered them into her ear all over again just now. She saw her little lips moving fast, frantic.

Fern's throat sealed tight. She should tell everyone, tell the deputies what her daughter had said, but the words lodged in her chest like a stone.

Because if she spoke them out loud, it would make them true.

One of the hounds groaned and plopped down in the leaves, panting. The other circled and circled, whining as it looked back at its handler in apparent confusion.

"Don't make sense," one of the handlers mumbled. "The dogs can't hold the scent. It's like she up and vanished into thin air."

A few other men slowed, watching the hounds. Lanterns swung uncertainly, their light bobbing over the leaves.

"Did it rain out here today?" someone asked. "Sometimes that'll mix up the smells."

A stout man in front of Fern, a volunteer fireman, she thought, stopped abruptly and swung his lantern wide. The light splintered through the branches, throwing strange, broken shadows across the forest floor. "Not likely," he said, voice gruff and deep. "Ground's too dry."

Fern swallowed hard, eyes straining against the dark, searching for any shape that might be her child.

"Hope she ain't wandered out to the creek," someone muttered.

Colene squeezed Fern's hand a little tighter.

The word *creek* hung in the air. No one spoke. Fern's stomach clenched as she pictured the steep bank. The slick stones.

"The rain we've had this year, I bet the creek's near bone-dry," the fireman said at last, breaking the uncomfortable silence. His eyes softened as they met Fern's. "She's little. Ain't but three. She'll be scared. I reckon she's hid somewhere close."

Fern clung to those words, squeezed them tight inside her chest like a prayer. *Lost. Scared. Hiding.* That was all.

They would find her. They had to.

Twenty

Shannon

August 12, 2022

THE WOODS LOOKED DIFFERENT now.

I'd walked past them a thousand times, but knowing what I knew now, that a little girl who lived in my house had vanished into those trees and never come back, made the shadows seem darker. Heavier. Like they held secrets.

I gripped Hazel's hand tightly as we crossed Sunflower Lane together. She skipped beside me, joyful and carefree, stopping to examine every rock she spotted on the ground. She didn't seem to have absorbed any of what Kim had just said, thank goodness.

I swallowed hard as our house came into view. A sweet, ordinary little country cottage. But I knew better now.

Fern Carlisle had never left this place. Not even in death. And after everything Kim had told me, I supposed I couldn't blame her. She was a mother who'd lost a child and never stopped anticipating her return. She'd sat on her porch for decades, watching the trees, forever waiting for Loretta to come back.

What else was she supposed to do?

If it were Hazel—God, if it were Hazel—I don't think I could leave, either. I couldn't imagine anything but waiting, aching, clinging to any scrap of hope that my little girl might come home.

As we crossed the yard, I looked up at the porch and saw it differently. The rocking chair in front of the window, the one that creaked in the breeze sometimes, suddenly seemed fuller. In my mind's eye, I could almost see her sitting there.

Fern Carlisle.

White hair swept back into a soft bun. Shoulders stooped with age. A worn cardigan buttoned over a floral dress. Wrinkled hands folded in her lap, eyes fixed on the tree line. Watching. Waiting. Hoping. Every day the same. Every breath a silent prayer.

A swell of grief rose up so quickly it nearly knocked me off balance.

Not my grief, but *hers*. My chest burned with it. I imagined her there on the porch so clearly, so vividly, it felt like *I* was the ghost, just passing through her life. Not the other way around.

This wasn't just our house. It had been Fern's first.

Her home.

Her heartbreak.

Her prison.

And for the first time, I didn't feel afraid of her.

I just felt sorry for her.

So deeply, achingly sorry for this mother who couldn't let go.

Maybe that's why she lingered in Hazel's room, because it had once belonged to Loretta. Or maybe Fern saw something of her daughter in mine.

I didn't know for sure. But I knew this much:

If Fern was still here, still watching, still waiting . . .

Then someone needed to tell her it was okay to stop.

After Hazel fell asleep in my bed that night, her little fists curled tight around the stuffed cat named Loretta, I crept out and walked back down the hallway.

The house was still in a way that felt . . . expectant.

I strode into Hazel's room, pulled open the bifold closet doors, and stared into the empty storage space.

My heart pounded. I drew in a shaky breath and began.

"Miss Fern?"

My voice came out thin, uncertain. I cleared my throat and tried again, a little louder this time.

"If you're here, Miss Fern . . . and I think you are . . . I, um, I want to talk to you."

I felt a little ridiculous. Like I was pretending to be Jennifer Love Hewitt on *Ghost Whisperer*. But I pushed on.

"I know you lived here. This was your family's home. Your husband built this place for you and your girls, and it meant everything to you."

I hesitated. The next part was harder.

"I also know you died here, Miss Fern. And I think . . . I think maybe you stayed. Because you're waiting."

The air in the room shifted, just slightly. I shivered as goosebumps rose across my arms.

I tried to convince myself this was good. That she was listening. I had nothing to fear.

"You're waiting for your little girl, aren't you? For Loretta."

I paused, blinking fast, my throat tightening.

"My name is Shannon. And I'm a mother too. I believe you know my little girl. Hazel."

My voice trembled.

"She's my whole world. And I can't . . ." I faltered, pressing my hand to my chest. "I can't imagine going through what you went through. I can't imagine the pain."

A tear slid down my cheek.

"You lived every parent's worst nightmare. All those years without answers. No closure. The world moved on without you and your daughter, and I'm sure you felt . . . left behind."

I shook my head slowly as my voice shrank to a whisper.

"I am so, so sorry, Miss Fern. I'm so sorry for what you endured."

The house went completely silent.

I could hear my own heartbeat thudding in my ears.

"I-I think you stayed in this house because it's the last place she saw you. Maybe you're afraid to leave, just in case she comes back. And I understand that. I might do the same."

I paused and wet my lips with my tongue.

"But . . . it's been sixty years. And I'm so sorry, Fern, I truly am, but . . . Loretta isn't coming back."

I paused, holding space for the words to settle.

"You don't have to keep waiting," I said gently. "It's okay to rest now."

I stood there, searching for the right words. The ones I might want to hear, if the roles were reversed.

"You did everything you could do. You were a good mother. I know you were, no matter what you think. I know you did your best. What happened to Loretta wasn't your fault."

Something in the air eased. Lightened.

"You don't have to stay anymore. Not for her. Not for anyone."

I exhaled slowly.

"You're free to go, Fern. Go on. Be at peace."

I waited.

"You deserve to be at peace."

Finally, I turned, leaving the closet doors open behind me, and walked away.

The house felt quieter.

For the first time in ages, I felt alone.

Not watched. Not followed.

Just alone.

I returned to my room and slid into bed beside my daughter. I pulled her close, spooning her, my belly against her back, my hand resting atop hers.

Her breath stuttered a little in sleep, and I pressed my nose into her hair, trying to memorize it all. Her smell, her smallness, this stillness, this moment where everything was okay again.

I whispered, "We're safe," though I don't know if I meant it more for her or for me.

Then, at last, I slept.

I don't know what woke me.

A cold draft, maybe. Or just the feeling that something was wrong.

I reached out instinctively and touched only sheets.

Hazel's side of the bed was empty.

I sat up, pulse racing. My phone lit up on the nightstand.

MOTION DETECTED – NURSERY

I snatched it up and ran down the hall, bare feet slapping against the hardwood. I hit the nursery door and pushed it open.

Hazel was standing in front of the closet.

The doors were wide open.

She was crying. Whispering through hiccupped sobs.

"—please come back, Miss Fern. I'm scared. I don't want to go with her."

My heart slammed against my ribs.

"Hazel," I breathed.

She turned.

The second she saw me, she clamped her mouth shut. Her eyes went wide. Guilty, startled, afraid.

I crossed the room in two steps and dropped to my knees, gathering her up in my arms.

She didn't fight me. But she didn't speak, either.

Her body shook against mine.

Over her shoulder, the closet stood open behind us—dark and empty.

But the air inside it felt different.

Charged.

Electric.

Fern

February 1963

THE CASSEROLES HAD STOPPED coming long ago, though Colene still brought Sunday dinner every week without fail. She left it on the porch with a soft knock, knowing Fern rarely felt up to conversation. Every Wednesday, she dropped a sack of groceries on the porch steps, too. Flour, canned goods, fresh produce when she could spare it.

Fern barely remembered to thank her anymore.

The house had gone quiet since October. The giggling, the tantrums, the sibling bickering—it was all gone now, all stripped away in a single afternoon.

Joyce sat on the sofa most days with her books, silent and solemn. She didn't ask about her sister anymore, though sometimes Fern caught her staring at the tree line, her gapped front teeth gnawing anxiously on her bottom lip.

Christmas had been the worst. Joyce begged for a tree, and Fern let her drag in a scrawny pine from out back. It sat in the living room past New Year's, unadorned but for a handful of sad, lopsided paper stars Joyce had cut from notebook paper.

Fern hadn't set foot beyond the yard in weeks, let alone thought about gifts. On Christmas morning, there had been only one package beneath the tree.

To: Mama. From: Joyce.

Fern's cheeks burned with shame as she unwrapped it. Inside lay a trinket box, sloppily covered with colorful magazine cut-outs. Birds, butterflies, flowers. Cheerful scraps of a world Fern no longer recognized.

"It's called *decoupage*," Joyce had whispered, eyes shining. "Mrs. Harris showed me how. She helped me make it at school."

Fern managed a stiff smile and a hollow *thank you*, but nothing more.

Joyce lingered, waiting for praise, enthusiasm, some spark of the mother she used to know. When nothing came, her shoulders slumped.

"You can, um . . ." Joyce twisted the hem of her dress between her fingers. "You could keep it on your dresser, if you want."

Fern nodded numbly.

That night, when Fern finally dragged herself to bed, she found the trinket box already waiting on her dresser, front and center atop one of her mother's handcrafted doilies. Joyce had put it there herself.

The shame hit her so hard it made her knees weak. She steadied herself on the dresser, eyes fixed on that little box.

It was meant to be a heartfelt gift, but it felt like an accusation. A reminder of her failures, of the love she couldn't manage to give back.

Fern clicked off the lamp and crawled into bed, but the image of the little box loomed in her mind.

The weeks that followed ran together. One day faded into the next, a dismal, colorless routine of obligation and painful silence. Joyce went to school. Fern stared at the front door for hours until she returned. Sometimes she managed to do a little housework, to cook them a real supper, but most days, it was Joyce picking up the slack. The eight-year-old child was surprisingly capable, which somehow only made Fern feel worse.

By February, Fern finally carried out the scrawny, brown pine from their living room and tossed the paper stars in the trash. The quiet of the house felt permanent by then. One of those rare Alabama snows had fallen, a heavy one that seemed to shut down the world.

The temperature dropped so low, it knocked out the power grid. The lights clicked off while they were eating supper one night. Joyce shrieked when the dining room went dark, and Fern fumbled around blindly through the kitchen drawers until she found a matchbook. Her fingers moved clumsily as she struck a match. The flame flared to life, filling the room with a weak yellow glow. She lit a candle and placed it on the dining room table.

The deepened silence was more oppressive than the cold or the darkness. No refrigerator hum, no rattle of the heater. Fern's ears rang in the absence of background noise. She lit two more candles, but it didn't seem to brighten the place at all.

"Mama," Joyce whispered, tugging her sleeve. "Do you hear her?"

Fern froze. "Hear who?"

"Loretta." Her wide eyes shimmered in the candlelight. "She's calling you."

Fern's heart dropped into her belly. She began to shake her head, but then she heard it too. A voice. Weak, muffled, like it drifted from the woods.

Mama...

Her entire body lurched. It was Loretta. It had to be.

"Stay here," Fern barked, snatching a candlestick from the table. Her pulse thundered as she darted to the door and tugged on her boots.

The cold bit at her skin as she burst onto the porch. "Loretta?" she cried into the night. The candle flame flickered wildly, threatening to wink out.

Another whisper slithered through the darkness.

Mama...

Fern blundered forward, boots crunching and sinking into the snow. Her entire body trembled in the icy air. Her sweater was too thin; she hadn't thought to grab her coat. Snowflakes were still falling, she realized. She blinked them from her eyes, shivering, and squinted in the dimness, scanning the backyard.

The blanket of fresh snow created an unfamiliar white landscape, yet the peculiar brightness of the ground made it easier to see in the darkness. She could clearly make out the shape of the barn. The oak tree. The black woods beyond.

A woman stood at the tree line.

Tall and thin, her stark white face and bare, too-long arms stood out against the shadows. A wild mane of long, black hair blended into her dark, shapeless dress that dragged in the snow.

Fern blinked.

The figure was gone.

Her throat seized, but she stumbled another step forward. "Loretta! Can you hear me?" The cry fell flat, muffled by the snow. Every nerve in her body strained against the uncanny silence, desperate to hear her child's reply.

"Mama!"

The wail came from behind her. Joyce on the front porch.

"Mama, come back!"

Fern stopped.

The woods loomed before her, black and endless.

She couldn't leave Joyce.

She stumbled back toward the house, clambered up the porch steps, and slammed the door behind them. Her candle had sputtered out, leaving only darkness and Joyce's sobs.

Fern pulled her little girl into her arms, mumbling empty reassurances. But even as she held her, her ears strained toward the woods, hoping.

Shannon

August 15, 2022

I THOUGHT I WAS helping. That was the worst part. I really believed Fern Carlisle's spirit just needed a little nudge to move on, to cross over to "the other side."

But whatever I did that night, it was wrong.

Fern was gone, yes, but now things were worse.

Hazel had been acting terribly strange since that night, ever since I'd caught her begging an empty closet to bring Fern back.

"I don't want to go with her," she'd cried.

Her.

I didn't know who she was talking about, and that terrified me. All I knew was that the air in the nursery closet had felt different ever since that night.

I barely slept. I didn't even try.

Hazel was curled on the couch beside me, bundled in her favorite blanket with Loretta the cat, thumb tucked in her mouth. She'd never sucked her thumb before, and we'd never even used a pacifier when she was a baby. But she'd started that two days ago, out of nowhere. It seemed like a bad sign.

She hadn't spoken since that night either.

Not a word.

Not even when I offered to read her favorite book, play dolls with her, or make homemade brownies together. She just sat in silence, blinking slowly, staring off into space.

The unease growing in my belly was wrought with guilt and dread. I didn't understand what was happening to my daughter, and I felt like I was the one responsible for it.

Presently, as we sat together on the couch, *Bluey* on the TV but neither of us really watching it, I slipped my arm around her shoulders and pulled her into me.

"You know you can talk to me about anything, right?" I asked, my throat tight as the words came out. "You can tell me whatever you're thinking about. Even if you think you might be in trouble, even if you're scared, you can always, *always*, talk to me. Okay?"

She didn't reply, but I felt her head loll over into my side, relaxing against me.

"The other night . . . in your closet . . . I heard you talking to Miss Fern. Is that the lady who lives in your closet? The one you called the closet lady?"

No reaction.

"You said you were scared, that you 'didn't want to go with her.'" I swallowed. "Who were you talking about?"

Hazel cowered against me.

I squeezed her a little tighter. "If you're scared or worried about something, please, Hazel, let me help you. We'll deal with it together."

She stayed silent.

I racked my brain for the right words. I'd already seen enough to shred my old belief systems, but I still couldn't grasp exactly what all this meant. My house was haunted, but was there a second ghost? Something worse than Fern?

I looked down at Hazel, tucked into my side, still staring at nothing.

What can I do to help her?

If she wouldn't talk yet, maybe I could at least make her feel safe. Bring her things she loved. Keep her close to me and away from that room.

Her picture books were still in there. Her dolls. Her dress-up clothes. All the little familiar comforts that might help her feel secure.

"Hang tight," I murmured, kissing the top of her head. "I'll be right back."

She didn't respond.

I stood and moved down the hall to Hazel's room, my sock feet silent on the old hardwoods. I pushed open the nursery door and felt a rush of cool air. Not freezing, but enough to raise the hairs along my arms.

I crossed to the bookshelf first, pulling *Corduroy* and *If You Give a Mouse a Cookie* and nearly a dozen other picture books she always asked for. I stacked them inside her plastic bin of dolls, then moved to the closet to grab a few of her favorite dress-up clothes.

I reached for her blue ice princess dress and stopped short, my hand hovering in the air as my nose crinkled.

Oh, God—had something died in here?

I sniffed again and nearly gagged. My eyes swept across the small space, searching for a rodent corpse. Maybe a forgotten apple core or a dirty diaper that had somehow fallen out of the pail long ago. Something, anything, that would explain the foul, sour stench seeping from the closet walls.

The longer I stood there, the more the scent took shape, coiling around me, thick enough to taste.

Dread washed over me. This wasn't normal.

I snatched the princess dress, gripping the gauzy, itchy fabric a little too tightly as I reached for a basket of clean laundry beneath it. Hazel's silky unicorn nightgown and a pair of purple footie pajamas sat on top. I grabbed them quickly. I sure as hell didn't want to have to come back in here at bedtime.

Eager to escape, I scooped up everything I'd come in for and hurried out the door. The cool air followed me, slipping past my legs like it had been waiting for a way out.

I set the bin down in the hall and pulled the nursery door shut behind me. But before I did, I turned the old brass lock into place. A flimsy attempt at control, but at least it would keep Hazel from slipping back in there alone.

Her eyes were on me when I came back, wide and unblinking.

"Alright," I said, conjuring a smile and my most cheerful voice. "I got all your favorite stuff. Books, dolls, princess dresses. We can leave it all out here for a while. I got some pajamas too, so we don't have to go back in there tonight." Any other clothes she needed, she could get from the laundry room; the neglected pile in the dryer was big enough to keep us dressed for a week.

I set the bin beside the couch and the smell hit me again. Rot. It had followed me.

Hazel didn't reach for anything. Her eyes slid past me to the hallway and landed on the closed nursery door.

"What is it?" I asked.

Her bottom lip trembled. She hugged Loretta the cat tighter.

"You locked it?" she asked, her voice barely more than a whisper.

I gulped. "Yeah. Now nothing in there can bother us."

Her eyes stayed on the door. Her thumb crept into her mouth. "That's gonna make her mad," she mumbled around it, so quiet I almost missed it.

A shiver crawled up my spine. "Who?"

Hazel's gaze darted to me, then back to the door. Her shoulders hunched.

"The . . ." She stopped, sucking harder on her thumb like she could pull the word back in. She hid her face in the cat's fur and wouldn't look at me again.

I went to her and rubbed her back gently. "Hazel, please, who are you talking about?"

Her head shook once, quick and tight.

"It's okay," I murmured. "You can tell me."

She leaned away from me, eyes still fixed on the locked door. When she spoke, her whisper was so faint I had to lean closer to hear it.

"The tricky lady."

The words came out in a rush, like she needed to get them over with before she lost her nerve. And then her thumb was back in her mouth, her gaze averted, as if saying it had already gotten her in trouble.

I caught the way her shoulders curled in like she was trying to make herself smaller.

There were rules here. Not mine. Not hers.

Rules she'd been given.

Rules she was afraid of breaking.

Almost an hour later, after I finally got Hazel calmed down with a snack and cartoons, my hands were still shaking.

I felt like I was gonna puke. Whatever lived in that closet had its sights set on my daughter. It was giving her instructions. Making her keep secrets from me. Terrifying the shit out of her. Out of both of us.

And I didn't know what the hell to do about it.

For half a second, I thought about calling Pastor Greg. He wasn't really *my* pastor, more my mom's back in the day, but I'd known him since I was a kid. Didn't people usually turn to church leaders in times like this? Supernatural matters usually required some sort of spiritual advisor, like a priest, at least in the movies.

But Mom had been Southern Baptist, not Catholic, and I wasn't sure what Pastor Greg would even do if I tried to explain that a ghost was stalking my daughter. Just imagining that conversation shut the idea down fast.

So where did that leave me?

I couldn't fight what I couldn't see. What I couldn't understand. I couldn't make Hazel tell me what the "tricky lady" wanted without increasing her fear and anxiety.

But . . . maybe a child therapist could.

They couldn't fix this. No shrink in a cardigan could help me evict a ghost. But maybe they could get Hazel to open up, give me details I could use to keep her safe. Maybe they could even teach her some coping strategies to help her work through this.

I pulled up the insurance portal on my phone and started searching.

The first three practices I called weren't accepting new patients. The fourth had a six-week wait. The woman at the fifth place told me they'd just lost their only pediatric counselor and had no idea when they'd hire another.

I got her on a waitlist at an office in Decatur. By the time I hung up, the sky outside had gone dark. My hands were shaking again.

There wasn't going to be help. Not anytime soon.

It was all on me.

Somehow, I'd have to protect her.

TWENTY-THREE

Fern

May 5, 1963

THE ARRIVAL OF SPRING did the Carlisles good. Joyce seemed lighter once the frost melted, when she was able to frolic around the yard again with her best friend, Shirley Henderson. Her sunburned face was bright and happy when she and Shirley played together. Fern tried to be thankful her eldest still laughed sometimes, even if she herself couldn't.

But if she was honest, the warmer weather had given her a boost, too.

She'd taken to sitting on the porch in her rocking chair while Joyce was at school, a glass of sweet tea sweating in her hand, watching the woods as though Loretta might walk out of them any moment.

Sometimes, she thought she heard her daughter's voice drifting through the hum of cicadas, calling her from the trees.

Mama . . .

She'd followed the sound a few times and found nothing.

She never told anyone about it.

Joyce had been spending more time with the Hendersons lately. They'd started taking her to Calvary Baptist on Sundays, and Fern hadn't fought it. She didn't have the heart to. She already carried enough guilt for abandoning the church herself. Everybody in town surely noticed her empty seat on the pew. But she couldn't bring herself to go. She couldn't stomach the inane small talk, the pitying stares. The despicable reassurances that Loretta's disappearance was somehow "God's will."

But Joyce needed Sunday School. She needed normalcy. She needed *something*. If Fern couldn't give her that, then she was glad Colene Henderson could. Maybe God would forgive Fern for letting someone else do the job she could no longer manage.

This Sunday, Fern was rocking on the porch when the Hendersons' old Plymouth rumbled down the gravel driveway. Joyce hopped out from the backseat, hugging her leather children's Bible close. She looked so grown in her canary-yellow dress and crisp white cardigan, the skirt flaring as she bounded up the steps.

Fern recognized the dress at once, a hand-me-down from Shirley, who was growing faster than Joyce. Colene had kindly passed it along, and Fern felt the familiar stab of guilt. Joyce's stockings were spotless, her hair ribbon tied just so. She looked polished, cared-for.

She looked like somebody else's child. Not Fern's.

Joyce took the porch steps two at a time. "Hey, Mama," she said brightly.

Fern's eyes stung as she beheld her. "Hey, sweetheart."

"I'm gonna go change," Joyce said. "This dress is itchy."

Fern nodded and watched her yank open the screen door and disappear inside the house.

Colene climbed the steps more slowly, balancing a covered dish in one hand. Her round, matronly frame was tastefully dressed in a blue houndstooth suit with a pleated skirt that fell just below the knee, her golden blonde hair flawlessly coiffed into curls that didn't budge in the breeze.

She always looked so put together. Fern caught herself wishing she'd spot a run in Colene's stockings, something small to make her seem less perfect.

She gave Fern a tired smile as she set the dish on the porch rail. "Pot roast. Should be enough to last y'all a couple of days."

Fern thanked her, then looked beyond her toward the woods.

Colene hesitated, then sank into the second, empty rocker beside her. "Fern, I've been thinking . . ." She smoothed her skirt with white-gloved hands, choosing her words cautiously. "Well, it ain't good for you, staying shut up in this house by yourself. I don't mean to be harsh, but . . . I think you should come back to church."

Fern swallowed.

"We all miss you, Fern. Somebody asks me about you every Sunday. Folks still care."

It didn't feel that way to Fern. She knew people had been gossiping about her ever since Raymond left.

"Being back in the Lord's house . . . I know it would do you a world of good," Colene went on. "And listen, we've got a tent revival comin' up this week. Brother Harold Birch and his wife Hilda. Have you heard of them? They're known all over the Southeast. Folks say his preaching's powerful. *Healing,* even."

Fern's shoulders tensed. "I don't think—"

"I know," Colene cut in gently. "I'm not sayin' it'll fix everything. Just come sit with us. For Joyce, if nothing else. You oughta see the way that child lights up at church, Fern. She truly loves the Lord." She paused. "And she needs to see her mama there, too."

Fern gulped, her eyes still on the woods.

"I'll . . . I'll think about it," she whispered.

Colene reached over and gave her hand a firm squeeze. "That's all I'm asking."

She let go, reached into her pocketbook, and extracted a folded sheet of paper. A flyer for the upcoming revival services. She passed it to Fern.

"All the information is on there," Colene said. "Joyce is excited about it. I hope we'll see you there."

Fern pulled on her Sunday best, a forest-green shirtdress sprinkled with tiny white polka dots. It had been cheerful once; now it was just sad. The fabric had faded at the seams, the buttons dulled from their original pearly shine. Even with her girdle on, the belt cinched unforgivingly at her waist. She'd set her hair in rollers the morning of the revival meeting, hoping fresh, polished curls might redeem her appearance. But when she stepped out into the muggy Alabama afternoon, the humidity wilted them flat.

"You look beautiful, Mama," Joyce told her anyway, beaming as they walked hand in hand to the Hendersons' Plymouth waiting for them in the driveway.

She squeezed her daughter's hand, reminding herself of why she'd let Colene and Joyce talk her into this. She wasn't going to this revival service for her own sake, but for Joyce's. If a week of tent meetings could give her poor child some kind of hope, Fern would force herself to get through it. After the last few months they'd endured, she owed her that much.

Her heart was pounding by the time Colene parked the car, and she feared her knees might buckle as she climbed out into the dusty churchyard. The sticky evening air pressed close and heavy. From the big white tent pitched in the field next to the sanctuary came the tinny, plink-plonk of an old upright piano hammering out a lively hymn, the kind of honky-tonk sound Fern had heard in country churches her whole life.

She hesitated, smoothing her skirt with clammy palms. Joyce tugged her forward, smiling, her yellow dress bright against the dimming dusk. Colene and Shirley walked ahead, chattering between themselves.

The tent loomed larger as they approached, its canvas sides rolled up to keep from slow-roasting the multitude of congregants. Fern followed Colene down a side aisle, passing rows of folding chairs packed tight. Women in floral dresses fanned themselves with paper fans, illustrations of Jesus praying in the garden of Gethsemane mounted on a wooden stick. Men dabbed handkerchiefs across their brows. Children wriggled, already restless, shushed by their parents.

An assault of smells hit her at once as she settled into a seat, a medley of overpowering floral perfumes and body odor. She caught one or two nods from familiar faces, polite but guarded, before she fixed her gaze on the front where a rotund woman pounded away at the piano.

Fern sat stiffly as more folks shuffled in. Sweat prickled her spine, and she was certain every eye in the place had turned on her.

Finally, the music clanged to a halt, and a hush fell over the tent. Coughs and rustling fans filled the silence until Brother Robert

Kingsley stepped up to the wooden pulpit, booming out a welcome and a prayer.

The hymns that followed his invocation all blurred together. Fern knew them all by heart. She sang along distantly, her mind elsewhere until the last chorus faded.

"We're in for a treat tonight, folks," the minister proclaimed at last. "Brother Harold Birch and his wife Hilda have traveled all over the South, sharing the Gospel with thousands. The Lord has His hand on these two, and y'all will see it tonight. Before Brother Harold comes up to share the word of the Lord, his wife, Sister Hilda, is going to bless us through song. Please make her feel welcome this evening."

Everyone clapped as Hilda Birch stepped to the lone microphone, eyes lowered. The evangelist's wife was younger than Fern expected, probably early twenties. Her slate-gray dress was drab and plain, overly modest and loose-fitting. Her brown hair was cropped short in a heavily hair-sprayed bob that resembled a helmet.

Hilda cleared her throat and leaned into the microphone. "The Lord gave me this song about two weeks ago, in a little motel room outside of Savannah, Georgia." Her speaking voice was soft and lilting, touched with a Southern drawl that made every word sound sweet. Yet Fern caught the timidity beneath it; a reluctance, as though she'd prefer to be on the other side of the microphone.

"Harry and I had just finished up a week-long revival. It was wonderful. We saw dozens of folks come to Jesus that week. But despite that, I found myself feeling a heaviness. I couldn't sleep because of this . . . this burden I felt on my heart. I sat up most of the night, prayin' for folks who were hurting, and well, these words came to me." She gave an unassuming little shrug. "I don't know who needs to hear this message tonight, but the Lord does. I pray you'll hear Him through it." She paused, and a shy smile broke across her features. "Just bear with me, this is the first time I've shared it with anyone."

A round of *amen*'s and *bless her Lord*'s echoed throughout the tent as the pianist struck slow, solemn chords. Then Hilda lifted her eyes and began to sing.

"Your weary heart, so heavy laden . . ."

Fern's breath caught. Hilda's alto voice was rich and velvety and unexpectedly powerful. It was like another woman had stepped forward, this one confident, commanding, and Spirit-filled. Her voice washed over the tent in a mournful sweetness.

"The night's been long, your burden more than you can bear,
But hear the Savior whisper through the darkness,
'Come rest, my child, you are not forsaken here'."

Fern's chest tightened as the words settled upon her. It felt like the lyrics were about her, written just *for* her. Weary. Heavy laden. Forsaken. She wanted to look away, but Hilda's voice captivated her.

By the time her final note faded to silence, Fern's eyes were burning. She blinked fast, refusing to let tears fall inside the crowded tent. Around her, people applauded and shouted, caught up in the Spirit. Fern just sat there, hands clenched tight in her lap, trying to steady her breath.

Then Brother Harold "Harry" Birch strode up, Bible tucked beneath his arm, and replaced his wife behind the mic. He was tall and broad-shouldered with dark hair slicked back. He seemed young for a traveling evangelist. Most revivalists Fern had seen were stern, white-haired, red-faced old men who showered the front row in saliva as they shouted about hellfire.

Harry, on the other hand, radiated energy and optimism. He preached with excitement and vigor, his voice strong and loud, full of conviction. His hands gripped the sides of the pulpit as he read from his open Bible. "'Be sober, be vigilant, because your adversary the devil walks about as a roaring lion, seeking whom he may devour.'" He paused, scanning the crowd. "Now church, I'm here to tell you that the devil don't always *roar*. Sometimes, he whispers."

Fern felt a chill on the back of her neck.

"In the book of Ephesians, Paul tells us, 'For we wrestle not against flesh and blood, but against principalities, against powers, against the rulers of the darkness.'" He glanced up again, his eyes dark and fiery as they seemed to meet Fern's. "Folks, I can attest to this. The darkness Paul writes about here is very real. My wife and I have seen a lot of things in our travels."

He leaned in as his voice dropped.

"We've seen marriages destroyed, families torn apart, children tormented in their sleep, people suffering from things doctors and medicines couldn't fix. We've prayed over houses where darkness walked the halls." He shook his head. "Don't be fooled into thinkin' the devil's only after the world out yonder. He comes for the righteous, too. Especially those who are going through trials. Those are brokenhearted, grieving. That's who he whispers to." A pause. "That's who he devours."

Fern's breath snagged in her throat. She felt Joyce's hand sliding into her own. Fern tightened her fingers around Joyce's.

"But verse nine says to 'resist him, steadfast in your faith.' That means we don't go down without a fight. The blood of Jesus has the power to fight on our behalf, the same power tonight as it did two thousand years ago. Power to drive out fear. Power to expose lies. Power to send the devil back where he belongs!"

A chorus of *amen*'s filled the tent once more. Someone clapped, someone else whooped. The Holy Spirit in the place was almost tangible. Fern couldn't move, couldn't look away.

"Our Lord and Savior Jesus Christ sent us here tonight to tell somebody in this place that you don't have to live under Satan's bondage. That shadow at your door, that weight in your home, it has no authority over the children of God. We've cast it out before, and by His power, we'll cast it out again!"

Ages later, when the benediction finally came, the tent erupted into chatter, folding chairs scraping against dirt as people began filing out. Fern stayed in her seat, heart pounding. She knew she should rise, follow Colene and the others to the car, but her legs wouldn't move. Not yet. Not when she could still feel the preacher's eyes on her, as though he'd seen right through her.

Joyce tugged on her hand. "Mama," she whispered, eyes wide and earnest, "we should go talk to them."

Fern's stomach lurched. "Talk to who?"

"The preacher and his wife. They can help us. I just know they can."

She swallowed, then glanced over at Colene, who was fully engaged in conversation with one of the mothers from the girls' school. Her eyes tracked to the front, toward the Birches, and she caught Hilda's gaze. The evangelist's wife gave her a small smile, so gentle and sincere Fern nearly cried.

"Alright," Fern said, despite herself. Joyce squeezed her hand, and together they stepped into the aisle and headed toward the front.

Harry was shaking hands with a cluster of men, but Hilda stood off to one side alone, as though she'd been waiting for them.

"Evening," Hilda said. Her voice was soft, almost shy, but she sounded genuine when she said, "I'm so glad you came."

"Th-thank you," Fern managed. "I enjoyed your song. Very much."

Joyce smiled at her. "You have a beautiful voice. Like Patsy Cline."

Hilda laughed softly. "I don't know about that, but that's awfully kind of you to say." Her eyes lingered on Fern, fixed and searching. "The Lord laid it on my heart to sing that song tonight. I just felt that someone here was carrying more than they could bear." She hesitated, biting her lip. "Sometimes He gives me that feeling, though I don't always know who it's for."

Fern's throat tightened, and she dropped her gaze, embarrassed.

"It's Mama," Joyce blurted. "She cries at night."

Heat rushed into Fern's face. "Joyce," she chided, picking at the fabric of her dress.

Hilda reached forward and touched Fern's arm lightly. "It's alright," she murmured, her gray-blue eyes softening. "This is what revival is for. That's what the word means. Restoration. Coming back to life when it feels like the end."

Fern blinked fast, fighting tears again.

Joyce squeezed her hand.

"I don't know what it is you're going through, but I believe the Lord crossed our paths tonight for a reason," Hilda told her.

Fern's heart hammered inside her constricted chest, but she let her voice break free. "When your husband preached about powers of darkness," she said hoarsely, "it sounded . . . it sounded like he was talking about our house."

For a moment, Hilda only watched her, an unreadable seriousness settling across her features.

A shadow passed over them. Harry Birch had stepped closer, evidently having caught enough of Fern's words to pique his interest. Up close, Fern was struck by how young he truly looked, no more than twenty-five, maybe younger, though the sharp lines of his jaw and the intensity in his dark eyes made him seem older in the pulpit. Standing this near to him, Fern felt dwarfed, not just by his height and broad build, but by the confidence radiating off him.

He looked down at Fern with a gravity that made her pulse quicken. "Forgive me, ma'am, but I couldn't help but overhear. You spoke of darkness in your home. Will you tell us more?"

Fern's lips parted, but no sound came. Where would she even begin? "It . . . well, it feels like our home has been under the devil's attack for quite some time."

The Birches waited for her to go on.

"It started with my husband leaving. He grew . . . restless. Bitter. Until one day, he was just gone. We haven't heard from him since." Her voice wavered, the words tumbling out in fragments. "And after that, things in the house . . . changed. Footsteps when no one was there. Unusual smells. My girls woke in the night, screaming.

They heard voices. Saw strange things." She paused to breathe. "It was almost like . . . something moved in when he moved out."

Harry and Hilda exchanged concerned glances.

She squeezed Joyce's hand hard as tears blurred her vision. "And then—" Her voice broke. "My youngest, Loretta . . . she's only three. She wandered into the woods last October and never came back."

Hilda's face crumpled, her breath catching as she pressed a hand to her mouth. "Oh, sister." She stepped closer and gently drew Fern's hands into her own. Her palms were soft, a little damp from the humid air, but her grip was steady. "When we prayed with your pastor before service, he asked us to remember a family by name. Carlisle." Her voice shook, but there was no mistaking the tenderness in it. "I've been carrying you in prayer all evening without knowing who you were until now."

Fern let out a shuddering sob.

Harry's broad shoulders shifted as he exhaled, his gaze fixed on Fern, unflinching. When he finally spoke, his voice came out low but resolute. "The devil preys on the broken. He'll tear a loving home apart, piece by piece, until there's nothing left but despair." He leaned in, conviction sharpening every word. "But he will not have the final word."

He glanced at Hilda, then back at Fern, his eyes burning with purpose. "If the enemy has staked claim in your house, then we'll meet him there. Tomorrow, sister. We'll come."

Hilda tightened her grip on Fern's hands. "You don't have to carry this burden alone anymore. The Lord puts people in our lives when we need them most."

Fern only nodded, unable to speak. She clutched Joyce's hand as though it were the only thing tethering her to the earth. For the first time in months, she felt a flicker of something she thought had been lost forever.

Hope.

Twenty-Four

Shannon

August 15, 2022

I TRIED TO TELL myself we were fine, that locking the nursery door and getting Hazel on that counselor's waitlist meant things were under control.

By nightfall, I couldn't shake the feeling that something in the house wanted me to believe that.

We'd spent the entire day in the living room, side by side. Hazel barely left my lap except to go to the bathroom, and even then, she pulled me by the hand along with her. We camped out on the couch. I set my laptop on the cushion next to me, trying to get some work done while Hazel watched TV, but it didn't take long to see this was not a day for productivity. I shut my computer and set it on the coffee table, resolving to devote all my attention to my daughter.

I read to her until my throat was sore. We played six rounds of *Candy Land* with Loretta the cat as player three and her stuffed unicorn, Carrot, as player four. We made homemade pizza for dinner, then after a bubble bath, we fell asleep snuggled together in my bed, her small hand curled around a fistful of my T-shirt.

When I startled awake hours later, the room was all shadows.

And my arms were empty.

"Hazel?" My voice was hoarse, half-asleep. I sat up and pushed back the covers, scanning the room.

She wasn't there.

Panic surged through me. I leapt out of bed and took off down the hallway.

The nursery door gaped open.

I'd locked it earlier. I knew I had. I'd even double-checked it before bed.

Dread gnawed at my insides as I stepped across the threshold. The nightlight threw a dull orange glow over the hardwoods, the flower-shaped rug, the rows of books.

Goosebumps prickled my arms as a draft rolled from the closet. The bifold doors stood slightly ajar.

I turned in a slow circle, my breath coming in quick, shallow gasps as I searched the shadows. "Hazel?"

A faint sound stirred behind me, a whisper of movement. I whipped around, heart hammering.

The old double-hung window was raised high. The curtains billowed gently as the night air crept in, thick and damp and cool, carrying the faint scent of wet leaves and earth.

That's when I saw her.

A small figure crossing the yard. Barefoot. Nightgown fluttering. Headed straight for the woods.

For a moment, my brain refused to process what I was seeing. Then instinct kicked in.

"Hazel!"

My voice cracked the silence like a gunshot, but she didn't turn. She moved with steady, unnatural purpose, like something was pulling her toward the tree line.

I ran.

Down the hall, through the kitchen, out the back door. It slammed behind me as I burst into the night.

A layer of fog hovered low above the ground, coiling through the yard and swallowing Hazel's ankles as she went. It shimmered faintly in the moonlight.

"Hazel!"

She kept walking.

The grass was slick with dew beneath my bare feet, the air sharp and heavy with the smell of rain.

"HAZEL!"

Finally, she stopped. Silver moonlight spilled across her features as she turned slightly, still not looking at me but toward the darkness in the woods. Toward something else.

I reached her at last, and I fell to my knees, grabbing her shoulders, pulling her into me. She was ice cold. Her little body shook against mine as I held her.

"What are you doing?"

"She called me," Hazel whispered.

I gulped. "Who? The tricky lady?"

She nodded, lips quivering. "I didn't want to go, but she told me she'd show me the other little girl. She said I could play with her."

"What other girl?"

"Loretta. She said I could go with her, now that Miss Fern isn't watching anymore."

Oh, God.

I crushed her against me, staring into the woods. Something moved there, too far to see clearly.

I scooped Hazel into my arms and ran for the house.

Inside, I slammed the deadbolt home. My pulse roared in my ears.

"We're leaving," I told her. She didn't argue.

I thought about packing, but the hallway stopped me cold. The air there felt heavy and charged, and when I managed to suck in a shallow breath, the reek of decay hit me.

We couldn't stay another second.

Hazel clung to me as I bolted out the front door.

The gravel driveway tore at my feet as I sprinted to the car, but I didn't slow down. I strapped Hazel into her car seat with shaking hands. I think I buckled her in too tightly, but I needed to know she couldn't slip away from me again.

Sliding into the driver's seat, I realized I had no plan.

But we needed to be anywhere but here.

Tires spun on gravel as I slammed it into reverse. I didn't want to look back, but my eyes betrayed me.

A figure stood in the front window, backlit, perfectly still. Watching.

Tears blurred my vision.

I floored it.

I didn't think, just drove. Down back roads, past sleeping houses, until at last, the glow of the city pulled me in. The first decent-looking budget hotel in Huntsville was enough.

My mud-caked bare feet sank into the worn carpet as I carried Hazel inside, her fingers still locked around her stuffed cat.

Behind us, the automatic doors closed with a hiss, sealing the darkness outside.

At least for tonight.

Twenty-Five

Shannon

August 16, 2022

I HAD TO SELL the house.

The thought hit me hard as I lay on the stiff hotel mattress, staring up at the moisture-stained ceiling tiles. For a long moment, I didn't move. My whole body ached. My shoulders and arms throbbed from carrying my daughter the previous night, my calves burned from running, and the soles of my feet felt bruised from walking barefoot across gravel and pavement.

Eventually, I groaned and sat up. Reached for my phone.

7:12 a.m.

I usually started work at eight.

That's when it hit me: I didn't have my laptop.

I'd left it on the living room coffee table, right where I'd been working yesterday afternoon before everything happened. Before we fled the house in the dark with nothing but the clothes on our backs.

Without that laptop, I couldn't work.

I made my own hours. I didn't have to check in with anyone. But I had a few active projects—unfinished files and unanswered client messages. Sooner rather than later, I was going to have to go back and get it.

The thought made me shudder. Even for a minute, even just to grab it and leave, I couldn't imagine stepping foot in that house again.

But one problem at a time.

A dozen other to-dos began circling my brain. I needed a plan. Before I could make one, I had to know where we stood. I unlocked my phone, opened my banking app, and thumbed through my checking and savings accounts.

$219.42.

The sum total of what I had left in checking until my next client payment came through.

I'd charged the hotel room—another hundred bucks—to the credit card. There was probably room on that card to do it again a couple more times. But I still had to figure out food. And after our days at the hotel were up, I had to figure out how to cover groceries, gas, and a place to stay for the rest of the month.

My savings account was worse—not even enough to cover a tank of gas. There was nothing left to fall back on.

I switched over to my credit card app, barely able to breathe as I waited for the balance to load.

Current Balance: $2,921.17.

Available Credit: $1,078.83.

Better than I expected. But a thousand dollars didn't stretch like it used to. The thought of racking up even more debt made my stomach turn, but it was the only lifeline I had left. It could buy me a few more nights in this hotel, just enough time to figure out what the hell I was going to do next.

Then what? Where could we go? Not back to the house. That wasn't an option.

I needed to call someone. A friend. A family member.

Who? Who was left?

I leaned back against the headboard, phone clutched in my sweaty palm, trying not to think about what this meant. How trapped I was.

I pulled my knees to my chest and stared at the wall.

My thoughts tumbled over each other, no order, no direction. I couldn't prioritize anything. There were too many needs, all of them urgent. How to work. Where to stay. What to feed my daughter.

At least the hotel offered a free continental breakfast downstairs. That would get us through the morning. After that, I'd need groceries. Something simple. Something that fit in the mini-fridge and could be cooked in the tiny microwave.

I needed to sell the house.

That was the only real way out. Sell it and start over somewhere else. Anywhere else.

I had to find a realtor.

I grabbed the hotel notepad and pen from the nightstand and started scribbling, trying to turn my internal chaos into an action plan:

Contact realtor.

Get laptop.

Finish current projects.

Groceries.

Find temp. housing.

I stared at the list, feeling no more prepared than I had a minute ago.

A faint knock sounded at the door.

My heart jumped.

Hazel, still sound asleep beside me beneath thin comforter, didn't even flinch.

I slid out of bed and peered out the peephole.

No one was there.

Something hung from the doorknob, though. I cracked open the door and found a plastic bag, the hotel's logo printed across it. Inside was a pair of pink dollar-store flip-flops, new with tags, and a folded note that read:

> *Thought you might could use these.*
> *- Front Desk*

Heat rushed to my face. I could picture the clerks at shift change, whispering about the barefoot woman who'd shown up at three in the morning with a little girl and no suitcases.

Embarrassment burned through me, but it eventually cooled to gratitude.

The flip-flops slapped noisily against the tile floor as Hazel and I trekked across the lobby toward the smell of coffee and waffles. As we passed the front desk, the woman behind the counter gave me a knowing smile.

I decided to stop and thank her.

"You the one from three-thirty-four?" she said, her voice gentle but curious. Her eyes slid to my feet. "I sent those up for you first thing, honey. 'Bout broke my heart when I heard you come in here barefoot."

"Yeah," I said, my face boiling hot. "It was . . . a rough night. Thank you. They're a perfect fit."

Her lips broke into a smile. "Girl, don't mention it. I've been in some sticky situations myself." She glanced down at Hazel. "Hey, there, sweetness. You hungry? We still got plenty of breakfast over there. Miss Frankie just put out some fresh bacon. Y'all go get you something."

"We're headed that way," I said.

"Good. And listen, honey," she lowered her voice, "if y'all need anything—any toiletries, extra towels, even just an ear to listen—you just ask for Latoya. I'll take care of you."

"Thank you, Latoya."

Her gaze softened. "It gets easier, you know. Leaving. It takes a while, but I promise you, it does."

I opened my mouth, then closed it. I wanted to tell her it wasn't an abusive husband I'd left, that it was something else. Something I couldn't understand. But I couldn't put it into words, not without sounding insane.

And maybe it didn't matter anyway.

Escaping is escaping, no matter what you're running from.

The free hotel breakfast felt like a luxury. Yogurt cups, pastries, a waffle maker, a hot bar with bacon, eggs, and buttery grits. My mouth watered, and Hazel's eyes glowed like it was Christmas morning.

We'd never taken a family vacation, but today, I decided we'd pretend this was one. After everything, we deserved that much. Maybe we'd even play in the outdoor pool.

We piled our plates with waffles, greasy bacon, and fruit. The coffee was bitter, but it did its duty of resurrecting me. Hazel happily chugged away at a cup of orange juice, a fact I would likely regret later when the blood sugar spike sent her bouncing off the walls. But I didn't care right now. I was just happy to see her happy.

My to-do list lingered at the back of my mind.

Find temp housing.

Get groceries.

My eyes drifted to the breakfast bar, quietly calculating what I could stash in my purse without drawing attention. How many yogurts could I sneak in there? How many bananas?

I thought of Granny Jean then, how she used to slip fried chicken and biscuits into her purse off the buffet at Shoney's. I'd been mortified as a teen. Now I understood why she did it.

God. I'd become Granny Jean.

Contact realtor.

Get laptop.

Ugh, I needed my damn laptop. I couldn't get any work done without it, and if I didn't work, we'd have no income aside from Marc's measly child support check, which wasn't due for another two weeks.

I took a sip of coffee. It tasted burned.

I had to go back to the house.

But maybe I didn't have to go back alone.

If I scheduled a meeting or a walkthrough with a real estate agent, at least I'd have a buffer. Another adult in the room.

I could grab the laptop then, pretend I'd forgotten it, make it casual.

In. Out. Done.

I grabbed my phone and thumbed through my contacts until I found the realtor who'd helped us buy the property back in 2019. Tom Altamira. He'd been easy to work with then, friendly yet professional.

I stared at his name for a long moment.

I'd call him as soon as we got back upstairs.

"Hello, this is Tom."

"Hi, Tom," I began into the phone, heart pounding. "This is Shannon Reed. You helped my—" I gulped, my chest tightening as I forced the words out, "—my husband and me a few years ago. We bought the old place on Sunflower Lane in Gurley."

"Oh yeah! Of course. How've you been?"

"Fine," I lied automatically. "How about you?"

"Great, thanks. How can I help you, Shannon?"

I swallowed. "I'm calling because I want to sell the house."

"Got it. I would love to help you with that."

I felt myself relax a little. "Great."

"We'll need to set up a walkthrough so I can get a feel for the place, get you a ballpark asking price. I remember you talking about some plans for updates back then. Did y'all end up renovating?"

"Um . . . yeah, we did do some renovating," I said. "We pulled up the carpet and found original hardwoods underneath. We did a lot of painting." I rattled off everything I could think of, though my brain tripped over the memories. It was hard to remember which of the projects we'd started and actually completed.

"Sounds like you put a lot into it," Tom said. "That's good news. And I don't know if you're aware, Shannon, but the Huntsville market's red-hot right now. I think you'll be happy with what it's worth."

My spirit soared at his words until I remembered *why* I was selling the place.

I didn't know what to say. Was I legally obligated to disclose the truth about the property? The things we'd endured there?

I wasn't sure, and I couldn't figure out how to ask him.

"I'd like to list it as soon as possible," I said instead.

"Of course. Let me check my schedule." I heard the rustle of pages. "I'm free first thing tomorrow. Is eight too early?"

"Eight would be perfect."

"Alright. I'll swing by in the morning and we'll get things rolling. I'm excited to work with you again, Shannon."

"Thank you so much," I said.

As the call ended, I stared at the screen.

I was doing the right thing.

I was.

Twenty-Six

Shannon

August 17, 2022

I EASED MY CR-V down the long gravel driveway at seven forty-five in the morning and shifted into park. Hazel and I stayed put, the SUV a barrier between us and the house while we waited for the realtor, Tom Altamira, to arrive.

I stared through the windshield at the place we'd once called home. It didn't feel like ours anymore. Even on this bright summer morning, bathed in golden light, the house looked wrong. Ominous. Like it was watching us. Most of the flowers I'd planted out front had withered or been choked out by weeds, but the wisteria vines endured. Now they curled up the porch columns in thick, twisted braids. Their blooms were lovely, yes, but almost grotesquely so; something trying too hard to be beautiful.

The rocking chairs hadn't moved. They sat stiff as sentries, waiting for someone to sit. To stay.

It all looked staged, like the house was pretending to be charming. I could see its mask now. I could feel its true nature.

My heart thudded as I scanned every window for movement, every shadowy corner for something that didn't belong. But I saw nothing.

While we waited for Tom, I pulled out my phone and started a list of everything I needed to grab while we were here. My work laptop and charger. A suitcase, which I would need to fill with more clothes. More toiletries. Toys and books for Hazel. Laundry detergent. Some kitchen basics. Photo albums. Important documents like birth certificates and such.

"I don't wanna go in there, Mommy."

I glanced up at the rearview and caught Hazel's reflection in the baby mirror clipped to the car seat. The distress on her face made my heart sink.

"I know, baby. Me neither. But we won't be alone this time. A nice man named Mr. Tom is coming over to help us sell the house so we can go live somewhere else."

The car went quiet as she processed this information.

"What if the tricky lady comes?"

I swallowed. "Then we'll run as fast as we can and drive far away from here."

She gave me a reluctant nod.

A few uneasy moments passed, then the crunch of gravel behind us signaled a new arrival. I glanced in the rearview mirror once more as a black Toyota Highlander rolled to a stop behind us.

"There he is," I told Hazel. "That's Mr. Tom." I climbed out and began unbuckling her.

Tom waited for me at the hood of his Highlander, tapping on an iPad. He glanced up and smiled, the same easy, genuine smile I remembered from three years ago when I was pregnant and hopeful and had no idea what this house would take from me.

He didn't seem to have changed at all. The same tidy curls in his hair, the same smooth copper skin and sharp jawline. Fitted blue button-down, neatly pressed khakis, polished shoes. Effortlessly put together, just like I remembered him, like someone who actually slept and drank water and didn't live off of dinosaur nuggets.

Meanwhile, I was wearing maternity leggings three years postpartum and the same stained, baggy T-shirt I'd run out of this house in a couple nights ago.

I felt my cheeks flush with embarrassment as I wondered what he saw when he looked at me now.

"Hey, Shannon," he said as I approached with Hazel on my hip. "Great to see you. It's been a while." His dark, chestnut brown eyes softened as they landed on Hazel. "And who is this?"

"This is my daughter, Hazel."

Tom lit up. "Hazel! It's so nice to meet you."

She shrank against me, clinging to me with both hands and bunching up the front of my T-shirt so tightly the collar drooped and exposed the worn gray strap of my bra. I tugged it back into place as casually as I could, pretending not to care, but I could feel the heat creeping up my neck.

"She's a little shy around new people," I said, offering an apologetic smile as I rubbed a hand over Hazel's back.

"I get that. Meeting someone new can be a little scary sometimes." His words came easily, calmly, suggesting a level of comfort around little kids that most men didn't have. "But I promise, I'm just here to help your mom."

Hazel didn't respond, but she peeked out at him for half a second before retreating again.

I gave a breathy laugh, all nerves. "She'll warm up."

Tom's gaze drifted toward the house.

"So, um . . . would you like to go inside?" I asked, pulse quickening.

"Sure, whenever you're ready." His eyes traveled across the house's façade, taking in the wisteria-draped porch and the sun-dappled siding. "It's cute. Honestly, you've got it looking like a real-life storybook cottage."

A storybook cottage like the Hansel and Gretel house, I thought. Sweet on the outside, while within, something evil waited to devour children.

We climbed the porch steps together. My fingers trembled as I slid the key into the lock. I wondered if he noticed.

Hazel tightened her grip around my neck and locked her small legs around my waist like she feared I might set her down.

I pushed the door open. The air inside hit me at once, a wave of familiar scents: aged wood, the lingering citrus oil from my diffuser, and something else. Something old and musty.

As I crossed the threshold, Hazel's body went rigid in my arms, a full-body clench. She wasn't letting go, and I couldn't blame her.

Tom followed, his footsteps steady on the worn wood planks. "Wow," he said, slowly glancing around the entryway. "It looks so different without the carpet. These are the original floors, right?"

"Yeah," I said. "We wanted to refinish them, but, well, we just never got around to it."

He nodded sympathetically and hunched down for a closer look. The oak boards were beautiful in places, dulled and warped from water damage in others. I'd covered the worst of it with rugs, but I wasn't going to point that out right now.

"Well, even as-is, they've got character. That'll stand out in the listing." He stood and moved into the living room, his eyes taking it all in. "I see you painted. Looks good. Neutral was a wise choice for resale, too."

I glanced at the walls we'd coated in a clean, crisp white. Snowbound by Sherwin Williams. "Thanks. We were going for light and airy. Something peaceful." *Peaceful*. Ha. That hadn't lasted long.

Tom stepped carefully around a scattered wooden puzzle and a crumpled blanket fort. "Did you repaint the whole interior?"

"Just the living room and the nursery," I admitted. "We meant to keep going, but . . ." I trailed off, unsure what to say.

He gave a soft nod of understanding. "Hey, life happens." He made a few notes on his tablet, then glanced up at me. "Alright. So. You thinking a full clean-out first, or staging it as-is?"

My stomach tensed. The idea of clearing out this place, sorting through every drawer and closet, coming back here again and again until the place was stripped bare, made my skin crawl.

But then I glanced around at the mess we'd left behind. Toys, picture books, and princess dresses littered the floor. Dirty dishes crowded the kitchen sink. Unfinished home improvement projects lurked in every corner: a bucket of drywall putty, a roll of electrical wire, several lengths of baseboard molding we'd bought and never installed, still leaning against the wall where we'd abandoned them two years ago. I'd gone to blind to it all.

I hadn't even considered tidying up before Tom arrived, and now, standing in the middle of it all, I felt like an idiot.

"I'm so sorry, I didn't even think about that." My cheeks were so hot, I probably looked like a tomato. And knowing that only made it worse. "I should've cleaned—"

Tom waved a hand, already moving toward the hallway. "Don't stress, Shannon. Seriously. Lived-in is normal, especially with kids in the house. But if you *do* want top dollar, a quick tidy and maybe some light staging could help. Nothing fancy. Just enough to help buyers picture themselves here."

I nodded, grateful for how kindly he'd phrased it.

He paused near the dining room entry, tablet still in hand. "Is Marc here today?"

The question was so casual, so gentle, but it still hit like a slap.

"No," I said quickly. "No, um, we're divorced."

I caught a flicker of surprise on Tom's face before he masked it with a polite nod. "Ah. Got it." He cleared his throat. "Well, for what it's worth, the improvements you made, even if they aren't what you planned originally, they'll help out a lot. This place is going to show well."

My fingers tightened around Hazel's back. "I hope so."

"Mind if I walk and take a look around? I'd like to see the whole place and make a few notes for the listing."

"Sure," I said, noticing how shaky my voice sounded. "Um, but would it be okay if we walked it together? I'd, uh, I'd just feel better sticking together."

"Oh. Yeah, of course." He sounded friendly, but his eyes darted past me, toward the hallway. The one that always felt too dark, even in the daytime. He shifted his weight, adjusting the strap of his bag. "You guys aren't staying here right now?"

I shook my head. "We're at a hotel. Just for now."

He blinked at that, just once, but I saw the way his gaze swept the room behind me. The furniture was all still here. A million toys. The mail on the counter, some of it unopened. Nothing packed.

"Oh."

That was all he said. It settled oddly between us.

I had the sudden urge to explain myself, but I held my tongue. What could I say? I'd brought this man here to sell this place. He needed to see it as a house. *Just* a house. Four walls and a roof.

But how much was I legally required to tell him?

They talked about that on real estate shows—stigmatized properties, haunted houses, places with histories that made buyers hesitate. But what was legal? What was *ethical*?

I looked back at Tom and found his eyes on me.

Something in his expression shifted, just enough to make my skin tingle, like he saw straight through me. Like he recognized something I hadn't meant to reveal.

"It feels a little . . . different in here than I remember," he said, giving the hallway a longer look. His gaze seemed to linger on Hazel's bedroom door.

I shifted my weight anxiously. "Different?"

He hesitated, eyes still on the door. "Hard to explain." One corner of his mouth ticked up. "My sister would probably call it *negative energy*."

I gave a short, awkward laugh. "Oh yeah? And what would you call it?"

"Just . . . different," he said, finally glancing back at me. His face was unreadable, but the air between us felt heavier. He straightened his tablet, breaking the moment. "Let's keep going."

TWENTY-SEVEN

Fern

May 1963

MORNING DAWNED BRIGHT OVER the valley, pouring gilded sunlight across the dewy fields. Inside Fern's house, the light stopped at the windows. She'd opened all of them to let the outside in, hoping a bit of fresh spring air might cut through the gloom. But the honeysuckle-sweetened balmy breeze was already thick with humidity, and the house only grew stuffier.

After seeing Joyce off to school, Fern spent the morning tidying with frantic hands. She dragged the Electrolux from the hall closet and ran it back and forth across the avocado green carpet until neat diagonal tracks striped the floor. She straightened the curtains, swept the kitchen, wiped the counters twice, though they were already clean. She caught herself twisting the dishrag in her hands repeatedly, wringing it until her knuckles ached, and she forced herself to set it down just as the knock she'd been waiting for came at the front door.

Harry Birch stood on the porch framed in dazzling sunlight, his Bible tucked firmly beneath one arm. Beside him, Hilda smiled softly, neat and composed, both of them looking so fresh and untroubled it made Fern's stomach ache a little.

"Good morning, Mrs. Carlisle," Harry greeted her. "May we come in?"

Fern gulped and stepped aside. "Of course. Please."

They crossed the threshold, their eyes roaming quietly over the entryway.

"Your home is lovely," Hilda offered.

Fern managed a faint smile. "Thank you. Can I get you something to drink? Coffee? Or sweet tea?"

Both shook their heads politely, so she led them into the living room, smoothing her skirt with sweaty hands as she went. The room was spotless, the furniture freshly dusted, every cushion plumped, lace doilies perfectly in place. But no amount of cleaning could banish the feeling of oppression, the sense that the house was brooding, prevailing against Fern's attempts to make it shine.

"Please, have a seat," Fern told them, motioning toward the sofa. She tried to sound warm and casual like a good Southern hostess.

Hilda lowered herself gracefully and folded her hands in her lap, her eyes wandering the room with restrained curiosity. Her gaze lingered on a framed photograph of Joyce and Loretta on the end table, both girls in matching Easter dresses, smiling shyly at the camera. Her expression softened as she stared at it, though she said nothing.

Harry didn't sit. He stood in the center of the room, Bible still wedged under his arm, his dark eyes drifting toward the hallway that led to the bedrooms.

A floorboard popped somewhere in the back of the house. Fern flinched. "It does that sometimes," she said, hating how brittle her voice sounded.

Hilda glanced at her husband, then back at Fern, her brow creased with concern. "It feels . . . heavy in here," she murmured.

Fern felt a flicker of relief at Hilda's words. If even a stranger felt it, then she wasn't crazy. The heaviness was real, not some invention of her weary mind.

Harry shifted his stance. "It does indeed. Mrs. Carlisle, I'd like to begin with a prayer," he said. "Then, if you'll allow us, we'll walk through the rooms together."

Fern nodded.

Harry drew the Bible from beneath his arm and pressed it to his chest as he bowed his head. "Heavenly Father, we come into this home asking for Your peace to abide here. I lift up Mrs. Carlisle and Joyce, and I lift up Loretta, wherever she may be. Lord, You know where her little feet have wandered. You know the sorrow that's settled over this house. You know their pain. Their fear. Cover them now with Your presence. Let no darkness linger in these rooms. Drive out the enemy in Jesus's name, and fill this house with Your light. Be our refuge and our strength. Guide our steps as we walk here today. In the name of Jesus, we pray. Amen."

The women echoed the final word, though it faltered halfway up Fern's throat. She hadn't prayed in months, not since those first desperate weeks after Loretta vanished. *Amen* felt strange on her tongue now, burdened by everything she had lost.

An uncomfortable silence settled over them then, and Fern gestured awkwardly toward the hallway. "Should I give you a tour?"

"Please," Harry told her. "I'd like to pray over each room."

She led the Birches to the kitchen first. Harry stopped at the living room threshold and placed his hand on the doorframe.

"Cleanse this house of evil, Lord. Send your Holy Spirit into this place."

Beside him, Hilda's voice sounded soft and sure: "'And the light shineth in darkness; and the darkness comprehended it not.'" She looked to Fern as she added, "John one, verse five."

The three of them moved from room to room—kitchen, dining room, laundry room—Harry praying, Hilda at his side, reciting scripture. Fern followed close behind, feeling uneasy as they approached the back of the house.

When they reached the dim, narrow hallway, the air shifted. It cooled, drastically enough to raise goosebumps on Fern's arms.

Hilda shivered. "'The Lord is my light and my salvation; whom shall I fear?'" she murmured.

The walls smothered their voices uncannily as they moved down the hall and into the master bedroom. They prayed over Fern's space, then Joyce's. Harry touched the girl's bedframe as he prayed, Hilda whispering, "'He shall give His angels charge over thee, to keep thee in all thy ways.'"

One room remained.

Loretta's.

Fern froze before the closed door. Her hand hovered over the knob, her breath shallow. She hadn't opened this door in weeks.

She felt Hilda's hand gently come to rest on her elbow. "You don't have to do this alone. We're right here."

With trembling fingers, Fern pushed the door open.

The room lay before them like a dark shrine, the morning sunlight strangled by pink ruffled curtains. Every toy and book sat neatly in its place on the shelves she and Raymond had painted together, but the precise order of everything only deepened Loretta's absence. Fern's eyes slid to the closet, the bifold doors shut tight.

A chill swept over them at once, fierce and unnatural, as if the cold was seeping from behind those doors. Cold that had no business in Alabama this far into May.

Hilda's voice trembled as she whispered, "'The Lord is nigh unto them that are of a broken heart; and saveth such as be of a contrite spirit.' Psalm thirty-four, verse eighteen."

Something small clattered to the floor. One of Loretta's wooden alphabet blocks had toppled from the bookshelf, though no one had gone near it. A second one, then a third, struck the hardwoods with such force, Hilda cried out, clutching her chest.

Terror throbbed inside of Fern as a fourth and final block clanged down next to the others. They moved together to get a closer look.

M I N E

Fern's knees nearly buckled as she read it. *Mine.* Could it be Loretta? Could she mean her room, her toys? Or . . . was this something else? Something laying claim to her house. Her daughter. Her family.

"No," she choked out, a sob catching in her throat.

Hilda clutched her hand tightly.

Harry's jaw clenched. He stepped forward, planting himself between Fern and the fallen blocks. "This is not your house," he declared. "This family is not yours. In the name of Jesus Christ, I command you to flee this place."

For a moment, silence settled around them. Then the closet doors shuddered violently, vibrating on their hinges. Hilda shrieked. Fern staggered back, eyes wide, panic clawing up her throat.

The doors rattled on, an unrelenting fury that seemed to stretch into eternity, until at last they stilled again.

The quiet that followed throbbed in Fern's ears. Her breathing was ragged, her hand still locked in Hilda's trembling grip. Harry stood frozen, clutching his Bible, jaw set tight. For a long moment, he said nothing, only stared at the closet as though sizing up the thing inside.

When he finally turned to Fern, there was a new solemnness in his eyes. "Only one kind of enemy fights this hard to hold its ground," he said.

"An evil spirit," Hilda breathed.

Harry nodded. "But it knows its time is short. Greater is He that is in us than he that is in the world. We'll come back another day, more prepared. Mrs. Carlisle, is there somewhere you and Joyce could stay in the meantime? Perhaps with some family?"

Fern stiffened. "If Loretta's still out there, if there's even a chance she'll come back, this is where she'll come." She swallowed. "What if she finds the door locked? No one waiting for her?" She shook her head. "No. I have to be here."

Hilda's lips parted as though she might speak, but she only pressed them back together, her features paling with a grief that mirrored Fern's.

Harry dipped his chin, the muscles in his jaw flexing around words unsaid. They didn't argue, and Fern took their silence as mercy.

Twenty-Eight

Shannon

August 18, 2022

I WAS BARELY HOLDING it together. I was trying to work, keep a three-year-old alive and entertained in a hotel room, and figure out how to sell the haunted house I'd fled in the middle of the night.

We'd been at the hotel less than three full days, and I already hated everything about it—the air, the lighting, the constant hum of the mini fridge. The way the room seemed to shrink every time Hazel had a meltdown.

Yesterday dragged by in a dull, miserable haze. During the house walkthrough, while Tom tapped through paperwork on his iPad, I made a frantic attempt at staging—scooping up dirty clothes, folding blankets, stuffing stray toys into a tote. I could only bring myself to tidy whatever room Tom was standing in. When I pulled out a suitcase and started tossing things inside, I caught him watching me. His brows pinched for a second, like he wanted to ask something, but he didn't.

We came straight back to the hotel and spent the rest of the day trapped in survival mode: endless snack demands, screen-time guilt, and Hazel careening between wild energy and full-on emotional collapse. She was completely out of sorts in the cramped room. More dramatic, more sensitive. Louder in every way. She screamed because her sock felt *"wrong."* She tried to scale the headboard like it was a jungle gym. Eventually, I surrendered and put PBS Kids on the hotel TV.

Now she was on the floor again, shredding pages from the hotel notepad into tiny confetti and murmuring to herself as she arranged the scraps into piles. I didn't ask questions. At least she was quiet.

Tom had called earlier to say the photographer was headed to the house this morning. Thankfully, I didn't have to be there for that. The listing was scheduled to go live tomorrow, assuming the place didn't show its true colors in the pictures. Part of me half-expected the photos to come back full of orbs and strange figures.

In the meantime, I was focused on catching up on work as much as possible. I sat on the edge of the bed, my laptop burning against my thighs, trying to finish a carousel of Instagram graphics for a daycare client who wanted everything to be "sunny, imaginative, and full of magic!" The contrast between that and our miserable hotel room was enough to make me laugh. Or cry.

I was lining up a quote about curiosity in a fun, bubbly font when a knock sounded at the door.

Hazel looked up from her paper piles. "Who's that?"

I stood, brushing granola bar crumbs off my leggings. I'd channeled my inner Granny Jean and swiped three of them from the breakfast bar downstairs earlier. "Probably housekeeping," I told her.

When I opened the door, Latoya from the front desk stood there, still in her work polo and khakis, holding a couple of Walmart bags. Her smile was tired but kind.

"Hey, sweetheart," she said. "I just got off work and ran over to the store. Thought you could use a few things."

Before I could say a word, she pressed the bags into my hands. A quick glance inside showed coloring books, a pack of stickers, crayons, and a variety of snacks.

My throat tightened. "Oh my gosh. You didn't have to do all this."

"I know," she said with a small shrug. "But I wanted to."

Hazel darted over to my side, unashamedly peeking into the bags. "Goldfish!" she squealed.

Latoya chuckled. "I hoped that'd get a smile."

"Thank you," Hazel said with a shy grin.

I tried to thank her too, but my voice faltered. I suddenly wondered if she'd seen me sneaking granola bars. The front desk had a clear view of the breakfast area. Of course she'd seen. Heat crawled up my neck.

Latoya's eyes met mine, and something in her gaze verified my suspicion. "Listen, I know how tight things can get. I've been there. More times than I can count, to tell you the truth." She glanced past me at our room. At my laptop open on the bed, Hazel's shredded paper on the floor, *Wild Kratts* on the TV. "I know hotel life can't be easy, especially with a little one."

I swallowed, unsure what to say.

"How long are y'all planning to stay here?"

"I, uh, I'm not sure."

"Well," Latoya said after a moment. "I wanted to tell you about a friend of mine. Miss Maureen. She goes to my church. Taught kindergarten for years and years back in the day. Sweetest lady you'll ever meet. Anyway, she keeps an extra room ready all the time, just in case a woman needs a safe place for a bit. She don't ask questions, she just helps. Says that's what we're supposed to do."

My chest ached. I tried to keep my expression neutral, but I could tell I was failing.

"She's wonderful with kids," Latoya went on. "If you want, I'll give you her number. She's not far. Just over in Madison. Thought it might help, even for a few days."

I didn't know what to say.

Latoya smiled. "No pressure, okay? Just think about it. Miss Maureen always says the Lord puts folks in your path for a reason."

She glanced down at Hazel, who was back on the floor, already flipping through the coloring book and humming to herself. "And I think that reason might be sitting right here."

Her words caught me off guard. I blinked hard, trying to push back tears. "Thank you," I managed.

Latoya squeezed my hand once. "You don't have to do this alone, sweetheart. Nobody should have to."

I called Maureen that afternoon. She had the voice of a teacher: calm, patient, and gently no-nonsense. The way she spoke to me, I felt like I already knew her.

"Just come on over whenever you're ready," she said. "I've got the room made up and ready for you."

I wanted to pack up and leave right then, but I'd already paid for the night, and the hotel had free breakfast in the morning. I wasn't about to waste either.

We left just after nine Friday morning. I looked for Latoya at the front desk when we checked out, but she wasn't there. It was a different clerk this time. She was younger, glued to her phone. I handed over the room key, relieved to leave the place behind us.

Maureen's house sat near the end of a cul-de-sac in an older subdivision where every house looked the same. Weathered brick, overgrown hedges, cracked driveways. Hers was a single-story ranch, tan with green shutters and a narrow carport shading a silver Honda. I pulled in behind it and let the engine idle.

My eyes followed a row of zinnias and marigolds blooming along the walkway to an unassuming concrete stoop, where a colorful wind chime featuring an iridescent hummingbird turned lazily in the breeze.

As I shut off the engine, I glanced in the rearview mirror. Hazel was quiet, her stuffed cat Loretta squished tight against her chest, eyes wide as she took it all in.

She caught my reflection and whispered, "Where are we?"

I swallowed. "This is Miss Maureen's house," I said carefully. "She's a friend. We're going to stay with her for a little bit."

Hazel kept staring out the window. Then, after a few seconds, "Is she nice?"

My chest tightened. "Yeah, baby. She's really nice. I think you'll like her."

She looked at the porch again, then nodded, serious. "Okay."

I unbuckled. "You ready to go in?"

"Can I bring Loretta?"

"Of course."

She hugged the yellow tabby tighter, and I watched the tension ease just a little from her shoulders.

As I climbed out and rounded the car, I heard the creak of a screen door behind me. I turned as a woman stepped out onto the front stoop, drying her hands on a dish towel. She had to be Maureen.

She was broad-shouldered and soft-bodied, with wispy white-blonde curls escaping from a claw clip. Her floral blouse fluttered slightly in the breeze, loose over drawstring denim capris.

She tossed the towel over her shoulder and raised a hand in a friendly wave. Her smile was wide and warm, like we weren't just expected, but *wanted*.

"Shannon!" she called as she crossed the lawn. "I'm Maureen. Welcome." She reached the car and peeked in. "Hey, sweet pea. You must be Hazel."

Hazel clutched Loretta but didn't look away. Just stared, watchful and quiet.

Maureen didn't push. She turned to me instead. "You need help with anything?"

"No, ma'am, I think I've got it," I said as I unfastened Hazel's car seat.

Maureen gave me space but stayed close. "I should've asked yesterday, but do either of y'all have any allergies or food restrictions?"

The thoughtful question surprised me. "Oh, uh, no. We're good."

"Oh, good. I put together a little welcome basket. Nothing fancy, just a few things to make it feel more like home. And I've got banana bread in the kitchen. Just came out of the oven."

"Thank you," I said, a lump rising in my throat. "Really."

"You're welcome. Take your time. No rush here."

She gave Hazel a gentle wave, then turned back toward the house.

I lifted Hazel out and grabbed our bags. She gripped my hand tightly as we followed the path to the front door.

The yard was quiet except for a robin chirping in the lone maple tree and the occasional soft creak of wind through its branches.

Maureen held the door open for us. "Come on in," she said.

I hesitated at the threshold. Just for a second, halted by a flicker of doubt. The feeling of stepping into someone else's life. But the heavenly smell of cinnamon and baked sugar beckoned me inside.

Maureen's living room furniture was mismatched in a way that felt intentional. Homey. Crocheted afghans draped over chairs. A whole gallery wall of framed kids' drawings. A big gray cat curled up on a windowsill, soaking up the daylight.

Hazel tugged on my pant leg and pointed. "There's a kitty," she murmured.

I smiled, relief rising in my chest. "There is."

"That's Eloise," Maureen said, gently closing the door behind us. "She's old and cranky, but she likes good company."

Hazel kept her eyes on the cat, clearly intrigued.

I dropped our bags near the couch and turned to Maureen. "This place is really lovely."

"Thank you. You're welcome to stay as long as you need."

The words settled into me like warmth from a cozy fireplace.

I had no idea what was coming next. But for the first time in a long time, I didn't feel like I was bracing for it.

Twenty–Nine

Hazel warmed up faster than I expected. She sat cross-legged on the living room rug, humming as she lined up a parade of wooden animals Maureen had pulled out. Eloise wandered over, sniffed her head-to-toe, then plopped down beside her like she'd passed the test.

I stayed on the couch, hands curled around a mug of fresh coffee. Maureen settled into the recliner across from me. The banana bread scent still hung in the air.

For a while, neither of us said anything. The silence was a little uncomfortable. I didn't know where to look, what to do with my hands. Sitting in a stranger's living room without an agenda felt incredibly strange.

Maureen watched Hazel for a beat, then glanced back at me. Her voice was soft. "You can breathe now, you know."

I blinked. "What?"

"You've been holding your breath," she said, gesturing gently toward me. "I can see it in your shoulders."

I laughed, but it came out shaky. "You're not wrong."

She didn't say anything else right away. Just sipped her coffee and let the moment linger.

"I don't even know how to talk about it," I said after a long pause. "Everything that happened. It's just . . . a lot."

"Oh, you don't have to tell me anything," she said. "But if you ever want to, I'll listen."

I nodded. "Thank you. I appreciate that."

Hazel made two wooden animals kiss and giggled.

Maureen smiled. "She's settling in nicely."

"Yeah, she seems comfortable here." I glanced down at my coffee mug, cream-colored porcelain printed with a faded apple and the words *#1 Teacher* in red cursive, something a student probably gifted her twenty years ago. I realized I'd been absently picking at the design with my thumbnail and forced myself to stop. "I'm pretty sure Eloise sealed the deal."

That got a chuckle from Maureen. "You know, Eloise doesn't usually make friends this fast. She's very particular about people."

We looked down at Hazel and Eloise as she said this. The cat curled against my daughter's knee, purring contentedly as if they'd been buddies for years.

Maureen took another sip of coffee. "Now, you mentioned you work from home, right?"

"Yes, ma'am. Graphic design. Mostly marketing stuff."

"Well, you've got Wi-Fi and quiet. If you need to get some work done today, don't let me hinder you. There's a desk in your room, but you're welcome to the dining room table too. It gets good light."

I looked at Hazel. "Are you sure? I don't want to impose."

"Oh, you're not." Maureen smiled, but her voice took on a wistful tone. "Frankly, I miss having a little one around. After thirty years in a classroom, the silence is too much sometimes." She caught herself and gave a small laugh. "Anyway, old habits die hard. I like feeling useful." Her gaze softened on me. "If I can help you catch your breath a little, I'd love to."

My throat burned as I nodded. "Thank you."

I set up my laptop in the dining room. Maureen was right. The lighting was perfect. A traditional oak table sat nestled in a cozy bay window nook, its surface worn smooth by decades of family meals. Daylight spilled through the glass, dappling the wood in soft, shifting patches of gold.

The sun warmed my back as I opened my laptop. From the front room, Hazel giggled. Maureen laughed with her.

It was all so . . . gentle.

Tears came without warning. A silent, sudden release. For the first time in years, I wasn't the only one keeping Hazel safe.

I'd needed this for so freaking long.

My phone buzzed beside the laptop. A text from Tom.

Listing's live and it's looking good. Already several views this morning and one showing booked for 5:30 tonight! I have a feeling the weekend's gonna be booked solid with showings.

I wiped my face and typed back quickly:

That's great news! Thank you!

Tom's response came a few seconds later:

Of course! You guys still staying at the hotel?

I hesitated, typing and deleting three different versions before finally landing on:

Not anymore. I met a woman at the hotel who helped us find a room at a retired teacher's house. She's very nice and is letting us stay for a bit.

Three dots appeared and disappeared. Appeared again.

That's great. I'm glad you guys are safe.

I stared at the screen. His reply felt . . . careful. Like he didn't quite know what to make of me opting to move into a stranger's spare room over going back to my own home.

Another message came through:

I'll keep you posted on the showings. Take care of yourselves, okay?

I exhaled and put away the phone.

For the first time in a long while, I felt safe enough to focus on work.

By that afternoon, I'd actually finished a full project—start to finish—without interruption. I sent the final files off to my client, and within an hour, she emailed back to let me know she was thrilled and no revisions were necessary. She even sent payment right away, with a generous tip, all before dinner time.

The weight that lifted off my shoulders felt almost unnatural, like maybe I was forgetting something. Work wasn't supposed to feel this easy.

Maureen asked what we wanted for dinner. She offered to cook or order delivery—her treat. I tried to argue, but she waved me off with a laugh.

"I've been craving Chinese all week," she said. "You'll be doing me a favor."

We ordered from China Dragon and spread the cartons out across Maureen's kitchen table. General Tso's chicken, spring rolls, egg drop soup, and crab rangoons. A feast for three people, but we didn't hold back. We ate until our stomachs ached, laughter mingling with the clatter of chopsticks and the kind of conversation that made us feel like old friends.

Now, with dinner behind us, the room had quieted. Hazel crunched on a fortune cookie while I folded greasy cartons into a trash bag, and Maureen wiped the table with a damp rag.

"Hazel made something for you today, while you were working," she told me, drying her hands on a dish towel. "I was going to tell you earlier, but . . . well, now feels better."

Hazel lit up. She slid off her chair and darted out of the room, returning seconds later with a piece of white construction paper clutched in her small hands. She held it out to me.

"Look, Mama," she said. "It's us."

I smiled as I took it, then froze.

Three stick figures stood beneath a yellow scribbled sun, drawn in thick, colorful crayon lines. Each figure was labeled in neat, adult handwriting—*Mommy, Miss Maureen,* and *Hazel.* A cartoonish house sat beside us. Orange roof. Purple door. A green chimney puffing out a gray spiral of smoke.

Behind it stood a fourth figure, drawn in black. Taller than the house. No face. No name.

It loomed behind the little house, arms stretching longer than they should've been, a dark scribble where its mouth belonged.

"Oh . . ." I breathed. My throat felt tight.

Maureen's gaze flicked down to the drawing. "I wrote the names for her," she said. "But the rest was all Hazel."

Hazel bounced on her toes and pointed at the image. "That's *here*," she said, tapping the house.

"Miss Maureen's house?" I asked.

She nodded.

I hesitated, then pointed to the dark figure behind it. "Who's this?"

"The tricky lady," Hazel said it so simply, so casually, that for a moment I forgot how terrified she used to be of that name. "She came with us from our old house. She missed me."

A chill crept down the back of my neck.

Maureen turned toward her. "What did you say, sweetheart?" she asked softly.

"She missed me," Hazel said. Her tone was sing-song, almost dreamy. "She said she didn't mean to scare me before."

The room seemed to tilt a little. My pulse thudded in my ears. "Hazel. What do you mean she's here?"

"She's outside now. Watching through the windows."

My stomach lurched, the half-pound of Chinese food I'd just eaten threatening a comeback.

The bay window stood tall beside us, its glass turned obsidian now that night had fallen. Our reflections hovered there, ghost-like and translucent, layered over the void of Maureen's backyard—my face pale, Maureen's unreadable, Hazel's still smiling vacuously as if she'd said something wonderful.

Goosebumps prickled my arms as I peered out into the darkness.

No. It wasn't possible.

Was it?

Maureen crouched down next to Hazel with an expert level of calmness. "You're such a good artist," she said. "Would you like to draw me another picture?"

Hazel beamed. "Yes!"

"There's more paper and crayons on the little table in the living room. I'd love to see what else you can make."

"Okay!" She sprinted out of the room, pigtails bouncing.

Maureen moved to the window. She slipped the beige curtains free from their metal tiebacks and pulled them closed in one fluid motion, sealing off the view outside.

Her smile was gone now. She glanced at the drawing again, then looked at me, her expression tight with concern.

"Shannon," she said, her voice low. "I've had students draw things like that before. It usually means . . . something's happened." She paused, carefully choosing her next words. "Something they don't know how to say."

I stayed quiet, my eyes fixed on that horrible dark figure.

Maureen's voice remained calm, but I could feel something shift underneath it. "Do you know who she was talking about? A tricky lady?"

I blinked.

"Somebody who might have followed you?" Maureen asked reluctantly. "I'm not trying to pry, and you don't have to tell me everything. But I need to know if there's any kind of danger. For her. Or for you."

My stomach twisted. I couldn't explain what I *thought* Hazel meant. I would sound insane.

"It's . . . um . . . it's not like that," I said, forcing my voice steady. "There's no one dangerous. No one's following us."

Maureen nodded slowly, not quite relaxed, but not pushing either. "Okay."

"I think my daughter just has a very vivid imagination," I said, cheeks burning hot with the lie.

"Mm, yes. That she does."

Maureen gave a faint smile that didn't reach her eyes, then carried the trash bag to the corner, setting it beside the back door instead of taking it outside to the bin.

I glanced down at the drawing in my hands, the faceless figure lurking there in thick black crayon.

I wanted to rip it up.

Instead, I folded it neatly and set it aside.

Shannon

August 20, 2022

I WOKE TO SOFT, golden light glowing through pale curtains, and for a few seconds, I didn't remember where we were. Then it came back in pieces: fleeing the house, staying at the hotel, Latoya the kind desk clerk, Maureen welcoming us into her home.

Hazel's drawing of the tricky lady.

My stomach clenched.

She came with us from our old house. She missed me.

She's outside now. Watching through the windows.

In daylight, it should've felt like nonsense. But after everything, I knew better.

Hazel was curled up next to me, hugging her stuffed cat from Grandy, her breathing slow and even.

I sat up and unplugged my phone on the nightstand. A new text from Tom waited.

Good morning! Just wanted to give you a quick update. The first showing yesterday evening went great. Client was very interested, and they might make an offer.

My heart leapt. A possible offer already?

I tapped open the message to reply and saw that Tom was typing. Three dots appeared and disappeared. Reappeared again.

The second showing was sorta weird though. They cut the tour short. Said the kid's bedroom made them uncomfortable.

A wave of dread rose inside my gut. It always came back to that room. That damn closet.

Three bouncing dots came onscreen again. Longer this time.

Gone.

Back again.

Finally:

They wanted to know if anyone had died in the house.

My stomach lurched as I reread the text.

Had anyone died in the house?

Technically . . . no.

Not *in* the house.

Just . . . in the backyard. Did that count? What was I supposed to say, legally? If someone asked directly, didn't I have to tell them?

My fingers hovered over the screen, trembling slightly.

I didn't know how to respond.

It wasn't violent. There'd been no crime scene. My dad had just collapsed. In the grass. In broad daylight. I had held his hand. Hazel had watched. The paramedics had tried—

I squeezed my eyes shut and forced the memory away.

What would Tom say, if I told him? Would he tell me not to worry, or would this change everything?

I scrolled back to his earlier message. Maybe if the first client made an offer, it wouldn't matter. Maybe this wouldn't come up again.

Finally, I typed:

Thanks for the update. Let me know if you hear anything else.

I didn't mention Dad's death. I couldn't. Not yet.

I set the phone down on the comforter, the unspoken truth burning in my chest.

Beside me, Hazel stirred. She rolled onto her back with a sleepy murmur, blinking up at the ceiling like she, too, was trying to remember where we were. "Is it morning?"

"It is," I said, putting on a smile for her.

She sniffed the air like a curious little animal, nose scrunching. "Is somebody cooking?"

I hesitated, then caught it too. The faint smell of bacon.

"Miss Maureen," Hazel said with certainty, already sitting up, eyes brighter now. "She's making breakfast!"

"I think you're right," I agreed, glad for the shift in focus. "Let's go see what she's got."

We stepped out into the hallway, following the sizzling and popping sounds to the kitchen. Maureen stood at the stove in a breezy V-neck T-shirt with a butterfly embroidered on the front and floral capris. She looked exactly like someone who'd been up since sunrise and had already prayed over the day, fed the cat, and watered her begonias.

"Well, good morning!" she beamed. "I was just about to come check on you two."

Hazel darted to the table and took a seat, looking very ready for breakfast.

Maureen chuckled at her eagerness, then handed me a coffee mug before I could even ask. "I checked the forecast," she said.

"It's supposed to be gorgeous today. Sunny, but not as hot. I was wondering . . ." She plated a crispy slice of bacon and glanced back at me. "What do you think about a little picnic? Dublin Park isn't far from here. It has a great playground, and I bet this one's got some energy to burn."

Hazel bounced in her chair and clapped. "Yes! Park picnic!"

I smiled, feeling the tension in my shoulders ease. "That actually sounds perfect."

Maureen nodded. "I think it might do us all some good to get out in the sunshine."

I couldn't agree more.

By late morning, we were settled atop one of Maureen's old quilts beneath the trees at Dublin Park. The sun was bright, but the heat not yet brutal, the sky overhead that crisp, clear blue that meant autumn was on its way soon. I sipped from a bottle of water as I watched Hazel run wild through the playground, climbing and sliding with giddy abandon. She ran over to us periodically, taking breaks for water and Goldfish crackers before darting back to the slide.

It felt so peaceful. So *normal*.

Maureen leaned back on her elbows beside me, eyes half-closed as she soaked in the sunlight. I had almost forgotten we were in survival mode.

My phone buzzed in my pocket.

Tom again.

Just a head's up, you've had showings all morning and the afternoon is booked solid.

A second message followed almost immediately:

Might be a good time to start thinking about what you're looking for in a new place. I have a feeling you'll get an offer before the weekend's over. Likely more than one.

My heart skipped as I read his words. It should have felt like good news, and part of me was relieved. But mostly, it made my stomach hurt. Selling the house meant moving forward. Making real decisions for our future.

What did I even want in a home? What could I *afford*?

What if I chose wrong again?

I forced myself to reply.

Wow, that's great! Thanks. I'll start thinking about it.

Questions swirled in my mind. What did *home* even mean now? What did Hazel and I need, now that it was just the two of us?

A small, low-maintenance yard. Something close to a library and a park. Sidewalks. A good school for Hazel. A newer build that needed no renovations.

A place near here would be perfect, I realized. I imagined us coming to this park regularly, going for walks on the paved trails, teaching Hazel to swim at the big outdoor pool we'd driven past, having playdates on the playground with the new friends we'd make here in Madison.

Where our little farmhouse on Sunflower Lane had been rural and isolated, our new house would be in a busy neighborhood with sidewalks and plenty of kids Hazel's age. We'd find a community. We already knew someone here. Maureen. She was so kind; I hoped we'd stay in touch and continue to be friends.

I reined in my thoughts, realizing I was getting a little carried away. But it was easy to, here, on this perfectly clear day.

"She's having a blast," Maureen commented, taking a swig from her water bottle.

"She is," I agreed, grinning. "I'm so glad you suggested this. She really needed it."

Maureen smiled. "I think we all needed this."

"True."

"I'd love to take y'all out for ice cream after this, if it's okay," she said. "We'll round out the afternoon. And our rear-ends."

I chuckled softly. "Hey, you'll never catch me saying 'no' to ice cream."

She sat up and propped her elbows on her knees. "You know, when my kids were little," she said, "We never really did fun stuff like that." She plucked a tall blade of grass from the ground and twirled it between her fingers. "I used to think if I just kept everything running— meals, school, baths, bedtime— that was enough. And honestly, that's all I could do. I swear I went years without taking a breath."

I nodded, understanding that feeling too well.

"Rick and I struggled a lot. Financially, I mean. We could barely pay the bills. There was no room for extras, like ice cream parlors." She paused. "You know, we never even took a vacation." She exhaled heavily then shrugged. "Things got easier eventually. But by then . . . my kids were half-grown."

She watched Hazel squeal as she flew down the slide. "I look back now and think, 'Dadgum. I missed it.' I was so busy surviving, I forgot to . . . be there." She sighed. Her voice was quiet when she added, "They don't come around much these days. Just holidays, if I'm lucky."

I glanced at her, surprised. Her expression didn't change, but there was something hollow in it. Not bitter. Just . . . tired.

"Being a parent is so hard," I said, not knowing what else to say.

She inhaled deeply. "It is. Even when you have help and support, it's never perfect. Rick and I had two incomes, we had childcare, and we still struggled. And that was, goodness, thirty years ago. I can't imagine how tough it is nowadays."

Her words hit a tender spot. I felt exposed, a little embarrassed.

Maureen seemed to sense it. She looked down at her hands, rubbing her thumb along the rim of her water bottle like she wasn't sure if she'd overstepped. She gave a quiet shrug. "When I see someone trying to hold everything together by themselves, I just . . . I just want to help."

I swallowed the lump in my throat. "Well, you are helping," I told her. "More than you know."

She didn't respond right away. She kept her eyes on Hazel, like the smile on her face and the sound of her laughter was healing something inside her.

"To tell you the truth, Maureen, I didn't think people like you existed anymore," I confessed. "Kind people. Someone who helps without asking for anything back."

That triggered a real smile. A soft one that crinkled her eyes in the corners

"Well now, don't go telling people that," she said. "I've got a reputation to uphold."

I laughed quietly, grateful for the joke.

We fell into a comfortable silence again, one that didn't need filling.

We watched as Hazel scaled the ladder to the big slide, beaming with pride. "Mommy! Miss Maureen! Watch me!" she called out.

"We're watching!" I yelled back.

She climbed all the way to the top and plopped down at the mouth of the tube slide with confidence. Without even hesitating, she dipped into the slide and out of sight.

My chest clenched in her absence, even though seconds later, she shot out the bottom end of the tube slide.

Maureen and I clapped.

Hazel glowed as she ran toward us. "Did you see me? I was brave!"

It sounded like *bwave*, and I melted.

"You were so brave!" I told her, throwing my arms around her.

She squeezed me, then took a big gulp of water and ran back to the playground. "I do it again! Watch! Watch me, Mommy! Miss Maureen, watch!"

Maureen leaned back on her elbows again. "She's gonna sleep good tonight."

I smiled, but a chill slid down my spine. One of those strange, inexplicable, motherly instincts, like the kind that used to jolt me awake seconds before baby Hazel cried out for milk in the night.

No, she won't.

The words came into my head uninvited, as clearly as if someone had spoken them aloud.

She won't sleep well at all. Something bad's coming.

I blinked hard and forced myself to look at the sky, at the lush green grass, at Hazel laughing on the slide.

But the dread forced itself deep.

No matter how bright the day was, I couldn't shake the feeling that something dark was already on its way.

Hazel was out cold in about two minutes, curled up on the queen bed in Maureen's guest room, clutching Loretta the cat tightly beneath her chin.

I checked my phone. Still no updates from Tom. Nothing but unread client emails that could wait until tomorrow. I set it down, tiptoed to the bathroom, and took a quick shower.

When I returned, Hazel hadn't moved. I stood in the doorway, watching her. The scene looked serene, but that feeling from earlier, the one that had wormed its way into my chest at the park, hadn't faded.

I pushed it down once more and climbed onto the queen bed next to her, clicking off the lamp on the nightstand as I settled between the sheets.

My own exhaustion was heavier than I'd expected. I drifted off quickly, too.

A faint sound jolted me awake seconds later.

Only it wasn't seconds later. My phone read 3:34 AM.

It was way too dark in the room, I realized. The nightlight was off. How had that happened?

I rolled over to check on Hazel. She was gone.

No, no, no. Not again.

The same cold rush from that last night at the house swept through me, hollowing me out. I ripped the covers back and lunged out of bed, every nerve in my body screaming as I scanned the shadowy room.

"Hazel?"

No answer.

I turned toward the doorway just in time to see a small figure slip past, rigid and silent, pale nightgown ghostlike in the dark.

My heart seized. "Hazel!" I hissed, bolting after her.

The hallway was deathly quiet. The air felt heavier than it had earlier, stuffy and warm.

A soft voice. Up ahead.

I followed it to the kitchen.

Hazel stood at the big bay window beside the table, one small hand pulling back the beige curtain, the other pressed flat against the glass. Moonlight washed over her, silver and otherworldly. Her lips moved in a whisper I couldn't make out.

A chill crept up my spine.

"Hazel," I said, trying to keep my voice calm. "What are you doing?"

She didn't turn.

I stepped closer, pulse roaring in my ears. "Sweetheart?"

I glanced at the window, bracing myself for something awful. But the yard beyond the glass lay empty, muted and gray in the darkness.

I reached out and touched Hazel's shoulder.

She flinched hard, and I jumped, a gasp catching in my throat. Then she blinked up at me, dazed and bleary-eyed. "Mommy?"

Relief crashed through me so fast my knees felt weak. I rubbed her shoulder. "Yeah, baby. What are you doing out here?"

She frowned and looked back at the window. "The girl wanted to play. But I can't see her now."

I swallowed. "What girl?"

She didn't answer. Just leaned forward and put her hand against the glass again.

"She's gone." Hazel yawned, her small frame sagging with sleep again. "She said her name was Viola."

I stared at her.

Viola?

The unfamiliar name meant nothing, but the old-fashioned sound of it sent a chill down my spine.

"You must've been dreaming," I said, though I didn't believe that.

Hazel rubbed sleepily at her eyes.

I scooped her up, my heart still pounding, and carried her back down the hall. The nightlight glowed again when I reentered the bedroom.

I tucked her in and lay down beside her until her breathing deepened.

But I didn't sleep.

I couldn't.

I lay in the dark, staring at my daughter, that name echoing through my skull.

Viola.

Who was Viola?

THIRTY-ONE

Shannon

August 21, 2022

I COULDN'T LIE IN bed a moment longer. The gray light creeping through the curtains told me it was morning, but my body felt like it hadn't rested at all. Hazel lay sound asleep beside me, grinding her teeth—a harsh, scraping sound I'd never heard from her. I winced as I stood, careful not to wake her, and crossed the room to the desk in the corner.

I powered on my laptop. Work meant normalcy. Bills paid. Control regained. After the incident at the kitchen window last night, with *Viola*, that was what I craved.

The screen's glow blinded me in the dim room. I squinted as I skimmed my inbox, half-reading a few client emails I didn't have the energy to answer. I picked the easiest-sounding job and got started.

Jim Thomas Realty had a new open house and needed his flyer updated with fresh photos. Same layout as last time. Easy. Reliable. I liked working with Jim.

A couple of minutes into the project, my phone buzzed against the desktop.

Incoming Call – Tom Altamira

My stomach tightened. It was barely eight o'clock. On a Sunday.

"Hello?" My voice came out rough.

"Shannon, hey, it's Tom," he said, his voice gruffer, lower than usual. He sounded tired. "Sorry to call so early."

"It's okay," I said, glancing toward Hazel. She hadn't stirred. "Is everything alright?"

"Yeah . . . I've got some news on the house. I'd rather talk in person, if you're able to meet up today. Would you be okay getting out this morning?"

"I don't know. I don't really want to leave Hazel right now."

Tom didn't ask for details. "No problem," he said easily. "I can come to you. What kind of coffee do you like?"

The knock came just after eight forty-five.

Maureen answered the door. She was already dressed for church, wearing a soft floral dress with a crocheted shrug, her white-blonde curls twisted back in an oversized claw clip.

I hovered awkwardly behind her in the living room as she opened the door.

"Good morning," she said, smiling politely at the man on the porch.

"Morning," Tom replied. "Sorry to intrude so early. I'm here to see Shannon."

"You must be her realtor."

"Yes, ma'am, that's right. Tom Altamira."

"Maureen Ledbetter. Come on in." She stepped aside as Tom entered. He held a cardboard carrier full of coffees in one hand, a bakery bag in the other, his iPad tucked under his right arm.

He was dressed more casually than I'd ever seen him, a look that suited him annoyingly well. Dark jeans. Fitted navy henley with the sleeves pushed up to his elbows, effortlessly stylish. The black curls atop his head were tousled like he'd just rolled out of bed, but in a way that worked for him.

I'd just rolled out of bed too, but it definitely didn't work for me. I'd yanked my limp hair into a lopsided ponytail, fished a wrinkled T-shirt from my suitcase, and pulled on the jeans I'd sweated through at the park yesterday.

I looked exactly how I felt: wrecked.

Tom's expression softened when he saw me. "Morning. I come bearing caffeine."

"That was so nice of you," I told him. "Thank you."

"Why don't you two take your coffee out back?" Maureen suggested, nodding toward the sliding glass door. "It's a nice morning. I'll keep an ear out in case Hazel wakes up. I'm heading to church in a bit, but y'all have plenty of time."

"That sounds great," I said, glancing toward Tom.

"Oh—also, I got Hazel a chocolate chip muffin," he added, holding out the paper bag. "Hope that's alright. I should've asked first."

My chest tightened a little as I took it from him. "That's perfect. She'll love it."

He shrugged like it was nothing, but it wasn't to me. He'd thought of Hazel, and that small kindness hit hard.

We moved together through the house to the dining room. I unlatched the back door and led the way out to Maureen's patio, a cozy stone pad decorated with wind chimes and a dozen potted plants. The morning air was crisp, laced with the scent of flowers and dewy grass. The well-maintained yard, boxed in on all sides by a tall wooden privacy fence, stretched out far beyond the flagstone, shadowed in patches from mature trees scattered across the property. Songbirds chirped above us, bright and cheerful, as they darted from one branch to another.

Tom waited for me to sit before taking the chair across from me at the small iron table. He slid one of the coffees toward me, the drink order I'd texted him after he practically demanded I choose something.

"Large latte with an extra shot of espresso," he said with a smirk. "Must've been some night. You okay?"

His concern caught me off guard. My whole body ached from the sleepless night, and my brain buzzed with static. I couldn't shake the image of Hazel at the window, hand on the glass, whispering to someone who wasn't there. The memory, paired with not knowing why Tom was here, set my nerves on edge.

My hand shook as I reached for the coffee. "I think so."

Tom was quiet for a moment, giving me a chance to elaborate. When I didn't, he set down his cup and grabbed his iPad. "Well. I guess let's get into it." He tapped the screen, his tone shifting into something more businesslike. "Here's where things stand."

I leaned forward, my palms suddenly sweaty around my latte.

"You've got multiple offers from Friday and Saturday's showings. Three solid ones." He swiped and tilted the screen toward me. "This first one came in yesterday morning. It's from an out-of-state investor. It's a cash offer, sight unseen. Full asking price, no contingencies, and he's able to close in fourteen days."

I gulped. "Oh, wow. That's fast."

"It is. It's easy, too. No financing delays, no inspections. But . . ." He hesitated. "It's an investment firm in North Carolina. They'll do a total flip and resale, or they'll rent it out."

That shouldn't have mattered. At all. I needed that house off my hands. But for some reason, the lack of emotion in such a transaction made me feel a bit sad.

Tom swiped again. "The second offer is from a local couple. It's under your asking price, as you can see. Conventional loan. They want to do a thirty-day close, and they're asking for closing cost assistance. Not a bad offer, just . . . slower. A little messier."

"Okay."

He paused before tapping to the third. "And then there's this one. Came in late Saturday afternoon."

Something in his voice told me this was the one.

"Conventional loan. They're offering five-thousand over asking price, and they already put down earnest money. It's a young family. They have a little girl around Hazel's age. Dad's an engineer, and they're moving to Huntsville from Colorado, I think. Anyway, they toured the house and fell in love with it immediately. They were so serious, they started the paperwork in the kitchen."

A lump formed in my throat as I stared at the numbers onscreen, trying to process it all.

Three offers.

A family who *loved* the house. Who stood in the kitchen, probably talking about paint colors and weekend projects while their daughter ran down the same hallway where Hazel used to play.

A sick, heavy dread pooled in my chest. If they moved in, if that little girl slept in Hazel's room . . .

Tom inhaled slowly, his expression tightening. He had more to say, and whatever it was, it didn't seem good.

"What is it?" I asked reluctantly.

He set the iPad down and clutched his coffee cup with both hands. "Right after that last family finished the paperwork, something happened. I didn't want to text it. I thought you should hear it from me."

My heart kicked in my chest, accelerating in a panic.

Tom took a sip of coffee, then set the cup down. His gaze dropped to his hands for a moment before he looked at me again.

"They were getting ready to head out," he said. "Belinda, their agent, was still in the kitchen with the wife and the daughter, while the dad went off to take one more look at the bedrooms. Belinda said he'd brought a tape measure, that he was doing some measurements. Like I said, they were serious about the house."

I said nothing. I could barely breathe.

"He was in Hazel's room when . . . he fell. Hard. He hit the wall going down, scraped up his arm, banged his head. It wasn't bad enough for the hospital, but it scared them all."

"Oh my gosh. He just . . . fell?"

"Well, that's the thing. He told Belinda he felt someone push him. From behind."

I stared at him, throat dry and clenched tight.

"Like I said, everyone else was in the kitchen. There was no one else in the house. But he swears he felt a hand between his shoulder blades, shoving him down."

I sat very still, every hair on my arms standing on end.

"After that, they packed up fast. The wife said the house felt *off*. Like all of a sudden, someone didn't want them there."

He paused, watching me carefully.

"I don't think they'll pursue anything legally," he went on. "But Belinda filed a report, just in case. We're required to when someone gets hurt during a showing, even if it's minor."

"Oh, jeez." I thrust my head into my hands.

"That's why I wanted to tell you about it in person. I figured you deserved to hear it from me, not in a text or some weird follow-up email from Belinda, in case she reaches out to you."

I swallowed hard, then whispered, "Are they pulling the offer?"

Tom hesitated. "Not yet. Belinda told them to sleep on it, but I think you should be prepared for that one to fall through."

I nodded.

"I don't want to push you into anything, but you've got two solid offers." He scratched the back of his neck. "I think you'd be wise to accept one of them and get this place off your hands."

I knew what he was saying without saying it. Before I could respond, his phone chirped out a cheerful ringtone, and he excused himself to take the call.

I remained seated at Maureen's wrought iron patio table, sipping my bitter latte as I stared into the yard, but I didn't see any of it. My mind kept looping Tom's words.

A man shoved from behind in Hazel's room.

The house feeling like it didn't want them there.

A thought bombarded my brain so hard I nearly spilled my coffee.

The camera.

I still had the security camera set up and running in Hazel's room. I'd turned off the app's notifications after we left the house. The curtain on the open window blowing in the breeze kept setting it off every five minutes.

But the camera remained vigilant.

My hands were clammy as I pulled out my phone and opened the app. A long list of unread notifications greeted me.

MOTION DETECTED - 4:13 AM.

MOTION DETECTED - 3:16 AM.

MOTION DETECTED - 3:01 AM.

I scrolled. There were tons of them. Why were there so many in the middle of the night? What was moving in that room?

I tapped one around midnight and waited for it to load.

The footage showed Hazel's room in grayscale, dim and still.

A light flickered across the wall. Just for a second. Just once. Like a power surge.

But I knew for certain there was no light mounted in that spot, no lamp or anything that could've come on.

I squinted at the screen as I replayed it.

There was no sound. No real movement. Just a weird flash of light.

I backed out to the main menu and watched some of the other footage captured during the night. It was all the same. A brief flash, a flicker of *something*.

I thumbed through the rest of the notifications until I reached Saturday evening, when the family would have been touring and submitting their offer.

MOTION DETECTED – 5:43 PM.

My pulse pounded as I tapped the notification. The recording took forever to load, spinning . . . buffering . . .

At last, it played:

Onscreen, an attractive woman dressed in a satiny purple blouse, black pencil skirt, and clacky high heels entered the room. She looked a little flustered as she dashed about, iPad in hand, vigorously typing on it as she moved. She held up the tablet, seemingly capturing a photo of the wall, then of the floor.

I suspected this was Belinda the buyer's agent making her incident report after the family had gone. I watched her as she worked, feeling a little creepy for doing so, then I clicked out of the video and scrolled back.

I selected the one before it—5:17 PM.

A tall, barrel-chested man with glasses and a neat, chocolate-brown goatee made his way around Hazel's room. He wore a gray polo and khakis. He held a tape measure in his right hand, which he expanded across the room, measuring the space's width. He produced a pen and a small notepad from a pocket and began jotting things down.

It was unsettling to see him there, a strange man amongst Hazel's things. I held my breath as I watched him, waiting for what I knew was coming.

The man tugged open the closet doors and inspected the storage area. He stretched the tape measure across the space, then made another entry on his notepad. Evidently satisfied, he closed the closet and turned away.

He lingered there for a moment, focused on his notes. The screen flickered with something like static, and the man lunged forward, hitting the wall with a sickening smack.

My hand flew to my mouth. I heard the man groan, watched him scramble to his feet, holding the side of his head. The fall had knocked his glasses clean off his face. I stared in shock as he fumbled to replace them on his nose, as he gaped around, stunned.

He looked back at the closet.

So did I. There was nothing to see.

I replayed the clip over and over, and one thing was clear: this hadn't been an accident. The man didn't trip.

He was standing there, making notes about the house, when something propelled him forward against his will.

Footsteps crunched softly on the flagstone behind me. I jumped and locked my phone screen, heart pounding out of my chest.

"Sorry about that," Tom said, stepping back out onto the patio. He looked faintly annoyed, but mostly tired. "That was Belinda, the buyer's agent."

I peered up at him slowly, still clutching my phone with a trembling hand.

"The family pulled their offer," he said, confirming what I already knew deep in my gut. "They said it just didn't feel right, not after what happened."

I stared at him, dumbstruck.

"Shannon?" he asked, his brow furrowing as he sank back into the chair across from me. "Are you okay?"

I turned my phone back around and held it out.

Quietly, I told him, "You need to see this."

Tom stared at the phone for several seconds after the footage ended. He didn't speak. Didn't move. His mouth hung open slightly, like he was still trying to process what he'd just seen, as the silence grew into something almost palpable.

"Belinda . . . she said he must have slipped on the hardwoods." He exhaled. Rubbed his palm across the lower half of his face. "That wasn't him slipping."

"No," I agreed. "He was pushed."

He nodded, slow and stunned, like the truth was gradually seeping in. He stared at me. Openly. "This isn't the first time something like this has happened, is it?"

I hesitated to answer.

"Is that why you and Hazel left? Why you went to the hotel?"

I managed a nod.

He released a heavy exhale and leaned forward in his seat. His dark eyes grew wide with concern. "Did one of you get hurt?"

"No," I replied. "But we came close." I paused. "Hazel . . . I had to get her out of there before something happened."

Tom's expression shifted. He didn't seem surprised, or skeptical, but more like he'd just confirmed a suspicion he'd never said out loud. "Okay," he murmured. "That tracks with . . . some things I've heard."

A jolt of surprise shot through me. *Some things he's heard? About my house?*

His gaze sharpened on me, his jaw tightening with resolve. "I think it's time you talked to my sister."

THIRTY-TWO

I KEPT CHECKING THE clock, counting down to two-thirty, the ETA for Tom's sister, Carmen. Apparently, she was the kind of person you called when strange things started happening and you didn't know what to do.

By noon, I'd already signed the investor's offer on the house. My fingers shook so badly I could barely click through the digital paperwork. Tom hovered nearby, answering questions, but I barely heard him. All I could think about was the time he'd told me clients were asking whether anyone had died in the house . . . and how I'd said nothing.

I'd lied by omission, hadn't I?

Now that the paperwork was signed and the sale in motion, the weight of my silence pressed heavier. I wasn't just selling a house. I was pushing that cursed place off onto some unsuspecting poor soul. How could I do that?

The video of the man in Hazel's bedroom looped in my head. The violent shove. The danger in that house hadn't left when we did. Someone else could get hurt, and it would be on me.

But Tom swore Carmen could help. I clung to that hope like a life raft.

The doorbell chimed right at two-thirty.

I set Hazel up with paper and washable finger paints on the patio, making sure she was close but out of earshot while I talked to the Altamira siblings.

The back door creaked open as Maureen stepped out. "They're in the living room," she said with a warm smile, giving my arm a reassuring pat. "Go on. We'll be just fine out here."

"Thank you," I murmured, genuinely grateful.

I slipped back inside and walked toward the living room. The woman beside Tom looked up as I entered, and something about her made me stand a little straighter.

She was tall, striking, and unmistakably related to Tom, though she had an edge to her that was all her own. She wore black scrubs beneath a long charcoal cardigan, her hair pulled into a thick braid, loose and unraveling after a long day. High cheekbones, copper skin, and dark brown eyes framed in smoky kohl gave her an almost startling intensity.

But her presence—that was what struck me. She was quiet. She didn't rush to fill the silence, yet she radiated something, some sort of cool, composed, commanding energy that made you pay attention even when she wasn't speaking.

Tom's voice broke through my thoughts. "Shannon, this is my sister. Carmen. She's, uh, she's dealt with this sort of thing before."

Carmen's gaze swept over me, measuring, assessing. She gave a small, polite smile. Not unfriendly, exactly. Maybe . . . cautious. She seemed to be reading the room. Reading *me*.

"Hi," I said timidly.

"Hello, Shannon." Her voice was low and husky, with the faint rasp of someone who smoked sometimes. She smiled softly again and glanced at her brother. "Should we sit?"

"Yeah, of course."

We each claimed a seat, me on the sofa, Tom at the other end. Carmen took Maureen's recliner, setting a large black canvas tote on the floor by her feet. Black leather clogs with chunky heels peeked from beneath the hem of her scrub pants.

I noticed her laminated nametag then, still pinned to her cardigan. *Carmen Altamira, RN, Haven Hospice.*

My stomach clenched. Mom had been on hospice, at the end. Memories of those final days flickered up without warning.

I couldn't think about that right now. I focused on Carmen instead, realizing she'd come straight here from a day spent caring for the dying.

I wondered what that did to a person. Spending every day with death. Knowing from the start there'd be no recovery. Forming bonds with your patients and watching them fade.

Maybe that was why Carmen didn't look the least bit rattled to be here.

"So, Shannon," she said, crossing her legs and resting her clasped hands on her knees. "Let's start at the beginning."

I took a deep breath, fiddling anxiously with the hem of my T-shirt. "Well, um, we moved in about . . . three and a half years ago."

Carmen tilted her head slightly. "What drew you to the house?"

The question surprised me. "I don't know," I said after a moment of reflection. "It was old and small, but . . . charming. I liked the country cottage feel that it had. You know? And the land it was on. It felt private. Peaceful. It all had so much potential, and at the time, it felt like something we could fix. Something we could make ours."

Tom nodded. "It had a ton of potential," he agreed. "And you had a vision. You and Marc. I remember that."

"I always wanted a house with history." I laughed dryly. "Guess I got more than I bargained for."

Carmen didn't smile.

I cleared my throat and pushed forward. "I guess the first big thing that happened was at Hazel's third birthday party."

I stopped. My voice was already shaking.

"We had a little party outside. My dad, he went into the house alone. To use the bathroom. And he . . . saw something." My throat clenched. "It scared him. Literally to death." I looked down at my hands. "He came back out white as a sheet. Clutched his chest and collapsed on the grass. The paramedics got there fast, but . . ." My voice trailed off. I didn't need to finish it.

Tom leaned back slightly, like the weight of what I'd just said had physically pushed him backward.

"Shannon . . . I had no idea . . ." he said, his voice low.

"I'm sorry I didn't tell you," I said. "I just couldn't. But my dad saw something in that house. And it killed him."

Carmen's gaze flicked sharply between us, but she said nothing.

After a moment, I went on. "The camera in Hazel's room . . . it caught . . . things. The closet doors moving on their own. Voices whispering. My dad stepping into the hall, freezing, clearly seeing something. The doors slam shut, and the video cuts off right after."

Neither of them spoke.

"After that day, I never looked at the house the same. I *knew* something was wrong. I talked to my neighbor and found out a little of the house's history. And it isn't good."

Carmen leaned forward slightly. "What'd you find out?"

"A family lived there in the sixties. Fern Carlisle and her two little girls. The youngest, Loretta, vanished without a trace. She was only three years old. No witnesses, no evidence. One minute she was playing in the backyard, the next she was gone."

Carmen shot Tom a look, and he immediately dropped his gaze to the coffee table, like the two of them had silently arrived at the same unsettling conclusion.

"What?" I breathed.

Tom sucked in a sharp breath and reluctantly lifted his eyes to mine. "I sold you the Carlisle house."

The Carlisle house. The way he said it made my stomach clench, like it was some well-known urban legend everyone was privy to except for me.

"I figured it out last night, when Belinda called me about the incident," he said, rubbing a hand over his jaw. "She mentioned the name Carlisle, and it all clicked. I'd heard the stories, but I never realized *this* was that house. The seller's name was Marshall. I looked it up again last night to be sure."

"Marshall was Joyce Carlisle's married name," I said. "She inherited the house when Fern passed a few years ago."

Tom sighed. "I can't believe I missed that."

"Well," I said, trying to steady myself, "my neighbor told me Fern never recovered after Loretta vanished. She stopped leaving the house. She died in there eventually. Maybe in Hazel's bedroom. That's where most of the activity seems to be happening."

"That's where that guy got shoved," Tom said.

I nodded, a shiver prickling along my spine. "I didn't believe in ghosts, but . . . after everything that happened . . . I became convinced that Fern *never* left the house."

They waited for me to say more.

I looked down, fiddling with my shirt again. "I tried to stay calm, to be logical, but I just couldn't rationalize it away anymore." I hesitated. "So . . . I did something."

Carmen blinked. "What did you do?"

"I went to the closet and, um, I talked to Fern. I tried to help her move on, to the other side, or whatever." A long pause. "And that's when everything got worse."

Tom shifted forward, alarmed. "Worse how?"

I drew in a deep breath and let the words fall out. "I found Hazel at the edge of the woods in the middle of the night."

Even Carmen looked rattled by that.

The tears came despite my efforts to hold them at bay. I wiped at my eyes as they spilled over. "I just—I grabbed her. We got in the car and drove to a hotel."

They listened intently.

"And on the way out, I saw a figure in the window. Staring out at me as I left."

Tom rubbed his forehead. "Jesus."

Carmen didn't flinch. Her gaze dropped to her lap, thoughtful and tense. When she finally spoke, her voice was low. "So you just told her it was okay to leave? Fern?"

I nodded. "I thought maybe, after being stuck there all those years, waiting for Loretta, maybe she needed someone to tell her she didn't have to stay."

Her expression softened, but concern shone in her eyes. "I understand why you did it. And it's definitely not the worst thing you could have done." She paused. "But in situations like this, it's best to put some protections in place before you open that kind of door. You never know what else might be listening."

My stomach tightened. "So I made it worse."

"Not necessarily." Carmen shifted in her seat. "But I've made that same mistake before."

Tom lowered his gaze like he knew where this was going.

"Several years ago, not long after I started working hospice, one of my patients passed unexpectedly. His decline had been slow—everyone thought he had at least a couple of months. The family wasn't ready." She clasped her hands tighter, knuckles going white as she remembered. "When he died . . . it was pure chaos. His husband collapsed, their daughter was screaming." Her bottom lip trembled. "The grief in that house was violent. When I went back for the bereavement follow-up, you could still feel it in the air. In the walls."

A faint, self-conscious smile curved her lips. "The family knew I was a little . . . witchy, I guess. I'd started dabbling in energy work in college. Researching old folk practices. I'd only read a few books at that point, I didn't really know what I was doing." Her smile faded. "But the husband asked me to do a cleansing ritual. I just wanted to help. To give them peace. So, I tried. I lit a bundle of herbs I'd ordered online, rang a little bell, and spoke a blessing I'd pieced together from a few sources that probably shouldn't have been mixed."

She swallowed hard. "I cleansed, but I never grounded the space. I didn't shield myself or the family." A beat. "Later that week, the husband called me. He'd started hearing something breathing by his bed in the night. He woke up with strange bruises and scratches all over his body."

I recoiled.

"That's when I realized it wasn't my patient's spirit," Carmen whispered. "Something else had come in behind the grief. Something drawn in by the opening I had made."

Her eyes locked onto mine.

"I blamed myself for months. But I learned what I needed to learn, and I went back and cleansed the space properly. And thankfully, things settled down after that." Her expression grew compassionate but grave. "I'm telling you this, Shannon, because whatever happened at your house, whatever door you might have opened, I need to see it. I need to understand exactly what we're dealing with before we can know what needs to be done."

Thirty-Three

I hugged Hazel longer than necessary before we left Maureen's. I buried my face in her hair, drinking in her sweet, familiar scent. I'd never left her with anyone but Marc. Ever. The idea of walking out that door without her felt like leaving a piece of myself behind.

But Carmen insisted she couldn't get a true read on the house unless one of the targeted people was physically present. And there was no way I was taking Hazel back there.

I barely knew Maureen, but at some point, I had to start trusting other people. If going back alone meant I could keep my daughter safe in the long run, then I would do it, even if it broke me a little to leave her now.

Tom's hands were tight on the wheel as he guided his Highlander down the highway. Carmen, in the backseat, had been quiet most of the drive. The vehicle slowed as we turned onto Sunflower Lane. The moment the street sign came into view, my whole body tensed. *Sunflower Lane.* It had sounded so idyllic at first, three years ago. The perfect name for a cozy little country cottage.

Now it was sickly sweet, full of artifice.

My stomach knotted itself as we crawled past my neighbor Kim Gillespie's brick house.

I saw our mailbox up ahead and gulped. The *For Sale* sign had been updated with a small placard that read *Under Contract.* Tires crunched over gravel as we turned down the long driveway. My intestines slithered as I saw the house again.

Realistically, the place looked no different. Nothing had changed. But . . . it felt so different. I couldn't explain it. The late afternoon shadows seemed all wrong. They stretched too far across the yard, curling around the base of the porch like fingers. The grass—which could use a good mowing—was too still.

The house didn't look empty. Maybe that was it. It seemed aware, like it had noticed us pulling in.

Tom parked near the porch and killed the engine. None of us moved.

Carmen broke the silence first. "Okay," she said, voice steady. "Let's go see what we're working with." She unbuckled and climbed out.

I didn't move right away. I wasn't sure I could.

Tom glanced over at me. "You okay?"

I nodded, even though I wasn't. "Not really, no."

He didn't say anything right away. Just reached over and rested his hand lightly on my forearm. His touch was warm, grounding.

"We'll stick together in there, okay?" he said gently. "Just stay close. Carmen will know what to do."

We got out together.

Carmen, a canvas tote slung over her shoulder, stopped at the front door and closed her eyes, like she was listening for something. A breeze caught the ends of her long cardigan, fluttering the fabric around her calves.

I climbed the porch steps with wobbly legs. I had the spare house key in my pocket, but Tom was already opening the realtor lockbox. He slipped the key into the deadbolt, unlocked it with a pop, and the door creaked open with a low groan.

The air that spilled out felt familiar at first, then suddenly too thick, too heavy. It pressed against my skin.

Behind me, Carmen murmured, "Don't go in yet." Her voice was low and sure. "Let me."

She moved past me over the threshold. Her clogs clicked against the floorboards. One step. Then another. She paused just inside the foyer.

I watched as she pulled something from her bag—a small black pouch—and held it loosely in one hand. "There's definitely something still active here," she said quietly.

The floor groaned under her next step. Carmen wandered deeper into the house, her expression unreadable.

I stopped in the foyer, eyes tracking across the living room. I took in my gauzy white curtains, the jute rug on the floor. The couch and its throw pillows, the coffee table with its stack of books, a half-burned soy candle, plastic plant. Tall wooden shelves packed with books and decorative knick-knacks. All still here. All still mine.

It hit me like a punch to the gut.

I would have to come back here. Again. And again.

How had I forgotten about this?

My contract gave me fourteen days. Two weeks to clear out an entire house, to pack up everything I hadn't already fled with, which was most of our belongings.

Years of accumulated stuff, and all of it had to go.

I would have to walk into this place, this horrible, haunted place, over and over and over, like it wasn't trying to kill me and my daughter.

My throat tightened. I turned to Tom and, with desperation in my voice, I said it aloud: "I still have to pack all of this."

He didn't hesitate. "I'll help. We'll get a crew together if we need—"

"And move it where?" I interrupted. My voice cracked. "Where will I even put all this stuff?"

The silence that followed was brutal.

Tom swallowed so hard, I saw his Adam's apple move in his throat. "Maybe a storage unit. We'll figure that out too."

I nodded, but the enormity of the task pressed down on my chest. All my books. Hazel's toys. Our dishes. Every room was full, every closet stuffed, every drawer packed.

And then I remembered the barn. The garden tools. The rototiller. The stupid galvanized steel feed bins we bought when we thought we'd raise chickens. I had no idea what Marc had taken with him. Probably nothing. Probably left it all for me to deal with, just like he had everything else.

My hands started shaking. Hot tears burned in my eyes as the overwhelm hit me. For one desperate second, I thought about calling Marc. Half of this crap was his. He should be here, helping.

But the thought died as fast as it came. He wouldn't show up. Or if he did, it'd be with that same smug, distant face he wore the last time I saw him, like all of this was my fault.

No. I wasn't giving him another minute of my time.

Tom stepped in close, his voice low. "Hey."

I didn't look at him. I couldn't. If I did, I'd fall apart, and this wasn't the time.

"This is a lot," he said gently. "It's too much for one person."

I exhaled a shaky breath, still staring at the cluttered room. My vision blurred from the pressure behind my eyes.

"But you don't have to do this alone, okay?"

A tense silence grew between us.

From deeper inside the house, Carmen's voice floated back toward us. "You guys should come back here."

Neither of us moved at first.

Our eyes met, and I saw an unspoken question in his eyes, a silent check-in. *You good?*

I nodded, weakly, and we walked together toward the hallway, toward Carmen.

As we crossed the threshold, the air shifted. It grew cooler. Denser. Carmen stood just outside Hazel's bedroom, facing the slightly ajar door. She wasn't moving. One hand clutched the strap of her canvas bag, the other hovered mid-air, palm open, as if telling someone to stop.

She turned when she heard us approach. "This room," she said. "Something's pulling me in there."

I swallowed. She'd found her way to Hazel's room without my guidance. I wasn't sure if this was reassuring or not.

The three of us stood there for a moment in uneasy silence, facing the door like it might open on its own. At last, Carmen reached forward and pushed it the rest of the way open.

Tom drew a little closer to me, and I didn't move away.

Hazel's room was just as we'd left it, yet it felt gutted. Empty. Not physically, but emotionally. Like something had been ripped out. The energy in the room was different. Too still. It smelled faintly of dust and something older. Something damp and earthy.

Her little bed sat under the window, neatly made. The flower rug was rumpled at one corner. Her bookshelf still held a line of toys along the top: plastic horses, a stuffed frog, a well-loved unicorn. Dozens of picture books remained on the shelves.

Everything about this room screamed Hazel. But it didn't feel like her space anymore.

Carmen took a slow breath through her nose and exhaled. "This room is bad." She looked at me. "This is where it started?"

I nodded. "It's where it always comes back to."

Carmen moved to the center of the room, fishing something small from her bag. She closed her fist around it and murmured words I couldn't catch. Her gaze cut to the closet.

The bifold doors were closed.

She approached them with deliberate slowness, then lifted her hand and rapped her knuckles against the wood. Three times. Quick and even.

The air changed. A chill swept over my arms.

Then, from within the closet—a faint tap.

I froze. So did Tom.

Tap. Tap. Tap.

Three slow, measured taps, mirroring Carmen's exactly.

She didn't seem fazed. "It's aware of us," she said, voice low. "It knows you're back, Shannon."

One of the bifold panels shifted. Just a fraction of an inch. The hinges gave a soft metallic squeak.

My pulse raced in my throat. I thought I might be sick.

CRACK!

Both panels snapped open at once, folding hard and smacking into the doorframe with a sound like gunfire. I stumbled back and nearly tripped over Hazel's rug.

Tom cursed beside me as something fell from the closet, tumbling end over end before landing at my feet.

A stuffed animal.

But not one of Hazel's.

This thing was old. Something from another time. A rabbit with faded pink fur and limp silk ears. A seam gaped along its side, white stuffing spilling out.

My stomach flipped. I took another step backward. "That's not ours," I whispered.

Carmen didn't flinch. She sidestepped the antique toy and crouched in front of the open closet, her eyes narrowing. She stared into the space, studying it for a long time before she spoke.

"It's not just one thing," she murmured. "I can feel . . . layers. This room is holding multiple energies." She hesitated. "I think there's more than one spirit here."

My lungs locked.

"Okay, Carmen," Tom's voice cracked. "Don't you think we've seen enough for one day? Let's get out of here."

I agreed wholeheartedly.

But Carmen didn't move. Her gaze remained on the closet. "Just one more minute." She inched closer to the void. "Then we leave."

"Let's not make it angry," Tom said tightly.

"I just need to find out what it is and what it wants."

My stomach churned as I watched Carmen kneel before the closet, her eyes closed, fingers splayed open toward the darkened space.

The pressure in the air shifted. I felt it in my ears, in my teeth.

Tom reached for my arm, steadying me as the temperature dipped again.

Carmen's breath caught. Her eyes popped open, and she recoiled, snatching her hand back from the threshold like she'd been burned.

"What?" Tom asked, alarmed.

She clambered to her feet and turned to us with a look that hadn't been there before. Somber, almost reverent. "You were right, Shannon," she said softly. "Fern is still here."

My throat cinched tight. "She is?"

"She's weak. Fading. Barely holding on. But she's trying." Carmen swallowed. "She's been trying to protect your daughter."

The room seemed to tilt around me. "What?"

"There's another presence here, too," Carmen said. Her gaze flicked toward the closet again. "Something darker. Older. And it isn't only haunting this house. It's *hunting*."

A cold shiver ran the length of my spine. "Hunting us?"

Carmen shook her head. "Not you, Shannon. I'm afraid this thing wants children." She glanced at the filthy vintage stuffed animal at our feet. "I think this belonged to the last one it tried to take. Or . . . that it *did* take."

Tom and I exchanged a glance.

"Loretta Carlisle," I breathed. "It took Fern's daughter?"

"I think so. And I think Fern's spirit has been holding it back, keeping it away from Hazel." Carmen's dark eyes locked onto mine. "But now that she's almost gone, there's nothing left between it and your daughter."

THIRTY-FOUR

Fern

May 1963

"Brother Jimmy said the tape might catch somethin' our ears don't," Harry Birch said, placing the portable reel-to-reel tape recorder on the bookshelf in Loretta's room. The thing was about the size of a shoebox, with spools and knobs and buttons that looked quite complicated to Fern.

The Birches had promised to return better prepared, and today, almost a week later, they had.

Fern watched as Harry threaded the brown ribbon from one reel to the other. His hands weren't graceful, but he seemed to know what he was doing.

Hilda stood stiffly next to her, hands clasped low across her abdomen. She held them there protectively, and the thought slipped into Fern's mind—was Hilda with child?

She forced her eyes elsewhere. "Brother Jimmy?" Fern repeated.

Harry kept his attention on the reels. "A pastor friend of ours up in Nashville," he said. "He's been my mentor for years. He's traveled a lot, studied strange things most folks won't speak of. He gave me several suggestions to try today."

Suggestions to try didn't sound very reassuring to Fern, but she kept that to herself.

"He specializes in deliverance ministry," Hilda added.

"You mean . . . casting out demons?" Fern asked.

Hilda answered with a reluctant nod. "He's more on the charismatic side. But the New Testament does have several accounts of Jesus and the disciples casting out unclean spirits."

Fern swallowed hard, her heart kicking in her chest. Was this what they thought of her? That she was like the lunatics in the Scriptures, crying out and cutting themselves with stones?

"Do you mean . . . me?" Fern asked finally, her voice sharper than she'd intended.

Harry looked up from the reels, startled. "No, ma'am. Not you. Demons don't always possess people. Sometimes they attach themselves to a thing or a place. Brother Jimmy says that's what hauntings are. Not ghosts at all, but soldiers in the devil's army. And we believe, after what we've seen here, that's what's happening in this house."

The thought of her home being inhabited by something unholy made her skin prickle. A demon from Hell under her roof, in her daughter's bedroom.

She noticed Hilda's eyes fixed on the closet. The bifold doors remained shut, but there was a sense that something lay behind them.

"Alright," Harry said. "Let's begin."

The switch clunked as Harry flipped it to 'record.' The reels squeaked and whined as they wound around and around. Harry pulled the corded microphone and raised it to his chin.

"Mrs. Carlisle, I want to begin by asking you a few questions. And I must warn you, some of them might be a little uncomfortable."

Fern blinked. "Okay."

Harry held the microphone close. "First thing we need to do is make sure there's no doors left open. So I need to ask you, Mrs. Carlisle . . . is there any unconfessed sin weighin' on you?" He hesitated before adding, "That could mean witchcraft, dabbling with cards or fortune-tellers. Sins of the flesh, such as addiction to drugs or alcohol. Runnin' around. Pornography."

Fern's face burned.

Harry cleared his throat. "Sometimes it's smaller things, too. Holdin' a grudge, carrying bitterness, letting anger set up in your heart. Any of those can be a foothold for the enemy."

That made her heart lurch. She thought of the resentment she held toward Raymond for abandoning them, for giving up on their marriage, their family. The bitterness she felt for having to carry this all alone. The fierce, profound anger she felt toward God for taking Loretta from her.

"If there is, Fern," Hilda said, her voice gentle and coaxing, "the Lord is faithful to forgive. Always."

Fern squeezed her hands together. *Anger. Bitterness. So much resentment.* These things had lived in her bones over the last year, but she said nothing.

The reels kept turning, hissing like an otherworldly being.

She lowered her eyes, heat crawling up her neck. *Lord, forgive me*, she prayed silently. *Forgive my anger, my hatred, my unbelief. I don't know what else to do.*

Overhead, the light buzzed and flickered, casting weird, undulating shadows across the closet doors.

Harry reached inside a leather satchel he'd set next to the recorder, removed a glass vial of golden liquid, and uncapped it.

"With all the strength of Jesus Christ our Lord and with all the power of Heaven, I expel any unclean spirits from this place," he proclaimed. He tipped the vial carefully, letting a few drops pool in his palm. He daubed his fingers with the liquid, then reached for the closet doors.

"Harry has oil that we've prayed over," Hilda narrated, perhaps for Fern, more likely for the audio recording. "He's now making a cross on the closet doors."

He dragged his fingers in two slow, intersecting lines across the wood panel, leaving behind a glistening oil cross. "This place belongs to the Lord," he declared. "In the name of Jesus Christ, we command all evil entities to flee!"

Hilda began to sing. "*Would you be free from the burden of sin? There's pow'r in the blood, pow'r in the blood.*"

The familiar melody of the old hymn filled the room, drowning out the hiss of the tape and the humming of the light still blinking above their heads.

"*Would you o'er evil a victory win? There's wonderful power in the blood.*"

Hilda nodded at Fern, gently urging her to join in on the chorus.

Harry put both hands on the closet doors and closed his eyes as he prayed over the space.

Swallowing her embarrassment, Fern cleared her throat and softly sang along. Her voice sounded weak and foreign to her own ears, but she kept going, hoping it would somehow help.

"There is pow'r, pow'r, wonder-working pow'r, in the blood, of the Lamb . . ."

The reel-to-reel recorder hissed louder, and a sharp crack split the air as the closet doors exploded open, sending Harry reeling back in shock. The oil vial fell, landing on the avocado green carpet with a dull crack. A tangy scent rose as the oil seeped into the carpet, darkening the fibers.

Fern gasped, clutching her chest. Hilda's song faltered only for a breath before she forced herself to go on, voice trembling.

Harry scrambled upright, his face drained of color. He pressed a hand against one of the open accordion doors, and the wood began to rattle beneath his palm.

Alive.

"I command you to leave in the name of Jesus Christ!" he shouted. "You are not welcome here. This house and this family belong to the Lord!"

The door gave one final shudder, then fell still.

Silence filled the room except for the rhythmic squeak of the tape.

Nobody moved.

Fern locked her eyes on the closet, waiting for another tremor, another sign of life.

Nothing happened.

"Harry?" Hilda whispered.

He didn't answer right away. Instead, he pressed his palm flat against one of the doors, testing it. He jerked slightly as a faint knock sounded in response.

Three slow taps.

Tap. Tap. Tap.

Hilda flinched and guarded her abdomen in that protective motion again, as if anticipating a blow.

Harry's jaw tightened. He pressed harder on the wood. "You will *not* have this house," he roared, face reddening with intensity. "In the name of Jesus Christ, you will *not* have this family. Be gone from this place. *Now.*"

A hush fell over them.

Seconds ticked by, turning into minutes.

Nothing else happened.

Harry exhaled. Slowly, he straightened. His fingers shook as he retrieved his handkerchief, wiped the oil from his hands, and folded it away.

"It's finished," he said at last, his voice low and raw. "To God be the glory."

Hilda let out a shaky breath, one hand still resting on her stomach. "Praise the Lord."

Fern tried to mirror their relief, but her heart wouldn't slow.

The closet stood wide open, dark as ever.

Fern watched from the doorway as Harry and Hilda made their way down the gravel driveway, the setting sun turning their retreating figures into silhouettes. Harry carried the reel-to-reel recorder like a trophy, his gait brisk, confident, certain. Hilda nodded at something he said as they neared their sedan.

The screen door eased shut behind Fern with a click.

Silence enveloped her.

She stood still for a long moment, expecting to hear a creak or a taunting whisper, some trace of what the Birches had driven out. But there were only the usual house sounds, the faint hum of the refrigerator, the tick of the grandfather clock in the living room.

Joyce was spending the night with the Hendersons. Hilda had suggested it, saying it could be dangerous for a child to be present during what they had to do. Fern had agreed, grateful at the time. Now, with the house devoid of her eldest's chatter and movement, the quiet felt suffocating.

She drifted down the hall into Loretta's room.

The oil cross glistened faintly on one of the parted closet doors, its shine dulled by the disappearing daylight. The air did feel lighter, she admitted. Still, her belly refused to unclench.

She lowered herself to the edge of Loretta's bed and smoothed the quilt beneath her palms. Her fingers picked at the stitched flowers absently. The sheets smelled like *her*. Her baby. Tears stung her eyes as she inhaled deeply, drinking in the lingering scent.

She wanted—needed—to believe it was over. That the Birches had done something real. That God had intervened on their behalf.

But she didn't trust the silence.

Her gaze slid to the open closet. A hollow ache unfolded inside of her as she eyed Loretta's little dresses hanging from the rod, all of them freshly laundered, waiting for her to put them back on again.

Her heart squeezed as a tear rolled down her cheek, and she whispered into the emptiness, "Please . . . just give her back."

No answer came. Only the steady echoing tick of the grandfather clock in the living room, counting the seconds of peace that couldn't possibly last.

THIRTY-FIVE

Shannon

August 21, 2022

MY STOMACH WAS IN knots all the way back to Madison, back to Maureen's quiet little cul-de-sac. By the time we pulled into her driveway, the sun had already vanished beyond the horizon and pitched the world into shadows. Tom parked the Highlander behind Maureen's car, and for a moment, nobody moved.

I felt drained. The house had taken something out of me, like it always did. But I was grateful to be pulling up to a house that felt safe. One where Hazel waited.

The smell hit me before we even opened the front door: garlic and freshly baked bread. Maureen had cooked dinner.

As we stepped inside, Hazel came barreling down the hall barefoot, her curly ponytail bouncing. "Mommy!" Her eyes lit up. "We made lasagna!"

I crouched down and scooped her up in my arms, squeezing her tight against me. "You cooked dinner? You and Miss Maureen?"

"Yeah!" Her arms wrapped snugly around my neck as she collapsed against me. "I sprinkled the cheese and did the noodles!"

"That's amazing, baby. I'm so proud of you."

When I finally set her down, I saw Maureen standing in the kitchen doorway with a glass serving bowl in her hands.

"I hope y'all are hungry," she said. "We made a big salad, too. And garlic bread." Her eyes landed on Tom and Carmen. "There's plenty for everyone, if y'all would like to sit and eat with us."

Her voice conveyed warmth, an easy Southern hospitality that sounded genuine. But her eyes lingered on the Altamiras a second too long, maybe wondering why my realtor and his sister were keeping company with me, a frazzled single mom, after dark. But she didn't ask.

"That sounds incredible, thank you," Tom said. "We'd love to."

The five of us ate around the big oak table, Hazel proudly narrating every step of her culinary contributions while Carmen listened attentively, smiling and nodding as if every detail were the most important thing she'd hear all day. Tom smiled through it all, too, though I could see the tension in his eyes, the same unease that buzzed in my chest.

When dinner was over, the table cleared, and the dishwasher loaded, Maureen wiped her hands on a checkered dish towel and leaned in close to me. "Everything okay? Y'all look a little . . . tense."

I hesitated. "Just a long day."

"I know selling a house can take it out of you. Gets real stressful."

I nodded, grateful she'd guessed the most normal explanation.

"Well, if y'all need to talk business, go on in the living room. I can get Hazel ready for bed."

"Are you sure?" I asked her, guilt rising in my chest. Hazel had been so proud of dinner, so clingy when I walked through the door. I felt like I hadn't really been *with* her in days, not fully. Part of me wanted to curl up beside her on the couch and pretend everything was fine.

But it wasn't. There were too many unanswered questions. Too much still hanging in the air after what we'd seen at the house. I needed to debrief with Carmen and Tom. To figure out our next steps.

I accepted her offer and kissed Hazel's forehead. "Okay, sweetie. Let Miss Maureen help you get ready for bed, and I'll come tuck you in after I'm done talking to Mr. Tom and Miss Carmen, alright?"

"Okay!" she said, already skipping toward the hallway.

I followed the Altamira siblings to the living room. Tom and I took the couch, Carmen the recliner again. I sucked in a deep breath. "So. What now?"

"We need to cleanse the house," Carmen said, leaning forward as she crossed her legs, "but not yet. I need a few days to prepare. Gather supplies, set intentions. Like I said before, you don't want to rush this kind of work."

My pulse ticked up. "The closing's in fourteen days."

"I'll be ready before then. Let's try for Sunday. That gives us a week. In the meantime, you should probably start packing."

I flopped back against the cushion. "Right. The other big problem."

"You shouldn't be over there alone," Tom said firmly. "And you definitely can't take Hazel back."

He was right, of course, but I felt a tug in my chest just the same. "I feel like I've barely seen her," I admitted. "She's used to being with me all the time, and now I'm leaving her with someone she just met while I deal with this nightmare."

"You're protecting her," he said softly.

Carmen nodded. "And it's temporary. This'll be over soon. Right now, you're making the best choice you can."

I swallowed hard. "Thank you for saying that." I sucked in a breath and tried to collect myself, to focus. "Okay. So. Tomorrow is Monday. I need to start packing."

"Is there anyone else you could call in to help?" Carmen asked. "Family? A friend?"

Her question stung. I knew she wasn't judging. Her voice was gentle, like she already suspected the answer but had to ask anyway. Still, heat rose to my cheeks. I looked down at my hands.

"No," I said after a pause. "My parents are both gone. Things got . . . weird with my friends after the divorce. You'd be surprised how weird people get when you stop being part of a couple." I attempted a shrug like it didn't matter. "And my ex . . ." I trailed off, shaking my head. "Not an option."

Carmen's brows pinched with sympathy. "I'm sorry," she said. "I didn't mean to pry. Just wanted to cover all the bases."

Tom spoke before I could reply. "We'll help. Between the three of us, it'll get done."

I looked at him. He was watching me with an intensity that made my heart skitter. "You really go above and beyond for your clients," I said, trying to keep it light.

"Anything for a five-star review on Google," he deadpanned.

I couldn't help but grin at that. It felt strange on my face. Good, though.

Carmen rolled her eyes, smiling too. "You need to update your business cards. *Tom Altamira: realtor, mover, and part-time ghostbuster.*"

He chuckled.

"Anyway, I can help you after work," Carmen said. "Tom?"

"I'm free during the day," he said. "And . . . I might've already texted some cousins. Diego has a trailer and a house full of strong teenage boys. We could clear the place out in a day."

I laughed, stunned. "You're serious?"

He smiled, soft and a little sheepish. "Told you. You're not doing this alone."

Gratitude filled me, loosening the knot in my chest.

"Now that getting you out of that house is sorted," Carmen sighed, "we need to refocus on the bigger, scarier picture. The other presence. The one that's not Fern."

A chill rippled through me, and for a second, I was back in Hazel's room. I heard the crack of the closet doors snapping open, saw that old stuffed rabbit tumbling out at our feet, felt the air thick with something that shouldn't have been there.

"We need to figure out what it is," Carmen continued. "It was old. Aware. And hungry."

Tom leaned back, his fingers drumming once against his knee. "Where do we start?"

"The land," Carmen said. "Before Fern. Before the house."

My stomach twisted. "Fern's husband built it in the early sixties. They were the first to live there."

"Then we go back further," Carmen said. "Who owned the property before? What's the history? We need to go deeper."

Tom straightened, all business now. "The county probate office will have land records. We can request them electronically, but they'll need at least a day to pull the old records out of the archives. I know someone there. I'll reach out first thing in the morning and see if she can possibly move us up the list."

"Perfect," Carmen said.

"They should have everything ready by Tuesday."

I nodded, letting it all sink in. "Alright. We'll spend tomorrow packing. Then Tuesday, we find out what that place has been hiding."

Thirty-Six

Shannon

August 22, 2022

Tom and I met at the house on Monday morning at nine. Going back there sucked, but having a plan helped. A purpose. A way forward. A way *out*.

I climbed from my CR-V and circled around to the back, raising the liftgate to grab the moving boxes I'd collected at the Publix down the street from Maureen's. A polite kid in the produce department had wheeled out a cart loaded down with banana boxes and handed them over with a smile. Now my entire car smelled like bananas, but I wasn't complaining. Free was free.

Tom pulled up next to me and hopped out, gravel grinding beneath his shoes as he crossed the driveway. For a moment, neither of us spoke. We stared at the house, its slightly sagging porch, the drawn blinds, the faint shimmer of heat above the roofline.

He spoke first. "Morning."

"Hey," I said, forcing a small smile.

"I just got off the phone with my friend at the probate office," he said. "She told me she'd give me a call as soon as it's ready. Should be before noon tomorrow."

"Great. Thank you."

"Here, let me give you a hand."

He loaded his arms with boxes and followed me to the porch. The steps creaked under our weight.

Inside, the air felt stuffy and dense. No lights were on, but a strange brightness filtered through the windows. Too golden, too sweet.

I paused in the doorway to the living room, surveying the space. The throw blankets folded on the couch. Toys tucked into corners. All the stuff we had to sort, pack, and get out of here.

Tom followed my gaze but said nothing. Instead, he set the boxes down by the coffee table and looked around, brows furrowing.

I felt certain he was thinking the same thing as me.

There was so much stuff.

Too much. I needed to do a lot of downsizing. I glimpsed a Barbie head floating macabrely in the corner and wondered if anyone touring the house had noticed it. A cracked Magna-Tile lay nearby. How long had I ignored literal garbage?

"Where do you wanna start?" Tom asked me.

I blinked at him, my brain going blank. "Uh, in here, I guess." I squatted down and grabbed both broken toys. "Maybe we should start with trash." I held up the toys to illustrate my point. "I'll grab some bags."

I ducked into the kitchen, the sound of my footsteps oddly loud in the stillness. I yanked open the cabinet under the sink, grabbed the box of trash bags, and hurried back, unwilling to be alone for long.

I unrolled a bag and shook it open. The Barbie head and broken Magna-Tile went in first.

Tom lingered a few feet away, shifting his weight like he wasn't sure whether to help or wait for instructions.

"Um, maybe set a box aside for donation stuff," I told him. "I'm sure I'll have a lot of that."

"Got it," he said.

I moved to the bookshelves, weighing how much I cared about my little tchotchkes, my thrifted vases and fake plants. I felt a pang of embarrassment when I spotted a ceramic pumpkin I'd somehow missed last November. I put it in the donation box.

The quiet stretched on between us awkwardly, and I found myself floundering to think of something to say.

"This is a nice room," Tom spoke up. He bobbed his head over toward the alcove by the front window. "I remember when you first saw the place, you said *that* was gonna be your reading nook."

I paused, my hand hovering over a stack of books I hadn't touched since Hazel was born. "I did say that, didn't I?"

"Yep. You had a whole vision," he said, glancing up at me. "Big armchair, string lights, shelves full of books. You were really excited about it."

I sighed. "Yeah. That sounds like me."

"You still could do that, you know. Somewhere else."

The words caught me off guard. I swallowed, staring at the shelf of unread volumes in front of me. My gaze skimmed the row of homesteading books Marc had insisted on buying. *Backyard Chickens for Beginners. The Weekend Homesteader's Guide to Self-Sufficiency. Harvest at Home: The Modern Gardener's Toolkit.* Their spines were bright and uncreased, reminders of everything we never started.

I blinked fast and looked away. "We had plans for everything back then, didn't we?" The bitterness in my voice surprised me, but I didn't try to suppress it. We were past that. "A big garden, fruit trees, chickens."

"Yeah. I remember."

"I really thought we'd grow old here," I admitted. "Before every-thing fell apart."

I turned away, moved to the entertainment center, and began rifling through the DVD collection. Anything to keep my hands busy. Plastic cases clicked loudly as I shuffled them.

"You know," Tom said after a long moment, his voice barely more than a whisper, "I was engaged once."

I glanced at him in surprise. "You were?"

"Yeah." Tom kept his eyes fixed on the floor. He paused be-fore continuing. "It was years ago. We'd been together so long, I thought we were solid. We'd already booked the wedding venue. We were saving for a down payment for a house. Then I found out she was seeing someone from work."

"God. I'm so sorry."

He shrugged. "I'd caught her lying a few times. Never anything dramatic, just small things that didn't add up. I kept giving her the benefit of the doubt for way too long."

I studied him for a long moment. "Because you're a good per-son."

He smiled at that, a half-hearted one that didn't reach his eyes. "Maybe. Or maybe I just didn't want to start over again. It's easy to ignore the cracks when you've built so much on top of them."

My throat tightened. I nodded, slowly. I knew exactly what he meant.

By sunset, we'd packed up the living room, hall bathroom, and a good half of the kitchen. Every box we sealed up with packing tape felt like a tiny funeral, one more piece of my old life being put away for good.

Tom and I locked up together before going our separate ways. I drove back to Maureen's, where another home-cooked meal waited for me. Roasted chicken with potatoes and green beans. Hazel chattered through every bite, happily recounting her day full of cartoons, coloring, books, and helping Miss Maureen in the kitchen.

Her joy was contagious. I let myself relax, pretending the house, the boxes, and the ghosts didn't exist.

As I tucked her into bed that night, I kissed her cheek and clung to the hope that, by this time tomorrow, we'd know more about the house, the land, maybe even about Fern.

THIRTY-SEVEN

Shannon

August 23, 2022

TOM CALLED A LITTLE after nine the next morning. His friend at the probate office had pulled the old land records and sent him scans first thing—deeds, plat maps, and a handful of names neither of us recognized.

"There's a lot here, actually," he said, his words coming fast, bright with an energy I hadn't heard from him before. "More than I expected. Now that we've got some names, we can dig deeper. You free to meet at the downtown library?"

"Absolutely. When's a good time for you?"

"The sooner the better," he said.

"Give me half an hour," I told him. I hung up, finished my coffee in one long gulp, and went to find my shoes.

By the time I merged onto the Parkway, the August sun had burned through the morning haze, the rising heat turning the asphalt before me into a shimmery mirage. I crawled along with the rest of the traffic toward the Huntsville skyline, a nervous energy pulsing beneath my ribs.

We finally had something solid to chase. We were going to find answers.

The downtown Huntsville library loomed ahead, large and imposing, a fortress of red brick and sharp, modern angles. *Fort Book*, some locals appropriately called it. Overhead, the Alabama state flag fluttered in the cool morning breeze beneath the American one.

Tom and I met up beneath the covered walkway, where arched brick columns and a teal metal roof formed a shaded corridor leading to the main entrance. He was waiting for me just outside the library's front doors, leaning against one of the brick columns like some kind of academic adventurer, a brown leather messenger bag slung across his chest. He wore a slate-gray button-down rolled to the elbows and khakis. The morning light caught in his black curls, mussed in that effortlessly stylish way.

He was as dashing and put-together as ever, but faint shadows beneath his eyes betrayed him. Like me, he was running on too little sleep.

"Rough night?" I asked.

He smiled faintly. "Yeah. I stayed up too late poking around online, looking up your property. I wanted to make sure I wasn't missing something obvious."

My chest tightened. "You didn't have to do that."

"I wanted to." With a wink, he added. "Above and beyond, remember?"

"Right, right. You're chasing my five-star review. Well, you are dedicated, I'll give you that. This is some intense customer service."

He grinned, tired eyes crinkling in the corners. "You haven't seen my full package yet."

I pressed a hand to my mouth, struggling to suppress laughter. "Oh my god. You really walked right into that one."

Tom exhaled through his nose, amused. "*Research* package," he clarified, shifting his bag on his shoulder. "Historical documents, old census records. I'm a bit of a history nerd. This stuff's thrilling for me." He gave a small, playful shake of his head. "Come on. Let's go inside."

I couldn't help but laugh.

He flashed me a sheepish half-smile as the automatic doors whooshed open, and we stepped into the library together.

The air inside was cool and faintly dusty with the pleasant, comforting smell of old books. We made our way through the atrium, past the circulation desk, then climbed the stairs to the second floor, where the Special Collections Department waited.

I'd never been up here before. Never had a reason to visit. The vastness of the space surprised me. Rows of towering shelves stretched across the room, filled to capacity with heavy, oversized reference volumes for viewing only, not checkout. County histories. Vintage periodicals. Military records. Family genealogies. Immigration logs. Slave registries.

My throat clenched at that last one.

The sheer number of books was overwhelming, and that was only what sat out in the open. To the left stood the rare book room, sealed behind a locked glass door. To the right, the archives room, accessible only with staff assistance.

A few computers hummed quietly beside a pair of machines for viewing old newspaper reels. Microfilm readers, according to the laminated signs reminding patrons to ask for help before using them.

"Alright," Tom whispered, unshouldering his messenger bag and plopping it down atop a study table. We were the only ones there, but it still felt right to speak in whispers. "Let me show you what Jada sent over this morning."

I took a seat across from him as he pulled out his iPad.

He tapped the screen a few times and began. "So. Fern's husband, Raymond Carlisle, purchased the property in 1959 from a guy named Ernest Wallace. Ernest inherited forty acres of land in the 1920s from his father, Asa Wallace."

"Okay."

"But here's the weird part." He tapped the screen again. "Neither of the Wallaces ever built anything on that piece of land. The younger Wallace divided up the land in the fifties, but the parcel Raymond Carlisle bought? Mostly wooded. No dwellings. However, she did find a survey from 1900 that showed an old barn there. That was long before the Wallaces owned it. No sign of a house, though. Whatever might've been there before was already gone by then."

I frowned. "So . . . who built the barn?"

"That's what I'm wondering. Whoever put it there, it predates anything else on the parcel. And for some reason, the Wallaces just kept it, along with the land, without ever living there." His eyes locked on mine, dark and focused. "Now, that survey from 1900 said the property belonged to a Malcolm Carruthers."

I nodded, but my thoughts were spinning. Why did that land sit empty for so long? If there'd once been a homestead to go with that barn, what happened to it? Or had it always stood alone, a random outbuilding in the middle of the woods? And why did my stomach flutter every time Tom spoke like this, like we weren't just unearthing history, but unlocking something bigger? Something buried. Something that didn't want to be found.

Tom's voice pulled me back.

"—October 1889," he read, "Malcolm Carruthers purchased the property from Madison County."

"From the county?" I leaned closer. "Not from a person?"

He nodded. "That usually means it was tax-forfeited or seized as abandoned land."

A strange chill prickled over my skin.

"There was a notation. Look." He turned the iPad so I could see.

The screen showed a scanned document with faded, cursive handwriting:

Previously registered to Samuel Ellison in 1870. Forfeited due to abandonment. No improvements on property.

"Samuel Ellison," I read aloud, pulse kicking up. "Why did he abandon it?"

"Good question. That's as far back as Jada could trace it. Nobody really kept records out in the county back then, or if they did, they're lost to time."

I stared, processing, not knowing what to think.

"But now that we have some names and date ranges, we can check genealogy records and old newspapers. See what else we can find."

Within minutes, we were splitting the work—Tom clicking through the electronic genealogy databases, me doing the same in the digitized newspaper archives. Unfortunately, I learned rather quickly that digitized papers only went back to 1991, so I went to the information desk for help.

A woman sat at the counter behind a wall of clear plexiglass leftover from COVID, her silver hair pulled into a tight knot at the nape of her neck. When she looked up, her smile was polite but a little distant. "May I help you?"

"Yes, ma'am," I started. "I'm looking for old newspapers, like, older than the digital database, and I don't really know where to start."

"You'll need the microfilm," she answered. "What dates are you looking for?"

I tried to recall the dates Tom had read from the land records. "Um, late 1800s? I'm looking for articles about the Ellison family in Gurley."

The librarian's expression grew weary, like she'd had this conversation before. "Unfortunately, you can't keyword search microfilm. You've gotta do it the old-fashioned way, which means you've gotta flip through every single page of every single paper, front to back. And keep in mind, they were released weekly, so that's fifty-two issues a year."

I gulped.

"Let's start with the year. Can you narrow it down to at least a month or two?"

I fished my phone from my pocket and opened the forwarded email from Tom, scrolling through the attachments until I found the notation about Samuel Ellison, who had purchased the property in 1870. The next recorded transfer was from Madison County to Malcolm Carruthers in 1889.

That left a nineteen-year gap.

My stomach turned, a queasy flutter taking over as I realized just how daunting this task was going to be. I had no idea where to look or what the hell I was even looking for.

I sucked in a sharp breath and said, "Can we start with 1870?"

"You said Gurley, right? We don't have any papers from Gurley that far back. You could check *The Huntsville Democrat*, but unless it was something sensational, rural families were hardly ever featured in the city paper."

I nodded, slightly defeated but still determined. If something had happened out there, it probably would have been sensational enough.

She led me to an alcove lined with rows of metal filing cabinets. I followed her to the back corner as she pulled open a drawer with a metallic groan.

Inside were dozens of small boxes, each labeled in neat, fading handwriting. She selected one marked *Jan 1870 – Dec 1873* and set it on the table at one of the microfilm reader stations. After loading the machine and giving me a quick tutorial on the knobs and dials, she left me to it.

For the first twenty minutes or so, it was actually kind of fun. The old headlines, the bizarre advice columns—some of them appalling, the rest unintentionally hilarious. The vintage ads were my favorite. So many of them were for tonics promising miracles, like *Henry's Constitution Renovator and Blood Clenser*, guaranteed to cure an impossibly long list of ailments.

The clicking and whirring of the advancing reel became soothing, hypnotic even, as I scrolled through the weeks and months. But as the minutes stretched on, my amusement faded. The dates crawled forward. October. November. December. By January 1871, the words were blurring together.

I pressed on, skimming now, searching for words like *Gurley* and *Ellison* and never finding them. Each reel frame came and went without success, a passing window into a bygone era that never captured a glimpse of the people I needed.

By June, my eyes burned. I was considering calling it quits when I advanced a couple more frames and froze.

FIRE CLAIMS ELLISON HOMESTEAD

The headline glared across the screen in thick, black letters. My hand stilled on the dial, heart hammering as the subheading came into focus:

> *Wife of missing Gurley man found dead after months of misfortune.*

My stomach dropped, a sudden, dizzying lurch that knocked the breath from my lungs. "Tom," I whispered.

In the silence of the library, he heard me.

He rose from his computer station, hurried to my side, and leaned in, the warmth of his body and the spicy scent of his cologne closing in as his eyes moved over the words.

"Ellison?" he breathed. "As in Samuel Ellison?"

I began to read, my heart pounding:

> ***Madison County, July 12, 1871—*** *A fire claimed the life of Mrs. Samuel Ellison early Sunday morning when the family's rural homestead northeast of town was destroyed. Her body was recovered from the root cellar by neighbors who arrived too late to intervene.*

The fire marks the third tragedy to strike the family in recent months. Mr. Ellison disappeared without word in May, and in June, their three-year-old daughter was last seen playing near the edge of the woods. No sign of the child was ever found.

Neighbor Horace Lynch, first to arrive at the scene of the blaze, remarked: "That land don't take kindly to nobody. Folks say it was grief made ol' Ada lose her senses, but I think the land's to blame. My daddy said them woods was cursed."

The property is expected to be turned over to the county.

I stared at the screen, the pit in my stomach caving deeper with every re-read.

"Jesus." Tom gave a shaky exhale after a few moments. "Shit, Shannon."

Our eyes met, and I saw the terror I felt mirrored in his eyes.

"They had a daughter who went missing," I whispered, my hands trembling. "She was three. The same age as Loretta Carlisle. The same age as Hazel."

The color drained from Tom's face.

We didn't say anything else. There was nothing to say.

Because we both knew this wasn't just history.

This was a pattern.

Thirty-Eight

With the librarian's assistance, we printed the article. I stared at it for a long time, focusing on the gaps between the words. The omissions.

It struck me that the newspaper never mentioned the names of Samuel Ellison's wife or daughter. Not once. They existed only in relation to him. *His wife. His child.*

That was the way history remembered women and girls like them: barely in the margins, unnamed, unimportant.

But the genealogical records Tom had uncovered filled in the blanks.

Her name was Ada Ellison.

Their daughter was named *Viola.*

My breath snagged in my throat when I read it.

Viola wasn't some eerie figment of Hazel's imagination. She was real. Another lost child. Three years old when she vanished.

And no one remembered her.

A slow, bitter fury curled in my chest. Ada and Viola had been erased, a vanished child and a distraught mother reduced to footnotes. It made me ache for them, for every forgotten woman lost to time.

We filled pages with notes, snapped not-great phone photos of documents on glowing screens, and printed whatever the old machines would allow. Articles about Loretta Carlisle's disappearance were easier to find. She even came up in the digitized archives, her story spanning decades, painting my house as a place of secrets and turning Loretta into both a cautionary tale and a local legend. Tucked between the lines was Fern, withdrawn and reclusive, a mother whose heartbreak no one seemed to understand.

As we waited for the printer to finish spitting out the last few pages about Loretta, a voice broke through my daze.

"You guys digging into the old Carlisle place?"

I turned. A young librarian with an auburn fringe stood a few feet away, carrying a stack of fragile-looking books in gloved hands. *Morgan*, her name badge read, dangling from a lanyard patterned with mushrooms, butterflies, and wildflowers.

Tom straightened, responding before I could find my voice. "Yeah, actually. We're trying to trace the property's history."

Her eyes widened, face lighting up with interest. "I recognized those articles." She bobbed her head toward the stack we'd printed. "That house comes up every few years. Usually around Halloween. Somebody always wants to research it. You guys working on a paper or something?"

My chest fluttered. People wrote papers about my house?

"Something like that," Tom said.

"Well, it's quite the rabbit hole," she said with a grin, setting the books down on a nearby cart. "The Carlisle place is like our own little Amityville."

I stared at her, pulse pounding in my ears. "It's . . . that well-known?"

Morgan hesitated, the grin fading into a more thoughtful expression. "I'd say so, yeah. In certain circles. Especially after those demonologists wrote about it in the seventies. That kinda turned the place into a local curiosity."

Tom and I traded a look.

"Demonologists?" I asked, stunned.

"Yeah. The Birches." She seemed surprised we didn't already know. "Harry and Hilda Birch, I think. They wrote a few books about their . . . encounters."

Encounters.

I felt like I might be sick.

Morgan kept going, oblivious to the ice sliding down my spine. "You'd be surprised how many amateur ghost hunters have tried to get inside over the years. Don't think any of them ever did, though."

My thoughts spun like a whirlwind. I can't imagine what my face looked like as I stared at her.

"Hang on a sec, I'll go look up that book for you." She darted behind the reference desk and tapped away at her computer keyboard. "Here we go. I'm pretty sure the Carlisle place is mentioned in this one. *Ministers of Deliverance.* Here's the call number. It should be right across the way there, in adult nonfiction."

She scribbled it on a piece of scrap paper and slid it across the counter with a friendly smile, completely unaware that her words had just splintered reality.

We found *Ministers of Deliverance* by Harry and Hilda Birch tucked low on a back shelf in the theology section, its cracked spine wedged between other forlorn paperbacks with dusty edges.

Tom slid it out and turned it over in his hands. The cover was a faded maroon, stamped with gold lettering in a questionable font that had almost rubbed away. The author photo on the back showed a prim-looking couple posed shoulder to shoulder, both wearing the tight smiles of a church directory portrait. He wore his hair in a tidy side part, slicked so heavily with pomade it looked like it might drip. Her puffy bouffant sat like a towering brown helmet, frozen in place by enough hairspray to withstand the Rapture.

They didn't look like experts in the supernatural. They looked like the kind of couple who left gospel tracts in gas station bathrooms and made special trips to pray over the beer aisle at the grocery store.

We huddled close together as Tom flipped through the yellowed pages, the faint smell of mildew meeting our noses. Each chapter title was centered in ornate cursive. *Chapter One: A Spirit of Division. Chapter Two: The Curse of the Odom Family.*

Tom froze mid-turn, the brittle page trembling in his fingers.

Chapter Three: The House on Sunflower Lane.

"Holy crap," I whispered.

Beneath the chapter heading, a black-and-white photograph took up half the page—unmistakably my house. It looked new, its clapboard siding bright and gleaming, the front porch *not* sagging. My house—Fern's house, then—captured in its prime.

I read the first line of the opening paragraph beneath it and felt my blood run cold:

> *In the spring of 1963, we were summoned to a modest home on the outskirts of Madison County, Alabama, where a mother and her young daughter reported disturbances too grave to ignore.*

My vision tunneled, my brain refusing to process the words. Fern and her daughter had experienced disturbances?

I stared at that first line until the words stopped making sense.

Tom closed the book gingerly, marking chapter three with his thumb, and nodded toward a study table at the end of the aisle. "Come on. Let's go find out what they had to say."

I followed him on shaky legs and took a seat next to him. He splayed the book open before us, and we began to read.

> *This was in the early days of our ministry, back before the Lord revealed our true calling in the field of deliverance. Back then, our focus was on evangelism; we traveled from church to church across the Southeast, spreading the Gospel and holding revival meetings wherever God led us. It was during one such meeting in Huntsville that this mother, whom we shall call Mary (name changed for privacy), approached us after the service, distraught.*

> *Mary explained that her family had been under the*

*devil's attack for many months. It began, she said, with
her husband's sudden change of nature. Once kind
and devoted, he had grown restless, bitter, and withdrawn until, at last, he abandoned his family without
a word.*

My eyes got stuck on that line. Restless. Bitter. Withdrawn.

I thought of Marc. The way he'd grown cruel and uncaring.
Started sleeping in his office. How he'd left us without a real explanation, without even a goodbye.

Then Samuel Ellison flickered through my mind, the husband
who'd "gone missing" in the eighteen-hundreds. It stood to reason
that he, too, fit this pattern.

How many men had walked away from that house?

How many families had it ripped apart?

*In her husband's absence, the atmosphere within the
home darkened. Mary and her two young daughters
began hearing footsteps. The children complained of
nightmares, of seeing a strange woman standing in the
corner of their room, whispering to them. Their mother
described the sensation chillingly: "It was almost like
something moved in when he moved out."*

My stomach turned in on itself.

How was this possible?

The manifestations increased as time went on, and the crisis came in October of 1962, when the youngest daughter—just three years of age—vanished from the backyard in broad daylight. A search was made, but unfortunately, no trace of her was ever found.

The ache in my chest deepened. This was where our stories diverged, because I'd woken up just in the nick of time. Because I'd run. Tears stung my eyes as the truth hit me: I'd come within inches of becoming Fern. Of losing Hazel to the same thing that had taken Loretta and Viola.

We agreed to visit Mary in her home the following morning. The atmosphere of the place was oppressively heavy. We prayed with Mary in her living room, then together, we walked through the home, praying over each room and quoting Scripture.

I read through the paragraphs that followed, taking in the account of their visits to the house, of how they "successfully" banished an unclean spirit from Loretta's—now Hazel's—bedroom. I balked at how they'd anointed the closet doors with oil. Sang some hymns and prayed some prayers.

Clearly, their confidence was misplaced.

It hadn't been enough.

The heavy atmosphere we'd experienced upon arrival had lifted, replaced by a sense of peace that could only have come from our Lord and Savior's holy presence. We gave thanks to Him and prayed over the house one last time before taking our leave.

At the advisement of a more experienced minister of deliverance, we made an audio recording of this final session using a reel-to-reel device. Several days later, while reviewing the recording, we made a most unsettling discovery.

For the first few minutes, the audio proceeded as expected. Then, at approximately the halfway point, we discerned several overlapping voices, all of them faint and garbled as though two radio stations were colliding together on the same frequency. Their exact words could not be distinguished, but one voice sounded markedly older, while another sounded like a small child crying. We determined these to be mocking imitations of our prayers and dismissed them as the enemy's attempt to sow discord and confusion.

As of our last correspondence with Mary, activity at the residence has ceased. Sadly, the missing daughter remains unaccounted for to this day, yet we rejoice that the unclean spirit's power over this household was broken. To God be the glory.

The chapter ended there.

Beside me, Tom exhaled, a shuddery sound that seemed too loud in the quiet library.

I shut the book, and their photo on the back cover stared up at us. Harry and Hilda Birch, all pious smiles, two strangers peering at us from the past, certain they had won.

I tried to imagine them, packing up and leaving Fern behind, telling themselves they'd defeated Satan. I bet they slept better for it.

I wanted to hate them.

But they'd been there. They'd *seen* it.

Were they still alive? Could I find them? And if I did, would they tell me what really happened that night?

Or would they just pray for me too, the way they prayed for Fern?

Thirty-Nine

We walked out of the library side by side in silence. The sunlight hit me like a slap to the face. Tom flinched beside me, pale and squinting, as if we'd stepped out of one world and into another.

That's exactly how it felt.

The parking lot shimmered in the afternoon heat, every car gleaming blindingly in the harsh light. I felt hollow and strange. Overstimulated from all we'd learned and overwhelmed by what it all meant.

In my arms, I carried *Ministers of Deliverance.* I'd used my library card to check it out, along with two more titles by the Birches we'd found on the same shelf: *Possessions and Exorcisms* and *Rulers of the Darkness.* I wanted to read more about them, get a sense of who they were.

As we neared Tom's SUV, he stopped and released a long exhale. He raked a hand through his hair and spoke in a voice so low, I strained to hear him. "I'm sorry, Shannon."

I didn't know what to say.

He shook his head, a humorless laugh slipping from his lips. "I grew up in Five Points. I've lived in Huntsville my whole life. I knew the stories. Kids used to whisper about *the Carlisle girl* on the school bus. Teenagers used to dare each other to drive out to her creepy old house at night. Some of them swore they saw her ghost in the front window."

I stared at him.

"But I never went out there," he said quickly. "I never had any idea where it actually was. Honest to God, Shannon, I didn't recognize it when I sold it to you. I thought it was just a story anyway. Just a dumb urban legend. I didn't believe in any of that stuff. That was Carmen's thing, not mine."

The guilt in his voice hit me hard. "You couldn't have known."

He winced. "But I should have. It's my job to know." He looked out over the parking lot, jaw tight. "Three years ago, I was new to real estate. I didn't have many clients yet, and every sale felt make-or-break." He paused, swallowing. "I was trying so hard to prove myself that I didn't question anything I didn't have to. And now . . . I just . . . I feel like I failed you."

My throat tightened.

"I should've put the pieces together. You trusted me, and I should've taken better care of you than that."

The Alabama heat hung between us, thick and stifling.

"I can't undo selling you that house," he said, his words heavy with regret, "but I can help you get out of it. Whatever it takes."

I nodded. "Thank you."

He drew in a deep breath and straightened. "That means I'm yours for whatever's left of the day. If you're up for it, we can drive out there now and keep packing."

My stomach twisted hard. It was the last thing I wanted to do, but I knew it was probably the best use of our time. "Alright. Let's get it over with."

He gave a small, encouraging smile. "We'll grab something to eat on the way. My treat. The taco bus is right down the road."

The thought of food made me queasy, but I couldn't go back to the house and pack all afternoon on an empty stomach. And the more I thought about carnitas, the less nauseated I felt. "That works," I told him.

The drive was short, and the smell of grilled meat that welcomed us cut straight through the heavy fog in my chest. We ate at one of the picnic tables beside the bus. Sunshine warmed my back, the breeze ruffled the wax paper to-go box liners beneath my street tacos, and for a moment, it almost felt like a normal lunch break.

Almost.

There was still too much to do, too much to face.

So I finished my meal, threw away the box, and climbed into the passenger seat.

Time to go back.

The drive out to Gurley was quiet. Highway 72 shimmered ahead of us in the scorching afternoon heat, the agricultural fields blurring past in a green haze. Neither of us said much. What was there to say?

Tom took a slight detour, pulling into the Piggly Wiggly to see if we could score some more boxes and a fresh roll of packing tape. Inside, the overhead fluorescent lights were too bright, the air-conditioning was too cold, and the whole place smelled like deli-case fried chicken.

He tossed a couple of bottled coffee drinks and a pack of gum onto the checkout belt while I grabbed a travel-sized bottle of ibuprofen—a last-minute impulse buy for the dull headache that had been growing behind my eyes since using the microfilm reader.

On our way out, the cashier pointed us toward a cart of flattened cardboard boxes near the door. We loaded as many as would fit in the back of Tom's SUV before heading out again.

When the familiar curve of Sunflower Lane came into view, my stomach tensed.

After everything we'd learned at the library, I saw the property with new eyes. The front yard, the line of trees, even the porch seemed altered, like the house had shed its disguise at last and laid itself bare before me.

Unmasked and exposed, there were no more secrets between us.

I scanned the land, wondering where the old Ellison homestead had stood before the fire had claimed it. Were there remnants of their lives still buried out here? Beneath this house, maybe? I pictured Ada Ellison standing in this same yard, calling for a daughter who never answered.

I imagined Fern doing the same after little Loretta vanished into the trees.

Harry and Hilda Birch arriving here like saviors, anointing doors and praying over the rooms.

I thought of the gawking teenagers who parked at the end of the driveway, windows rolled down, hoping for a glimpse of Loretta or Fern in spirit form. The ambitious local ghost hunters who'd undoubtedly crept around the property, searching for a way inside.

Everyone had known this house was haunted.

Everyone except me.

I let out a heavy sigh. The ghosts had always been here. Long before Fern, before me, maybe even before the Ellison homestead was built. I was just the latest chapter in a centuries-old story.

Tom opened the hatch of his SUV and handed me a box. "Ready?"

I wasn't, but I nodded anyway.

We picked up where we'd left off yesterday: the kitchen. Tom reconstructed a detergent box while I padded the bottom of it with a few grocery bags I'd been saving beneath the sink.

We worked together in silence for a while, the steady rhythm of motion somewhat comforting. We wrapped the plates and glassware in dish towels, careful not to chip the edges. When those ran out, I raided the master bathroom for hand towels.

"I can't stop thinking about that couple investigating this place," Tom said suddenly, breaking the quiet. "The Birches."

I glanced up at him from the coffee mug I was enveloping in a washcloth. "I know. I still can't believe it, really." I shook my head and tucked the wrapped mug inside the box. "Do you think they're still alive?"

"Maybe. They'd be pretty old, but it's definitely possible."

I chewed on my bottom lip as a thought struck me. "What if they know something that could help us? Maybe they have notes or records or something that didn't make it into the book." The idea unsettled me and thrilled me all at once. "Do you think they'd talk to us?"

"Only one way to find out." He finished swaddling a glass tumbler and pulled his phone from his pocket. "Let's see if they're still around."

I peered over his shoulder as he typed their names into the internet browser, and within seconds, he'd found an ancient, poorly-formatted website. My graphic designer brain died a little inside as I took it in.

A banner with a pixelated cross and the text *Birch Deliverance Ministries* in beveled gold 3D text (not Comic Sans, but an equally outdated serif font that looked like Copperplate Gothic's primitive ancestor) suggested it hadn't been updated in at least a decade. Maybe two. The background was white marble, clearly chosen to look "elegant," but the result was just tacky.

"Wow," I murmured. "This isn't looking too promising."

"Yeah. Looks like the last update was . . . 2004," Tom said, scrolling carefully, as if the page might break. He tapped a link labeled *Contact Us*.

The email listed was an @aol.com address. That felt about right.

But beneath that, wedged above a low-res clip-art dove, was a phone number and a post office box in Decatur, Alabama.

"Decatur," he said. "They might be local."

My heart skipped. "Should we try calling the number? What do we even say?"

"I don't know," he admitted. "But before we worry about all that, let's see if anyone's even still answering it."

I held my breath as he tapped the number and hit *call*. He put it on speaker, and together, we waited.

The call connected with three beeps followed by an automated voice. *"We're sorry. The number you have dialed has been disconnected or is no longer in service."* A mechanical *click*, then a flat, emotionless, *"Goodbye."*

Tom glanced at me. I shrugged.

He went back to the search results, thumbing through a few links before stopping.

"Well," he said, voice low, "here's Harry's obituary."

He tapped it open, and I leaned closer to read it.

Reverend Harold "Harry" Lawrence Birch, 75, passed peacefully into the arms of his Savior on January 29, 2016, surrounded by his loving family. Born in Clay County, Alabama, in 1940, Harry answered the call to ministry at an early age, preaching his first sermon while still in high school. He married his childhood sweetheart, Hilda Mae Williams, in 1959, and together they devoted their lives to sharing the Gospel.

The couple began their work through Birch Evangelistic Ministries, conducting tent revivals and worship services throughout the Southeast during the early 1960s. In later years, they co-founded Birch Deliverance Ministries, where they dedicated their efforts to spiritual restoration for families in crisis. Reverend Birch co-authored several books on this subject with his wife, and they worked alongside one another in ministry until his retirement.

He is survived by his wife, Hilda, who continues the work of Birch Deliverance Ministries from their home in Decatur, and by their daughter, Rebecca Birch Griffiths, of Huntsville.

"Hilda's still alive," I whispered.

"Maybe," Tom said. "At least she was when this was written."

In 2016, I noted. Tom did a quick search for *Hilda Birch Decatur Alabama.* No obituaries came up, but a White Pages listing did—with an address.

"312 Sherman Street," Tom read aloud. "Current property records are public. We can run it through the Morgan County tax assessor's site and see if she still owns it. Want to find out?"

I nodded, though a flicker of unease curled in my stomach.

In less than a minute, Tom had pulled this year's tax record for the property and verified the owners were still listed as *Birch, Harold and Hilda.*

He glanced up at me, the glow from his screen reflecting in his dark eyes as he asked, "How do you feel about a little road trip?"

FORTY

Shannon

August 24, 2022

WHEN WE CLIMBED OUT of Tom's Highlander, my nose wrinkled. The air smelled like cat food. We'd passed the Meow Mix factory on the Tennessee River a few minutes earlier, when we'd first crossed the bridge into Decatur, and even here, in the charming Albany historic district, it still lingered.

I wondered if cats all over Decatur spent their days drooling.

The smell was incongruous with the beauty of the neighborhood: manicured lawns, tidy sidewalks, old trees arching over the street, and some of the prettiest Victorian homes I'd ever seen.

Tom had been letting his history-nerd flag fly all the way down Sherman Street. "They named it after General Sherman, the Union general," he'd said, and now, as we met at the hood of his car, he picked up where he'd left off. "It was an attempt to appeal to Northerners, to convince folks to move down here after the yellow fever epidemic wiped out so many of Decatur's citizens. Grant Street's just over that way, too. They were really trying to mend fences."

"Sounds awfully progressive for Alabama," I said.

"Well, we did just pass two streets named after Lee and Jackson, so there's that," he said with a small smile. "But yeah, it's a nice neighborhood. I love bringing clients over here to tour these old homes."

He cut himself off, realizing he was rambling, probably from nerves, and turned toward the reason for our forty-five-minute drive to Decatur.

The Birch house was a small Craftsman bungalow tucked behind a row of overgrown azaleas. A gigantic magnolia shaded most of the yard, too late in the season for blooms, its broad, waxy leaves whispering faintly in the muggy August breeze.

Morning sunlight glinted off the dormer's short windows, the glass so clouded with age, it barely reflected anything at all. The siding's once-forest-green paint had faded to pale celadon in spots, and the ivory trim was chipped and peeling. Four tapered columns supported the deep porch, brick at the bottom giving way to wooden shafts painted the same tired ivory as the rest of the trim. Beside the front door sat two wicker chairs, their cushions sun-faded and flat.

My heart climbed into my throat as Tom and I approached the entrance. He pressed the doorbell, and we heard a faint chime sound from within. We exchanged nervous glances—half expectant, half uncertain—as we waited for someone to answer.

The paneled oak door pulled open with a creak, and a small, stooped woman appeared in the gap. She was older than I'd expected, well into her eighties, with narrow shoulders rounded by time and a faint tremor in her hands. Deep creases framed her gray-blue eyes, which met mine first. Her eyes seemed to smile at me before her lips did, warm and kind, and I felt the nervous tightness in my chest ease.

"May I help you?" she asked. Her voice was soft and honeyed, her vowels stretched in that slow, old-timey Southern way.

"Mrs. Birch?" I began. Something about her face, about her presence, made me feel safe enough to spill everything in a single, breathless rush. "I'm sorry to just show up like this, but my name is Shannon, and this is Tom. We drove here from Gurley. I was hoping we could talk to you about my house. I think you and your husband went there in the sixties to help the woman who used to live there. Her name was Fern Carlisle."

I'd let the words tumble out too fast. As soon as I stopped, I winced inwardly. Too much, too quick, to an elderly woman who might not have even caught half of it.

But the shift in her expression told me she'd heard me just fine.

"Fern Carlisle," she repeated, almost to herself. Her eyes flicked to Tom, then back to me. "Yes, I remember her. That poor woman. Y'all better come on in. It's too hot to stand out here."

Hilda held the pitcher steady as iced tea streamed into a set of textured amber glasses, each one half-filled with ice. The cubes cracked softly as she poured.

She slid a glass toward each of us and lowered herself onto the empty chair on the other side of the kitchen table. "You did right to leave that place when you did," she told me. Her face had gone pale while I told her what had happened.

Her kitchen was small but tidy, a hodgepodge of decades. A shiny new stainless refrigerator stood beside a stove that might've been here since the eighties, both tucked between original midcentury cabinets painted a soft butter yellow. Lace curtains softened the daylight, scattering it in odd patterns across the faded floral tablecloth before us. In the center of the table, a bowl of plastic fruit gleamed, glossy under the light.

Granny Jean had always kept the same plastic fruit on her kitchen table. This place reminded me of her house in other ways too, with its cozy clutter and old-fashioned warmth. Even the smell was familiar, a mix of lemon polish, old coffee, and something else I couldn't pin down.

Hilda's eyes glistened with tears as she studied me. "I truly thought that house was at peace." She shook her head. "Did Fern have any more trouble after that, or did it not begin until you moved in?"

"As far as I know, not until we moved in," I said. "I mean, Fern lived there for the rest of her life."

Hilda fell silent for a moment, her gaze distant. "I remember that summer clear as day," she said quietly. "I was expecting then. My daughter, Rebecca." Her lips trembled in something like a smile, but it faded before it formed. "I remember feeling uneasy the whole time we were there. Fern's little girl had gone missing not long before, and I couldn't stop thinking about her. Being pregnant, it just . . . it sat heavy on me." Her eyes met mine. "They never did find her, did they?"

I shook my head. "No, ma'am."

Hilda drew in a long breath. "From everything you've just told me, the spirit at that house seems drawn to a particular kind of family," she said at last. "Young parents. Young daughters."

Tom nodded. "There's definitely a distinct pattern to it."

"Yes, a pattern," Hilda agreed. "Or perhaps . . . a cycle it *has* to repeat."

"Have you ever encountered anything else like that?" I asked her.

"No. Not exactly. That's what's got me so confounded." Her hand shook as she cupped her chin. "My husband, Harry, used to say that every supposed 'haunting' was just the same old devil wearing a different mask. And for a long time, we both believed that." She glanced down at the bowl of fake fruit. "But I've had a lot of years to think since then, and I'm not so sure anymore."

Tom leaned forward. "What do you mean?"

Hilda hesitated. "Some of the things we dealt with . . . well, over time, I realized a lot of those so-called possessions were actually untreated mental illness."

The admission surprised me. I hadn't expected someone like her to say that out loud.

"In some cases, yes," she went on, "something unclean had taken hold of a person. And when we called on the Lord, when we stood our ground and commanded it to leave, it did. But others?" Her voice faltered. "Others felt different, to me. I don't quite know how to explain it."

We waited quietly for her to find the right words.

"I guess you start to notice things after a while," Hilda said. "Certain places just . . . feel wrong. You can walk out onto a property and sense it immediately. The air gets all thick and heavy, almost like that feeling in the air right before a storm."

I gulped. I'd experienced that exact feeling at the house more times than I could count.

Her eyes unfocused as her thoughts drifted somewhere else. "There was one place I'll never forget. An old plantation house down near Selma. Enormous white columns, front porch bigger than my whole house. The couple living there called us because their son was having awful nightmares and waking up with these strange welts on his back and scratches on his arms."

She folded her hands on the table before her, the tremor in them more noticeable now. "This was in the early seventies, if memory serves. We thought we knew what we were walking into, but I suwannee, the moment we stepped out of the car, I felt it. The air had that heavy feeling; it about made me sick. Harry insisted it was the devil, same as always, but I wasn't so sure. That land, those old cotton fields, they'd been cracked open by pain and sorrow. It was like the soil had soaked up too much suffering, too much cruelty. Maybe that wound invited something in, or maybe it just *became* something on its own. I don't know. Either way, the land was alive. And wrong."

A shiver crept up my arms.

"We prayed over the place, of course. The little boy's nightmares stopped, but you know what? The mother reached out to me the next spring and told me that every plant on that land died all at once. All their crops. The family moved out not long after that."

Silence settled over us, the soft whir of the ceiling fan above us filling the quiet.

"That was the first time I realized a place itself could be bad," Hilda said. "And those hills out where your house is, Shannon? That stretch of woods? It carries something, too. I remember feeling that same way out there. Old pain. Old sorrow."

I gulped as a sense of dread settled in my gut.

"There's an awful lot we don't understand about this old world, things we *won't* understand until we meet the Lord face-to-face. I reckon hauntings are one of those mysteries." Her fingers absently traced the rim of her glass. "Still, I've come to believe that some pain is so deep, so fierce, it never dies. It just seeps down into the earth and lingers there."

Forty-One

Traffic had crawled to a stop on Interstate 565 East, an endless snake of brake lights stretching toward Huntsville. The midday sun burned overhead, glinting harshly off the back of the Mercedes in front of us.

I fiddled with the air vent and stole a glance at Tom. His left elbow rested on the door, fingers drumming absently against the steering wheel. Sweat shimmered across his temple, dampening the curls near his hairline. He wasn't looking at the road—wasn't looking at anything, really. Just lost in his thoughts.

The air between us had felt tense and uneasy since leaving Hilda's. She'd insisted on coming to the house herself later in the week, promising that she and her daughter, Rebecca, would spend this afternoon digging through her old case files until they found everything connected to the house on Sunflower Lane, including the reel-to-reel recording they'd mentioned in *Ministers of Deliverance*.

Though I appreciated her insight and was eager to hear that recording, the thought of her going back there unsettled me. She'd seemed so certain, so calm about it, like it was nothing more than a simple errand. But Hilda was well into her eighties, and she still felt like she owed something to that place. I didn't know whether to admire her or beg her to stay away. Mostly, I just felt guilty for ever reaching out in the first place.

Tom's phone lit up in its dash mount, the buzz breaking the silence inside the car.

"That's Carmen," he told me, swiping to read a new text message. "She says she gets off at two and is free to come by and help pack after."

"Oh, that would be great. Tell her thank you."

He nodded and started typing.

The line of cars ahead of us inched forward about two feet, then stopped again.

I sighed, checked my own phone, and sent a quick text to Maureen.

Hey, just checking in. Everything going okay with Hazel?

The reply came a minute later.

She's doing great. We just finished sidewalk chalk drawings and now we're making cookies. She's happy and safe.

I smiled at that, then looked back out at the stalled traffic. "God. It feels like we've been sitting here forever."

"I know." Tom exhaled and returned his phone to the dash mount. "Must've been a crash up ahead."

I peered through the windshield. Heat shimmered above the hood, undulating in slow waves. It warped the air just enough to make the world feel surreal.

"What Hilda said about the land," I began, unable to hold it in any longer. "Did it remind you of the article we found about the Ellison fire?"

Tom turned to me. "What do you mean?"

"It quoted a neighbor, remember? The neighbor who found the fire and Ada Ellison's body, I think. He said something about the land being to blame, that the woods were cursed." I swallowed hard. "It sounds a lot like what Hilda was saying."

His jaw tightened. "Damn. That's right."

"That would mean the Ellisons were just another part of the pattern. Another family the land . . . took."

A siren wailed somewhere up ahead.

"But the property records didn't go back any further," I murmured. "There's nothing before the Ellisons. Nothing about who lived there first, what the land was before they settled there."

Tom gave a solemn nod. "Well, there *was* someone there before them. Folks lived all through those woods long before the Ellisons showed up." He paused. "They just didn't get to leave the same kind of record."

A pit opened in my stomach as I realized what he meant.

"When Hilda talked about the land soaking up sorrow," Tom said, his voice low, "it made me think of something."

He didn't look at me as he spoke. He stared straight ahead, jaw clenched, fingers flexing around the steering wheel. "The Trail of Tears passed right through Gurley in the 1830s, just about where Highway 72 runs now. Families were forced out. Marched across the mountains. A lot of them didn't make it."

Silence settled between us, heavy as the humid air outside.

"You ever noticed that historical marker right by Madison County High School?" When I shook my head, he went on. "It says a group of over a thousand Cherokee people were forced through there by the militia. They camped out where the school is today. Terrible conditions. No supplies. People were sick, exhausted. About three hundred of them escaped to the hills, but the rest were forced to march west."

He exhaled through his nose. "Over four thousand people died on that trail. All of that pain . . . right here on this land."

A tight ache swelled beneath my sternum. I tried to picture it—all those families forced from their homeland, marched through all kinds of weather, with inadequate food and no shelter. Mothers clutching their children, trying to soothe crying babies. Elders too weak and frail to walk. People starving and stumbling and suffering.

The land here had known heartbreak long before Fern Carlisle or Ada Ellison ever set foot on it.

The line of cars finally loosened, and the Highlander rolled forward, slow at first, then picking up speed as we passed the Memorial Parkway exit. Flashing lights and a tow truck on the exit ramp marked the aftermath of a wreck.

My stomach tightened at the sight of someone else's misfortune.

We eased past, the lanes opening before us. A green sign ahead marked the transition of I-565 to Highway 72.

This was the road to Gurley. To my house. I'd driven this stretch a thousand times, unbothered, untouched by the history beneath the asphalt.

But it felt different now.

Forty-Two

"At this point, I'm about ready to light a match," I muttered as Tom and I stood in the doorway of my bedroom closet, staring at the mountain of clutter before us.

Tom blinked. "Pretty sure your buyer wouldn't love that."

"Right." I gestured at the mess. "Well, what if it came fully stocked with crap instead?"

He grinned as he shook open a garbage bag. "Man, it's too late now, but I could've put all that in the listing. 'This charming country cottage comes fully furnished with a thoughtfully curated wardrobe, dozens of shoes, a yoga mat, a curious number of old curtain rods, and . . .'"

He stopped as his eyes caught on a row of men's button-downs and flannels. Marc's. All of his clothes hung there, untouched, like they were awaiting his return.

Heat crawled behind my eyes. I stared at my favorite pair of fall boots, unable to meet his gaze. "All of that can go to the thrift store."

Tom nodded.

After an uncomfortable beat, he squinted at a shelf. "Is that one of those folding things for shirts?"

"Yep. New and unopened."

He perked up. "Okay, yeah, I'm taking that."

I laughed, grateful for the break in tension. "Take anything you want, please."

We tackled the closet together, filling up half a dozen trash bags with clothes to donate. I no longer cared about the too-small clothes that hadn't fit in years, or the fast-fashion trends I'd never quite pulled off. I even parted ways with my comfiest maternity leggings. I folded Marc's things fast so I wouldn't think about him, wouldn't breathe in his smell that still clung to the fabric.

A horn honked out front a little before three, announcing Carmen's arrival. She climbed out of her beat-up Subaru with a travel mug in one hand and a canvas tote slung over her shoulder.

"How's it going?" she asked as she stepped inside, taking in my face first, then the row of trash bags lined up in the entryway.

"Alright," I said. "You can see the back of my closet now."

"Yeah, it got brutal in there," Tom added. "She Kon-Mari'd the hell out of that place."

Carmen's eyebrows shot up, impressed. "Nice." Her eyes swept the living room, assessing the stacked boxes and remaining clutter without a hint of judgment. "So, where do you need me?"

"Well, we're almost finished with my closet." My throat tightened as soon as I said the next part. "I'm thinking . . . Hazel's room." I swallowed. "We've been avoiding it."

Carmen responded with a slow nod. "Of course." She gave my arm a gentle squeeze. "We'll face it together and take it slowly, whenever you're ready."

The three of us finished the master closet in under half an hour. Tom handled the obvious donate-or-toss items, Carmen set aside the few things that needed thought, and I made the final decisions. No overthinking, just forward motion.

When Tom tied off the last bag, I paused in the doorway, bracing myself on the frame. The closet was empty now, all bare shelves and naked rods, the same blank slate it had been when we'd moved in three years ago.

I let out a slow breath. "Okay," I said at last. "Hazel's room."

We moved down the hallway gingerly, the aged hardwoods creaking and popping loudly beneath our feet. Hazel's door stood open. I wasn't sure if I'd left it that way or not.

The room looked so innocent from here. Her flower-shaped rug, her little bed. My pulse accelerated anyway, the air getting tighter the closer we got. My body remembered what my mind tried not to replay: the violent flutter of that dingy vintage rabbit launching into the air from within the closet.

Carmen slowed beside me, like she could feel something shifting too. Tom stayed a step behind, gripping a broom and dustpan like a sword and shield he might need against some invisible foe.

I nudged the door with my fingertips.

Hazel's room sat untouched, deceptively sweet in the golden afternoon light. Toys in their baskets. Books on their shelves.

Carmen turned to face the closet.

I held my breath as she reached out and parted the bifold panels.

The doors slid open on their tracks with a soft, familiar clatter, revealing rows of little clothes in soft pastels and floral patterns.

Nothing happened.

Nothing moved.

"Okay," Tom murmured, leaning the broom and dustpan against a wall. "I'll go grab some boxes."

I took a reluctant step forward, eyes drifting across the closet's contents.

On the top shelf sat several boxes labeled in my careful handwriting: *Newborn. Three Months. Six-to-Nine.* Each one was a time capsule of sleepless nights and milk-drunk smiles and a different version of Hazel I could barely picture anymore.

I reached up and pulled down the *Newborn* one. I set it down on the dresser, lifted the lid, and the smell hit me.

Baby shampoo and breast milk and exhaustion. My knees nearly gave out beneath me.

Tiny onesies. The hospital hat. Those super-soft muslin blankets I used to swaddle her in.

I swallowed hard as I went to lift out her first dress, a pink one with miniature owls printed across it, but my fingers stopped just shy of it. This was a terrible idea. I couldn't do this. Not right now. Not here.

I felt Carmen's eyes on me.

I shouldn't have started with the newborn stuff, of all things. What was I thinking?

"I'm gonna keep this box," I said, shoving the lid back onto it. "But I think the others should go to another mom who needs them."

Carmen nodded. "I drive past the women's shelter on my way home. I can drop them off for you, if you'd like."

Relief flooded my chest. "Yeah. That would be good. Thank you."

"Of course."

Tom returned with flattened boxes tucked under one arm and a roll of packing tape in his hand. He paused in the doorway, reading the room, eyes roaming from Carmen to me to the closed *Newborn* box. He opened his mouth to speak just as my phone buzzed in my back pocket.

I jumped, then fished it out.

An unfamiliar number. Decatur, Alabama.

My stomach flipped. "Sorry," I said. "I need to take this."

Tom stepped aside, giving me space to pass by as I hurried out of the room and pressed the phone to my ear.

"Hello?"

"Shannon, this is Hilda Birch," came her honeyed drawl. "I found that recording. My daughter can drive me out to Gurley on either Friday or Saturday. Which one works best for you?"

My thoughts spun, struggling to map out our schedule for the coming days. "Friday," I managed. "Friday sounds great."

"Alright, dear, we'll be over, say, ten o'clock Friday morning? Y'all be careful."

When the call ended, I stared at the phone screen, pulse pounding in my throat. Hilda Birch. The recording. The house exorcism they'd attempted in the nursery decades ago.

It was real.

And soon, I'd hear it.

We got Hazel's room packed that afternoon. I loaded her things into my CR-V to take back to Maureen's house, and Carmen took the old baby items. We filled Tom's Highlander with overstuffed garbage bags and made multiple trips to the thrift store until nothing but furniture and stacked boxes remained. That stuff would wait until the weekend, when Tom and Carmen's cousins could help haul it.

It felt good. Strange, but good. I felt lighter, as if I had finally shed a layer of dead skin I'd been afraid to let go of.

And then there was the barn.

The dreaded barn. That thing was packed to the rafters. I hadn't gone out there in a year. I had no idea what was waiting for me.

But it was time to find out.

FORTY-THREE

Shannon

August 25, 2022

THE SKY WAS THAT clear, endless, impossible blue you only get in North Alabama right before fall. A gentle breeze carried the first hint of cool in months, stirring the leaves at the tree line, whispering promises of changing seasons.

It should have felt comforting. Poetic, even. A new season, a new chapter. A clean slate.

Instead, unease coiled low in my stomach as Tom and I crossed the yard toward the barn. The day felt too bright, too perfect, as if something dark beneath it was waiting to surface.

The barn door groaned loudly as I tugged it open, metal grinding against metal. I braced for hornets, rats, something alive to explode out, but the shadows stayed still.

I slid the second door open, forcing sunlight into the dim space. The sight inside filled me with dread. It was worse than I remembered; not just cluttered, but suffocating. Plastic bins stacked to the rafters in leaning towers. Old paint cans and tubs of drywall putty. A barely-used tractor. Lumber. Tools. Rolls of hardware cloth still sealed in plastic. All the projects we'd planned, all our big ideas, piled atop the Carlisles' abandoned things. Two families' failures pressed together and left to rot.

Marc hadn't taken a single thing.

My stomach churned. "What do I do with all this?"

"Sell it?" Tom offered, not unkindly.

"We don't have time. Or energy." My throat tightened. "We barely have a week before closing."

He stepped forward and popped the latch of a rusty toolbox, brows lifting. "Could be worth some serious money, though."

I knew he was right. Anyone with half a brain would sell it all, get something back for the years I'd lost here. But the thought of photographing and listing it all and meeting strangers from Facebook Marketplace in parking lots made my chest clench tight.

"You could just open the doors and let people in to shop," he said with a shrug. "A yard sale."

I let out a weak laugh. "Yeah. Maybe." The idea wasn't bad. Extra money would help, and I'm sure the buyer would appreciate a cleared-out storage space.

"You don't have to decide right now," Tom said gently. "Let's just make a path, see what all's out here."

I sighed. "Yeah. Okay."

We began the excavation, hauling out one piece at a time. The air inside the barn was stale. Everything smelled like rat pee and old hay with a hint of dead mouse. We rolled out a rickety wheelbarrow, a broken-down lawnmower, several plastic storage bins filled with tangled Christmas lights and corroded extension cords.

A spider the size of a quarter darted across the top of one bin, and I yelped, dropping it hard enough to pop the lid loose.

Tom laughed but didn't say anything, which I appreciated.

We moved deeper, carving a narrow path through years of neglect. Dust coated my tongue. Sweat soaked through the back of my shirt, and my ponytail stuck to my neck. I pulled it free and kept going.

Tom lifted a quaint wooden tool carrier, open on top with a simple wooden handle. It looked hand-carved. "Man, some of this looks antique," he remarked.

"It probably is," I said, wiping my forehead. "The barn was full of old junk when we bought the place."

"Oh yeah, I remember. Marc acted like he hit the jackpot."

I remembered, too, how giddy both men had been when they realized the barn hadn't been cleared out. Marc had seen it as a gold mine. A treasure trove of tools, lumber, and parts, all for "free."

"Whoa!" Tom cried out.

My eyes snapped to him, heart pounding in my throat. He was standing near the back, glancing down at something.

"There's a chest freezer back here," he said.

I breathed, relieved his exclamation had been over something mundane. "Yeah, that thing's ancient. It was the Carlisles'."

The old chest freezer sat like a dingy, ivory sarcophagus in the back corner of the barn, streaked with rust, bannered with cobwebs, and sprinkled with rodent crap. Someone, probably Marc, had piled a bunch of junk on top of it.

"Looks like it's intact," Tom said. "You ever open it?"

"Nope." I stepped closer, swiping a cobweb out of my face. "Marc always said he was going to haul it out, but . . . yeah. We just started piling stuff around it and forgot it existed."

"Think it's empty?"

"I don't know. Probably. There's no power out here. We've never plugged it in."

"Hmm. Might be worth testing it out. This thing could be worth a small fortune if it still works."

"True," I said. "I guess we can try to get it out of there."

Less than enthused about the endeavor, I helped him clear off the debris—boxes, a broken dining chair, half a bale of moldy hay, a bucket filled with more extension cords.

And wedged behind the chair leg, the hand-painted wooden sign I'd forgotten about.

Joyce's Clubhouse
LORETTA KEEP OUT

Those uneven letters hit differently now that I knew the whole story.

I wondered if Joyce had ever looked back on the day she painted those words and wished she could scrub them clean. If she'd thought about the sign while the search parties combed the woods for her little sister. I held it out for Tom to see.

"Oh, wow," he breathed, taking it from my hands. "Looks like there was a bit of sibling rivalry between those two."

I nodded, but I couldn't stop picturing Joyce's obituary photo. That haunted look in her eyes.

Silence stretched between us for a moment, then Tom cleared his throat and set the sign gently on a nearby shelf.

"Alright," he said, forcing brightness into his voice. "Let's see what's in here." He gripped the grimy freezer door handle, lifted it, and peered down into the thing. "Wow."

Reluctantly, I joined him and found the interior to be in shockingly great shape. My overactive imagination had been expecting everything from a decayed corpse that had been stashed away for decades to a nest of rats, but the deep cavern was clean and appeared fully intact.

"Man," Tom said, running a finger along the edge of the chamber. "I bet you can get some good money for this thing."

Based on the interior's condition, I felt like he might be right. We closed the lid and, feeling a bit more motivated now, began to inch the massive thing forward.

My lower back wasn't happy, but together, we managed to drag it across the dusty floor, inch by inch. A patch of something darker revealed itself beneath it.

Wood. Old floorboards, blackened at the edges, warped and brittle, clearly different from the dirt-packed floor that made up the rest of the barn.

Tom and I spotted it at the same time.

We exchanged confused glances before abandoning the freezer.

As Tom crouched down to examine it, I heard him gasp. "Uh... Shannon?"

"What is it?"

"Look at this."

I squatted beside him, following his gaze. Set into the wood was a rusted iron ring.

"No way," I whispered.

"Trapdoor. Looks old."

My mouth went dry. "How the hell did we not know this was back here?"

"It's been covered up this whole time. 'Cause no one moved that heavy-ass freezer."

We both stared at the hatch, an uneasy tension settling in the air around us.

The freezer hadn't been sitting there by accident. It was hiding something.

"What do you think is down there?" I asked, pulse racing. I already knew I didn't want the answer.

He inhaled sharply. "Old barn like this? Could be a storm shelter. Or a root cellar."

We stared at each other in nervous silence.

"Wanna open it?" he asked.

I did, but everything inside me screamed to leave it alone. Ultimately, my curiosity won out. I nodded.

My heart pounded against my ribcage as Tom grabbed the ring and pulled. The door groaned as it opened, resisting at first, then giving way with a *pop*. Wood scraped against wood, and a cloud of dust billowed up, spilling out cold, damp air laced with the scent of earth, ash, and decay.

Beneath us, narrow stone stairs disappeared into the dark.

Forty-Four

I WENT DIZZY AS I peered into the gaping blackness below, my knees suddenly unsteady. I reached for Tom's arm without thinking, grounding myself in the solid weight of his forearm. Embarrassment flared through me when I realized how tightly I was gripping him, but I didn't let go.

There was something ancient in the air wafting up into my nostrils. Something still. Undisturbed for decades. It felt like a crypt.

Tom reached into his back pocket and pulled out his phone. He tapped the screen, clicking on the flashlight. The beam barely pierced the shadows.

"We've gotta see what's down there," he told me, his voice low, nearly a whisper.

I swallowed hard. "Do you think it's safe?"

He shrugged as he glanced at me, something unreadable passing through his eyes.

My pulse roared in my ears as I stared down into the darkness.

Tom went first, testing each step cautiously before fully committing his weight. I followed close behind, my iPhone held out in front of me, flashlight function engaged.

The deeper we descended, the colder it got. The air was damp and cave-like, tinged with rot and something faintly metallic.

We swept our flashlights slowly across the space as we reached the bottom. The floor was compressed earth, smooth and even. Stacked, raw-cut stones composed the walls, sagging in places where time had taken its toll. I had a sudden fear that it would collapse around us, burying us alive.

Wooden shelves lined the area, packed with food miraculously preserved from another era. Glass jars of fruits and vegetables. Crates full of fossil-like remnants of tubers, potatoes or beets.

A root cellar.

Goosebumps lined my arms as the newspaper article I'd found at the library slipped into my thoughts. The one that said Ada Ellison's body had been recovered from the root cellar by neighbors who arrived too late.

I wondered if Tom remembered. I couldn't bring myself to ask. It felt like we weren't supposed to speak down here.

In the far corner, our lights caught on something unusual, and my stomach turned.

A dark woolen blanket stretched across the floor, a flimsy pillow left behind at one end. A chipped enamel basin sat nearby, along with a rusted tin cup and a lidded mason jar long emptied of its contents.

Someone had been living down here.

Tom moved toward it cautiously, so I did too.

I gasped when I saw the rest.

A child's belongings had been arranged in the center of a pale linen cloth, now yellowed with age. A tiny calico dress, patterned with delicate blue flowers. A pair of scuffed leather shoes, their toes pointed outward, as if their wearer had only just stepped out of them. A bonnet, soft and threadbare with frayed edges, still held the ghostly shape of a little girl's head.

Next to the clothing rested a simple rag doll with a hand-stitched smile and dark button eyes. It would've been the creepiest thing I'd ever seen if it hadn't been so heartbreakingly sad.

I bent down, breath shallow. A ring of little carved wooden animals encircled the rag doll. A rabbit, fox, squirrel, bear, and deer. Imperfect edges and faint knife marks told me these creatures had been whittled by hand, lovingly shaped and sanded smooth. My stomach sank as I imagined Samuel Ellison making them for his daughter by firelight, before he vanished.

A leather-bound Bible sat nearby, the spine cracked, the faded gold lettering barely legible. A dried purple flower lay across it, pressed paper-thin, almost glowing in the light from my phone. It reminded me of the wild violets that sprouted along the tree line in early spring.

A viola. Of course it was.

I reached for it before I could stop myself. It was so brittle, it crumbled to dust beneath my fingertips.

My breath caught in my throat. Something about it broke me. This beautiful, fragile, little thing, preserved all this time, undone in an instant. By me.

The air thickened, heavy with grief.

Tom's flashlight beam wavered as he stood. "You okay?"

I nodded too quickly, already stepping back. "Yeah. Yeah, I just... I don't think I can be down here anymore."

"Yeah," he echoed, his voice tight. "Me neither."

We climbed back up the stone steps, neither of us saying another word.

The harsh midday sunlight blasted my face with heat as I pushed my way out of the barn. I squinted against it, dizzy and disoriented from the contrast. Birds chirped. A breeze rustled through the trees. The scattered mess of junk and tools spread across the yard assaulted my eyes.

It was jarring. Too bright. Too loud. Too *alive*. I felt like I'd crawled out of a grave.

Tom looked just as shaken. His face was unusually pale as he ran a hand through his hair.

We both stood there, not moving, not speaking. Just absorbing what we'd found.

I watched Tom tapping his phone. He met my eyes as he pinned the device to his ear. "I'm calling Carmen."

A good idea. We could use her help. This discovery changed things. I was no witch, no psychic, but even I could tell the vibes down there were way off. I wanted her to come over and check it out. Who else would know what to do with something like this?

He held the phone to his ear as he paced. "Yeah. We just found something. A root cellar, under the barn. Totally untouched. A kid's stuff. It's—yeah." A pause. "Weird energy down there."

I hugged my arms around my body. My skin crawled like something had followed me out. Like the root cellar was breathing down the back of my neck.

I turned away, walked a few feet into the grass, then sank to the ground. My knees gave out, or maybe I let them. The earth was cool beneath me. I closed my eyes, breathing deep, trying to push the heavy feeling off my chest.

After a while, Tom appeared beside me. His expression was tired, solemn.

"Carmen's on death watch," he said quietly. "Her patient's fading fast. She promised the family she would stay until the end. She'll come tomorrow, first thing."

Tomorrow was Friday, I realized then.

"Hilda's supposed to be here tomorrow," I said.

We both looked back at the barn. The doors remained open wide, revealing the chaos we'd dragged out into the yard. Junk everywhere. It looked worse than when we'd started.

The freezer was still sitting where we'd abandoned it, inches away from the hatch, looking ominous now that I knew what had been hiding beneath it.

I didn't know what to say. What to do.

Tom let out a heavy exhale. "We've been at it all morning. Want to take a break? Get outta here for a bit? Maybe we could grab some lunch . . . if you think you could eat."

I hesitated. My stomach didn't want food, but my body needed to be somewhere else. Anywhere else.

"Yeah," I said finally. "Getting out sounds good."

He gave a faint nod, reached for the barn doors, and tugged them closed with a thundering clang.

Forty-Five

Arlene's Kitchen out on Highway 72 looked like it hadn't updated a thing since perms and shoulder pads were all the rage. Tom parked the Highlander in front of the white cinderblock building capped with a red tin roof. A neon OPEN sign flickered in the window, and from my seat in the car, I could make out a chalkboard sign propped next to the door that read:

THURSDAY PLATE LUNCH: CHICKEN 'N' DRESSING $7.95
VEG OF THE DAY: TURNIP GREENS, SWEET CORN
PEACH COBBLER WHILE IT LASTS!

We stepped out into the sweltering afternoon and made our way to the entrance. Tom got the door for me, a jangling old cowbell announcing our arrival. The sunlight had felt unnatural after the root cellar, but the fluorescent lights in here were even worse. A wave of cornbread and fryer grease hit me like a wave. Why had I agreed to food?

It wasn't busy inside. The lunch crowd was long gone. I saw only a couple of elderly folks at the counter and a waitress wiping down tables with a rag that had seen better days.

We slid into a booth by the window. The vinyl seats were the color of faded rust, cracked and patched in places with silver strips of duct tape. The table wobbled slightly when I leaned on it. It was one of those old laminate-topped ones with a clear plastic cover, beneath which a collage of local business cards had been wedged over the years. Tow trucks, lawn care, a gospel quartet, plumbers. I spotted Tom's company logo on one and almost smiled, then I saw the name. *Lance Burrell*. Not Tom.

"You know this guy?" I asked, tapping Lance's smiling smug face.

Tom eased forward to look, squinting. "Oh. Yeah. Lance." He didn't bother to suppress an eye roll. "That guy's a hotshot. And he owes me lunch."

I felt my lips stretching into a grin at this new side of Tom. "Maybe you should sneakily replace his card with one of yours," I suggested.

"That's tempting," he said, grinning back at me. "But I bet you anything Lance checks this table once a week to make sure his face is still front and center."

I smirked. "What a shame. This could've been your claim to fame."

Tom leaned back in the booth with a low chuckle. "Trust me, if I ever make it onto one of these tables, I'll have officially peaked."

A silver-haired waitress approached us with a warm greeting and handed us menus. I wasn't hungry, but I ordered a sweet tea and the special with fried okra and corn just to feel normal.

Tom ordered sweet tea and the pork chop plate with mac-and-cheese, fried okra, and peach cobbler like it was his go-to. I wondered if it was.

Our drinks arrived in ruby red plastic Coca-Cola tumblers, syrupy sweet tea poured over tiny nuggets of ice. My favorite. I took a tentative sip, but it was practically medicinal. I instantly felt better.

We nursed our teas in silence, watching dust motes swirl through a sunbeam like tiny ghosts.

"I keep seeing that little dress," Tom said finally. "The shoes. The bonnet. I don't know, it was . . . sad." He paused. "Worse than sad."

I swallowed hard. "I know."

"It felt wrong being down there," he added. "Like it was something private. Like no one was meant to see it."

I ran my fingertips down one side of my cup, tracing the familiar ridges of the cheap plastic. The texture grounded me, something nostalgic and familiar in a day that had been anything but.

"Do you think Ada Ellison stayed down there after Viola disappeared?" I asked quietly. "Like she was waiting for her to come back?"

Tom nodded, his brown eyes locked on mine. "The same way Fern waited for Loretta."

I didn't realize I'd stopped breathing until my chest began to ache.

"And that article," he went on, softer now, "said her body was found down there."

My stomach twisted. The root cellar had felt like a tomb from the second we stepped inside. A place where pain and grief and death had soaked into the walls and never left. "You don't think she starved," I said, more statement than question.

"No. Those jars down there, they're old. Really old. I'd bet they've been down there since Ada's time."

"Then . . . what happened to her?"

Tom didn't answer right away. He stared past me, eyes fixed somewhere behind my shoulder, like he was mentally still in that underground tomb.

"She might've suffocated," he said at last. "If the fire spread far enough. Smoke might've made its way down there."

"Wouldn't there be signs of that?" I asked, though I didn't really want an answer. "Wouldn't there be fire damage?"

"There *was* fire damage," he said. "There was charring on and around the trapdoor, on the outside. The fire couldn't have gotten down to where she was, but the smoke could've. And if she was already weak, or . . ."

He left it at that.

I imagined it then. Smoke creeping in, slow and silent. Ada curled up asleep on the blanket next to her little girl's things, waiting for her return, unknowingly breathing it in.

After a few moments of tense silence, our waitress brought our food. The plates clinked noisily as she set them down before us. The country cooking smelled wonderful, but neither of us dug in with much enthusiasm.

Tom stabbed a piece of okra with his fork, but didn't eat it. "You gonna be able to sleep tonight?" he asked.

I let out a long breath. "Probably not. You?"

"I doubt it." He gave a tired shrug. "Might just pop some popcorn and turn on *Frasier* reruns."

I blinked, surprised into a breath of laughter. "Wait, *Frasier* is your comfort show?"

He glanced up, mock-defensive. "Don't hate. That show was smart. Witty."

"Oh, no, I always liked it too, I just haven't heard anybody talk about it in, like, twenty years. You do kinda give me Niles vibes."

"*Niles?* Really?"

"Mm-hmm. Well, minus the opera. And the neuroses. And… most of it, actually." I took a sip of sweet tea. "But I did notice the way you dodged those cobwebs and mouse turds in the barn."

"I would've Lysol'd if I could've."

"I knew it."

Tom shook his head, still grinning. "Alright, then. What's *your* go-to show when everything's gone to hell? *Gilmore Girls*?"

"… *The X-Files.*"

Tom snorted.

"Don't judge me. It's weirdly comforting."

"Right, nothing like a good government conspiracy to soothe the soul." He finally popped the okra on his fork into his mouth. He chewed it, swallowed, and said, "Man, that show freaked me out as a kid. I saw Mulder's sister get abducted when I was, like, six. Scarred me for life. I couldn't sleep unless I had one foot on the floor, like that would do anything to stop the grays from beaming me up."

A genuine laugh escaped my lips, real and warm. It felt mildly restorative, loosening the tightness in my chest. After the root cellar and everything we'd seen down there, this little moment, joking about *Frasier* and alien abductions, felt like a healing balm.

"Maybe I'll try that tonight," I said. "If the ghost acts up, I'll just dangle a foot off the bed."

"Hey now, I never got abducted, did I? Maybe six-year-old me had a pretty solid strategy."

"That is true."

Feeling lighter and emptier now, I reached for my fork and sampled the cornbread dressing. It was savory and rich and immediately comforting. It tasted like Thanksgiving dinner at Granny Jean's house, a taste memory so vivid it nearly brought tears to my eyes. Suddenly famished, I went in for more.

Tom's phone buzzed beside him on the table. Once. Twice. Three times. He finally looked at it, brows knitting together as he set down his fork.

I paused mid-bite, the warmth of the dressing fading in my mouth as I watched Tom's jaw tense.

The air around us seemed to shift again, like the spell had been broken. The heaviness we'd shaken off was creeping back in, crawling across the floor, and climbing up our legs.

"Everything okay?" I asked, though I could tell it wasn't.

Tom hesitated. "I, uh, I just got some texts from a client. I showed him a bunch of houses a couple weeks ago and never heard back from him." He paused, forehead creasing as he continued. "He wants to look at a few more properties this weekend."

Despite the irrationality, my stomach sank. "This weekend?"

"Yeah. He's pre-approved and ready to buy. Like, now." He rubbed his face. "I can refer him to someone else—"

"And lose your commission?" My heart ached, but I couldn't let him do that for me. He'd already put time into this other guy. He had bills to pay. A life. I couldn't ask him to put it all on hold just to deal with my mess.

"Hilda's coming over tomorrow," Tom said. "And Diego's bringing the trailer Saturday."

I didn't know what to say.

He sighed, flipping his phone face-down on the table. "Worst timing ever."

"Yeah."

We both stared at our plates for a long moment. My appetite had vanished once more.

Tom sat back and raked a hand through his hair. "Listen . . . I can do both. I swear. I'll go back to the office this afternoon, line up a few showings, get my ducks in a row. But I'll be back at Sunflower Lane tomorrow morning."

I studied his face, and he meant it. He was trying. "Okay. Well... what about this afternoon? We've got junk everywhere. The barn's still a wreck." I hated to bring it up, but there was no way I could go back out to the barn alone. Especially not after what I now knew lay beneath it.

Tom winced. "I know. I was thinking maybe we could knock out a little more when we get back. Just an hour or two. Then I'll head to the office and get the weekend scheduled. That way tomorrow's clear for Carmen and Hilda."

I bit the inside of my cheek, unsure.

"I'll be back in the morning bright and early," he added. "I swear on Martin Crane's armchair."

That made me crack a smile. "That's a serious promise."

"Sure is."

I looked at him for a long moment, then gave a nod. "Alright. As long as you're sure it isn't too much for you to juggle."

Tom gave me a crooked half-smile. "I'm okay at juggling."

Back at the barn, we worked hard and fast during Tom's last hour. We moved things around, tossed out obvious garbage, and made a pile of everything that looked valuable. It still looked like chaos—just slightly reorganized chaos. At least there was now a clear pathway in and out.

My eyes kept drifting to the hatch, to the root cellar. To the hidden shrine beneath our feet.

Eventually, Tom's phone dinged again, and I knew it was time for him to go.

He sighed and wiped his hands on his pants, glancing at me with reluctant apology. "I've gotta run."

I nodded, trying my best to keep my face neutral.

"I'll be here early tomorrow. With coffee," he promised. "Seven o'clock?"

"Sounds good."

"Okay. Now get the hell out of here." Tom gave me a strained smile, and he was gone. I watched his SUV back away, taillights flashing red as he disappeared down the long gravel drive.

I stood there a moment, just listening.

The barn loomed behind me, silent.

No wind. No birds. Nothing. I could hear my own heartbeat, and it was accelerating now that I was alone.

I didn't *want* to go back in, but I'd set my phone and keys on the workbench just inside the door. I'd tossed them there without thinking earlier.

I crossed the threshold and stopped cold.

The trapdoor to the cellar was open.

We had closed it.

Tom had pulled it shut before we left for lunch. Neither of us had touched it since.

Now it gaped open, the darkness within impenetrable. Cold air crept out from it and brushed against my skin. It felt charged, that just-before-a-storm feeling Hilda had talked about.

I took a single step forward to retrieve my things, and that's when I smelled it.

Smoke.

My throat tightened as I inhaled it. Burning wood. I scanned the space and saw no inky cloud, no haze. No flicker of firelight.

It vanished as quickly as it came.

I snatched my keys and phone off the bench and backed out of the barn without turning around.

Forty-Six

THE COMFORTING SCENT OF laundry detergent hit me the moment I opened Maureen's front door. The smell was familiar. Safe.

Maureen appeared in the kitchen doorway, curls frizzed out, a sheen of sweat above her lip. "Hey, Shannon. Thought I heard you pull up. We've been playing in the backyard." Her brow creased as she studied me. "You feelin' okay?"

I gave her a tired smile. "Yeah."

Before she could call me out on the lie, I heard the slap of little bare feet on linoleum. "Mommy!"

Hazel sprinted toward me, arms wide, grinning. I crouched and caught her, burying my face in her sun-warmed curls.

"Ah, I missed you!" I said, squeezing her close. "What've you been up to today?"

"Miss Maureen let me play in the hose!"

"The hose?"

Maureen nodded. "I hooked up my old sprinkler. We had ourselves a grand old time."

I laughed, though the sound came out thinner than I intended. "Sounds like fun."

"I made you a picture!" Hazel said, tugging my hand. "Come see!"

She dragged me toward the coffee table where a pile of crayons and paper had taken over. She rifled through her stack of creations and pulled one out with both hands, beaming. "See? That's you."

She pointed to a stick figure with brown hair and a blue scribble of clothes. Big, jagged crayon strokes in red, orange, and yellow surrounded the figure, swallowing up most of the paper. "And that's fire."

My knees turned to gelatin as I stared, taking it in.

She pointed to another figure drawn beside mine. This one lay on the ground, consumed by flames. Its face was blacked out violently in thick black scribbles applied with such pressure, it had torn the paper.

"Do you like it?" Hazel asked.

I couldn't find words to reply.

"The lady that lives under the barn told me to draw it for you," Hazel said, like it was nothing. "She said it was important."

I felt like my legs might buckle under me. I needed to sit. I scrambled for the couch and sank onto it, not taking my eyes off the drawing for a second.

I heard Maureen clear her throat behind me. I glanced up at her and found her gaze fixed on me intensely, concern etched all over her face. She gave me a wordless we-need-to-talk-now look.

"Hey, sweet pea, do you wanna watch something?" Maureen suggested, grabbing the remote. "How 'bout I turn on *Bluey*?"

Hazel perked up. "Okay!"

Maureen switched on the TV, pulled up the beloved cartoon, and started a familiar episode. We waited until Hazel was safely engrossed before we moved together into the adjacent dining room.

"That picture . . ." Maureen began softly, then trailed off. She leaned against the table, gripping the edge with tight fists, knuckles pale. "It's like something out of a nightmare."

I nodded, still clutching the drawing in my hand. The flames seemed to pulse on the page if I looked at it too long.

Maureen raised her eyebrows. "And what in the world did she mean by the lady that lives under the barn?"

I stared at her. For days, I'd avoided the truth, letting Maureen believe we were here because of vague domestic troubles. I could keep doing that. It would be easier.

"Maureen, if I'm going to answer you honestly . . . I have to tell you why we're here. Why we left."

She didn't speak, just waited.

I slid my sweaty palm over my face. "Our house has a history," I said, my tongue going dry. "A little girl named Viola vanished from there in the 1800s. Her mother died in a fire soon after. And in the sixties . . . another little girl disappeared. Loretta Carlisle. Both of them were Hazel's age when it happened."

Her eyes widened and, for a moment, she looked past me toward the living room. "Loretta Carlisle," she repeated, her voice low. "I think I've heard that name before."

I slid out a dining chair and sat down hard. "It's not a coincidence, Maureen. It's a pattern. And I think—" My voice shook. "I know it sounds insane, but I think whatever took them is still there. And now it's found Hazel."

Maureen rubbed the side of her face like she was trying to make sense of it all. "So, what are you saying? You really believe your daughter's been talking to . . . to some dead woman? From under your barn?"

I looked down at the drawing again, afraid to meet her eyes. "To tell you the truth, I don't know what I believe anymore."

Maureen folded her arms across her chest. "Do you . . ." She faltered, her voice dropping to a whisper. "Do you think something *evil* is in that house?"

The word *evil* hung heavily between us.

"I think . . . something's wrong," I said carefully. "Very wrong." I paused, heart pounding in my chest. "And Hazel is somehow connected to it."

Maureen glanced toward the living room, toward Hazel's silhouette illuminated by the soft flicker of the animation onscreen. Her face was tight. "Lord have mercy."

There was a long silence. Bluey and Bingo giggled in the background.

"I thought getting out of there would keep her safe," I said, voice cracking. "But I think it followed us."

Maureen's lips pressed together, and I saw something shift behind her eyes. Fear, yes, but something else. "You're telling me something evil has followed you here. Into my home. And it's got its sights set on that little girl."

I couldn't think of a response.

Her expression hardened with resolve. "Then we close every door to it. The Scriptures say not to give the devil a foothold. If it thinks it can take one step in here, it's wrong."

I opened my mouth, but she raised a hand to stop me.

"I'll pray over her tonight, Shannon, and over you. And I'll pray all over this house, asking the Lord to drive it out. Every room, every corner."

She reached for the drawing. "Whatever this is, it's not welcome here. I rebuke it in the name of Jesus, and I claim this home for the Lord."

I wished the Lord lived closer to the barn.

Forty-Seven

Shannnon

August 26, 2022

I left Maureen's before sunrise on Friday, the roads black and empty except for my headlights. I hadn't really slept, just drifted in and out of shallow, anxious dreams until lying in bed became unbearable.

Hazel's drawing hovered at the forefront of my consciousness the whole night.

Fire swallowing me. A scribbled-out face.

The lady that lives under the barn told me to draw it for you.

I gripped the steering wheel harder.

By the time I turned onto Sunflower Lane, my stomach was in knots. The closer I got, the harder my body fought. My muscles tightened, breath shortened, like every cell inside me was scream-ing, *Abort mission! Turn around!*

As I inched toward the house, I wanted to keep driving, to pretend none of this had touched my child, or me, or the life we once had.

But I couldn't do that.

I forced the CR-V down the gravel driveway.

The sun hadn't fully climbed the horizon yet. Pastel light washed over the yard as the sky blushed shades of peach and lavender, too beautiful for this place.

Fog crept low across the field, dense and white, rolling in slow, curling ribbons that drifted and coiled around the grass. It gathered thickest where the yard met the tree line, swallowing trunks and branches into fragments, like the woods themselves were dissolving.

The mist had claimed most of the barn, too. Only the roofline showed, while the rest of it disappeared into the white.

I eased to a stop and cut the engine.

The house rose before me through the smoky haze, edges softened by the patchy film, windows dark and impenetrable.

For a moment, I sat there in the heavy quiet, watching the fog shift and glide as my own breath misted in the cold air inside the car.

I checked the rearview mirror out of habit, checking Hazel's car seat in the back. She wasn't there, of course. My chest clenched at the empty space.

Headlights appeared through the fog at the far end of the driveway, two pale beams cutting through the mist as a familiar black SUV rolled toward me.

Some of my anxiety eased as Tom pulled up beside me.

We got out at the same time and met between the cars.

"Morning," he greeted me. He carried a white paper bag and two coffees. He held one out for me to take. "Large latte with an extra shot of espresso. Figured you probably slept about as well as I did."

I managed a smile and thanked him as I brought the cup to my lips. The espresso was bitter and sharp. Good. I needed the sting.

"I also brought breakfast." Tom lifted the bag slightly. "Bacon and Gouda paninis from that hipster place at Lincoln Mill. And, uh, also . . . two cranberry orange scones. Because I panicked and ordered both."

A nervous laugh escaped me.

We didn't move toward the house. We didn't move toward the barn either. Instead, we hovered there beside our cars, staring at the thick fog curling around our ankles.

Tom blew out a breath. "Man. Just when you thought this place couldn't get any creepier."

I appreciated his attempt to lighten the moment and tried my best to match his tone. "Yeah. I almost turned around twice."

"Only twice? Now I'm embarrassed."

A smile tugged at the corners of my mouth, but didn't quite make it. The mist settled on my skin like damp, clammy hands.

"Okay," he said, shifting the bag in his hand. "We can't face evil on an empty stomach. That's where I draw the line. Car picnic?"

I huffed something close to a laugh. "Sure."

He opened his passenger door for me, the glow of the dome light cutting into the mist.

We ate in quiet, coffee steaming in the unseasonably chilly morning air. It felt strange to be eating breakfast out here, like we were casually tailgating a haunted house. *My* haunted house. But better out here than in there, I decided.

After a few bites, I cleared my throat. "Did you hear from Carmen?"

"Yeah. Her patient passed a little after midnight." His voice softened. "She stayed with the family until they were ready to let her go."

"Let *her* go?"

He nodded. "Sometimes families don't want the nurse to leave. Once she goes . . . the moment becomes real."

My heart sank.

"She texted me when she got home," he added quietly. "It was around three. She said she'd rest a bit and be here by ten."

"That's a lot."

"I know," Tom murmured. "I don't know how she does it, but she does."

He sipped his coffee as he stared out the windshield at the fog-shrouded barn.

"Carmen's built different," he said simply. "Always has been."

I dabbed a paper napkin across my lips as I waited for him to go on.

"When we were kids, our abuela got sick." His voice softened. "She was placed on hospice, at our house. Carmen sat with her for days. Holding her hand. Talking to her. I couldn't even go in there." He shook his head. "I was eight. Scared outta my mind. The whole house smelled like candles and medicine, and I just—I couldn't do it."

His fingers flexed on the coffee cup, remembering.

"Carmen was twelve," he said. "*Twelve.* Sitting there, watching someone go like she'd been doing it her whole life."

He finally turned to me. For a split second, I didn't see the man sitting there, but a scared little boy, lurking outside a bedroom door he couldn't make himself walk through.

"She's always been braver than me. Stronger."

A lump rose in my throat. "Tom," I breathed. "You were just a kid."

He didn't answer at first. Just peered out the windshield as the fog pressed against the glass, his jaw set tight, coffee in his hands. "Guess I still feel like that kid sometimes," he said at last. "Which is why I'm damn glad she's coming here today."

Eventually, we forced ourselves out and headed back toward the barn. Unlike when I'd left yesterday, the trapdoor was shut. Maybe a gust of wind had blown it closed overnight. I didn't want to entertain other possibilities, not if I expected to stay out here and function.

We kept our distance from that corner and moved through the clutter like we had a plan, which we did not. I divided things into piles. Tom snapped pictures of tools and farming equipment, texting a few contacts to see if anyone was interested. I didn't stop him. The tractor, hardware cloth, and an antique saw all had interested buyers within the hour.

Rifling through the mess helped. It gave my hands something to do and my brain something to focus on that wasn't a stone staircase disappearing into the earth.

But every so often, I felt my eyes tug back toward that closed hatch, and by nine-thirty, my nerves felt stretched thin. I kept glancing toward the driveway, hoping for and dreading Hilda's arrival in equal measure.

Right at ten o'clock, the crunch of gravel caught our attention.

My heart kicked hard. I wiped my damp palms on my leggings and watched as a white sedan rolled up the drive and stopped behind Tom's SUV, engine idling for a long moment before cutting off.

Hilda Birch stepped out first, her petite frame swallowed by an oversized quilted jacket in a powdery blue that nearly matched her eyes. Her snowy hair was pinned back in a dignified bun.

Her daughter emerged from the driver's side. She was taller, with a stouter build, soft features, and neat silver curls cropped at her chin. She wore a silky emerald blouse, tailored gray trousers, and expensive-looking black leather loafers that made me feel under-dressed in my grimy T-shirt and leggings.

As Tom and I moved forward to greet them, I wondered what they saw when they looked at this house. What did they feel standing on this land?

What exactly had I dragged them into?

Hilda shaded her eyes and smiled when she spotted us. "Morning," she called out in that sing-song lilt of hers, leaning heavily on a wooden cane as she crossed the gravel with small, cautious steps.

Her daughter followed closely, one hand clutching a stylish leather tote, the other gripping the handle of a small, rectangular case.

"Hi, there, I'm Rebecca," she said brightly, offering a cheerful smile as though visiting haunted properties was something she did between salon appointments and Pilates class.

She looked so thoroughly unfazed, I wondered if she'd grown up like this. Riding around bored in the backseat while her parents investigated haunted houses and places marred by old tragedies. Was this just normal life for her?

"Thank you so much for coming," I managed, sweeping my hands self-consciously across my thighs to knock away the dust. "I know it was quite a drive here from Decatur."

"Oh, we enjoyed it," Rebecca insisted. "Mother hasn't been out this way in years."

"Yes, so much has changed," Hilda murmured. Her gaze lifted past us, landing on the house. With a slight shake of her head, she added, "But not this place."

Her tone held a gravity that made my stomach drop, like the years separating us from Fern had collapsed. History was no longer behind us. It had circled back.

I swallowed. "Well, um, should we go inside?"

Tom and I led the way up the porch steps. The old boards groaned beneath our feet, like the house was complaining about our presence. Hilda followed slowly, her cane clunking against each step in a steady rhythm.

I pushed open the door. Tom and I crossed the threshold, but Hilda stopped.

She paused at the doorway and pressed her palm against the frame. Rebecca waited behind her, patient and composed, as though she'd watched her mother do this a hundred times.

Hilda bowed her head reverently. "We enter this place in peace," she said to the house, to whatever listened. "In the name of Jesus Christ, you will return that peace to us. No harm will come to those under His hand."

Only then did she and Rebecca step inside.

Hilda's gaze moved slowly over the entryway, taking it in with a quiet solemnness. I imagined her here six decades ago, stepping into this same room with her husband to pray over Fern Carlisle.

What had it felt like back then? Had Fern stood in the same spot as me, spine stiff, palms sweaty, trying to pretend she wasn't terrified?

Tom and I had shoved all the furniture against the walls in preparation for moving day tomorrow, leaving the living room too open, too bare. It felt uncannily exposed, like we'd peeled off the house's skin and were staring straight at its bones.

I hovered awkwardly, unsure what to do or say. This was still my house, technically, and instinct tugged at me to play hostess. To offer a seat, a drink, something. But that didn't feel right.

I didn't get the chance anyway. Rebecca set her tote and the small case on the coffee table and immediately got down to business. "I think we should begin by listening to the recording," she said.

She flipped open two silver clasps on the case and lifted the lid, revealing a row of buttons and a smooth metal face with two empty spools for eyes. A compact, vintage machine that I'd only ever seen in old detective shows I'd watched with my dad as a kid.

A reel-to-reel tape recorder.

"I tested it this morning," Rebecca said. "Still works just fine."

"Wow," Tom breathed, gaping at the relic with wide eyes.

With careful precision, Rebecca set the reel into place and threaded the thin, fragile tape through a narrow path of metal pieces, winding it onto the empty spool on the right.

A knock at the front door nearly sent me through the ceiling.

"Jesus," I breathed, hand flying to my chest.

"That should be Carmen," Tom said. To the others, he added, "My sister."

Pulse hammering, I crossed the room on shaky legs and pulled open the door.

Carmen Altamira stood on my porch, long black dress brushing against her sandaled feet, a belt of brass rings gleaming at her waist, her dark curls gathered beneath a knotted black scarf. Her eyes were clear and steady for someone who'd stared death in the face only hours ago.

"Hey," she said, voice low. "Did I miss anything?"

"Nope. We're about to listen to the Birches' recording. Come in."

I made the necessary introductions, and we all took our seats.

A hush fell over the room.

"This recording was made here in May 1963," Rebecca said, "in the nursery."

My heart thudded in my throat as her finger hovered over the switch marked *Play*.

"Around the ten-minute mark, there are voices," Hilda said, her eyes meeting mine. "Harry and I never could make out what they were saying. I'm curious what y'all hear."

My mouth went dry. I nodded, bracing myself.

CLICK.

Forty-Eight

The tape crackled. A low hiss filled the room.

A man's voice, garbled and staticky, formal in that stiff, mid-century way:

"Mrs. Carlisle, I want to begin by asking you a few questions. And I must warn you, some of them might be a little uncomfortable."

A pause.

Then a woman's quavering reply, barely above a whisper:

"Okay."

My heart lurched.

Fern.

Reading about this moment in the Birches' book had been one thing, but hearing Fern's voice? Hearing the tremor in her breath, the hesitation before she forced out the single word? It made her real in a way that sealed my throat.

My eyes stung as I listened to Harry Birch pressing her to reveal unconfessed sin, to the crackling silence where Fern couldn't answer, to Hilda's soft encouragement about the Lord's faithfulness to forgive.

As the questioning dragged on, Rebecca reached over and turned up the volume.

Hilda's voice came through louder, narrating her husband's actions:

"Harry has oil that we've prayed over. He's now making a cross on the closet doors."

Rustling. Movement. Then Harry's Southern-Baptist-preacher voice erupted:

"This place belongs to the Lord. In the name of Jesus Christ, we command all evil entities to flee!"

Hilda began to sing, her smooth alto warped by age and tape distortion:

"Would you be free from your burden of sin? There's pow'r in the blood, pow'r in the blood . . ."

Before me, seated on the armchair in my living room, elderly Hilda closed her eyes, as if bracing for a blow she already knew was coming.

I leaned forward, breath held, listening harder.

A woman's whisper surfaced in the static, too faint to make out against the background noises, but unmistakably human. And terrified.

My skin turned to ice.

"There is pow'r, pow'r . . ."

Another whisper layered over the first, higher, urgent, strangled at the end like someone was holding the speaker underwater.

". . . wonder-working pow'r . . ."

A child whimpered.

". . . in the blood of the Lamb . . ."

A woman's pleading gasps tore through, the same desperate syllables repeated over and over until they withered beneath her weeping.

I glanced at Carmen, whose unruffled gaze was fixed firmly on the spinning reels.

We listened to the rest of the tape, hearing the complete session the Birches had documented in *Ministers of Deliverance*. At last, Rebecca shut off the player with a clunk.

Silence flooded the room. We all sat there staring at the machine.

Rebecca cleared her throat softly. "What we just heard," she said at last, "is EVP. Electronic Voice Phenomena."

Hilda nodded. "Harry and I thought, when we first replayed this recording all those years ago, that these voices were demonic spirits. Toying with us. Trying to frighten us. All of it was hard to make out, but you might've noticed some words weren't even in English."

"Latin?" Tom ventured, the sort of guess anyone made when horror movies were your only reference point.

"That's what we thought too," Hilda said. "Or maybe Hebrew or Aramaic, one of the old biblical languages twisted in mockery. We just didn't know anyone who could help us understand it back then."

Carmen shifted in her seat. "It didn't sound like any of those," she murmured. "Not that I'm an expert, but it didn't sound quite right."

"No, it didn't," Hilda agreed. She drew a thin, shaky breath. "And I no longer believe it was the Enemy on that tape." Her hand trembled against her cane. "Listening now . . ." She swallowed hard. "It sounds too human."

A chill crawled up my spine. She was right. Those repeated syllables, buried under all that sobbing, weren't meant to frighten us. They were a broken, desperate plea. The sound of someone's grief.

Someone's pain. Raw and unbearable and bottomless. Deeply human.

Tom spoke up, his voice barely above a whisper. "Those were people." He stared at the recorder. "Echoes of people. Trapped in this place."

Hilda gave a solemn nod. "Something terrible happened here," she said. "And this place has seen nothing but sorrow ever since."

My stomach rolled. The room seemed to tilt, like the floor had shifted under us.

I remembered the trapdoor. The smell of raw earth. The buried shrine Tom and I had uncovered only yesterday.

"There's . . . um," I began weakly, "there's something we need to show you."

Tom pulled open the hatch, and a gust of air rushed up to meet us. This time, it wasn't just cool, it was frigid. I shivered.

We'd come prepared with flashlights this time, which I distributed among our group. As I flicked mine on and angled it into the opening, Rebecca frowned at the narrow stone steps leading down into darkness.

"Mother, you don't need to go down there," she said gently. "It isn't safe."

Hilda lifted her chin and met her daughter's gaze. "I have to," she said. "I have to see what we missed."

Her words carried a weight that stilled all of us.

Rebecca pressed her lips together but didn't argue.

Carmen went first, taking each step gingerly in her sandals, a silver anklet with a moon charm jangling softly as she descended. Tom followed close behind her.

I went next, pressing a hand against the rough wall for balance. Cold radiated from the stone, seeping straight into my skin. With each step, the weight of the air thickened, pressing against my ribs.

Behind me, Rebecca supported Hilda as they took one cautious step at a time. The soft tap of Hilda's cane against each stone echoed thinly.

"Easy," Rebecca murmured, her voice tight with worry.

"I'm all right," Hilda assured her, though her breath sounded strained.

Carmen reached the dirt floor and moved forward into the cellar with a wariness that wasn't like her usual confident stride. She scanned the room slowly, sweeping her flashlight in a slow arc across the space.

Tom joined her. I stepped off the last stair a moment later, then finally Rebecca and Hilda, who lingered at the bottom, close enough to see everything, to feel the shift in the air, but not far enough to risk stepping fully inside.

Everything was just as I remembered.

The blanket.

The pillow.

The little dress. The toy animals.

Hilda's breath hitched sharply behind me.

"Oh, my word," Rebecca exhaled.

We'd already told them what Tom and I found down here, but knowing it and *seeing* it were two very different things.

Carmen turned slowly. "The grief here . . ." She lifted her gaze to us, eyes shimmering with tears. "It's heavy. But it's not just grief. This is a place of devotion. Of waiting. She loved her child so fiercely, she refused to let go, even after death."

Tom glanced around uneasily. "Ada Ellison?"

"She was here long before Fern ever came. I think . . ." Carmen paused. "I think she never left."

Hilda took in a slow, shuddering breath. "All those years," she murmured, "we thought the Carlisles were battling demons. But it was a grieving mother's cry we were hearing. And we called it evil." Her jaw quivered as her eyes fixed on the blanket. "We were so sure back then. So certain we understood." A tear slipped down her cheek. "But we didn't. We didn't understand anything at all."

Rebecca rested her hand tenderly on Hilda's arm. "You couldn't have known, Mother. No one could've." Turning to Carmen, her voice wavering between logic and fear, she asked, "But if this was a mother's grief, if Ada Ellison never moved on, does that mean she's the one who's been taking the girls?"

Carmen grew silent for a moment. "I don't think so. The energy down here doesn't feel malevolent. It's just . . . sorrowful."

The space began to feel even colder, and I wrapped my arms around myself.

"She and Fern have both been trying to reach you, Shannon," Carmen said. "They're more than just residual sadness. They're still *here*. Trying to keep you from joining them."

Tom's brow knitted with concern. "What do you mean, joining them?"

Carmen turned to him. "They were both mothers who lost their daughters. They stayed here, rooted to this place, waiting. And now . . ." Her eyes met mine. "You're a mother living here too, with your little girl. They recognize the pattern."

The air thickened, slow and suffocating. I felt it in my throat, in my chest, like trying to breathe through smoke.

"So, if Ada and Fern are stuck here, trying to protect Shannon and Hazel . . ." Tom's voice shook. "Then who's the threat?"

We fell into a tense silence. A faint creak sounded above us. None of us moved.

The flashlight beam in Carmen's hand flickered. Once. Twice. She gave it a little shake, but the light dimmed again, struggling to hold.

On the floor before us, one of the little carved wooden animals toppled onto its side.

No one had touched it.

A chill skittered down my back.

Rebecca whispered, "Did you see that?"

Carmen's eyes were scanning the room again, slower this time, more careful. "Something's changed," she breathed. "Someone wants to be seen."

Her flashlight beam moved across the floor toward the little shrine in the corner.

That's when I saw it.

I froze.

Tom tilted his head, frowning slightly. "Was that Bible open like that before?" he asked.

"No," I said immediately.

The old leather King James Version with its faded gold lettering had been closed. I remembered this clearly, because a dried viola had rested on top, and I'd crushed it by accident. It had felt like a desecration.

But now, the book lay open. Resting on its pages was a bundle of yellowed paper, folded neatly, curling at the edges.

"Those weren't here before," I said. "I swear they weren't."

Carmen turned to me, her expression serious. "Are you absolutely sure?"

"Yes. I looked right there."

Hilda drew in a shaky breath. "That's a sign," she whispered. "Someone's reaching out."

"Mother, don't go over there," Rebecca insisted softly, pulling her a half-step back.

I swallowed, throat tight, and crossed the small space on unsteady legs. My heart hammered as I crouched down and picked up the papers with trembling fingers. Beneath them lay a stubby little graphite pencil, its end crudely whittled into a blunted point.

I unfolded the paper bundle and discovered several loose sheets, some filled with cramped handwriting, others still blank.

Tom and Carmen moved in close on either side of me. Together, we leaned in, our flashlights spotlighting the pages. The cursive handwriting was tight and slanted.

January 1, 1871

"These are . . . I think they're Ada Ellison's journal pages," I said aloud, as much to myself as the others.

I scanned the page, unable to focus, glimpsing words like *cold, Viola, beginning* written in small, delicately curling script.

BANG.

Something slammed hard against the wood above us.

Hilda flinched violently, grabbing for the wall. Rebecca caught her by the elbow and pulled her close.

Tom's flashlight swung upward. "Someone's up there."

A cold bolt of fear shot down my spine.

I imagined it instantly: the trapdoor slamming shut. The deep freezer rolled back over it. No one knowing we were down here.

No way out.

"We need to go," I said, my voice shaking.

Rebecca slipped her arm firmly around Hilda. "Come on. Let's get moving." Her voice was tight and controlled, an inadequate attempt to conceal her terror.

Hilda nodded weakly and began up the stairs with her daughter, the uneven taps of her cane striking the stone more sharply than before.

I hauled myself out of the opening and into the barn with the others, sucking in a shuddering breath the second I was on solid ground. I looked toward the source of the noise, but there was nothing to see.

The barn was empty.

Everything was exactly where we'd left it. Not a single thing had been disturbed.

"There's no one here," Tom said.

But it didn't feel like no one.

I sensed someone, or *something*, lurking just out of sight.

"Something wanted us out of there," Carmen said, her voice low. "Or maybe it didn't want us to read more."

I glanced down at the bundle of Ada Ellison's papers in my hands. I folded them and clutched them tightly.

My phone buzzed in my back pocket.

I jumped hard enough that Rebecca flinched beside me.

I pulled my phone out with numb fingers and found a text from Maureen:

Are you on your way back soon? Hazel's acting strange. Something is wrong.

Forty-Nine

I was shaking so badly, Tom insisted on driving me to Maureen's. He didn't argue when I said we had to take my car. Hazel's car seat was in the back, and I wasn't about to leave it here. Not when I had no idea what we were walking into.

Carmen followed close behind us in her beat-up Subaru, eager to help however she could. Hilda had wanted to come too—had tried to— but Rebecca stopped her.

"Mother, no," she'd said. "This is too much for you. We'll only slow them down."

Hilda's face had crumpled in a way that made my heart ache. "This is happening now because I didn't understand what was really happening back then," she said. Her hand found my wrist, her skin papery and delicate against mine. "I've caused enough harm thinking I understood this place."

Tears welled in her eyes as Rebecca gently tugged at her arm.

"I won't get in your way," Hilda said, voice breaking. "Go. Save your little girl. Do what I couldn't."

"I don't know how!" The words tore out of me before I could stop them. My voice cracked, raw and panicked. "I don't know what to do, Hilda. I don't know how to help her."

Hilda took my hand between both of hers, her grip trembling but strong. She nodded toward Carmen. "Let her lead. You're not alone in this. Just get to your baby. We're praying for you."

Now, in the car, the only sounds were the low hum of tires on asphalt and the occasional squeak of the wipers as a light rain began to fall. The sky had gone gray, and the road ahead blurred in the drizzle.

The weight of what we'd just experienced pressed down on Tom and me both. I couldn't stop hearing that sound we'd heard in the root cellar. The slam above us. The chill that followed. The heavy sense that something wanted us out.

I still hadn't let go of Ada Ellison's journal pages. I flipped through the bundle with care, skimming the slanted cursive, the writing faded but legible. Each entry began with a date, and something about seeing them, those preserved fragments of a life lived so long before mine, made the hair on my arms rise.

I needed to understand where it started. So I shuffled through the pages until I found the earliest one.

January 1, 1871.

As I began to read, however, I was surprised to realize these weren't journal entries.

They were letters.

January 1, 1871

Dearest Mama,

I rose before the sun today. The cold air nipped at me

through my shawl, but I stood outside and watched the frost glittering on the pines, silver and serene. It was so quiet I could almost imagine the earth itself was waiting, holding its breath for the year to begin. I thought of you. You always loved the first of the year and the promise of hope it brings. A fresh start, a new beginning.

I whispered a prayer in my heart. For strength. For peace in this house. For Viola's and Samuel's health. For the Lord to make something good of this land. I don't know what this year will bring, but I want to believe it can be better than the last.

Samuel hasn't smiled in ages. His silences stretch longer. When he does speak, he is often harsh and unkind. But he did give me these papers and pencils for Christmas. He remembered that I love to write. Paper is so dear now. I will try, likely in vain, to be brief.

It feels important to begin something new today, of all days. So I will write to you. Not because I expect you to answer, of course, but because you are the one I would've written if I could. Maybe I just need to feel like someone is listening.

Viola is three now. She is so bright. Always listening, always watching, absorbing everything around her. She speaks with the vocabulary of a much older child.

It is often easy to forget she is but three! And my, the strange things her curious little mind concocts. She is a queer one. I hope you do not think me unkind to say such. Once, I caught her whispering to the empty corner of the room. I asked who she was talking to and she said, "She talks to me when you're busy."

When I asked who "she" was, she only shrugged and changed the subject. I expect it's an imaginary friend. She has no other children to play with, and we're far from neighbors. She must be lonesome. Still—I worry. She is too quiet sometimes. She listens to things I cannot hear.

But perhaps she is not so different from me. After all, here I sit writing to you, dearest Mama, long after you're gone. Maybe we all just need someone to talk to.

Please keep watch over us.
With all my love,
Ada

I stopped, the page fluttering in my shaking hands.

I blinked and glanced at Tom, who kept his eyes focused on the rainy road before us. "They're letters," I said softly. "From Ada. To her mother."

He frowned slightly. "She never sent them?"

I shook my head. "It sounds like her mother had already passed. I think . . . I think Ada wrote them because she was lonely. Because she missed her."

Tom didn't say anything. Just kept one hand on the wheel, the other resting near the gearshift like he was lost in thought.

Rain fell harder against the windshield, and he flicked the wipers up a notch.

I glanced back down at the letters, straining to read Ada's tight, antiquated cursive in the dim gray light. I found the next one, dated January 12.

January 12, 1871

Dearest Mama,

The days have turned colder, and the wind has not let up. It howls against our roof at night like a living beast, shaking the shutters and rattling the door latch until I begin to pray aloud. I try not to let Viola hear my fear, but she is a sensitive child. She asks me why the wind is angry. I tell her it's only winter. She doesn't believe me.

Samuel came in late tonight. I don't know where he had been. His boots were muddy, and his face was pale as fresh snow. When I asked if he was unwell, he muttered something about needing to clear his head and went to bed without supper.

I miss the sound of his laughter.

*There is no one to talk to but you. I hope you can hear
me, wherever you are.*

With all my love,
Ada

I blinked, the words blurring as tears threatened to come. The
way she described Samuel—withdrawn, distant, unreachable. It
was too familiar.

I thought of Marc. How he'd stopped eating with us. How he'd
vanish for hours with no explanation, only to return angrier than
when he'd left. How I had missed his smiles and laughter, too.

And then there was how she painted Viola. Sensitive. Strange.
Talking to someone who wasn't there. Hazel had always been
the same way. Tender-hearted. Dreamy-eyed. Hearing things I
couldn't hear. Seeing things I couldn't see.

The parallels were too sharp. I couldn't read anymore. Not right
now. I folded the pages carefully and laid them back in my lap.

Outside, rain lashed harder against the windshield. My heart
climbed into my throat.

I was glad Tom had driven.

I suddenly felt more afraid than I'd ever been in my life.

I unbuckled the second the CR-V rolled to a stop, before Tom even shut off the engine. The moment he did, I launched myself out of the vehicle and into the pouring rain.

Maureen creaked open the screen door as I scrambled up the walkway. She held it open for me, face blanched, features tight with concern.

"She's in the guest room," she said. "She's alright, but she won't talk to me. And Shannon . . ." She stepped aside, lowering her voice. "There's black stuff on her hands. All over her clothes. It looks like dirt. I don't know how it got there."

A car door slammed behind us, and my head snapped toward the sound. Carmen had arrived. I watched as she and Tom dashed through the rain to join us.

We hurried into the living room alongside Maureen.

"Tell us exactly what happened," Carmen told her.

"She told me she was tired, so I put her down for a nap. I figured she must've meant it. How often does a kid say that on their own? Anyway, I got her set up in the guest room, then I went and did some housework. A little while later, I thought I heard the back door open. I went to check, and I found Hazel standing out in the backyard, in the rain, staring at the trees."

Maureen shivered a little, like saying it aloud made it more real.

"She was barefoot," she added. "Just standing there, soaking wet, like she didn't even feel the rain hitting her. I asked her what she was doing, and she just . . . looked at me. Like she didn't know me. Then she went back inside and wouldn't say another word."

"She's still not talking?" I asked.

Maureen shook her head. "Wouldn't even look at me after that. She just climbed back into bed. When I went in a little later to check on her, that's when I noticed the dirt."

I was already moving. I rushed down the hallway, my shoes squelching on the linoleum. The guest room door was cracked open. I pushed it gently with the tips of my fingers.

Hazel lay outstretched on the bed, her back to the room, her wet hair fanned out across the pillow. She wore a pink tank top with her favorite princesses on it and purple shorts. Both were streaked with dark smudges. As I moved closer, I saw her hands were smeared with dark, gritty soil, packed under her nails, streaked up her arms.

A faint earthy smell hung in the air.

My heart raced as I crouched down beside her. "Hazel?"

Her eyes were open, but she didn't move. She stared behind me, fixed on nothing.

"Hazel," I whispered. "It's Mommy."

She stirred slightly. I watched as her blue eyes unclouded and found me. Her lips parted and, in a hoarse whisper, she said, "She saw you down in the root cellar. Touching her things. She didn't like it."

My blood ran cold.

Behind me, I heard a sharp intake of breath. Carmen stood at my side. Tom lingered in the doorway.

"Who saw us?" I asked, my voice barely above a whisper. "The tricky lady? Hazel, what do you mean?"

She blinked slowly, then closed her eyes like she was drifting back to sleep.

Carmen moved beside me. "We have to protect her."

Her face was tight with concentration as she leaned over the edge of the bed and passed her hand slowly over Hazel's body.

"She's still connected to the house," she said quietly. "Whatever is doing this, taking the girls, it's latched onto her."

My stomach dropped. "What does that mean?"

Carmen looked at me, her eyes dark with urgency. "It means it followed you. Not all of it, but enough. A tether. A thread. She's marked. And if we don't sever that connection soon . . ."

She didn't finish. She didn't need to.

I glanced at Hazel. Her eyes were still closed, her breathing shallow. She looked so small. So fragile.

Carmen reached into her bag and dug around through its contents until she found what she needed. A small black stone. "This is obsidian," she murmured. "For protection. It will help absorb the darkness." She gingerly slid the stone beneath Hazel's pillow.

From a side pocket, she retrieved a small spray bottle. "Florida Water. It cleanses the energy." She gave a few quick spritzes above Hazel's body, then closed her eyes, swept the air with her palm, her lips mumbling something unintelligible as she moved.

Carmen's eyes roamed from me to Tom and back to me again. "She's still connected," she said softly. "But this will shield her long enough for us to figure out what to do next."

Tom frowned. "What *do* we do next?"

"We need to do a severing ritual as soon as possible."

I blinked. "Okay. What does that entail?"

"I'll need a few things from my car and some space to work. We'll do it tonight. Before this thing digs in any deeper."

Fifty

I sat cross-legged on the queen bed in Maureen's guest room, the soft whir of the ceiling fan buzzing above me. Hazel lay curled up beside me, her chest rising and falling in the rhythm of deep sleep. I couldn't stop watching her. Couldn't stop thinking how easily I might've lost her. Again.

I'd left her alone for days, trusting that distance from the house meant safety. But whatever haunted that place had followed us.

Down the hall, I heard muted voices. Tom and Maureen, maybe, speaking with Carmen as she prepared for the ritual. I didn't know what they were discussing. I wasn't sure I wanted to know.

Ada's bundle of letters lay in my lap. I desperately wanted to read more of her story. I needed to; maybe there was an answer to be found within it.

I picked up where I'd left off.

January 18, 1871

Dearest Mama,

Last night I woke to a strange sound in the walls. Not wind this time. Certainly not mice. It was a slow, heavy movement, something dragging across the boards out-side. Viola woke too. She climbed into bed with me and whispered, "I think someone's trying to come inside."

I lit a candle and walked the house. I found nothing. But the feeling stayed, Mama. That dreadful feeling of being watched—not by man or beast—but as if the walls themselves had eyes. Something that knows us but does not care for us. I felt it watching, and every part of me knew not to speak to it. Not to name it. Not even to look too long at the corners where the shadows gathered together. So I blew out the candle, climbed into bed beside Viola, and let sleep take us both.

Samuel never came to bed. I found him in the barn this morning, fiddling with something he wouldn't let me see. When I asked if he'd heard anything strange, he stared right through me, as though I hadn't spoken at all. He's changed, Mama. I scarcely recognize the man I married. He walks like he's burdened, not just by labor, but by something heavier. Some secret too dark for words.

I pray it's only the winter. You know how the bleak cold months can break one's spirit. My deepest hope is that he will thaw with the spring.

All my love,
Ada

I let the letter fall into my lap, Ada's words echoing in my mind. That feeling of eyes in the walls. Her husband slipping into silence. A frightened little girl who clung to her.

I glanced instinctively down at Hazel. She was still asleep, her long, pale lashes resting on flushed cheeks.

I sifted through the following pages, scanning dates and opening lines. One letter blurred into the next. Talk of chores and chickens, muddy floors, the dwindling firewood supply because Samuel couldn't be bothered to chop wood. All ordinary things.

Until I reached March.

March 16, 1871

Dearest Mama,

Viola cried out in her sleep last night. She said she dreamed of fire in the sky and a woman with no face who crawled out from under the floorboards. I held her while she trembled and sang her an old hymn until she calmed.

I knelt by the hearth afterward and prayed. I begged God to cover this house, to drive out whatever darkness dwells here. The shadows in this place do not feel natural. They seem to move and breathe.

But I fear there is more. Samuel did not come home last night. He returned at dawn, soaked in creek water and smelling of earth. When I asked where he'd gone, he looked through me and told me to mind my own business. I lost my temper then. I shouted, told him I needed a husband, Viola needed a father. I told him he was scaring us. He looked at me with something like pity. "You think this is about you," he said. "But it was never about you. Or the girl."

He said the girl, Mama. Not our daughter. And then he went back into the woods.

What am I to do? I cannot manage this homestead alone. Samuel needs help, and I no longer know how to reach him. I pray, but my prayers are going unanswered.

Please, tell me what to do.

I stared at Ada's words, my pulse thudding behind my eyes.

"It was never about you. Or the girl."

That line sat like a stone in my gut. Because it *was* about her. About Ada. About Viola. About Fern and Loretta. About *me* and *Hazel*.

Raymond Carlisle left. Samuel Ellison left. Marc left. The men always leave—whether by madness, fear, or some twisted call that only they can hear. And we're the ones left behind to make sense of the wreckage. To hold the house together while things fall apart. While the daughters start hearing things. Seeing things.

I pressed the heel of my hand to my chest, trying to slow the heat rising under my skin. Not fear. Not grief. *Rage.*

Whatever this thing is, maybe it doesn't want the men to stay. Maybe it breaks them first, hollows them out, and sends them wandering. So the women are alone. So the girls are vulnerable. So it can do what it's *always* done.

Samuel Ellison was wrong. It was always about us. The women. The girls. Because we're the ones who stay. And apparently . . . that's what it needs.

I *had* to know what happened next. What Ada did. I knew how their story ended. Samuel vanished in May, Viola in June, and the house burned shortly after. I needed to know how they got there. I moved to the next letter.

April 3, 1871

I barely skimmed the first line before a soft knock pulled me out of the moment.

"Shannon?" Carmen's voice came through the door. "Can you come out for a second?"

My heart fluttered with nerves.

I inhaled shakily and returned the letter carefully to the bundle. Whatever Ada had written next, whatever horror she'd faced in that house, I'd have to face it later.

Right now, I had to face my own.

I opened the bedroom door. Carmen stood just outside, her hands folded loosely at her waist. The look in her eyes told me everything

I needed to know. Tension radiated from her, a storm barely suppressed beneath the calm.

"Everything okay?" I asked.

"Maureen needs to talk to us," she said. "We're in the kitchen."

My stomach flopped. I followed her down the hall, passing the living room, and froze for half a second. The coffee table had been moved aside. Carmen had set a small circle of candles on the rug, but none were lit yet. The sight alone made my chest clench. If Maureen had seen that . . .

In the kitchen, Tom stood by the sink with his arms folded, looking like he wished he could disappear into the cabinets.

Maureen sat at the table, posture stiff, hands clasped tightly together. She looked up when I entered. "Shannon, honey, can you sit a minute?"

I slid into the seat across from her, my guts tightening like I'd just been called into the principal's office. Carmen stayed by the doorway, quiet.

Had I broken a rule? What was going on?

Maureen hesitated. She looked down at her hands, then back at me with eyes that were kind, but firm. "I hope you know how much I've come to care about you and Hazel," she began gently. "I opened my home because I believed you needed somewhere safe. I still believe that. I love y'all. Truly. I do."

I nodded slowly, unsure where this was going but already feeling a pit of dread growing in my belly.

"But what y'all are fixin' to do tonight . . ." She looked toward the living room again. "The candles. The supplies. The . . . ritual." Her mouth struggled to form the word. She glanced toward the living room. "This isn't something I feel comfortable allowing in my home."

There it was.

Carmen's head lowered slightly, acknowledging the boundary. "I understand," she said.

Maureen nodded once, relieved to avoid an argument. "It's not about you. Or what you believe. I was just raised to keep certain things out of my home. I'm trying to be respectful. I hope y'all can be respectful of that, too."

"We're only trying to help Hazel," Carmen said. "We mean no harm."

"I know," Maureen said, and she did. The honesty in her eyes proved it. "But I still can't allow it. Not here. I have to draw a line."

Tom cleared his throat. "We can go to my place."

I turned toward him. "Tom, I couldn't—"

"You can," Tom cut in softly. "There's really no other option. It's safe there. And we can do what needs to be done."

I didn't know what to say. My eyes burned. Carmen glanced at him, surprise flickering across her face before she gave a small, appreciative nod.

"I'll still help you however I can," Maureen said. "But this?" She paused, choosing her words carefully. "It's not of the Lord. It opens a door to something I don't want in my home."

That landed harder than she meant it to, I could tell. She glanced over her shoulder at Carmen, then back at me, her expression shifting into something close to regret. "I'm sorry. I hope you understand."

I did. And I didn't.

I understood where she was coming from. Anyone raised around here would. But still, I felt the ground shifting under me again. Another rejection. Another safe place, slipping away.

I closed the guest bedroom door behind me and leaned against it, letting myself breathe for a moment.

Hazel was still asleep.

I sighed and moved quietly around the room, trying not to disturb her, gathering the things we'd unpacked and tossing them back into our bags. Some picture books. A couple of dolls and stuffies. Our toothbrushes and toiletries in the bathroom. A stack of clean clothes that smelled like Maureen's laundry detergent. We'd only just settled here. And now we were leaving.

Again.

I tried not to let the self-reproach rise, but there was no stopping it. A *good* mother wouldn't be dragging her daughter from house to house, begging favors from strangers. A good mother would've figured this out by now.

The guilt bloomed in my chest, unexpected in its sharpness. This would be the third time I'd moved my daughter in two weeks. From the hotel to Maureen's and now to Tom's. Another new place. Another unfamiliar ceiling to wake up under.

What was I even doing?

Fifty-One

"SORRY ABOUT THE SHOES," Tom murmured as he held open the front door of his apartment for me. He nudged a pair of gym sneakers out of the way with his foot.

I stepped inside, Hazel still asleep in my arms, her breath warm against my collarbone. The air was cool and clean, carrying the familiar trace of Tom's spicy, cedary cologne.

The shift from Maureen's cozy, crowded house to this was a little jarring, even though his place was everything I'd expected: tidy, modern, minimal. Clean lines, neutral colors, dark hardwood floors. The kind of space that looked like it had been assembled deliberately, one well-chosen piece at a time.

A sleek black leather couch that looked expensive and barely used. A pair of framed vintage National Parks posters above the TV. A potted snake plant in the corner. On the floating shelves nearby sat a row of carefully arranged books, a few framed photographs, and some kind of artsy glass sculpture that looked *very* breakable. My stomach clenched just thinking about Hazel's curious little hands.

"This okay?" Tom asked, setting my suitcase down by the door. He glanced at Hazel, then at me.

"Yeah," I said quickly. "Of course. This place is beautiful. Thank you."

A tired smile curved his lips. "Guest room's this way. Sheets are clean."

I followed him down the hallway, my arms aching from the weight of my daughter, my chest aching for other reasons. My grubby toddler and I didn't belong here, in this lovely, curated space. I felt like a stain. A smudge on clean glass. But I was grateful to be here anyway.

"Bathroom's in here," Tom said, reaching into a doorway and flicking on a light to reveal a sparkling restroom. "If you need anything, seriously, just ask."

"Thank you."

"Carmen was right behind us, so she should be here any second. But I thought you might wanna get Hazel settled first."

I nodded and moved into the guest room. It was just as immaculate as the rest of the apartment. A queen bed with an oversized, pillowy comforter the color of charcoal, a small dresser, and a couple of antique maps on the walls. I laid Hazel down as gently as I could, trying not to wake her. She shifted once, curled onto her side, and went still again. I pulled a blanket over her and just stood there for a moment, watching her sleep.

She was safe. For now.

When I stepped back into the hall, Tom was still there. He gave me a slightly awkward smile. "I'll, uh, I'll clear some space in the living room," he said. "Figured that'd be the best place for Carmen to do her . . . thing."

"Are you sure you're okay with this?" I asked.

His smile was crooked but earnest. "I mean, I never imagined hosting a witchcraft sleepover, but hey. Life's full of surprises." He glanced toward the closed door behind me. "Look, I can't say I understand any of it, but if it helps Hazel, then yeah. I'm more than okay with it."

Before I could respond, a soft knock echoed from the front door.

Carmen.

Tom let her in. "Ay, Tomás," she said, eyes sweeping the spotless apartment as she kicked off her sandals. "Still living in a museum, I see."

"This is what actual cleanliness looks like. Not that you'd know," he shot back. He gave me a sideways look. "There's a reason we're not doing this at Carmen's place."

Carmen dropped her rain-speckled tote by the couch and arched an eyebrow. "A little clutter adds character. And you know, some of us don't dust our baseboards for fun. It's called having a life."

He gave a theatrical scoff, then in a tone that imitated hers, "It's called hygiene, Carmen."

"Of course it is." She turned to me. "This man vacuumed his vacuum once. I was there. Saw with my own two eyes."

I couldn't help it, I laughed.

Tom rolled his eyes but smiled. "Okay, okay, you two can roast me later. Where do you want to set up?"

Carmen surveyed the living room with a thoughtful squint. "We'll need some floor space."

He spread out his arms, gesturing broadly. "Again, we're not at your place, so we're in luck."

"So rude." Carmen shook her head and turned to me. "Don't let him fool you, Shannon. He only gets this place spotless by shoving everything he owns into closets and cabinets and drawers and pretending he's a minimalist."

Tom held up a hand. "Lies."

Still looking at me, Carmen quipped, "Go open a closet. I dare you."

"Don't pull our guest into this."

"Oh, Shannon's not a guest anymore, manito, she's in the inner circle now."

I laughed again. As the two siblings bantered, I felt something soften in my chest. Their easy back-and-forth put me at ease, showed me we were welcome, that they'd made room for us without question.

"I'm sorry you had to witness that, Shannon," Tom said, still smirking.

"Yeah. But fair warning, you should probably get used to it," Carmen added with a wink. "We're in too deep together at this point."

I smiled, but it faded quickly. They were trying, genuinely, to make me feel at home, and it was working, for the most part. But the calm felt fragile. I could feel something else stirring beneath it—restless and impatient.

Carmen's gaze flicked to mine, sensing it first. Tom felt it too. The banter drained away, replaced by silence as they both moved toward the coffee table, each taking an end.

"Oh, before I forget," Tom said as they lifted it aside, "Diego, our cousin, texted. He and his boys are coming over with the trailer at eight in the morning."

Right. The move. I'd been so overwhelmed, I'd forgotten that was actually happening tomorrow. My pulse fluttered, equal parts relief and guilt. "Thank you."

They set the table down in its new spot, and Carmen gave my forearm a light squeeze. "You're almost out of there, girl."

The reassurance should've comforted me. Instead, it only highlighted how precarious everything felt. *Almost* wasn't safety. Not yet.

I watched as Carmen bent to open her tote and began pulling out candles and strange little jars that clinked as she set them on the hardwood.

I lingered near the hallway, uneasy.

"Um, is it okay if I wait with Hazel while you set up?" I asked sheepishly. "She's still out cold, but . . . I just want to keep an eye on her. Plus, if she wakes up, you know, I don't want her to be confused by where we are."

"Of course," Carmen assured me kindly.

I gave a grateful nod and slipped down the hall, back to the guest room. Back to Hazel and the lingering sense that something unseen still had its eyes on us.

"Everything's in place," Carmen murmured through the door a while later. "We just need you two."

I brushed Hazel's hair from her forehead and stood, heart thudding like a drum. I scooped her into my arms and followed Carmen.

They'd closed the blinds and drawn the curtains tight, muting the last of the daylight until Tom's apartment was cloaked in shadows. A dozen candles flickered across the living room. The air smelled faintly of beeswax and something herbaceous.

In the center of the room, Carmen had formed a wide circle of fine white powder. Salt, I assumed, though knowing her, it could've been something else. Something stronger.

Tom knelt on the floor, just outside the ring. His eyes met mine, calm and steady.

"You'll sit inside the circle," Carmen instructed me gently, gesturing toward the space she'd prepared. "You can keep Hazel in your lap, if that feels right. Just make sure she's entirely within the boundary."

I glanced down at the powdery ring. It looked fragile, like one wrong move could shatter the spell.

Tom scooted back as Carmen spoke, but he didn't move far. He stayed just beyond the circle, hands in his lap, eyes flicking between me and my daughter.

"I'll be right here," he told me quietly.

I nodded, too full of nerves to speak.

Carmen knelt on the opposite side of the circle and began lighting the remaining candles. Shadows danced across her features as the flames caught. "I'll start by stating our intentions. The red thread will symbolize Hazel's connection to the house, whatever ties her to it. When the time comes, I'll need you to speak, Shannon. You don't have to know the right words, just do your best to describe the thing that's latched onto her. I'll guide you. But for now, just hold her. Keep her close."

I tightened my arms around Hazel and stepped carefully into the ring. Her warm, soft body remained limp with sleep, her head lolling against my shoulder as I cautiously lowered myself to the floor.

"We'll need something from the house," Carmen said. "I was thinking Ada's letters. They should hold a lot of energy we can use."

"Oh. Okay. They're on the bed in the guest room."

"I got it," Tom offered, already on his feet.

He returned in seconds with the delicate bundle of papers and handed them to his sister.

She took the stack with reverence, then laid it just inside the circle, careful not to let the curled edges brush the line of white.

"Alright," Carmen said, her voice low. "Let's begin."

She reached forward and gently placed a small clay censer near the edge of the circle. From her tote, she pulled a stick of incense and lit it with a steady hand. Sweet, resinous smoke spiraled upward. Something woody.

When she spoke again, her voice had changed. It was still hushed, but it carried something deeper now. A weight. A power.

"This is a severing," she said. "We are letting go of what does not belong. What was never invited. What is not welcome here."

She reached for the coil of red thread. With steady fingers, she unwound it and stretched it out, then draped it across Hazel's small, sleeping body.

"This represents the connection," Carmen continued, "between her and what followed you. Between her and the house."

She laid a hand atop Ada's letters and closed her eyes. "These hold memory," she said. "They remember what did this."

I clutched Hazel a little tighter, her warmth grounding me as the smoke curled higher around us.

Carmen sat back on her heels and looked me in the eye. "Now you'll need to name it, Shannon. The thing that's binding her."

My stomach turned. Name it? What was I supposed to say?

Carmen must have seen the panic on my face. "You don't need its true name," she said. "You only need *your* truth." She nudged the thread slightly with one finger. "Just describe it. Say what it feels like."

I touched the thread where it lay across Hazel's chest. My fingers trembled. I still felt so clueless, so lost. How could I put this into words?

I opened my mouth and stammered, "Fear." It came out weak and unsure.

Carmen nodded gently. "Keep going."

I looked up, first at Carmen, then at Tom.

He remained on the floor just outside the circle, but his eyes locked on mine with quiet intensity. His face was pale, jaw tight. He was just as scared as I was. But he didn't look away. He gave the smallest nod. *I'm here. It's okay.*

It helped.

I looked down at Ada's letters. I remembered her words, felt the despair that was so tangible in the root cellar. "Loneliness," I tried. "Grief. Pain." Feeling inadequate, I shrugged. "I don't know."

Carmen's voice was soft. "How did it feel for *you* when this started with Hazel?"

I swallowed hard. My eyes burned as I forced myself to *really* think about that. "Like I was failing," I admitted. "Like I was losing her, and I couldn't explain why. I kept telling myself it was stress.

Exhaustion. That I was imagining it. But I knew. Something was wrong."

The incense smoke curled between us, slow and heavy. Hazel stirred, her fingers curling into my shirt sleeve.

"Keep going," Carmen repeated.

"Um . . . well . . . I've been scared since the moment she was born," I confessed. "Not just of this, whatever this is. I mean scared that I'd mess up. That I'd ruin her somehow. That I'd do the wrong thing and . . . and she'd be gone."

I gulped, my voice thin and shaking.

"I used to worry that I'd fall asleep while I was nursing her and drop her. Or that I would fold her swaddle wrong, and she'd get tangled up in her blanket and suffocate. I dealt with a lot of postpartum stuff, but I think most mothers feel that way at the beginning. I mean, it's terrifying suddenly being responsible for this whole other tiny person who is completely depending on you for everything." I paused to draw a breath. "It's like . . . I kept waiting for someone else to step in. For the real grown-up to show up and show me how to do this. But no one ever did. No one ever does."

I looked at Tom. He hadn't moved. His eyes were wide now, glassy in the candlelight.

"And then . . . that night . . ." I stopped, pressing my cheek to the crown of Hazel's head. "That night, when I found her, out at the edge of the woods in her nightgown, just standing there, something broke inside me. Because all those things that I'd feared? The worst-case scenarios I used to invent in my head at three in the morning? They came true. They weren't just in my head, dammit. Something got to her. Something *found her*."

The red thread trembled.

I clutched Hazel tighter, the memory sharp in my mind.

"I didn't think it would follow us. I thought if we just got out of that house, if we left, if I never took her back there, she'd be safe." I paused, my entire body shaking as I admitted this aloud. I looked down at my daughter. At the dirt still on her hands, her little outfit. "But I left her alone with someone I barely knew. I let it find her. And now I'm doing this, something I don't understand, trying to undo something else I don't understand, all because I couldn't keep my little girl safe."

I felt tears sliding down my cheeks.

Hazel was still in my arms. Warm, solid, breathing. But it didn't feel like enough. Not after everything. Not when I kept dragging her from one place to the next, relying on strangers for help, hoping to patch together some kind of safety I couldn't seem to provide on my own.

I was supposed to protect her. That's what mothers do. And I'd failed. Over and over.

The red thread twitched.

The breath caught in my chest. The air shifted. Carmen's eyes flicked down to the thread, then back to me.

"That's it. Keep going."

"The thing in that house . . . it doesn't just feel like fear," I breathed. "It feels like abandonment." Something inside me cracked open, and the words came tumbling out. "Every woman that house has touched—Fern, Ada—they were left behind to deal with the wreckage. They waited for someone to come back. For someone to help. But no one ever did. The world forgot about them and their little girls. No one cared."

The candleflames fluttered.

"I know what that feels like," I said. "Being the one who stays. The one who handles things. The one who doesn't get to fall apart."

My voice cracked. "It feels like anger. Staying and doing it all and being pushed to your limits because *someone* has to. Like holding everything together with bleeding hands, and it's still not fucking enough."

A candle near the bookshelf hissed and went out.

Carmen's gaze didn't waver. "You're doing it," she said softly. "That's the truth. That's the name."

I blinked through tears, jaw quivering. "It feels like rage, for having to handle it all, alone. For being the only one standing in the wreckage. Always."

I looked up, breath caught in my throat.

Tom hadn't moved. He sat motionless, his hands clenched into fists, knuckles white. But his eyes—his eyes were on me like nothing else existed. Wide. Shining. Unflinching.

He saw me. Not just the mess. Not just the mother.

Me.

And somehow, that made the pain sharper and softer all at once.

Carmen reached forward and pulled my hand into hers. She didn't speak, just gave my hand a gentle squeeze, then released it and reached for the thread.

She picked it up carefully, like it was alive. Like it might bite.

The incense smoke thickened.

Carmen held the thread taut between her fingers. Her other hand reached into a velvet pouch, retrieving a narrow, dark dagger.

"We sever what clings, and we send it to rest."

She raised the blade.

Hazel whimpered. "Don't."

It wasn't her voice. Not quite. It was higher. Foreign.

Carmen's face didn't change. Her hand didn't shake. "She doesn't belong to you," she declared.

She sliced the thread.

It snapped with a sharp sound, and the candle flames flickered violently, three of them going out in a sudden whoosh.

Hazel's hands flailed, her body jerking like something had just been yanked out of her.

Then she collapsed into me.

Carmen dropped the thread into an iron bowl and lit a match. It smoldered until it was gone.

"It's done," Carmen said. "You did it."

Before I could respond, Tom was there. He crouched next to me, his expression raw, like he'd just witnessed something sacred and terrible. His hand found mine.

I looked at him through the blur of tears.

He didn't let go.

Fifty-Two

When Hazel woke up, she was all giggles and boundless energy, like nothing had happened. As Carmen and Tom packed up the ritual space, I got Hazel into a bubble bath. I scrubbed the dirt from her skin, worked the tangles from her hair, and changed her into clean clothes. The bathroom filled with steam and the scent of strawberry soap. I kept one hand on her the whole time, like I still couldn't quite believe she was real. Whole. Safe.

Tom ordered pizza for dinner, and it felt like a celebration. Hazel was bright and bubbly again, drawing pictures with Carmen at the kitchen table while we waited for the food. She drew normal kid things. Sunny skies with big rainbows. Cats. A picture of Tom that she said looked like "a rectangle with hair." Carmen laughed so hard, she cried.

When bedtime came, I pulled her onto the guest bed beside me and curled around her. I cried into her hair, silent and shaking, holding her so close I could feel her heartbeat through her back. I didn't let go for a long, long time.

Eventually, her breathing deepened. The apartment went still. But I couldn't sleep.

I slipped out of bed quietly, stepping over a stuffed fox and the edge of the blanket she'd kicked off. I moved toward the living room, planning to camp out on the couch for a while. Maybe I'd scroll on my phone for a bit. Or maybe I'd go back to Ada's letters, try to piece together the last of her story.

But when I turned the corner, I stopped.

Tom stood in the kitchen, backlit by the fridge light. He hadn't noticed me yet. He was just standing there, staring into the open refrigerator, one hand on his hip.

"Couldn't sleep either?" I asked softly.

He looked up. His eyes softened when they found me. "Nope. Thought I'd go looking for a midnight snack instead. Bad habit."

I shrugged. As I moved closer to him, I could see he had changed into a worn cotton T-shirt and soft, heather gray joggers. He was barefoot. I'd never seen him like this. Casual and comfortable, a stark contrast to his usual pleated slacks and ironed button-downs.

Seeing his hairy toes felt a bit too intimate. It threw me a little.

"I'll settle for sparkling water." He pulled out a can and extended it toward me. "Want one?"

"Sure." As I took it, our fingers brushed lightly. "Thanks."

Tom grabbed one for himself and closed the refrigerator. He turned away as he snapped up the top of the can, trying to muffle the popping sound in the quiet apartment, for Hazel's sake. I did the same.

"Is she sleeping okay?" Tom asked.

I nodded. Fruity bubbles tickled my nose as I took a sip from the can. It tasted like cherries.

"Good," he said. "It was really good to hear her laughing tonight."

I smiled. "It was." I looked down at the can in my hands. "I was afraid I'd never hear that sound again."

Tom took that in. He opened his mouth to speak, then hesitated. Finally, he said, "You were really brave tonight."

"I didn't feel brave," I replied, keeping my eyes on the can. "I felt like I was falling apart."

"That's what real bravery looks like though," he said. "Showing up anyway."

The silence between us turned comfortable. I didn't look at him, but I felt his solid presence there beside me.

"I should feel better now. And I think I do." I fiddled with the pop top. "But . . . I can't shake this feeling like . . . it's not over."

"Well, Carmen still has her cleansing ritual planned for Sunday, after everything's moved out. Maybe that's why it feels like that."

"Maybe." I tilted my head toward the living room. "I was thinking of going back through Ada's letters. There's still several I haven't read yet."

He straightened. "Okay. Want some company?"

"Sure."

"That sounds a lot better than *Frasier* reruns, which is where this night was headed." He smiled at me. "Well, maybe not better. But close."

We padded into the living room together, and I retrieved the bundle of Ada's brittle pages from the table where Carmen had left them. Tom clicked on a lamp and sank onto the far end of the couch. I sat cross-legged near him, letters in my lap.

The apartment fell into a hush around us, nothing but the faint noise of city traffic passing by outside.

"I've been reading them in chronological order," I told him, keeping my voice low. I handed him the one from January 1, 1871. "This is the first one."

He accepted it with careful hands, something like wonder or awe flickering in his eyes.

I took a breath as I thumbed through the other letters, passing him the ones I'd read, stopping when I reached where I'd left off.

May 8, 1871

To my dearest Mama,

I have not heard a word from Samuel in four days. Not a soul has seen him. Yesterday, I walked as far as the river bend, hoping—though I dare not say for what. A trail? A boot print? A body, perhaps. But there was nothing.

This morning, I went all the way to the MacRaes' farm to ask if they'd seen him. Mrs. MacRae only clucked her tongue and said, "Men do what they will, Ada. You just worry about that little girl now." As if I hadn't done just that every hour of every day. I told her I feared something was wrong. She only said, "Then let the Lord deal with him." And I suppose I must.

But the shameful truth is this, Mama: I don't believe he's lost. I believe he left. Of his own choosing. I have thought on every word I spoke to him in these last days. Was I too cold? Too sharp-tongued? Did I wear him down with my worries and grievances? These months have been full of trials. And I can't help but wonder—if I had only bridled my tongue, if I had borne our burdens without complaint— would he still be here?

I feel it in my bones, Mama. He did not meet misfortune. He walked away from it all. His family, his land, all his worldly possessions. And now I remain alone in the ruin he left behind, striving to be both mother and father beneath this godforsaken roof. I labor from one dawn unto the next, and still this house and this land demand more.

Viola asked me this afternoon if the lady in the trees would bring Papa back. I told her there was no one in the trees. She merely smiled, like she knew something I did not. I do not know what to make of it. But my soul is weary with unease.

Oh, Mama, I am so very tired. How I long for your presence, for your arms around me, for the soothing sound of your sweet voice humming those precious hymns in the dark. I miss being someone's daughter. I miss it with a grief I cannot name.

You were steadfast and gentle, everything a wife and mother ought to be. And now here I am, frayed and fumbling, trying to fill every role that has befallen me.

I fear I am not enough. I fear I am coming undone.

That letter ended with no signature. Perhaps she was too weary to finish it.

Tears welled in my eyes as I stared at the yellowed paper. I didn't have to imagine her mental state. I'd lived it. Reading the ache in her words felt like standing before a mirror, looking back at my own grief.

I miss being someone's daughter.

My mom died of cancer when I was a sophomore in college. She was the epitome of strength and warmth. She used to hum when she cleaned the kitchen. Soft, aimless little tunes, half old-sixties rock, half her own melodies. It annoyed me as a teen, but I'd give anything to hear it now.

She used to hold me when it felt like my world was ending. If I ever needed a hug from my mama, it was now.

Because just like Ada Ellison, here I was, trying to keep my daughter safe, feeling like I didn't measure up. A less-than mother, trying to be more-than. Attempting to wear all the hats, juggle all the roles, and failing miserably.

I could've written that same damn letter. Only the names would have changed.

I remembered Tom's presence then. He was still sitting next to me on the couch, Ada's earlier letters fanned across his lap. But he wasn't reading anymore. He was looking at me.

He didn't say anything. He just reached for my hand.

The contact startled me. It was unexpected, but . . . nice.

I squeezed his hand back, wiped my face with my other, and reached for the next letter.

May 15, 1871

Dearest Mama,

Something is wrong with this land. I found the chickens lying in a circle this morning, all of their necks broken. It could not have been a fox or coyote, not a hawk or snake. For what beast kills without spilling blood, then arranges them in such a purposeful formation? It was as though some vile person had arranged them to be seen. But who?

I buried the poor things at the edge of the corn patch and breathed a prayer to Heaven as I worked, but my words were hollow. I do not believe they reached Heaven. Forgive me for saying so, Mama, but I fear this place is far too removed from Heaven for my cries for help to reach our Father's ears.

Viola is not well. She lingers at the edge of the woods, talking into the shadows, using sticks to draw unholy things in the dirt.

I remember Reverend Pierce once saying the Devil can use grief to open doors. I did not understand what he meant at the time, but I think I do now. I fear something evil has taken root here.

And part of me wonders, did Samuel leave to escape this?

I closed the letter with shaking hands.

One thing was becoming clearer with each letter: Ada Ellison wasn't the evil thing haunting the house. She wasn't the tricky lady, as I had once thought.

Ada was me.

She was Fern.

Just another woman trying to survive the cycle of something ancient and cruel.

So if Ada wasn't the evil in that house . . . then who was?

The question sat with me all night. It followed me into sleep. And it was still there the next morning when I got up to face what came next.

Saturday. Move-out day.

Fifty-Three

Shannon

August 27, 2022

I HAD TO FIGURE out what to do with Hazel. I hadn't heard a word from Maureen since that talk in her kitchen. Knowing she was an early riser, I'd texted her first thing this morning, but she hadn't responded. I couldn't blame her. I'd dropped something dark and unexplainable on her doorstep, and she didn't owe us anything.

Still, it left me with a knot in my gut and no one to call.

Tom found me standing in the hallway, phone in hand, frozen. "No luck?"

I shook my head.

He hesitated for a moment, then said, "She can stay here. With Carmen. They'll hang out, color, watch cartoons. They got along great yesterday. She'll be fine with her."

"But Carmen still has to go back," I said. "To finish it."

Tom nodded. "She will. But not until the house is cleared. Not until we're all ready."

I let out a shaky breath. "Okay."

"She'll be safe," he said. "Here. With Carmen. I promise."

I believed him. Hazel would be safe here.

I just wasn't sure the same could be said for the rest of us.

I drove this time. Tom's Highlander was still sitting in the driveway on Sunflower Lane, abandoned after everything that happened yesterday. Tom rode shotgun with two boxes of Bigfoot's miniature donuts balanced across his lap. A Styrofoam cooler of bottled water and Gatorade sloshed quietly in the backseat. It wasn't much, but it was something, some small offering to Tom and his cousins for spending their Saturday helping me haul away the final remnants of my time in that house.

The sun was already high when we turned down the driveway, already too bright and too hot through the windshield. A hefty silver pickup truck and long trailer sat parked in front of the house, trailer gate down, a couple of dollies and moving blankets already laid out. Three figures stood in the gravel near the porch. Not working, not talking, just . . . watching the house.

"They're already here," I said, surprised.

"Oh yeah. The Altamiras are a punctual bunch." Tom squinted at his family. "They look weirdly quiet."

He wasn't wrong.

As I killed the engine, one of the younger guys—tall and lean, buzzed head, a Monster energy drink clenched in his fist—nudged the other with his elbow. The older man in the middle, broad-shouldered with polarized sunglasses and a dark beard peppered with silver, gave us a nod that was polite but strained.

We climbed out.

"Morning!" Tom called. "Y'all beat us."

"By a while," said the bearded man. His voice was low and smooth but laced with something tight. His thick brows arched high above his sunglasses. "You brought snacks?"

Tom held up his hands, a box in each. "Donuts. Shannon's treat."

That got a faint smile from the shorter of the two younger guys. His eyes flicked shyly before settling back on the donuts. He looked about eighteen, baby-faced, with a mop of black curls barely contained beneath a backwards ballcap.

"Ooh, from Bigfoot's?" he asked.

I smiled. "Yep."

"Nice. I think we just became best friends," he said with a grin. "I'm Mateo, by the way."

"Elias," contributed his buzz-cut brother, raising his energy drink in a lazy salute.

"It's nice to meet you. I'm Shannon."

The older man finally stepped forward and shook my hand. His grip was firm. "I'm Diego. Tom's cousin. These two are mine—when they're behaving."

I gave a polite laugh.

"They seem suspiciously well-behaved this morning," Tom remarked, eyeing them. "Makes me nervous."

Diego didn't even crack a smile. "They're a bit freaked out," he said, voice lower. He cast a wary glance in my direction. "This place feels . . . off."

He turned toward the house again. The front door stood cracked open, just wide enough to be noticeable.

Had we left it unlocked yesterday? Everything after Maureen's text had been a blur, but I knew the door hadn't been left *open*.

Tom noticed it too and frowned. "You went inside?"

"No, man," Elias said. "We didn't even touch that door. It was shut when we got here, then it creaked open by itself when we started rolling the dollies off the trailer. Swear to God."

"Did you go inside?" Tom asked.

"Hell no," Elias said.

Mateo scratched the back of his neck. "Also . . . there's a dead bird on the porch."

My stomach turned. "What?"

He pointed toward the steps. "Like, right at the top." He cringed. "I almost stepped on it."

Elias crinkled his nose. "Gross."

I moved to look. The others followed.

It was a mourning dove. I recognized the soft brown-gray feathers, the delicate shape. Its body was curled slightly, wings tucked close, like it had laid down and never gotten up. Its neck, though, bent unnaturally. Sideways, like it had been snapped.

There was no blood. No other sign of trauma. I thought of Ada.

I found the chickens lying in a circle this morning, all of their necks broken.

I shivered.

Mateo shifted closer to me. "Is it, like, an omen or something? Carmen said this place had *energy*."

I didn't answer.

Tom moved beside me, his voice low. "You okay?"

I nodded. But I wasn't. "Let's just get this done," I said.

I stepped over the bird's corpse and pushed open the door the rest of the way.

FIFTY-FOUR

THE AIR INSIDE THE house felt even heavier than I remembered. It was almost palpable today, like it resented being disturbed.

The Altamiras filed in behind me. Tom stayed close, following me without hesitation, but the others lingered at the door. Diego looked uneasy as he crossed the threshold. His sons came after him, slowly, silently, their bravado left on the porch.

Everything appeared the same as we'd left it. Mostly-empty rooms, a few stacks of boxes, my furniture pushed against the walls. Dust swirled in the beams of sunlight that gleamed through the blinds.

Mateo and Elias made a show of grabbing donuts before we got started, like they needed one last moment of normalcy.

I leaned against the frame of the kitchen doorway and watched them. Men trying to act like the atmosphere of this place wasn't bothering them, who'd clearly already *felt* it before we got here. "Thank you guys so much for being here," I told them. "You have no idea how much your help means to me."

Elias looked at me as he scarfed down a donut, his fingers sticky with vanilla glaze. "It's no problem. We've helped plenty of people move. Usually, the houses don't feel like they're gonna murder us, but hey, first time for everything."

Mateo smirked.

"Seriously," I said, voice low. "I don't know what I'd have done if you hadn't offered to help."

That sobered them a little. Mateo's smile softened, while Elias gave a quick shrug that meant *you're welcome* even if he didn't say it.

Diego met my eyes and nodded. "We got you," he said. "Tom said it was a tough situation. We didn't ask for details. Just tell us what goes where, and we'll get it done."

That hit me harder than I expected. The kindness. The lack of prying.

"Alright," Diego said, clapping once. It echoed loudly in the space. "Let's knock this out."

Mateo brushed the powdered sugar from his hands onto his jeans. "I bet I get more loaded than Elias."

Elias snorted. "Nah, little guy, you know I always smoke you."

"Not this time. You just ate, like, a whole dozen donuts by yourself in like five minutes. You're gonna be on the toilet half the day."

"They were tiny."

"Tiny sugar bombs, and you washed them down with a Monster."

"That's *fuel*, Mateo. And I need it to deal with you all day."

"No, bro, it's *gastrointestinal suicide*. And you better hope Shannon hasn't already packed up the Poo-Pourri."

That got an actual laugh from Tom, which he quickly smothered with a cough.

Diego released a weary sigh as he glared at them. "You two gonna yap all day or lift something?"

"I *am* lifting," Mateo said, grabbing a box. "Lifting morale."

Diego shook his head and muttered something in Spanish.

I smiled as they disappeared around the corner, but it didn't last. The moment they stepped into the hallway, it felt as though a blanket had been thrown over the whole house.

The air changed. The easy rhythm of laughter evaporated.

I stood there for a second, box in hand, my chest and my belly clenching back into that familiar tightness.

This wasn't just a move. It wasn't just furniture.

This was a goodbye.

And the house knew it.

We'd been at it for almost an hour. Most of the furniture was loaded, some of it already strapped down, ready to be hauled off to the storage unit. Only a few big pieces remained, plus some boxes and other odds and ends.

And Hazel's room.

I stood in the hallway, staring at her door.

We'd saved it for last, not on purpose, but not by accident either. It just kept getting skipped. Passed over. Avoided.

The hallway was too quiet now. The house had been noisy with motion all morning, filled with footsteps and scraping furniture and dumb jokes meant to lighten the mood. But with each item we carried out, an eerie kind of heaviness replaced it, a weighty silence filling in around us like steadily rising water.

I felt it again, that awful prickle at the back of my neck. The feeling of something watching. Waiting.

Behind me, the aging floorboards creaked under work boots. "You want help?"

I turned. Mateo stood behind me, wiping sweat from his brow. His curls had escaped from beneath his backwards ballcap in the humidity, and there was a streak of dust across one cheek.

"Sure, thank you," I said. "I was about to start cleaning out my daughter's room."

He gave me a crooked grin that reminded me of Tom. "How old's your little girl?"

"She's three."

His grin widened with pride, deep-set dimples appearing in a way that only added to his cuteness. "I've got a three-year-old sister at home. Gabriela. She's a little handful. Thinks she runs the house."

I smiled. "Sounds familiar."

His warm, honey-brown eyes followed mine to the door. It stood ajar, shadows pooling beyond the threshold. He didn't seem to notice my hesitation. Instead, he reached ahead and nudged the door open for me.

"Whew," Mateo said, leading the way inside. He tugged at his shirt collar, swiping it over his face to clear away the sweat. "Finally. Somewhere that isn't an oven."

He was right. But the coldness in Hazel's room wasn't refreshing to me. It clung to my skin like frosty, wet fabric. I paused just inside the doorway, heart ticking faster.

It seemed silly to feel so terrified in a place like this, with its soft mint walls and glittery accents. A bright, cutesy space once filled with toys and giggles and princess everything. Now there was nothing but furniture, packed boxes, and lingering dread.

Mateo moved toward the vanity dresser, the heaviest piece of furniture in the room. Solid wood with a tall, plain mirror bolted to its back, the clunky old thing was a thrift store find I'd dragged home years ago and painted white. Hazel had since decorated it with a sprawl of cartoon cat stickers.

"Should we start with this?" Mateo asked.

"Sure," I said with a shrug.

He ran a hand over one of the stickers, a calico cat sitting in a teacup. "Nice touch. Gabriela loves cats, too. Let's take this mirror off first."

"It won't come off," I told him, wincing. "The screws are stripped out. It was like that when I bought it."

Mateo ducked behind it, running a hand over the brackets on the back side. "Ah. Yeah, I see what you mean."

A faint creak interrupted him. Wood shifting, maybe. The house settling.

Or not.

I turned, pulse quickening, but the space behind us was empty.

Still, the air felt different now. Charged and electric. Like we weren't alone.

I glanced at Mateo, wondering if he felt it too. But he was crouching beside the dresser, angling the heavy frame away from the wall.

"That thing's pretty heavy," I warned.

"No worries." He slid out one of the drawers and set it aside. "We can make it a little lighter." He removed the other two, stacked them neatly, then gave the dresser a testing rock. "That's better."

I nodded, though unease ripped through my gut, sharp and instinctive, like my body discerned something my mind couldn't.

The light shifted, just barely, and the hairs on my arms stood on end. The air in the room dropped ten degrees in an instant.

A foul stench seeped in—wet earth and rot, decay dragged up from below.

Mateo planted his feet, braced his hands on the frame, and tilted the dresser forward. Muscles tightened across his shoulders as the wood groaned.

In the corner of my eye, I saw one of the bifold closet doors shift behind him. It began to fold inward, inching along the track with a slow, grating groan.

I opened my mouth to call out.

The dresser lurched violently, yanked out of Mateo's hands as if some invisible force had seized it. One end slammed to the floor with a deafening *crack*. The mirror shattered. Glass exploded outward in a burst of jagged sparkles, raining down to the hardwood with a sound like breaking ice and ringing bells. Mateo flinched back—too late.

The dresser pitched forward, struck him square in the chest, and sent him sprawling onto the shards. Then the full weight of it crashed down on top of him.

He screamed—a raw, primal sound that sliced through me. Blood pooled beneath him, streaming across the floorboards.

I rushed forward, hands trembling. I heard someone screaming. It took me a second to realize it was me.

Tom and Elias were suddenly at my side.

Elias dropped to his knees, hands already on his brother. "Shit—shit—Mateo. Hey, hey, stay with me."

Mateo whimpered beneath the dresser's weight, his face chalky white.

Tom was talking into his phone, voice tight and urgent. "We need an ambulance. Right now. My cousin's pinned, he's bleeding—"

His words blurred together, drowned out by another voice in my head. The echo of another call. A different body on the ground.

He's not breathing—

Sir? Sir, can you hear me?

My dad on the grass outside the barn, paramedics pumping his chest for far too long, the icing on Hazel's cat cake melting in the sun.

My knees hit the floor. I couldn't move. Couldn't speak.

I think someone was calling my name, but I couldn't answer.

Fifty-Five

The ambulance was gone. Mateo was on his way to the hospital. We wouldn't know anything for hours.

I sat on the front porch steps, sobbing next to the dead dove.

The paramedics, in their rush, had rolled the gurney right over it. Feathers were scattered across the walkway.

I couldn't stop staring.

Not at the blood on my hands. Not at Diego's abandoned trailer in the driveway.

Just the bird. Crushed under all that weight.

The front door squeaked on its hinges behind me. Tom stepped out, carrying a cardboard box marked *Toys*.

He didn't look down at the dove. He didn't ask if I was okay. He just kept moving, his motions automatic as he set the box on the trailer and turned back inside for another.

I made myself stand and follow. We didn't speak.

There was nothing to say.

Inside, only a few boxes remained, but the place didn't feel empty. The lighting looked wrong somehow. Dimmer, even though the sun was out in full blast. The walls felt closer. The air felt oppressively heavy.

With all the furniture gone, area rugs rolled up and carried out, the sound was different, too. Every noise echoed and made me jump. Every step we took, each creak of the floor, every inhale and exhale felt uncannily loud.

Tom and I carried the rest of my things out in silence until finally, the house was stripped bare.

Yet it remained full of something we couldn't name.

I paused in the hallway one last time.

A strange melancholy settled over me as my eyes swept the emptied space. This was the place I'd brought Hazel home from the hospital. I could still see that day so clearly: her in the little striped hat they'd given her at discharge, impossibly small and bundled in my arms when I crossed this threshold.

Flashes hit me all at once. Hanging Hazel's *Baby's First Christmas* ornament on the tree by the front window. The slap of little bare feet on the floor as she learned to walk. The quiet afternoons on the couch with her asleep on my shoulder.

Those memories felt oddly distant now, almost like they'd been pulled out of me. Like the house had swallowed them, too.

It had only ever known how to take.

My father. My husband. My marriage.

My sleep. My peace. My sense of self.

It had tried to take my daughter.

And minutes ago, it had taken Mateo.

But it hadn't started with me.

It had taken Fern. Loretta. Raymond from his family.

Viola from her mother. Samuel from Ada. Then Ada herself.

It didn't matter the decade. It didn't matter who moved in.

This house only knew how to destroy and devour.

Families. Joy. Futures.

Whatever dream we'd had when we bought this place had rotted from the inside out.

And now, standing in the hollow shell it left behind, I couldn't mourn it.

I could only hate it.

Tom called my name from the door.

I turned away without a word, and I didn't look back.

At the storage unit, Tom and I unloaded the trailer in silence. Box after box. *Kitchen. Laundry room. Holiday decor.* It seemed to take forever, but neither of us complained. We just kept moving, jaws tense, sweat soaking through our clothes as we team-lifted the furniture.

Halfway through, Tom's phone dinged. He yanked it from his pocket and cursed when he saw the screen. "That client," he said quietly. "Dammit, I forgot all about it. I'm supposed to meet him at three o'clock."

I swallowed. Checked the time on my iPhone. *1:45 PM.* My stomach sank. "I-I can finish up alone," I said stupidly, eyeing the huge load left on the trailer.

Tom turned and gave me a hard look. "No, you can't."

I sighed in defeat.

As he put his phone to his ear, I kept moving, grabbing another box, but I could hear his voice behind me, calm and composed like none of this had happened. "Hey, Gordon, this is Tom Altamira." A quick pause. "Listen, man, I'm so sorry. I had a family emergency come up, and I'm not going to be able to make our three o'clock showing. Can we push it to tomorrow or maybe early on next week? If not, I can have a colleague come out and meet you instead. Just let me know what's best for you."

He paused, listening.

"Sure, of course. Totally understand. I'll follow up later this week. Thanks, Gordon. Appreciate it."

Tom ended the call and slid the phone into his pocket. He stared at the trailer like he wasn't seeing it anymore.

"He said he'll reschedule next week," he muttered. "Didn't ask questions."

Silence pooled between us.

He looked at me, and there was something in his face I hadn't seen all day. Not just the tension. *Grief*. Raw, unspoken grief clung to his features.

"This wasn't supposed to happen," Tom exhaled. "Mateo . . . he's just a kid. He was helping. He shouldn't have—" His voice caught, and he turned away for a second, blinking hard at the asphalt.

And just like that, my own guilt surged.

I looked down at my hands, blackened by dirt from the trailer, the edge of my palm crusted faintly red. Mateo's blood. I hadn't even realized. I rubbed at it in a frenzy, but it wouldn't come off. "I should've said no," I muttered. "I should've never asked for help. If I'd just—if we'd waited—"

"Don't."

"I let him go in there, Tom. I knew something was wrong with that room. I've known for weeks. And I still let him . . ." My voice cracked. "I still let him go in."

He was quiet, his expression unreadable. For a moment, I thought he was angry. At me. Then he said, barely above a whisper, "The way he screamed."

I nodded, tears streaking down my cheeks because I could still hear it. That terrible, guttural wail.

"It's going to stay with me," Tom said. "That sound. For the rest of my life."

I wiped at my face, but it didn't matter. More tears just kept coming.

"I keep replaying it," he said. "What if I'd gone in there with you instead of him? What if I'd carried that dresser?"

"Then *you* would've been hurt."

"Yeah." His eyes burned into mine. "Better me than him."

We both fell silent. The afternoon heat pressed down around us, heavy as the guilt we carried.

When neither of us could stand it any longer, we picked up the next box.

There was nothing else we could do.

Fifty-Six

HAZEL'S LAUGHTER GREETED US as Tom and I returned to his apartment, the bright, giddy sound of it so wildly at odds with the day we'd had, I almost cried.

We found Hazel and Carmen sitting together on the living room floor, both of them wearing crowns made from construction paper, surrounded by a sea of glittery costume jewelry and stuffed animals.

"I hereby decree," Carmen intoned dramatically, waving a wooden spoon around like a royal scepter, "that Princess Hazel shall rule over all stuffed bears, unicorns, and kitties alike."

Hazel giggled and clapped, then spotted me. "Mommy!"

She ran at me full speed. My tired arms ached as I scooped her up, every muscle screaming, but I held her tight and breathed her in like oxygen.

Tom met Carmen's eyes over Hazel's head. Something passed between them—something weary and wordless.

Carmen stood, brushing glitter from her black skinny jeans. "You two look like hell."

"You don't say," Tom muttered.

"Sit. I'm making dinner."

"You don't have to—" I started.

"Shannon." Her tone softened, but it held no room for argument. "Let me take care of you tonight."

Tom collapsed onto the couch. I followed, Hazel climbing onto my lap and settling against me with a contented sigh.

"You stink, Mommy," she said.

Tom barked out a laugh.

So did I. It felt good to laugh. I ran a hand down her back. "We've been working hard, remember? We moved everything out of our old house."

"Where is our stuff?"

"In a storage unit for now," I said. "We'll get it later when we find a new house to live in."

She nodded, like that answer was enough for her. I wished it was for me.

Carmen returned with two frosty cans of sparkling water. She handed them to us, looking between us, then down at Hazel. "Hey, princesa," she said gently. "Wanna come help me make dinner?"

Hazel hopped up eagerly. "Can I wear my crown in the kitchen?"

"You *have* to," Carmen said with a wink. "You're royalty."

As they turned toward the kitchen, Carmen paused just long enough to meet my eyes. "Rest. Ground yourself. You'll need it for tomorrow."

"Why tomorrow?" Hazel asked, dragging a step behind her. "We're not going back there, are we?"

The room fell still.

Carmen didn't flinch. "Just the grownups," she said softly. "But don't worry, okay? Whatever happens, we'll make sure you're safe."

Hazel seemed to accept that. She gave a solemn nod and followed Carmen into the kitchen, her paper crown slipping to one side.

I sank deeper into the couch cushions. "We can't take Hazel back there," I said, my voice barely carrying over the jangle of pots and pans in the kitchen. "I've gotta go back with Carmen. We have to finish this. But . . . without Maureen's help . . . we're in a bind."

My mind flicked to Hilda and Rebecca. They'd want to help. Hilda especially. But she could barely handle the cellar stairs, let alone keep up with a rambunctious three-year-old. It wasn't fair to ask her for help.

Tom leaned forward, elbows resting on his knees. "I can stay here with Hazel," he offered. "While you and Carmen do whatever it is you need to do."

I blinked. "You'd do that?"

His eyes met mine. "Of course I would. You need to go back without worrying about her."

"You're sure?"

"I've watched Diego's kids plenty of times. I still keep the youngest every now and then when Diego and Rosa need a night out." He bobbed his head toward the hallway. "I've got a bin of toys in the hall closet. Some books. Stickers. Should be enough to keep her happy for a few hours." He paused, then added, softer now, "She'll be okay with me. I promise."

I believed him.

But as his words settled, the pit of dread in my stomach only deepened. Because leaving Hazel here with Tom meant *I* still had to go back.

Back into that house.

Back to face the thing waiting for us inside, one last time.

I needed something to fight back with. If there was anything that could help—any clue, any warning—it had to be in Ada's remaining letters.

She and Fern, somehow, had been with me all along, invisible witnesses in the dark, gently guiding me forward. I couldn't shake the feeling that Ada had nudged me toward those letters in the first place.

Maybe they held nothing useful. Maybe it was already too late for answers. But if there was anything left she wanted me to know, I had to find it.

If I was going to face the thing that had devoured them, I had to read the rest of Ada's letters tonight.

Fifty-Seven

It was just after eight o'clock. I'd bathed Hazel and tucked her into bed while the Altamiras cleaned up the kitchen. The scent of enchiladas still lingered—corn tortillas rolled with beans and cheese, topped with red sauce and baked until bubbling. She'd served them with arroz con maíz and a side of sweet cinnamon-spiced roasted plantains, something Hazel had devoured giddily with sticky fingers.

In the kitchen, Tom and Carmen moved quietly, the soft clink of dishes and low murmur of their voices drifting through the apartment as they wrapped up for the night.

I settled onto the couch, legs folded beneath me, the fragile bundle of Ada's letters in my lap. I found where I'd left off.

May 30, 1871

Dearest Mama,

I do not sleep anymore. Not truly. I drift off for minutes at a time before waking to creaks and whispers, to the rustling of corn stalks that move without wind. Last night, I heard a woman weeping. A distressing, sorrowful wail, as though she were mourning a loss too terrible to speak of. Beneath her cries were faint words in a language I did not know, the same syllables over and over.

I thought perhaps I was dreaming, but Viola sat straight up next to me and whispered, "Mama, she's sad again." When I asked who she meant, she said, "The Indian lady who lost her little girl." Her nonchalance frightened me more than the weeping itself.

I froze, Viola's words landing like a gut punch. The voice on Hilda's tape, the language we'd failed to recognize. Not Latin. Not Aramaic.

Indigenous.

That car ride rose in my mind—Tom's eyes locked on the road as he talked about the Trail of Tears cutting straight through that stretch of land. All those families forced to march. To endure agony. I thought of Hilda, how she said the ground could soak up human suffering and change because of it.

My mind reeled. It was clear from Ada's writings that whatever haunted that place hadn't begun with the Ellisons. The land had been tainted before they ever set foot on it.

Could she have been the first? An Indigenous woman, grieving a child lost on that despicable march. I imagined her left behind, or maybe forced onward without her husband, without protection. What if her grief, her sorrow, had somehow seeped into the soil and opened a wound that never closed? What if the land had taken her pain and twisted it into something . . . alive?

I didn't know.

I forced myself to keep reading.

Viola has taken to sleeping beside me since Samuel's departure, and twice now I have awoken to find her gone. The first time, I found her crouched beneath the kitchen table, murmuring to someone I could not see. The second time, I found her standing barefoot at the tree line, dew on her nightgown, her eyes distant. I felt a dreadful presence out there, as though someone else—or something else—were lurking in the shadows, watching us. I gathered Viola into my arms and hurried us back inside, afraid to look over my shoulder.

I long to take her and flee this cursed ground. But where would we go? I have no money, no kin nearby. Still, I have given thought to Huntsville. Perhaps I could find work there—washing, sewing, anything that might keep us fed. I might inquire near the square, or call upon the Reverend Morgan's widow, if she is still there. I do not know what welcome we would find, but surely it would be more merciful than what waits for us here.

There is no sense in staying here, not anymore. The crops are failing, the neighbors keep their distance, and

Samuel is not coming back.

I keep thinking of what old Mrs. Adcock said shortly after we arrived, how "some land's better left alone." I'd taken her for a bitter old gossip, someone set in her ways, who'd lived here too long and come to resent newcomers. But now, her words return to me like a warning.

I recall another woman too, from the church—her name escapes me now—who lowered her voice when I mentioned where our homestead stood. She said there were old stories about that patch of woods, "not the kind to be repeated in godly company." I'd laughed then, unsure if she meant it. But I do not laugh now.

What if they knew something? What if there's a reason no one welcomed us, a reason no one else settled near this stretch of land? Some history passed down in whispers, too dreadful to speak aloud in the house of the Lord.

Every part of me longs to leave this place behind. I pray only for the strength to gather our things, take Viola, and never look back.

Ada

They warned her. The old woman. The church lady. Not with the truth, but with scraps of it, just enough to plant fear, but never enough to help. They left her to figure it out alone.

And the worst part?

Ada wanted out. Like me.

Wanted to save her daughter. Like me.

Ada's fear, her exhaustion, her desperation to protect her daughter at all costs, it rang so familiar I could barely breathe. She had begged God for the strength to leave. I, of course, knew exactly how it felt to want to run, to pack your child up and never look back.

But Ada never got the chance.

With a sick twist of dread, I unfolded the next letter.

June 5, 1871

Dearest Mama,

Viola is gone.

I have searched the woods until my legs gave out beneath me. My skirt is torn to ribbons from the bramble, one of my boots split at the heel. I called her name until my throat was raw, but there was no answer.

I have not slept these two nights. I sat in the rocker by the door, my Bible in my lap, the shotgun within reach. I prayed with every breath that I might hear her small voice cry out, "Mama."

But the only voices I heard were not hers. They circled the cabin first. Then they came closer. They came inside. I tried to tell myself it was the wind, or hunger, or the grief turning me mad—but no. It is not madness. It walks. It breathes. I feel it when I lie still. I feel it behind me when I turn. And worst of all, I feel it watching from behind the stove, the very place I'd once found Viola whispering to the wall.

I left a candle burning in the window. I set a dish of beans before her seat at the table. I laid out a clean dress, hoping these things she knows might somehow call her home.

But she did not come.

I stared at the words, heart hammering, throat tight.
Viola is gone.
I had known it was coming, and still, it knocked the breath out of me.

The grief in Ada's voice cut through the years like it had just happened. Her hope, clinging by threads. The beans. The dress. The candle in the window. I could see it all so vividly, it made my stomach turn.

She hadn't given up. She had waited. Prayed. Set a place for her child to return.

And something else had come instead.

A chill rippled down my spine.

There were still two more letters.

The next one didn't have a date or a formal salutation:

It has been days since I sent word to town about Viola's disappearance. And when no one came, I rode into Huntsville myself. I must have looked like a madwoman when I arrived, with my tattered, muddy dress and my ruined boot heel dragging with each step, my skin covered with sweat and dirt, my eyes red from crying and sleepless nights.

The sheriff met with me, though I could see from his first glance he'd already decided what kind of person I was. I told him everything—Viola's disappearance, the strange happenings, the feeling that something unnatural had taken hold of our home. He nodded the way men do when they've already made up their minds. Then he said it: "Could be your husband came back for her."

As if Samuel were somehow the hero of this story. As if I had driven him to it. As if I were too unstable to raise my own child.

He asked if I'd been eating. Sleeping. If I'd felt "troubled" lately. He never said the word "mad," but I heard it in every pause. He promised to send someone to look, but I saw the way he avoided my eyes. I do not believe he will.

And then, last night, I heard her. Viola. I swear I did. She was crying. "Mama," she said. "Mama, I'm cold."

But when I opened the door, there was no one. Only the darkness pressing in from all sides. But I know what I heard. I know my daughter's voice.

I no longer believe she is truly gone. Not like Samuel. His soul feels distant.

But Viola? Perhaps I am mad, but I feel her. I believe she is still near. Caught, somehow, in whatever net this cursed land has woven. Her voice, her presence—they linger. She is close. And I cannot help but hope, perhaps foolishly, that she might yet return to me fully.

Meanwhile, the house feels as though it has turned against me. The voices, the whispers, they press upon me so I cannot bear it. I cannot sleep beneath its roof. The root cellar has become my sanctuary—the only place I can think without hearing footsteps or breathing that is not mine.

I have moved down what little I need. Blanket, pillow,

lamp, my writing utensils. I have all of Viola's things prepared for her return. I light a candle in vigil as I pray for her. As I listen. As I wait.

My fingers shook as I stared at the letter.

Maybe Ada *had* gone mad in the end. Maybe the grief had split her open and let the dark inside. But I didn't think so.

Not when I'd felt it, too; when I'd sat up at night, heart racing, afraid the house was listening. Watching me.

A desperate Ada had ridden into town to ask for help, but she'd received nothing but dismissal. No one listened. No one cared.

My thoughts drifted back to that night in Maureen's kitchen. She hadn't yelled. She hadn't called me crazy. She'd just told me the ritual couldn't happen in her house. But somehow, that was almost worse. To be told, *I care about you, but not enough to stand in the darkness with you.*

And Marc? He'd given up on us a long time ago.

But not everyone had turned away. Tom had made space for us. Carmen had stepped forward to help us without hesitation.

That was the difference, wasn't it?

Ada had no one. I had *them.*

And yet, even with them, the fear still crept in.

The fear that maybe that house, that land, could still take everything from me. The fear that no matter how much I loved Hazel, it wouldn't be enough. That something ancient and hungry had marked this land, and it had a pattern—one that started with the men, continued to their daughters, and always ended with the women.

With the mothers.

I was changing. I could feel it. I was becoming someone harder, quieter, more watchful. But I wasn't sure if I was becoming stronger . . . or just closer to madness.

Like Ada.

There was one letter left.

Dearest Mama,

You came to me last night. Not in a memory. Not a dream, for I was sleeping and then woke to find you sitting beside me on the floor of the root cellar, just as plain as day. The lamp had burned low, but I saw you clearly in that soft light. Your favorite Sunday dress. Your hands folded in your lap. Your eyes full of sorrow and something resolute.

You reached for me. Brushed the hair from my face as you said, "Child, it's time."

And I knew what you meant.

This house is no longer mine. Perhaps it never was.

We built our home atop the bones of something old and wicked. I thought if I prayed hard enough, if I stayed righteous, I might be spared. But this thing—whatever it is—it does not care for righteousness.

It craves grief. It feeds on it.

This land is cursed, Mama. The house is defiled. I see that now. And at last, I know what I must do.

You and Father taught me the Scriptures, you know how they speak of the Refiner's Fire. How gold is tried by flame, how silver is made pure only in the crucible. "And I will refine them as silver is refined, and test them as gold is tested . . ." If this is my trial, then I will meet it with open eyes.

I have plenty of lamp oil. The floorboards are dry. I will strike the match at first light.

This root cellar, my sanctuary, will become my tomb. Let whoever finds me say what they will. You and I know that I did not run. I chose to stand. To fight back.

I have left a candle burning for Viola. A light to guide her home, if there is still a path to reach it.

If God still watches this place, may He accept my offering. May the fire cleanse this place for all future generations.

See you soon, my dearest Mama.

Love always,
Ada

I didn't realize I was crying until a tear struck the page. I wiped it quickly, afraid I might destroy her final words the way I'd accidentally crumbled that little dried flower down in the root cellar.

Ada hadn't run.

Not like I had.

She had stayed. She had fought. And in the end, she had burned it all down.

I could almost see her there in that root cellar, lit by lamplight, her mother's spirit beside her. I imagined the match in her trembling fingers. The strength it must've taken.

Ada hadn't been mad or hysterical or weak.

She had been brave.

But it hadn't been enough, had it?

The Carlisles proved that.

And now, more than one hundred and fifty years later, the land still whispered. The house still breathed. The taking of little girls hadn't stopped.

Would Carmen's ritual be enough?

I didn't know.

But this time, I wouldn't run.

I looked down at Ada's words again, the page still damp with tears.

She had risen against the darkness in desperation, a mother turned warrior—one hand igniting the flame, the other forever reaching out for her child.

She had made her stand.

Now I would make mine.

Fifty-Eight

<hr>

"She burned it down."

Tom and Carmen went still at the sink and looked at me, their identical deep brown eyes gleaming in the flickering candlelight. A scented WoodWick candle snapped softly on the breakfast bar between us, casting gentle shadows across Tom's kitchen.

Its flame crackled steadily, drawing my attention—rhythmic and alive, yet safely contained within its glass jar.

Unlike Ada's fire.

Tom tilted his head. "Who burned what down?"

"Ada Ellison," I said. "I just read her last letter. She started the fire at their homestead."

Carmen stood up straighter, concern blooming across her face. "What did she say?"

"She thought fire would fix it. She thought the house was wrong, that the land itself was cursed. She believed if she burned it, it would cleanse whatever evil had taken root." I leaned against the counter. "But it didn't, obviously."

I passed the letter to Carmen. She dried her hands on a dishtowel and took it with care, smoothing the creases with cautious fingers. Her lips moved silently as she read. Tom shifted closer, peering over her shoulder.

When Carmen reached the end, she held it for a moment longer before setting it gently on the bar. Her eyes met mine. "She died trying to purify the land."

I nodded. "She tried to fight back. Alone. No one believed her. Not the sheriff. Not her neighbors. And she did it anyway."

Tom rubbed a hand over his face. "But it didn't work. Whatever haunted her then is still there. If fire couldn't stop it . . . what the hell will?"

Carmen didn't respond right away. She kept her gaze on the candle, as if searching for something in the flame. "Fire is cleansing," she said softly. "But it's not magic, necessarily. Not by itself."

"What do you mean?" I asked.

"Fire is in almost every purification practice I've ever studied. Across cultures, across faiths. But for it to work . . ." She trailed off.

Tom raised an eyebrow. "But for it to work, what?"

"Fire alone isn't a cure. It's a symbol. A tool. You can't just burn the house down and expect whatever's bound to that place to disappear. Not if your soul is still clinging to what was lost."

My stomach twisted. I thought I knew where she might be going with this.

"She stayed," I said. "In the root cellar."

"She set that fire, then she waited. She left a candle for Viola. She still hoped her daughter might come back," Carmen said. "That unwillingness to give up hope? It anchored her spirit to the land, and that gave the evil something else to feed off of. That's what kept the door open. Her grief kept feeding the cycle. And when Fern came . . . the land was already soaked in sorrow. It just picked up where it left off."

A heavy silence settled over the room.

I felt a chill ripple through me. I watched Carmen as I asked the question I wasn't sure I wanted answered: "So . . . if I try the same thing, burn it all down, would it stop it from repeating again?"

Tom shifted his weight from one foot to the other. "Okay, we can't actually be talking about burning down the house, right? I mean . . ." He gave me a look that was half concern, half warning. "The place is under contract. We close in six days."

"I know," I said softly.

He waited for more.

I had nothing else to say. Because deep down, at this point, I wasn't sure I could promise him anything.

"We'll do the house cleansing as planned tomorrow," Carmen said finally, her eyes fixed firmly on mine. "I have tools and knowledge that Ada didn't have available to her back then. Hopefully, it will be enough."

"And if it isn't?"

Carmen swallowed hard. "You'll have to do what Ada couldn't."

Fifty-Nine

Shannon

August 28, 2022

Tom's guest room was dark when I opened my eyes, the last fragments of a dream slipping from my mind. I couldn't remember a single detail, but I had the nagging feeling that I should. Like I was forgetting an important warning.

I pushed myself up from the mattress and dressed in the shadows.

Hazel lay still beneath the quilt, squeezing Loretta the cat close to her chest. I watched her, transfixed by the soothing rhythm of her breath. She looked so peaceful, like nothing could ever touch her. But I was about to walk straight into something that might prove that wrong.

I leaned down and kissed her forehead. "I love you," I breathed, tears burning behind my eyes. She stirred but didn't wake. "I love you so much."

I lingered for a moment longer, memorizing this image of her safe and sound as my throat grew tight. I turned away before I could second-guess myself.

I grabbed the canvas tote Carmen had told me to pack the night before. Every item had a purpose. I didn't ask questions. I just followed instructions.

I found Tom in the kitchen. He sat on a stool at the breakfast bar, coffee mug in hand, staring at nothing. He looked up as I entered, his expression unreadable in the soft glow of the stove light.

"Got a text from Diego a few minutes ago," he said, bobbing his chin toward his phone. "Mateo's stable. He's resting. Looks like he's gonna be fine."

A shaky exhale escaped my lips. "Thank God." The weight in my chest eased slightly.

"And Carmen just pulled up outside," he went on. "She's waiting out there. Said she needed the quiet."

I nodded.

He set the mug down and rose from his seat. "Listen," he said quietly as he closed the distance between us. "If anything feels off... feels wrong, even for a second, just walk away. Okay? Just get out of there."

My mouth went dry. That was a promise I couldn't make. The stakes were too high. But I didn't argue. Instead, I gave him a weak nod and murmured, "Okay."

Tom pulled me into a hug.

It caught me off guard, but I didn't pull away. His arms were solid and warm around me. I let myself lean into him, just for a moment, resting my cheek against the smooth cotton T-shirt that covered his chest. The dread I'd been carrying, the nerves, the ache of leaving Hazel—it all eased, just a little.

I closed my eyes and listened to the steady, calm rhythm of his heartbeat.

Something unspoken passed between us. Something we weren't ready to name. It felt like more than a goodbye.

When he ended the embrace, his hand remained on my elbow, fingertips brushing the edge of my sleeve.

"Text me the second you're done," he said, voice quiet but firm. "I mean it."

I managed another nod, but my throat was too constricted to speak.

As I turned toward the door, I felt the ghost of his touch still clinging to my arm.

It would've been easier if he hadn't done that.

I couldn't afford to feel anything remotely close to that right now. Not the warmth of him. Not the sudden, aching wish that this was something I could come back to.

Because I wasn't sure there'd be a "coming back" after this.

I slipped out the front door into the dark, the parking lot hushed and still. The only sounds were the low hum of the lampposts, a few cars zipping past on the highway, and Carmen's old Subaru idling, its engine rattling anxiously like it was barely holding itself together.

Same as me.

I opened the passenger side door. The inside of her car smelled like lavender oil, stale coffee, and the faint skunky edge of weed. A string of crystals dangled from the rearview mirror, a silver triple moon pendant shimmering at the bottom. I spied a wad of fast-food napkins, a water bottle, and an old ChapStick on the floorboard.

It was messy. Lived-in. A little wild.

As I hesitated at the door, Carmen reached over and yanked a granola bar wrapper off the passenger seat, crumpling it into a fist without a word.

She was dressed all in black—a long dress layered beneath a fringed shawl, her thick braid draped over one shoulder. A leather pouch hung from a cord around her neck.

She wasn't wearing any makeup, I noticed. Her eyes looked smaller without her usual smoky shadow and cat-eye liner. She looked softer, more vulnerable somehow.

She didn't wave or speak, just met my eyes and gave me a small, solemn nod.

Neither of us spoke during the drive. There was nothing left to say. Only something left to do.

As the house came into view at last, dread coiled tight inside me.

It wasn't just watching us.

I could feel it.

It was expecting us. Like it had always known this moment would come.

It was ready.

Sixty

Carmen stepped onto the porch and crouched near the threshold. The boards groaned under her boots, but the sound felt muted, like the air had solidified around us.

I looked down at the boards in a panic, eyes searching the wood, but the dead bird was gone. No feathers or bones remained. Just a dark stain on the warped wood, like the house had somehow absorbed it.

A wave of nausea rolled through me. I told myself a stray cat must've carried it off, or some other hungry wildlife, doing what animals do.

I watched as Carmen pulled a small glass jar of salt from her bag. Her hands moved without delay as she poured a thin white line across the doorway. Not a barrier to keep evil out, but a trap to keep it *in.*

Carmen stood, stepped back from the salt line, and gave me a single nod.

I paused. I knew what I needed to do, but every nerve inside my body was screaming at me to run. Tom's words echoed in my head. *If it feels off, get out of there.*

I swallowed my fears and moved to the door with resolve, slipping my key into the lock. As I pushed open the door, I could smell mildew. Old wood. The familiar scent of this place. Bitter cold whispered against the back of my neck, a sensation like static brushing my skin.

The house groaned.

Not from wind or age. It sounded almost like a voice. A greeting.

Welcome back, Shannon. We've been waiting for you.

Carmen followed close behind me and shut the door. The latch clicked into place.

I held my breath as I flicked on the lights, expecting some dark figure without a face to pop up in front of me like a horror movie jump scare. The overhead lights hummed to life, spilling yellow light into the living room, illuminating the empty walls and bare floorboards. It looked so hollow without my things. Gutted. Unrecognizable.

Carmen squeezed the black shawl tighter around her shoulders, the fringe brushing her hips as she moved. It looked old—handwoven maybe, something passed down through generations. I had the feeling it belonged to someone who had walked through darkness before her, and today, she was bringing them with her.

"I need to seal the back door," she said softly. "We can't leave any openings."

I didn't say anything. I wanted to follow her, but I stood frozen in place as she disappeared into the dim hallway.

As soon as she was gone, the silence changed.

It deepened. Sharpened. My spine prickled with the crawling sense that something had been waiting for her to leave me alone.

Panic surged in my chest as I braced for an attack that never came.

And then—footsteps.

Brisk. Familiar.

Just Carmen.

She returned without incident, the salt jar in her hand, her expression unchanged. But I noticed the way she adjusted the shawl again. She'd felt it too.

As her gaze drifted down the hall, I knew where we had to go next.

We moved together down the narrow corridor toward Hazel's room. The air grew colder with every step. And heavier. The creaking floor planks beneath our feet didn't sound right. With all the furniture and rugs gone, there should've been echoes, but the thick air swallowed each sound too fast.

The nursery door stood open.

I stared into the shadows beyond the threshold, thinking of the last time I'd gone into that room. With Mateo. His screams reverberated through my skull again, and it took everything inside me to move forward.

Carmen tapped the light switch.

Tom and I had cleaned up the broken mirror pieces yesterday, but I still saw them there in my mind, scattered across the floor, glittering, their jagged edges razor-sharp.

Mateo's blood was still there. A rust-colored stain spread across the floorboards where he'd fallen. Tom had tried to clean it, but it hadn't worked. Though it had only been there a day, it looked dried and old.

Carmen knelt beside it, barely flinching. She unslung her bag from her shoulder and set it on the floor beside her.

"We'll start here," she murmured. "This is where it broke through."

I stood rooted to the floor, watching as she unpacked the contents of her bag one item at a time. She laid down a square of black woven cloth in the center of Mateo's blood, smoothing it flat over the stained boards.

In the center of the square, she placed her clay censer, the one I recognized from the severing ritual.

She struck a match and lit something in it, waited until it glowed red, then sprinkled herbs onto the ember with a whisper I didn't catch. Smoke lifted at once, sharp, bitter, woodsy. It rolled out in thick tendrils, the smell stinging my nose.

"May I have the items I asked you to bring, please?" she asked as her eyes met mine.

I passed her the bag, a crumpled, neon-pink tote with the words *Strong as a Mother* printed in bold, cheerful letters across the side. I'd gotten it for free at some mom expo at the Von Braun Center, back when I was pregnant. It had been filled with coupons and formula samples I'd never used.

Now it held bait for the thing that wanted my daughter.

Carmen reached inside and removed the items one by one, placing them at each corner of the cloth.

First, the stack of letters written by Ada Ellison.

Then Fern Carlisle's faded rose corsage, the one I'd found in the bathroom drawer when we first moved in.

Next came one of Hazel's drawings, the one of me and the flames and the burning figure on the ground. I felt sick looking at it now.

And lastly, the photo Dad had snapped of Marc, Hazel, and me that Christmas we ended up eating out in Albertville.

My gaze locked on the photograph. Marc's hand on my shoulder, baby Hazel on my lap, all three of us grinning like we weren't already falling apart. God, had those smiles always looked so fake?

"Shannon?"

I glanced at Carmen. She beckoned me closer with a flick of her wrist and pressed a smooth, dark crystal into my palm.

"For protection," she said simply.

I curled my fingers around it and nodded.

Carmen pulled a coil of dark cord from her bag, twisted and rough like something hand-crafted with purpose. She unwound it with care and handed one end to me. It smelled faintly of smoke and herbs.

"Hold this," she instructed. "Keep it taut. Don't let it go slack."

I pocketed the stone and pinched the cord between trembling fingers.

Carmen remained on the floor, kneeling, her head bowed as she looped a length of black cord through her fingers. As she worked, she whispered in Spanish.

My Spanish was awful. I dropped it in my freshman year of college after flunking the first exam. I'd told myself it didn't matter, that I'd probably never need it anyway. I regretted that now.

Her words sounded low and melodic, though not quite a chant. Perhaps a prayer, something meant to be spoken from the heart.

As she rose to her feet, I saw that she was tying a knot in the cord. "This is for Viola," Carmen said. "The first we know by name. You are not forgotten."

She tied a second knot.

"This one is for Ada. You saw the truth and had the courage to face it. We name you now, as witness and protector."

A third knot.

"This is for Loretta. You were taken, but never forgotten. We speak your name now. You are not lost."

With each knot she tied, the room seemed to tighten, to shrink, like the walls were inching inward, closing in around us.

"This is for Fern. This house could not erase you. We see you, and we thank you for your protection and guidance."

A chill skittered across my arms, and I hoped it was her. Fern. Still here, approving of what we were trying to do. I couldn't bear to think of the alternative.

Carmen's hands remained steady as she tied a fifth knot, but I saw the sweat beading at her temples. The tension building in her jaw.

"This is for Hazel." Her voice was firm. "You will not be taken. We tie this knot to keep you safe."

My chest clenched, locking the breath in my lungs, and for a second, I couldn't even swallow. All I could see was my daughter's face, her curls, her grin, the way her eyes lit up when she saw me.

I'd almost lost her. The darkness in this house had come so close to taking her the way it had taken the others. I tightened my grip on the cord, trying to ground myself, and blinked hard against the sudden sting in my eyes.

I'd failed her once. I wouldn't fail her now.

Carmen's sixth knot came together more slowly. She looked up and met my eyes as she tied it.

"This is for Shannon," she said, her voice thick with emotion. "You came back to this place. You chose to face it."

Something cracked open inside me when she said that. Something deep, the part of me that always cowered. Always ran.

I was still afraid. But I was here, standing my ground, for Hazel. That meant something.

The light overhead flickered once, twice, as Carmen tightened the final knot.

"And this," she said, "this is for all the others lost to time. For those we cannot name. We see you. We acknowledge you."

As Carmen's words hung in the air, my mind flickered to the woman from the recording, the one Ada had written about, the one who had wept for her lost child long ago. This was for her. Someone was honoring her at last, even if we didn't know her name.

After a reverent pause, Carmen drew a breath, her voice taking on a fierce tenacity. "This is where it ends."

She stayed still, hands clasped around the final knot. I didn't move either. The cord stretched tight between us.

The smoke from the censer curled lazily upward, slow and steady now.

We waited.

There was no shift in the air, no groan from the walls. No sound at all, actually, aside from the faint, dry crackles of burning herbs.

For one breathless moment, I let myself believe it had worked.

Then my stomach turned, sharp and sudden, like I'd swallowed something rotten.

The room felt wrong again, but worse.

Goosebumps bloomed across my skin as the cord twitched once, twice, then ripped clean out of my hands.

The cord writhed between Carmen's fingers now like a live snake. Her grip held steady, but I heard her gasp. I glanced down and saw why.

The knots were *untying themselves*.

One by one, they loosened, the untangled bits of cord falling slack.

Viola.

Ada.

Loretta.

Each one unbound as if it had never happened.

"No!" Carmen shouted, diving for the cord as it flew from her hands, but it slithered away, faster than her hands could follow.

The final knot—the one for the forgotten dead—pulled tight, snapping the cord in two. The split pieces fell to the floor with a thump and lay still.

The knot ritual had failed.

And the house . . .

The house was awake.

Sixty-One

As the vile stench of decay seeped into the room, my heart felt like it was going to beat right out of my chest. I was certain my legs were going to buckle, that I was going to hit the floor and pass out right next to the ripped cord pieces.

If anything feels off, feels wrong, walk away. Just get out of there.

We were way past that point. We were in over our heads. It was time to run.

But damn it, we couldn't.

We had to end this, somehow.

Carmen pulled her shawl tighter around herself and closed her eyes, lips moving in a steady whisper. She drew in a sharp breath. When she opened her eyes again, they burned with purpose.

"I see you," she said, her voice low but unshaken. "You are old. You are powerful. You are hunger without end."

Carmen's eyes scanned the space, dark and intense, as if tracking the unseen entity's movement.

"You were drawn to this place. Called to it. This land was wounded when you found it, torn open by human cruelty."

My stomach twisted.

"You sniffed out that sorrow and clung to it," Carmen went on. "You fed on it. Made a home from it. You survive on grief and pain. You are a leech, and nothing more."

I stood frozen as Carmen began to walk the length of the room.

"That first, original grief shaped you. Not because it belonged to you, no, but because you could *use* it. A mother's sorrow, her daughter stolen away. You learned the pattern there, and ever since, you've been repeating it. Again and again. Different centuries, different families. Same ending. Until now."

The air shifted, tight and electric.

"Hazel saw you for what you are," she said. "She called you the tricky lady. A fitting name, because you lie. You whisper in voices that are not yours. You lure and deceive, repeating the shape of an old wound over and over again. But that pattern ends tonight."

She raised one hand toward the center of the room, fingers splayed.

"You have taken enough. I invoke—"

Her words cut off mid-syllable as she stumbled forward, shoved by an invisible hand.

Then she flew backward, her body slamming into the wall behind her with a sickening crack. She slid down it and crumpled to a heap on the floor.

"Carmen!" I screamed.

I scrambled to her side, moving without thought. My knees smacked hard against the floorboards as I knelt beside her, my hands hovering above her reluctantly, afraid to touch her.

"Carmen, can you hear me?"

Her eyes were closed. She didn't react.

My fingers shook as I reached for her wrist, checking for a pulse. I pressed down and felt it—slow, but there.

The tiny hairs on the back of my neck stood on end as the space behind me grew heavy with presence.

A whisper cut through the silence:

You should've run.

My belly cramped with horror.

An indiscernible second whisper overlapped the first.

Then another.

Then a flood.

Dozens of voices layered atop each other. Men, women, children. Some crying, some laughing, some praying, some screaming.

"Don't leave me here—"

"I want to go home."

"Too late, too late—"

"My baby!"

"Hazel! Come here, Hazel—"

"Jesus, be my shield and my salvation—"

"Run, Shannon, run away now—"

"They took my baby! My child!"

"We're still waiting for Hazel. She'll join us soon."

I caught terrible bits and pieces from the whirlwind of suffering and madness that surrounded me. Echoes of this property's past.

Warnings.

Pleas.

Lies.

I covered my ears, too overwhelmed by the rush of noise.

Then one voice cut through it all, drowning out the others:

"You must do what I could not."

Ada.

I knew it the moment I heard her.

The others kept screaming. But I had my answer. I knew what I had to do.

My eyes swept from Carmen's motionless form to her bag of supplies. I'd seen a little of what she had inside.

The cacophony of voices grew louder around me, so loud I could feel them vibrating in my chest. I had to act fast.

I rifled through the bag with trembling hands until my fingers closed around something smooth and cold. A small glass bottle. I barely glanced at the label: *Santa Muerte Oil.* I didn't know what it meant, but the word *oil* was promising.

I rose up on quivering legs and strode to the closet, unscrewing the bottle cap as I moved. Without pausing to second-guess myself, I tilted the bottle and sloshed the oil out onto the floor.

I drenched the closet and worked my way backward, splashing a line of the flammable liquid across the room.

"You aren't going to win," I declared, heart pounding in my throat.

I dampened the old floorboards, the woven black cloth, Ada's letters.

"You can't have my daughter. Or me. Or Carmen. Or anyone else ever again."

I turned to the censer and kicked it hard.

The clay bowl flipped and shattered against the floor. Smoldering herbs spilled out in an arc, scattering across the oil-soaked cloth with a hiss. A flash of orange followed at once, bright and hungry.

Ada's letters ignited at once.

I knelt down and slipped an arm beneath Carmen's back.

"Come on, Carmen," I gasped. "Please, come on."

I hauled her upward with everything I had within me, slinging her arm over my shoulder and clambering to my feet. Adrenaline must have kicked in and done its job, because her weight didn't feel much heavier than hauling Hazel around.

Heat licked at my face and smoke stung my eyes as I lumbered us toward the door and out of the room, out of the house, for good.

We stumbled out onto the porch, into fresh, crisp morning air, and collapsed on the dewy grass.

I cradled her, half-sobbing, half-choking on the smoke still caught in my lungs.

"Carmen," I coughed, brushing her hair from her face. "Please wake up."

For a moment, nothing.

Then her fingers twitched. Her eyes fluttered open, glassy and confused at first, but the spark of recognition found its way in fast. Her lips moved, dry and cracked.

"You did it," she rasped.

I nodded, tears slipping down my face.

The fire roared behind us, devouring the house that had taken so much.

We lay there, watching the flames clawing at the windows, the smoke billowing up in thick, black plumes.

Beyond it all, the sky was changing.

Dawn had come.

Sixty-Two

We got the hell out of there fast, before the fire department could show up. I didn't want to run into anyone, especially not nosy neighbors like Kim Gillespie, who'd have a hundred questions and an audience ready for gossip. I needed to be far away from the property before anyone could start pointing fingers.

I drove us back to Huntsville, all while Carmen kept insisting she was fine. She waved off my concern, but after watching her slam into that wall, I wasn't convinced. She winced every time we hit a bump in the road, yet she refused to let me take her to the ER.

"We smell like smoke," she said. "We're covered in it. We show up like this, they'll start asking questions we can't answer."

I hated that she was right.

I took her back to Tom's apartment instead. He didn't ask questions—not at first—but I caught the way his eyes widened when we stepped inside. Carmen limping, both of us covered in soot, our clothes smelling like a bonfire.

He didn't press.

Carmen camped out on his couch for the rest of the day. Hazel brought her a blanket and insisted they watch a Disney movie together. Carmen looked wrung out, still wired from everything, but when Hazel curled up against her, Carmen folded an arm around her. I watched her soften as she pulled Hazel close and let herself breathe.

Tom brewed fresh coffee. DoorDashed some food. He kept things light, even cracked a few jokes. He never asked what we'd done. Maybe he didn't want to know. Maybe, because of his job, he couldn't afford to know.

I sat on the recliner, sipping lukewarm coffee, watching Carmen finally relax as Hazel nestled against her, eyes still glued to the TV.

I let myself celebrate our safety.

I'd done it. I'd actually done it.

But . . . what the hell had I done, exactly?

I'd set fire to a house that wasn't mine anymore. A house that was under contract, set to close this week.

The questions came fast and unrelenting. Would the fire department suspect arson? What if they found something in the ashes, something that pointed to us? Could I be arrested? Could Carmen?

Would the insurance cover it? What if they called it fraud?

I didn't just set that house on fire.

I might've burned down my own future with it.

The next two days were filled with paperwork and phone calls I couldn't avoid. I gave my statement to the fire department, dodged their more pointed questions, and tried to sound appropriately shocked and upset when they told me the inferno had destroyed the house beyond salvaging. Things went similarly with the insurance company. I answered what I could and left a lot out.

I did, however, ignore three voicemails from Kim—aside from sending a quick, vague text to let her know we were alive, just in time to prevent the tragic tale of our demise from making it to Facebook.

Carmen was still stiff and bruised but on the mend. It was my turn to take care of her now. She was a reluctant patient, but I insisted. I brewed her tea, brought her over-the-counter pain meds, and forced her to take it slow.

I cooked for her, too. *Really* cooked. No microwaving or frozen foods involved. I slow-simmered a big pot of my mom's made-from-scratch chicken and dumplings, thick and savory and healing in the way only Southern comfort food can be.

Hazel stayed glued to Carmen's side. At one point, I found them cozied up on the couch with a heating pad and a stack of picture books between them, both fast asleep.

By Tuesday, the calls slowed. The official reports were filed. The house was ash. Tom went back to the office. Carmen returned home, planning to go back to work on Wednesday morning.

We were moving forward.

Finding a new normal.

Around noon, I was perched on a stool at Tom's breakfast bar, laptop open in front of me as I tackled a new design project I'd accepted, an e-book cover for yet another fairy romance novel. Hazel sat cross-legged on the living room floor behind me, surrounded by dolls and stuffies who occupied a city built from magnetic tiles.

The front door clicked open. Tom burst inside.

He looked like the Tom Altamira I'd first met. Crisp Oxford shirt, satiny tie, pleated slacks, perfectly styled curls, spicy cologne.

Hazel jumped up and ran to hug him. He crouched down without hesitation, scooping her in his arms like it was totally natural. He asked about her morning, complimented her magnetic tile constructions, and let her bubbly chatter reign the room for a while before rising to his feet.

Then he looked at me, eyes sparking with unspent energy. Something pulsed under his skin, some barely contained urgency that made the hair on my arms spring up.

I knew something was coming. My gut clenched as I braced myself, as he stepped closer, his eyes locked on mine.

"Well," he said at last, voice low and incredulous. "You're never gonna believe this."

My stomach churned. "What?"

"The guy buying your house? He still wants it."

I felt my mouth drop open.

"He said he planned to bulldoze it anyway. Called the fire a blessing in disguise."

I stared at him in disbelief. "Are you . . . are you serious?"

He nodded, grinning. "Completely. He said the house was too outdated and didn't fit his 'vision'." He emphasized this with air quotes. "All he cared about was the acreage."

I had no words.

My skin buzzed as he rested a hand on my forearm.

"We're still closing on Friday," he told me. "You're free, Shannon."

I released a slow breath, one I felt like I'd been holding for months.

Free.

The word echoed through me, unreal and weightless.

After everything the house had taken, after everything I had done, it was over.

I had no idea what came next.

But for the first time in a long time, the future didn't scare me.

Sixty-Three

One Year Later

THE HOUSE WAS SMALL. Eleven-hundred square feet, a garage barely big enough to squeeze my CR-V into, and a backyard so tiny, I could push-mow the whole thing in five minutes.

But it was mine.

I still couldn't believe it sometimes, but between my share of the property sale from Sunflower Lane and a major boost in income from taking a full-time job at a graphic design firm, I had managed to pull this off, all on my own.

It was a new build, too, in one of those cookie-cutter neighborhoods popping up all over every inch of Madison County. I used to hate those neighborhoods. But after what we'd been through, a bland cookie-cutter was the goal.

Today, our tiny backyard felt bigger than it was. Pink and purple party streamers strung across the privacy fence whipped in the breeze. One foldable table covered in a plastic Dollar Tree tablecloth sagged beneath the weight of hot dog and burger fixings, cupcakes, fruit skewers, and party punch. A second table held half a dozen brightly wrapped gifts.

Folding armchairs dotted the lawn, occupied by moms chatting as they watched their kids running through a sprinkler, giggling, screaming with glee.

As I stood there, watching the laughter and color swirl around me, an old weight tugged at my chest. We were outside then, too, with balloons and cake and bright summer sun. A cat-themed party by the barn. And by the end of that day, my father was dead.

I swallowed hard and blinked away the image. It was impossible not to think of it today, but I knew I couldn't let Hazel's birthdays carry grief forever.

The sound of Tom's laughter pulled me out of my head. He stood before the grill in a linen button-down, cargo shorts, and flip-flops, a spatula in one hand and a bubble wand in the other. I watched him blow a cascade of bubbles toward Hazel. She squealed as she ran through them.

Carmen chased after her, still in her scrubs from her earlier shift.

Maureen was there, too, laughing at their antics from a fold-up chair in the shade as she sipped punch from a paper cup with unicorns on it. She'd made the fruit skewers, actually. We'd been mending things over the last few months, and I was thankful for her friendship.

I'd made so many new friends in the last year, my heart felt so full. A couple of colleagues and a few other moms from Hazel's Pre-K class. My co-worker Heather sat next to a new mom friend on the lawn now, engrossed in conversation, and I felt a deep sense of satisfaction for having created a whole new life. A new job, a new house, a new social circle. Here I was, even hosting a big, successful party.

My phone chimed with an alert from my video doorbell. Another guest had arrived.

I made my way through the house and opened the front door to find Hazel's school friend Jabari, his baby brother, and his mom,

Malika. She had her hands full—a baby in the crook of her left elbow, a gift bag in one hand, and a store-bought bouquet of yellow flowers in the other.

Sunflowers.

"—sorry we're late," Malika was saying. "I meant to text you, but God, I'm such a mess today."

I stared at the thick green stems, the bright heads with their dark, heavy centers.

Just a coincidence. Just a flower.

"—and the baby had a blowout just as soon as I buckled him—"

Malika's voice drifted in and out, and I made myself look up. I found her face and focused on it, noting the sheen of sweat on her skin, the damp curls sticking to her forehead. A wet stain darkened the front of her top. Baby spit-up, I was pretty sure.

A look I knew quite well.

"No, no, don't worry about it, you're perfectly on time," I assured her, forcing a smile. "The food isn't even quite ready just yet. Come on in. Here, let me give you a hand."

I took the bag first, and then, after a beat of hesitation, the sunflowers.

"Thank you so much, Malika. These are beautiful." My tongue felt dry as I said it, but I tried to keep my face neutral.

"I just saw them and thought of you," she said, smiling now. "I never got you a housewarming gift." She shrugged. "Nothing warms up a house like fresh flowers."

"That is true," I agreed. I carried them to the kitchen and slid them into a mason jar full of water, chatting with Malika and Jabari as I did so.

I carried the jar outside and set it on the gift table. It should've been the perfect addition—bright, summery, cheerful. But they seemed *too* cheerful, like they knew something I didn't. I swear, it felt like those yellow faces were watching me.

Jabari sprinted off to join Hazel and the other kids at the sprinkler, and I introduced Malika to the grown-ups she didn't know from Pre-K.

The party was in full swing now. My stomach rumbled as the smell of burgers wafted toward me. The food was almost ready. Someone turned up a Bluetooth speaker playing a Disney playlist on shuffle. The kids darted around the grass, having a blast. The adults were talking. Everyone we'd invited was here, and everything seemed to be going just fine. I could relax and enjoy it.

I wandered over to the folding chairs, where the moms were gathered. Malika had settled in and was bouncing the baby on her knee while my co-worker Heather handed her a napkin for a spit-up accident.

Naomi, whose daughter was Hazel's shadow at school, waved me over with a potato chip in hand. I took a seat between her and Erica, one of the most hands-on moms in Hazel's Pre-K class; she was always volunteering for everything.

Erica sat cross-legged, sipping from a giant Stanley tumbler. "So," she started in a too-casual voice. "Did y'all hear about that little girl that went missing?"

A hush fell over the group.

"It was all over Facebook this morning," she continued, her eyes wide. "She's the same age as our kids. Just three or four years old. Her mom posted that she was playing in the backyard one second, and the next?" She snapped her fingers. "She was just gone."

"My god, where was this?" Naomi asked.

"Just over in Gurley," Erica replied.

I went cold.

"Jesus," Malika whispered, pressing a palm protectively over her baby's chest. "That's not far from here."

"No," Erica agreed. "It's not. Shannon, didn't you used to live out that way?"

I nodded weakly.

"I saw that post," Heather chimed in. "They said their house is right up next to the woods. Maybe she wandered off and got lost out there?"

"Maybe," Erica said. "Or some pedo took her. I tell you what, the world gets scarier and scarier every day for these babies."

Their voices faded as I watched Hazel leap barefoot through the sprinkler, shrieking with joy, untouched by the weight that had settled over the grown-ups.

I scanned the yard for the Altamiras.

Carmen had gone still, her spine rigid, eyes locked on the group.

Tom turned from the grill, the color drained from his face, his spatula held aloft like he'd forgotten what it was for. His eyes found mine across the yard.

We didn't speak. We didn't need to.

The jar of sunflowers, golden and bright, taunted us from the gift table.

A Note from the Author

THANK YOU SO MUCH for reading *The House on Sunflower Lane*. If you would be so kind, please take a moment and head over to Amazon, Goodreads, or anywhere you review books, and leave a rating or a short review. I'd love to hear your thoughts, and your ratings and reviews greatly help other readers determine if the book is right for them.

If you'd like to receive updates about upcoming releases, sign up for my newsletter at GwennaMcAllis.com.

Thank you again, reader. It's been an honor and a lifelong dream to have you here.

Acknowledgements

Jayne Hoen and Jessica Thornton—thank you both for reading this story early on and caring enough to point out what didn't work and what did. Your feedback played a huge role in how this book turned out.

Monika Mandikova—thank you for your thoughtful insight and careful attention to detail. You have a knack for spotting the plot holes I'd rather just brush under the rug.

Kathy Peterson—thank you for your kind words, sharp eye, and for taking the time to flag typos and errors. Thoughtful readers like you mean so much.

The cover design team at Miblart—thank you for always doing such an amazing job bringing my visions to life.

Cait Monroe with Special Collections at the Downtown Huntsville Library—thank you for taking the time to answer my questions and help me make the research scene in this book as realistic as possible.

My girls—thank you for the constant creative fuel. I always thought creepy kids in horror movies/books were cliché and un-realistic . . . until I became a mom. I'm so proud of both of you, and I love you so, so much.

My husband—thank you for your support and for all you do for our family.

And to the readers who choose indie books, who take chances on unknown authors with tiny followings, this book exists because of you. Thank you!

About the Author

Gwenna McAllis grew up in Alabama where she spent her childhood buried in stories about ghosts and things that go bump in the night. She later earned a B.A. in English with a creative writing focus from the University of South Alabama in Mobile and now writes supernatural suspense. She lives in North Alabama with her husband, two young children, and an aging rescue pup. For more about Gwenna and her writing, visit www.gwennamcallis.com.

www.ingramcontent.com/pod-product-compliance
Lightning Source LLC
Chambersburg PA
CBHW061044310726
48969CB00004B/1080